MAROC

A Snowdonia Thriller

Keith Williams

Amazon

ISBN: 9798815904880

Cover design by: Art Painter
Library of Congress Control Number: 2018675309
Printed in the United States of America

To Kathy Ross, without whose help and encouragement, this book would have remained unwritten.

Aros mae'r mynyddau mawr,
Rhuo trostynt mae y gwynt

The great mountains remain,
The wind roars above them

JOHN CEIRIOG HUGHES (1832-1887)

INTRODUCTION

Peter Maroc is ex SAS. Three years ago, his wife banished him from their home. Her father, Max Southwell, a retired college professor, still resents him for the neglect of his daughter.

He returns from Germany to his home village in Snowdonia to find his father-in-law has been left to die by his grasping sons. Meanwhile, his estranged medic wife is trapped in an African hospital and is powerless to help. Maroc makes it his mission to return Max Southwell to health and regain his wife's affections.

When a kidnapping goes wrong, Maroc is left suffering almost total amnesia. His wife's return from Africa forces him to fight for his family's survival against a ruthless enemy.

The action switches between the beautiful mountains of Snowdonia, the underbelly of Manchester's crime scene and Albania's bandit country.

PROLOGUE

Arrival

Two shots merged as a single sound. Two rounds from a Zastava M76 slammed into the right side of his body, spinning and pushing him backwards and down. However, the angle of impact, together with his body armour, had worked in his favour.

Dazed but with cruel clarity, he could see the shooter taking his time for a headshot, his expression neutral. Another day at the office.

He woke to his screaming as he jolted upright, his naked body soaked with the slick distillation of his terror. A timid dawn light tugged him back into a reality he could not yet allow

Peter Maroc sat unmoving for a full ten minutes, hugging his suffering close like a sickly child. His dark hair, allowed to grow wild through lack of opportunity or care, part hid his brooding countenance.

A four-day growth lent his gaunt face a certain savagery. It was not an unfair reflection of what lay beneath.

He'd arrived late, in darkness. The small Welsh town

in the heart of Snowdonia huddled furtively below, its presence betrayed only by dim points of lights. He'd rented the small cottage for the winter. Cheap and anonymous; it was all he needed.

It was getting lighter. He would have to surrender the dubious refuge of Morpheus and...what? The thought of breaking cover from his newfound foxhole made him uneasy. He would delay the inevitable walk to the village.

Things turned around in his head, spectres he could not yet understand. They circled like orbiting moons around a doomed planet, threatening his already tenuous hold on reality.

Tea; always a panacea. He sought and found a large mug he'd used the previous evening when he'd first arrived at the cottage. He wasn't a real tea man, where the correct ritual was strictly adhered to. As long as it was strong, he didn't much care.

As boiling water hit the tea bag and the pungent aroma reached his nostrils, his mind briefly captured a fleeting image of solemnity and absorption. Oriental eyes, a fragile beauty, serious with intent.

The old grandmother clock on the far corner table murmured its soothing counsel. 'Plenty of time, plenty of time'

Maroc took his time, relishing the hiatus afforded by the careful sipping. Like a gambler throwing dice, he shook his head violently, hoping to throw a pattern he could understand.

He dressed slowly against the winter cold. Pulling on heavy boots, the sharp stab of pain in his lower back vied for attention with his slowly healing ribs, still protesting their neglect.

Maroc stepped out through the low front door of his poorly lit man cave and started the half-mile trek to the small town below. The surrounding beauty of the bleak mid-winter was lost on him. His reality lay somewhere in a brutal past.

There was no future, no plans in the making. Except to put one foot in front of the other and breathe.

Important that last part Peter.

A forgotten voice arose from his obscured past.

Important to breathe, but oh so bloody painful, he thought, with unpractised humour.

He had the information written in a small notebook. 'Bryn Awel.'

No street name or further clue as to location. The agency had assured him it would be easy to find.

It's only a small town, just ask anybody there; they'll tell you.

A couple of men stood in the doorway of an ironmongery shop. They seemed at ease with their surroundings as only locals can be. He paused, his aching back and side glad of the break, and asked directions to the house.

His accent was wrong. The faint hint of a Welsh lilt, attractive to many, was too subtle for these boys. One was tall and wiry, the other medium height and built like the proverbial brick outhouse. Both had closely cropped dark hair.

They stared in sullen unison. As if responding to some unspoken signal they promptly turned away to continue their smoking and conversation. Maroc shrugged, realising for the first time how physically vulnerable he had become.

There was a time in which he would have made

his displeasure known. Damn the fallout. Now, he acknowledged his frailty. A new experience.

Approaching a small cafe, a single table circled by four chairs stood somewhat optimistically just left of the entrance door. The large window revealed the occupation of a couple of the tables. As Maroc tried to penetrate the dark interior for a better view, he barely avoided colliding with an exiting customer.

He came face to face with an attractive woman in her mid-thirties. Close to him in height, she was slim and... he knew her, but how, and from where? His mind tried and failed to make sense of this contextual quandary.

'What on earth...,'

she began, just as bewildered as he.

They stood facing one another, each trying to find reason in the encounter.

'What the hell are you doing here?'

Her beguiling and rather posh English voice only added to the air of dislocation.

She shouldn't be... here. Should she? What the hell was going on?

'You look like you've been to hell and back.'

He gave an involuntary bark at the irony.

'What's so funny?'

She seemed furious with him. Why? He decided to wing it.

'Jesus, is this Twenty Questions? Which do you need answering first?'

She smiled, a fresh-faced generous smile, and he knew that somewhere in his hidden past, he had liked her.

CHAPTER 1

They moved silently through the mountainous terrain of Gjirokastër County. Each man had his special skills. They were the perfect fighting unit.

The SAS patrol of four had entered Albania from southern Italy. Their mission was to disrupt the Albanian Mafia's cannabis and hard drugs operations in Lazarat.

For the past year, the particular clan or *Fare* in that region had raised flags with British and American intelligence and most other security services in Western Europe.

For years, the Albanian authorities had fought a losing battle against the powerful and well-organised Mafia within their borders. It had not been enough.

Drugs from their country were still hitting Europe. From there they were shifted to every lucrative market around the globe.

Recently, the Fare had upped their game. Always on the lookout for new opportunities, with increased margins, the organisation had added heroin and cocaine to their product line.

The big game-changer happened when the Albanians began buying cocaine directly from the Columbians at around £4,000 to £5,500 per kilo. This enabled them to outsell their rivals, who bought their supply from Dutch wholesalers at £22,500 per kilo.

The Albanians could lower their price and increase the purity of their deadly merchandise. The first-world narcotics markets began obtaining their cocaine almost exclusively from them.

The British government became concerned when huge consignments began arriving at UK ports. Something had to be done and done quickly.

Led by Peter Maroc, each trooper knew his role in the operation. Each carried in his head a plan of the mountainous region.

As part of a broader strategy with the Albanian special forces, this would be the first of a series of visceral strikes on the Fare. All operations had been fully sanctioned by that country's government.

Mark Fisher was the new guy. Older than the rest, Fisher had done sterling work in Iraq and Afghanistan. He had also participated in covert operations with the SAS in Bosnia and later in Kosovo.

Around five-nine and solidly built, he was the shortest of the four. A demolitions expert and an excellent marksman, his skills would be put to good use on the mission.

Once again, Maroc reviewed the plan in his mind. There were two main objectives.

The first was to clean out the organisation's coffers, secreting the money in one of the many caves in the region's hilly terrain. The other was to destroy as much of their stock of cannabis and cocaine as was possible in one strike.

In darkness, they would enter the Fare's operational buildings. Once inside the main office, Niels Johansson would use his refined skills on their office safe.

The Semtex had been brought to destroy the unprocessed marijuana and the cocaine. It would also provide a dramatic diversion for their escape.

Dave Blandford would drive the pickup they had 'acquired.' Not exactly the ideal getaway vehicle, Maroc hoped the element of surprise and confusion would afford them a good head start.

The initial plan had been to lay mines along their exit route. The M18A1 Claymore, directional anti-personnel mine would have been an ideal choice in disabling pursuing vehicles. The idea had been scrapped when the new rules of engagement were revealed.

Their revised brief was to keep the enemy body count to an absolute minimum. This was not to appease the Albanian government, but rather to prevent it from being accused of using foreigners to kill its own people.

While this position was fine with Maroc, Niels Johansson considered the order impractical. He had made his views clear. Political sensitivity was for politicians, not soldiers. Maroc thought he had a point.

Maroc sat next to Blandford in the front seat. The silence between them was not unusual. It allowed each man to mentally rehearse the tasks ahead.

Blandford was the first to spot the lights up ahead. Leaving the vehicle, a hundred yards away, they approached the main compound with practised stealth.

The main entrance on the north side of the large enclosure had an inner door. Someone had thoughtfully left it unlocked.

They stepped through like ghosts. Maroc

immediately spotted one of the guards standing around ten meters inside the compound.

He had his back to them and failed to hear Johansson's approach. The man turned around just as the Norwegian reached him.

One swing of his small weighted club had the man crumpling gracelessly to the floor.

Further inside the compound, a small cabin with large glass windows housed a second guard. A powerfully built man, his head completely shaved, he sat in blissful ignorance with his back to them.

He was fully engrossed in a magazine and failed to hear Maroc approaching. The SAS trooper employed a choking technique he had used many times.

Hadaka jime is a simple but highly effective chokehold applied from the rear. Quick and painless, the opponent usually passes out in seconds. He quickly bound the man's wrists and ankles, using a third rope to connect the bindings.

Trussed like a turkey, a gag in his mouth, he was going nowhere. He turned to see Johansson observing him. He gave Maroc a sardonic grin. It was not his style.

Once again, Peter Maroc considered their mission purpose. They were there to create as much chaos and destruction as possible, with minimum casualties. The Fare was about to have its first taste of official disapproval.

The ultra-light night vision goggles were an essential kit. Apart from the two they had disabled their use had already helped confirm there were no other guards on duty. Was it going to be that easy?

Apart from his combat knife, Maroc carried one weapon. This was a Sig Sauer P226 9 mm pistol.

It was not his weapon of choice; however, he still considered the Swiss-made gun reliable and accurate. The Sig was heavier than his favoured Glock 17. Although it carried two fewer rounds, it felt solid in his hand. He prayed it would not be used.

The Fare had one disadvantage. They were not yet aware of the presence of a deep-cover agent. Albanian intelligence officer Dalmat Dushku had been in place for six months.

Over that period, his feigned loyalty and dedication to the Fare had been demonstrated many times.

Sickened by some of the tasks he had carried out, Dushku rationalised his actions served a greater purpose. To be accepted and trusted by the Fare, he was obliged to abandon his moral compass; become less than human. His bathroom mirror had become an object to shun.

Dushku had provided Maroc and his team with a detailed plan of the compound. Concealed at a designated drop a mile outside the Fare's headquarters, it marked the location of all their targets.

The marijuana stock, together with the cocaine, would be the last task. The SAS patrol would first relieve these robber barons of some hard cash, a great deal of it.

It would take Mark Fisher some time to set up his pyrotechnic display. He had two targets to locate; the first comprised three large warehouses containing recently harvested marijuana. The second was a separate storehouse of cocaine, a much more valuable trophy.

Together with the Semtex, Fisher had brought in a couple of gallons of petroleum. It would aid in the destruction of most of the marijuana. However, to demolish three warehouses, two gallons would not be enough. Fisher hoped the Semtex would make up for the deficit.

Dushku's detailed plan had simplified his task, and, within minutes, Fisher had spotted the warehouses on the far side of the compound. He offered a silent thanks to the brave Albanian.

Three long low brick buildings with corrugated iron roofs stood side by side. Behind stood a smaller structure. It was where the Fare kept their newest addition to their product line, high purity cocaine. Fisher concluded he had reached his objectives.

He felt vulnerable with his hands engaged in carrying the Semtex and petroleum. If challenged, he would be slow in accessing his weapon. Not an ideal position for a soldier.

Johansson, Blandford and Maroc made their way to the central office building containing the cash and whatever else of value they could acquire. Once inside, the Norwegian would work his magic on their office safe.

On paper, Maroc thought, it was an uncomplicated plan. The team would be out and away, job done.

Maroc hoped the gods would be on their side, and their movement across the large compound would remain in near darkness. It gave his team a massive tactical advantage. Night vision would have them fighting, or rather evading, blind men.

Maroc was aware there could be a worse scenario. He was conscious of the dozen or so arc lights fixed high up on aluminium poles. Strategically positioned on the perimeter of the compound, each lamp pointed inward.

He knew if they were triggered, the patrol would show up like a circus act. The advantage offered by the N.V goggles would be reversed. They would be the blind men.

Their primary aim was to avoid confrontation, to evade the enemy. It was their speciality. When the warehouses went up, they would be inside their vehicle on the narrow track out of Dodge. As Fisher had put it, a simple plan for simple men. Was there such a thing in their line of work? Maroc had his doubts.

Johansson had never explained his proficiency as a safecracker. Not even to Maroc.

He had made vague allusions to an uncle who was a locksmith. It would not have come close to explaining the Norwegian's skills set.

Maroc had concluded it was none of his business.

He watched as Johansson delved into a small canvas bag. Muttering to himself, as he often did when concentrating, he produced an array of small electronic instruments.

As he hunched on his knees in front of the massive safe, the Norwegian's soft cursing increased in volume. Turning his head, he glared at his friend. Maroc took the hint and left him to it.

There could be no further action until they opened the safe. Maroc and Dave Blandford sat in the small anteroom just off the main office, not unlike a couple of expectant fathers. Twenty minutes later, they heard a triumphant, 'yes!'

Leaping to their feet, they entered the large office to find the safe open. Johansson was busy cramming bulky wads of large denomination banknotes into one of the voluminous bags brought for the purpose. Maroc left him and Blandford to finish the job.

Moving like a shadow, he made his way to the warehouses. The third and furthest one had light leaching out from the main entrance door.

Maroc entered and found Fisher making last-minute adjustments to some rather complex wiring arrangements. He looked up quickly, reaching for his sidearm. On seeing Maroc, he visibly relaxed.

Standing up, Fisher pulled out something small from a pocket in his combat trousers. Maroc guessed it was a detonating device.

Looking up at the patrol leader, Fisher grinned his pleasure. He was a man indulging in his favourite pastime.

'One receiver for all three warehouses, same frequency. Enough Semtex to do a nice job when I press this little fellah.'

Maroc grinned and gave him a thumbs up.

'And the cocaine?'

Fisher looked up.

'Sorted. I've put in enough Semtex plus a timer fuse. Set to go up in...'

He looked at his watch.

'Just over ten minutes. In any case, the explosion from this little lot should take care of the cocaine warehouse.'

Once outside, they could make out two figures coming toward them. Maroc signalled Fisher to stop. Johansson and Blandford appeared clear in his N.V. Maroc raised his arm. Blandford gave an answering wave.

When Maroc and Fisher reached their two friends,

Johansson signalled they needed help with the heavy lifting.

The patrol members, carrying large bags packed with banknotes, moved silently towards the exit. They were stepping through the gate leading to the outside when the door to the living quarters opened. Light spilt out, revealing two figures silhouetted at the entrance. The men stepped out of the building.

Maroc looked ahead, seeing Johansson and Blandford had noted the men's presence. Both had stopped and waited.

Their directive was clear, minimum casualties. So far things had gone as planned. They had not engaged the enemy.

The Mafiosos were lighting cigarettes and laughing at some private joke, oblivious to the SAS presence in their midst. Maroc noted one man was facing away from them while the other stood side-on. He gave the signal to wait.

A full minute passed; the men still chatted. Maroc heard a sound coming from the front cabin, holding the previously unconscious guards. Before he could stop him, Johansson had covered twenty yards, moving like a shadow towards the hut.

He disappeared inside. There was a slight scuffle, then silence.

Maroc began moving forwards. He reached the glass-panelled cabin just as his friend emerged. He looked past the Norwegian into the cabin. Maroc saw the man he'd incapacitated was in much the same condition as he had left him. Giving the Norwegian a quizzical look, Johansson shrugged.

'He'd woken up. Short sharp punch to the jaw.

Nothing more.'

His hands held out, palms forward, the Norwegian looked like a naughty schoolboy. Maroc, stifling the urge to laugh, gave a curt nod.

'Let's get the hell out, Niels.'

He signalled the other two and continued forwards. They came across the first guard the Norwegian had dealt with. He was still out cold. Perhaps Johansson's method had merit after all.

Once outside, Dave Blandford made his way to the small pickup parked a hundred yards from the front gate. Heaving his overfull bag into the back of the truck, he opened the driver's door.

Maroc joined him in the front passenger seat. Johansson and Fisher heaved their bags into the back of the open pickup truck and leapt on board. Both lay flat, the bags acting like expensive mattresses.

That was when Fisher activated the transmitter. There was a moment of pregnant silence, followed by an ear-splitting roar as the Semtex ignited. Every warehouse door was blown out, chased by orange and white flames. Fisher gave a nod of satisfaction.

The Honda may have been old, but it was proving reliable. It started on the first turn, and Blandford gunned it out of the parking area, heading for the narrow track leading north.

Fisher and Johansson were busy making sure the flashbangs were ready for deployment if needed.

Johansson would have preferred the Claymore anti-personnel mines for the job. However, Maroc had ruled for the less damaging flashbangs when or if the time came.

A flashbang, lobbed in front of a travelling vehicle,

would more than disorientate the driver. The others, except for Johannsson, agreed.

They had been driving for around five minutes, and there was still no sign of a pursuing headlight. Given their dramatic and highly noticeable exit, Maroc thought, it could only be a matter of time.

Johansson spotted a bright light behind them, steadily getting nearer. He and Fisher had a fair idea of what was about to catch up with them. Loud banging on the back window caused Maroc to turn around.

He saw a grinning Johansson holding up a couple of G60 flash-bangs. The stun grenades, strategically pitched, would definitely play their part in impeding their pursuers.

Maroc gave a thumbs up, and Johansson disappeared from view. The light grew steadily larger and brighter as the pursuing vehicle gained on the ageing Honda. Spotting a muzzle flash, Fisher hit the deck pulling Johansson with him. The Norwegian crawled to the cab and again rapped on the window.

'Incoming, get your bloody heads down.'

Fisher could see it was an army jeep. It would probably be a lot newer and faster than the pickup.

The jeep was rapidly devouring the dividing distance, and he thought he could make out a light machine gun mounted on a tripod set up at the back. However, the blinding spotlight made it impossible to be sure.

Fisher and Johansson continued to stay low as rounds passed over like angry fireflies. A few struck the top of the cab before continuing their whining journey into the blackness ahead. It was nothing they had not experienced before. Both men waited for an

11

opportunity to counter the action.

A sharp right bend appeared in front of the pickup. The Honda drifted into it, its wheels fighting for purchase on the dusty surface. Blandford somehow managed to keep the vehicle from veering off the track. Johansson stood up, and with legs spread wide, both his feet jammed against the sides of the narrow vehicle, he armed and threw the first flashbang.

It fell short of its target, exploding as it hit the road before the vehicle passed over it. It was enough to disorientate the driver.

The jeep swerved, threatening to leave the track. Somehow, the driver steered the vehicle back on course. It kept on coming.

Johansson picked up his second load, prayed to Odin and threw. The second flashbang was on the money, dropping neatly over the windscreen at the driver's feet. Given the stun grenade's proximity, the effect of detonation on the driver was devastating.

The jeep veered sharply left, its front wheel making abrupt contact with a large rock. Momentum did the rest, the jeep's abrupt halt causing it to catapult all three occupants out and onto the road.

For a few seconds, the vehicle stood vertically on its bonnet. Like some mechanical gymnast, it fell forward, continuing its journey for a short distance before coming to rest with its wheels still spinning.

Blandford stopped the pickup, and all four disembarked. They walked cautiously towards the pursuit vehicle with weapons drawn.

Using his Maglite, Maroc could make out the bodies lying further back and to the left of the stricken vehicle. On approaching, he could detect no movement. Steam whistled noisily out of the jeep's radiator as the four men moved cautiously forward.

Maroc and Fisher checked the prostrate bodies for signs of life. At first sight, it would seem the gods had decided there would be no deaths that night. So far, things were going to plan.

Two of the men were unconscious but breathing, the third was starting to recover. He was on his knees, attempting to stand. Maroc bent down to check on the unconscious men. He could not be certain, but his army medical training left him fairly confident there would be no lasting damage to either.

Once again, Johansson did his usual thing of striking the struggling man on the jaw, laying him out cold. *No real harm done then,* Maroc thought.

A different protocol would have had the SAS team dispatching all three with little compunction. For Peter Maroc, tonight's scenario was a better fit.

Maroc looked back along the narrow track, looking for signs of a further pursuit by the Fare members. There was nothing.

So far, things had gone their way. He knew however, they could ill afford to slow down now. Maroc could imagine the mood back at the compound and was sure of one thing. If the opposition was to catch up with them, they would have a hell of a fight on their hands. A fight they might not win.

Returning to the pickup the patrol continued at a more measured pace. They had travelled less than a couple of miles when Maroc turned to Dave Blandford.

'Another couple of hundred yards Dave.' He looked around, but the other two had their backs to the cab's rear window.

Blandford slowed the pickup, finally parking it by the side of the track. Running from the track to the right was a rocky path into the hills. They decided not to risk the vehicle on such rough terrain.

Maroc and Blandford joined the others at the rear of the pickup. They managed between them to haul the heavy bags over the last quarter of a mile to the designated hiding place.

The cave was around six feet high and went back twenty feet. It was concealed by tall bushes which grew well in the dry soil, Maroc thought it ideal for their purpose.

Between them, they carried the money inside, placing the bags at the farthest end. The rubberised lining meant water damage would not be an issue.

Johansson walked over to the pick-up and, reaching in, heaved out a large, extra bag. He looked up from the task and noticed Maroc observing him curiously.

The Norwegian gave his friend a cryptic smile.

'We have a bonus. Quite a large one.'

'What sort of bonus.'

'I think you're going to like it.'

Johansson was being enigmatic, a posture he knew Maroc found irksome. The Norwegian decided not to overplay the drama.

'Our Mafia friends left us a little extra. I found this in a metal chest next to the vault. The padlock was so basic, a child of nine could have opened it.'

Johansson carefully placed the heavy sack on the floor. He reached inside and withdrew a couple of thick plastic bags, handing them over to Maroc.

After attempting and failing to see beyond the thick, opaque plastic, Maroc looked up and gave

Johansson a questioning look. The Norwegian tilted his head thoughtfully.

'My guess would be cocaine, maybe heroin.'

Maroc shrugged, concluding this was not the time for close examination and discussion; he returned both bags to Johansson.

'Could be both. How much of the stuff?'

Johansson made a show of hefting the bag while closing his eyes.

'Maybe twenty-five, thirty kilos?'

Maroc whistled, impressed at his friend's enterprise.

'Ouch! That's going to hurt the bastards. Come on, let's get it into the cave with the rest of the swag.'

'Swag?'

Johansson looked perplexed.

'Not now, mate. I'll explain later.'

Maroc shook his head.

Flashing his Maglite around the cave's interior, he checked for signs of animal residency. Having found no evidence, he still decided to take one extra precaution.

Looking around outside the cave, he found what he wanted. There were rocks strewn over the whole area. The medium-sized ones would be ideal for providing an extra layer of security.

Between them, they carried the rocks into the cave and stacked them onto the tough canvas bags. The heavy stones would also help conceal their booty if someone did enter the cave.

Job done, the team headed back to the pickup. Hiding the money had taken twenty minutes. There was every possibility the Fare had organised another pursuit or called for outside help to cut them off before they hit the main road. With this in mind, the patrol had no intention of hanging around for further engagement.

In their line of work, safety was a relative term. Each man had his definition.

Ten minutes up the track, they swung their pickup onto the main road.

The day had gone well. Peter Maroc felt their present position warranted a few high fives.

CHAPTER 2

Bill Gordon's day had not gone well. Not even close. One phone call can deliver devastation on many levels, and Gordon had received that call.

Now at home and wanting to begin immediate enquiries into his friend's death, his wife Jean had been firm. She had ordered him to take a long hot bath. It was something she knew had helped him in the past.

As Gordon surrendered to the herb-scented warmth, some of the day's stresses began draining away. His lean combat-scarred body was not yet fully relaxed, but he was getting there.

Jean was downstairs in the living room. She would not disturb him. Not out of fear. That had ended years earlier.

Gordon still went for counselling once a month. Visiting the Combat Stress centre, he could meet others exposed to the same horrors. Occasionally, a familiar face he had worked with would turn up. That was usually good. Not always.

He no longer frightened her with his violent outbursts. She had borne it because she loved him. Understanding the underlying causes helped.

The eruptions were always verbal, never escalating to the physical. For Jean, that would have been the end. Never the target, she had been collateral damage.

His ranting was mainly self-recriminatory, his self-loathing palpable.

Over time and with good help, he had begun to understand the origin of his rages. He had learnt to recognise the triggers, to diffuse them in time.

Her mind travelled back to earlier days. Her husband would find, what to Jean was an unfathomable solace in drunken violence. He would invariably end up in a police cell. She would collect him the following morning, docile and contrite.

Tonight, she would allow him his personal space. He still had a lot to process. Please don't let this set him back.

Sipping freshly brewed coffee, Jean made another attempt to get into her novel. Finally giving up, she sat and fretted.

The call had come from the Hereford constabulary. They had found the body of David Blandford. He had been savagely beaten by assailants unknown and left at the roadside.

Spotted by a passing driver, the man had stopped to investigate why a car would park with its driver's door open. He had found Blandford laying a few feet from his vehicle.

Later, the Good Samaritan reported he had uttered a few words before losing consciousness. Blandford had died minutes before medical help arrived.

As well as being Gordon's business partner, Dave Blandford was unarguably the best instructor in *Manshield Security Training*. He was also his closest friend.

Twelve years in the regiment, both had seen action in the Balkan conflicts, Iraq and Afghanistan. Always in the thick of it, each had watched the other's back.

Before Gordon could check himself, the selfish part of his mind had turned to business. He realised how much the company would miss Blandford's contribution. He began mentally running through the bookings that would be lost without his key man.

He realised where his thoughts had strayed and felt the shame of betrayal. These issues were so bloody trivial when measured against the real reasons why this man would be missed.

People like Blandford were as rare as hen's teeth. Bright, funny and fiercely loyal to friends and family, the man was irreplaceable.

Hearing a sound behind her, Jean turned anxiously as her husband appeared in his dressing gown. She studied him briefly. His face was ashen, his sandy hair a tangled damp mess. He looked defeated.

Holding out her arms, his wife waited. He made his way to her, moving like a man much older than his forty years. He stopped; hesitated, not sure what she required of him.

Silently she reached out, taking both his hands. She made soothing noises as she drew him to her.

Jean led Gordon towards the large settee, guiding him down. Her practised fingers slowly disrobed him. He was passive, allowing it. They began gently, their actions, driven more by care than passion.

Jean felt his body tighten against hers as their movements became more urgent. He gripped her hair, driving into her, burying his face in her neck. She heard him cry out in pain of loss as he sought and found brief oblivion.

Peter Maroc ended the day's close protection class

with a talk on operational planning. His present job at the Academy, situated just outside Dusseldorf, suited him well enough. Having been there for just over six months, he had made friends, most of them within the Academy.

A few of the instructors were ex Kommando Spezialkräfte. The German Special Forces Command, KSK was a highly regarded unit, and he had found the ones in the Academy to be good lads. The good-natured banter between them was a constant currency, and it was nice to feel a part of the team. The daily exchanges had also improved his German.

Friendly and conducive to his present needs as this environment was, Maroc hated being on someone's payroll. He needed the autonomy of self-employment, or at least to be part of something in which he had a stake.

He was gathering the course papers into a folder when his mobile rang. The soft Edinburgh accent was immediately recognisable. Memories flooded back like old friends.

The last time he had seen Bill Gordon was in Albania. Their joint op had gone well enough, with Bill showing his usual competence in the field. The man he referred to as his favourite jock had not changed.

They had first met in West Germany. Bill had been in 22 SAS and, rumour had it, had served in the shadowy E Squadron. In a previous incarnation, this unit had been called The Increment.

Usually drawn from members of the British special forces, E Squadron often worked with the Secret Intelligence Service (SIS,) also known as MI6. A bunch of ruthless individuals, the elite squadron specialised in black ops.

Peter Maroc had long been aware of his friend's struggle with what Bill referred to as the dark forces. Maroc's support had been unstinting throughout. With help from the army's psychiatric unit, and their skill in dealing with combat stress, the big Scot had emerged into the light. He had one big gun in his arsenal, his amazing wife, Jean. There had always been a special bond between the two men.

'Us Celts must stick together, laddie.'

When Bill eventually revealed the real reason for his call, Maroc had been deeply shocked. Dave Blandford was a friend. He was also a man you could count on to take care of business.

Like Maroc, he had been in 21 SAS. Dave had also been on the extraction team in the Chechnyan operation. He and Maroc, together with Niels Johansson, had been the lucky ones. Maroc remembered Dave at the door, urging them out of that hellish room. By fighting in tight formation, the trio had blasted their way out of the building. They were finally able to reach the RV point with almost empty mags.

Maroc remembered Blandford urging him to get the hell away, telling him their friend Tony was gone. Now, he would be another of the band of brothers to bury.

Bill was quiet for a few seconds, then:

'Peter, how are you fixed for work at the moment?'

Maroc was aware of Bill Gordon's set-up in the UK, and its success had come as no surprise. Gordon had been a brilliant operative. He had also served a term as an instructor at SAS H.Q, Credenhill, Hereford.

Bill continued.

'Thing is, I need someone to replace David, mate. Can't think of anyone better than your good self.'

'Despite me being a part-time trooper?'

It had been a running leg pull, a reference to Maroc being in 21 SAS, a reserve regiment. Maroc had always gone along with it, never responding with more than a grin.

'True. But I managed to get you knocked into shape, you bastard. So, what do you say?'

Working with Bill Gordon was something Maroc had often considered. Fearing it would be an imposition, he had always felt reticent in voicing the question.

It would be an opportunity to get back to the UK. To Wales. Who knew who he'd bump into…? He realised there was nothing of urgency keeping him where he was.

'Give me a day to think on it, Bill. Sounds good, though.'

Three days later, Maroc drove through Germany towards the Dutch border, his destination the Hook of Holland. He would get onboard a Stenaline, sailing over to Harwich. Then a leisurely drive up to North Wales in his beloved Maserati Quattroporte Sedan.

He had bought the car in Greenwich a few years earlier. The body had needed work, but for the price…? Driving it from London back to Wales and hearing that throaty sound as he accelerated, he knew he had made the right choice.

An arrangement had been arrived at with the owners of a local car body shop. He had hired a spot inside their spacious workshop and, using some of their tools, done most of the restoration work himself.

Maroc had mentioned to Bill that he'd be staying with a relative in the small Welsh village of Beddgelert. Bill and Jean would have none of it.

'Our house is massive. Tons of room.'

It was settled.

The house was indeed massive and Maroc became more impressed on each visit. It was a late nineteenth-century Victorian manor house; it stood in its spacious grounds on the outskirts of the Roman town of Caernarfon in North Wales.

Maroc, on first seeing it had jumped at the opportunity of teasing Jean. He had offered that it was 'very nice.' Bill had taken this up, matching his underwhelm. Jean Gordon was more than up to their game. She had smiled at the pair, shaken her head and departed to the kitchen.

The evening was a homage to David with business off the menu. Jean Gordon had gone to great lengths to make the evening a success. Never viewed as the little woman indoors, unless, of course, you had a death wish, it was everyone's good luck she was an excellent cook.

For Jean, preparing fine cuisine was never a chore. Her best reward was seeing her husband and their good friends enjoying her efforts.

That evening, Maroc and Gordon sat at the large dining room table and waited in anticipation. They started with an excellent Scotch broth, followed by the main dish.

Devilled kidneys was a long-established favourite. There was a hoot of delight when it emerged from the kitchen. Bill kept an excellent cellar which was supplemented by Maroc whenever he came to stay.

That day, the three fully intended to drink a fortune in wine.

The meal started well, the sheer pleasure of eating and drinking extending to late evening. Tales of heroism in extremis abounded, and there was much bawdy laughter. It served to keep the tears at bay.

Tomorrow would be time enough to return to the world of men. The bastards who killed Dave would not go unpunished. Tonight, they would reside within the comforting delusion of boyish bravado.

CHAPTER 3

It was to be a late start for all three, with even Jean uncharacteristically struggling. Maroc offered to treat them to breakfast in town, then realised they were all well above the alcohol driving limit.

When he suggested drinking plenty of water, Bill gave him a look and went off to brew tea. He returned with three steaming mugs. They sat in one of the smaller sitting rooms, each tending their grief. Finally, Bill broke the silence.

'OK, we can't just sit and mope. Let's have a change of scenery.'

They decided on a gentle walk to the nearest pub. A very gentle walk.

At The Traveller's Rest, they huddled like conspirators around a table near the bar. Bill ordered coffee for everybody. This morning, David's death would not be mentioned. The time for talking was over. Action would be taken soon enough.

Bill Gordon had put in place an expansion programme that had David Blandford as chief coordinator. Maroc, not wishing to dictate terms, had nonetheless explained his position to Bill.

His time would have to be divided between Gordon's programme and Maroc's schedule. His friend had assured him he would not be required to work full-time for at least six months.

The overall project involved extending the academy to include an improved facility dedicated to hostage retrieval training. Maroc's job, over the next six months, was to develop new programmes and improve existing ones. He would need to be fully available on completion of the building work.

This arrangement suited Maroc. It would allow him to visit his home village in Snowdonia; seek out friends and family. The wild and rugged beauty of North Wales was a strong motive for Maroc's return to his birthplace. It was not, however, the main one.

Peter Maroc was not over his wife, not by a long shot. He fervently hoped she harboured the same feelings for him. He was aware reality could not be forged by wishing, or else she would be with him now.

Every day since their separation, he had asked himself the same questions. Had his selfish behaviour completely wrecked his chances of reuniting with his wife? Had his constant disappearance from her life killed the love he knew she once had for him?

Maroc was aware he had a darker side, a part of him that needed the closeness of death to feel alive. Now, he realised the presence of Emily in his life was an even greater need.

Before her, he had never needed another to complete him. As a child, he could turn inwards and find that still place no matter how bad things got. A refuge where he felt safe, contented.

This trait could be found in many of the successful members of special forces. It allowed them to operate under conditions that would break most men. However, such a lifestyle could be addictive. For peter

Maroc, it had become his drug of choice.

Bill gave his friend a brief outline of his plans for the centre. The details could wait for clearer minds. It would not be an energetic day.

By early afternoon, Jean had recovered well and was planning dinner. The weaker sex was allowed a siesta. Serious business could wait until tomorrow.

Today would be a gentle day. One of quiet and respectful reflection.

Maroc was showered and dressed by seven the following morning. Downstairs, he found Bill sitting at his office desk sipping coffee. A printer on a nearby shelf noisily spat out sheets of paper.

Gordon looked up from his untidy desk, giving his friend a lopsided grin.

'Coffee's brewed, mate. Help yourself.'

He rose from his desk, gathering up the stack of printed sheets.

'Your homework.'

He grinned at Maroc.

'I'll stick them in a folder.'

Maroc gave a small bow and started for the kitchen.

Jean had a full cafetiere of the black stuff waiting for him, and as usual, the smell worked its magic. He walked into her spacious kitchen and sat at the large pine table. Her smile, morning fresh, she poured him a full cup, sliding it over.

Not for the first time, Maroc marvelled at this exceptional woman. Her dark brown hair displayed a little grey with the casual indifference of maturity. But it was her brown, luminous eyes that drew attention. In looks, she was Emily's opposite. In temperament, they could have been sisters.

'Like the table, Jean. Antique?'

It's new, actually. I paid to have it distressed. Give it a bit of character.'

'The cost distressed the hell out of me. Could have done it myself with a hammer and a bicycle chain.'

Bill had his empty cup in one hand and a folder in the other. He placed the cup on the table. Turning to Maroc, he handed him the folder.

Jean's smile was saccharine sweet.

'More coffee, darling?

The day passed comfortably, with Bill Gordon showing Maroc around the academy. Given Gordon's SAS background, the layout inevitably reflected his training. The SAS was still the template for most other Special Forces programmes. Maroc was comfortable with the setup.

Dinner passed pleasantly enough, with the conversation consciously kept away from the elephant in the room. Maroc, however, was not surprised when Bill Gordon grew tired of keeping up the facade of normalcy.

Turning to Maroc, he pointedly asked if he knew who the perpetrators were. Maroc agreed to look into things through his contacts, both in the UK and Europe.

Jean was quieter than usual. Maroc had noticed that she kept giving her husband concerned looks. He decided to not get involved. Bill was a proud man and preferred his private life to remain private. They would sort it out between them. They always had.

Maroc left early the following morning with conflicting emotions playing havoc with his peace of mind. While it had been good seeing his old friends,

Blandford's death had deeply affected him. Yet another tear in his already damaged psyche.

Thirty minutes later, Maroc arrived at the small town of Beddgelert. He decided he would call at The Prince Llewellyn. He needed something to take the edge off the pain of loss before visiting his only remaining relative, his mother's brother, George.

His favourite of all his relatives, Uncle George, was a true mountain man. Next to his father, the old bugger had been his principal influence growing up. It had been four years since the tragic death of his parents in a car crash in the French Alps.

Maroc and Emily had been married a year. News of the tragedy had been revealed to them by friends of his parents. They were a French couple who often holidayed with Maroc's mother and father. He had known them since childhood. They had been in the lead car, travelling about half a mile in front.

When his parents' car had failed to appear at a designated stop, the French couple had driven back to discover the cause for the holdup. The car had left the road, broken through the protective barrier and plunged a couple of hundred feet to the valley floor.

At the point of the accident, a small group of people stood around, waiting for the emergency services. Further investigation of their wrecked car had left the police unclear as to the cause of the tragedy.

Since their death, for Maroc, returning to Beddgelert had always been difficult. George and his wife, along with Emily, had supported Maroc throughout the investigation into the accident. The couple had accompanied him to France. In their quiet way, they had looked after him. He knew a visit to

Wales without seeing them was never an option.

When dealing with his parents' not inconsiderable estate, Maroc found his father had kept good records of all his business dealings. These included investments in the stock market. Maroc had found himself a modestly wealthy man.

He still owned the family home but had opted to rent it rather than occupying a place so full of ghosts from his past. He knew he would lay them all to rest one day. One day soon. Not yet.

Stepping through the door of 'The Prince Llewellyn, he was assailed by memories of his youth. They hailed him with the familiarity of old friends. He was sixteen again, downing his first pint of best.

Sitting at the bar, acknowledging old faces, listening to his mother tongue, Peter Maroc waited for the usual burn of grief. This time it never came. He smiled and gave a contented sigh. It was good to be back in the country he would always call home.

CHAPTER 4

Uncle George greeted Maroc at the door of the old terraced house where he and his wife Mary had lived for the last thirty years. A vigorous man in his mid-sixties, he could outwalk and out-climb most men half his age.

Maroc winced as his uncle shook his hand. He was never prepared for the bone-crushing grip, and the old bugger always managed to catch him out.

Uncle George gave Maroc an appraising look. He scratched his cropped grey hair and grinned at his nephew.

'Lost some weight, lad. Been in the wars again?'

As Maroc followed his uncle into the front hall, he absorbed the familiarity of the place. There was an old-fashioned warmth to this household. For Maroc, it was a place where he had always come to for solace; for family.

Mary Edwards had been a beauty. In Maroc's eyes, she was still an attractive woman. On hearing his voice, she joined her husband at the door.

He loved these two people. Their steadfast loyalty and affection since the death of his parents were one of the few constants in his life.

As though his visit had been expected, a cup of tea materialised on cue. Uncle George suggested a snifter.

Mary was ahead of the game as she placed a bottle of eighteen-year-old Glenfiddich on the table. This was a special occasion.

'I'll bring glasses.'

She beamed at her favourite bad boy. Disappearing back into the kitchen, she returned with three whiskey glasses and a small jug of water. George grimaced as she diluted her drink.

'It's how the Scots drink it. That face you make will stick one day.'

George looked up in mock irritation.

'I know. If the wind changes.'

She winked at Maroc.

Toasting his return, they warmed the parlour with their small talk. Inevitably, the conversation turned to family. Uncle George's expression became serious.

'Don't know how much you've heard, Peter but Emily's mum passed away a year ago. Max's taking it bad'

Maroc was shocked. Why had he not been told by Emily, by anyone?

Maroc had always liked Katherine. He had always thought Emily had inherited her looks from her mother and, most definitely, not from Mr Grumpy.

'Max has been bedridden these last few months. I've been to see him a couple of times, but...'

Mary's voice trailed off. She looked at her husband as if he could better clarify.

George shook his head.

'Broken-hearted, poor bastard. As far as I can see, he's just been left to die in that bloody bed. Sons are like vultures, waiting for him to pop his clogs.'

'You mean John and Malcolm?'

'Right. Oh, don't get me wrong, no one could accuse them of anything. Far too clever. For those who know Max, it's as clear as day. He's just been left to sink. Killing him with kindness like.'

He looked up at Maroc.

'They can't wait to get his bloody money.'

'Did you say money? He was a college lecturer, not a merchant banker. Anyway, don't they have a tidy business of their own, in Australia.

'No idea about that. Yes, real money. Max invested wisely.'

He glanced at his wife, who nodded her agreement.

'Bit of a whiz kid with the stocks and shares. He's pretty well off.'

Maroc gave a rueful smile, aware this man held more information on people than the Mormons.

'How do you know all this, Uncle George?'

George smiled back, tapping his nose.

'Got my sources, lad.'

Mary rolled her eyes but said nothing. George continued.

'Why not call in and see for yourself. He might be glad of a bit of real company.'

Mary looked doubtful. She turned to Maroc.

'How long has it been since you last saw Max? You two...'

She hesitated, trying to find the right words.

'Never really, what I would call, hit it off, did you?'

Maroc looked at her, grinning.

'Not his favourite person, aunty Mary. Not since the split with Emily.'

He added, almost to himself.

'Come to think of it, I never was.'

Maroc hesitated for a moment before asking.

'I'm curious. What about Emily? What does she think of the setup?'

'You don't know, do you, lad?'

George looked at Mary before continuing.

'Emily's in some bloody awful place in Africa. She's been stuck there for months.'

His aunty took over the story.

'She's been doing work for The World Health Organisation.'

She looked at her husband for confirmation. He gave a qualifying nod.

'Some sort of epidemic in that region. Poor girl can't get home because of the quarantine still in place.'

It was a lot to take in. A lot to be concerned about. He had hoped to come back to North Wales and by chance or guile, bump into his wife.

Things were turning out to be very different. And very alarming.

The hell with it. Welcome or not, he would find out for himself.

There followed more updates about the goings-on and scandals in the area before Maroc said a fond goodbye to the couple. He promised faithfully to call in as often as his schedule would allow.

Max Southwell lived less than a half-mile outside the village, and Maroc enjoyed the gentle walk leading to the imposing Victorian house. The granite building was as solid and sombre as its owner. Standing within spacious grounds, it could not fail to impress.

The tall black painted iron gates were there when Max and Katherine had bought the place eight years ago. Its most prominent feature was a rather outsized

Welsh dragon incorporated into the design. This had been garishly picked out in red by the previous owners. Katherine had loved it, had insisted it would not be changed. He remembered how fiercely proud she had been of her Welsh heritage.

Maroc loved the large garden. Its lack of structure and formality resonated with him. As a child growing up in the village, Plas Meurig had been forbidden territory. This greatly added to its attraction.

He had often scrumped apples and plums from the previous owners. On his first visit to the house with Emily, he had felt a boyish frisson of apprehension. Was he still on record with the new people?

Now, stepping through the gate, he was taken aback. Almost totally reclaimed by Mother Nature, this was a far cry from the garden Katherine had been so proud of.

As he walked up the path towards the house, he thought of Emily. The times they had strolled around these lovely grounds.

How had he allowed their life together to slip away from him, and for what? The dubious lure of danger? The sheer selfishness of his actions now appalled him.

A woman around his age opened the door. Wearing a crisp blue uniform, she affected the manner of a nineteenth-century English butler addressing a tradesman.

'Can I help?'

Her voice was crisp, her stare bold and direct. He introduced himself as family, which was more or less the truth. An upward tilt of her chin, a slight hesitation, then somewhat grudgingly, she stood to one side. Maroc entered, attempting one of his more appealing smiles. It was not returned.

Visually, things were as he remembered, the large entrance hall as imposing as ever. The odours, however, were decidedly medical. The nurse, which he assumed she was, had indicated he remained in the hall. Maroc, faintly amused at her outmoded manner waited to be summoned.

He entered the large room and then stopped. The sight that greeted him was not what he had expected.

CHAPTER 5

Maroc had a hard time convincing the nurse that not only was he fully qualified to look after Max Southwell, but all had been fully sanctioned by his daughter, Emily.

'Yes, Mrs Maroc has given her full approval.'

Fingers crossed behind his back at the blatant lie, he continued.

'I'm to be given full details of her father's condition.'

Maroc was not proud of his duplicity or the ease with which he employed it. The talent, however, had saved his life and those of his comrades on more than one occasion. He was back in enemy territory and was secretly enjoying himself.

Maroc's training and experience with special forces had added much to his medical knowledge. His time in the East conferred another dimension to that knowledge. It was enough to help him convince nurse Price he was more than capable of looking after her ward.

Price's resistance had gradually weakened. She gave a final show of face-saving disapproval before allowing him access to Southwell's medical notes. Peter Maroc could be very plausible.

As she handed him the notes, he wondered what the hell he was thinking of. This reckless decision to step into such a position of responsibility had been taken by some insane alter ego. As was often the case with Maroc, his actions were reflexive, the rationale to be added later.

He scanned the folder content, giving Price informed and cogent comments on various points. It demonstrated to the nurse that he was at least competent enough to understand her notes. She visibly thawed as he allowed her to impress him with her knowledge of Southwell's condition.

After the death of his wife, Katherine, Max Southwell had deteriorated both physically and mentally. Often drifting into a fugue state, he would become angry in his denial of such lapses.

He accepted his final surrender to despair as righteous punishment for surviving his wife. It began affecting his health. His eldest daughter Emily and youngest son Malcolm looked on. The former with growing dismay, the latter already savouring his share of the inheritance.

Emily Maroc was an excellent physician, but coping with her father's mental state was taxing. He had announced, that there was nothing to live for. Emily had found this hurtful to hear.

As her medical practice consumed more and more of her time, it became obvious that her focus on her father could no longer be sustained. The periods away from her job were becoming more difficult to justify.

She felt frustrated and, at times, defeated. She also felt guilty, knowing that much could be done for her father. She should be pushing harder.

Southwell had shown early symptoms of fibromyalgia and irritable bowel syndrome. He would refuse to leave his bed, declaring it to be 'too bloody painful.'

Emily had remonstrated with him, suggesting gentle exercise would be beneficial. His depressions, however, took him down the path of least suffering. He became stubborn, insisting she had no idea what he was going through.

She failed to understand the advice and insistence of her brothers. It went against her every instinct as a doctor. Damn it; she was the professional. Their suggested course of action failed to make medical sense.

Her eldest brother John would phone from Perth with repeated admonition. She was not to cause her father further discomfort and suffering. Emily was made to feel guilty for taking the medically appropriate action. It frustrated and baffled her in equal measure.

Max Southwell did succumb to her nagging, and she would take him on gentle walks around the garden. Forced to respond to the massive workload thrust upon her by an understaffed health service, Emily had been obliged to take up the slack. She would return from her work to find her regime undermined; her good intentions thwarted.

Emily's trip to Africa could not be put off for much longer. A coherent plan of action had to be set in place before her departure. She had made contact with the local doctor in Llanberis.

Dr Gareth Llewellyn, a tall lean man in his early sixties, had a solid reputation for being a no-nonsense physician. He had agreed that much of Max Southwell's condition was psychosomatic, exacerbated by his increasing sense of futility. He was further concerned by some underlying issues regarding the older man's health.

Llewellyn promised he would monitor her father's progress and continue Emily's regime of exercise and movement. He further suggested sessions of professional counselling. These would help address his deteriorating state of mind.

Emily felt happier about leaving, having set in place a course of action that would best benefit her father. She knew he was in capable hands and her wishes for his ongoing care would be carried out. The brothers, however, had other plans.

Malcolm and John put in place a system of their own. One which would guarantee Southwell would not recover. They had brought in their people and introduced a new regime of care. The youngest son had convinced his father that rest was the best medicine. It had been an easy sell.

Malcolm informed Dr Llewellyn his services were no longer required. The doctor, insisting on talking to his patient, was dismayed at being told by Max Southwell he was no longer prepared to endure his harsh regimen. It was unnecessary pain and suffering. He had had enough.

Without daily movement and stretching, many of Southwell's problems returned. The loss of muscle tone rapidly affected his mobility. He had been warned by Emily and Llewellyn. If you don't use it, you'll lose it.

In a weakened state his apathy having returned, Southwell found it increasingly harder to fight the pain. He had demanded as much pain-relieving medication as possible. His demands had been eagerly granted. The outcome was inevitable.

Inactivity, depression and pain worked in synergy, pushing him into a downward spiral. Malcolm gave an award-worthy impression of the much-concerned son. His dwindling resistance rendered the older man open to infection. Southwell caught a heavy cold. Inevitably, it turned into a chronic chest condition.

Mentored by his older brother, Malcolm facilitated his father's decline. The patient's bed was brought downstairs into the living room. Southwell no longer needed to climb the stairway to his room.

An act of kindness. His fate was sealed.

Southwell became increasingly confused, his behaviour, at times unreasonable and obstinate. It was all the justification John needed to relieve him of his independence.

He worked through his brother Malcolm to skew the legal process to their benefit. Max Southwell was deemed psychologically unfit to run his affairs.

A full-time carer was brought in to attend to their father's every need. Southwell witnessed his autonomy dwindle and did not much care. He became feeble, his muscles atrophying through lack of use.

Both John and Malcolm insisted all further treatment would be palliative. This action was taken under the pretext of sparing their father's unnecessary suffering.

To an outside observer, they were loving sons, assuring his last days were comfortable. His daughter Emily would have seen through their ploy. But Emily was not there.

During a long conversation from Perth, John had managed to make Emily feel bad for wanting to prolong her father's agony. He had called her selfish.

Informing his sister that he had conferred with several specialists on their father's condition, Emily had capitulated. John Southwell had assured her he was merely guided by their advice.

Emily would later learn that the medical authorities he had referenced were either quoted out of context or, in some cases, their opinion manufactured. Side-lined, her medical credentials disregarded, Emily Southwell had never felt so frustrated or angry.

Peter Maroc walked into the large sitting room where Southwell lay on a king-sized bed placed in the far left-hand corner. The older man scowled at the intrusion, his displeasure becoming palpable at seeing who his visitor was. Maroc mentally shrugged. It had been anticipated and, as equally dismissed.

He was aware of Southwell's impatience; could feel his hostility. Still, he took his time. Maroc carefully examined the room's layout. He turned to face the man he had always viewed as the mighty patriarch.

Even in this weakened state, Southwell's ego was in evidence, his expression that of a man not used to being a secondary consideration.

On seeing Southwell, Maroc was taken aback. No longer the powerhouse he remembered, his father-in-law looked very much the invalid. In truth, he looked bloody awful.

Max Southwell might be a pompous bastard, but this was not right. A professor of philosophy at Cambridge, he had been a person of consequence. Maroc was now looking at a bad-tempered shadow of that old warrior.

Nurse Price had given a quick breakdown of Southwell's progress over the last six months. At first, despite his melancholy, he had been a lion, fighting over every yard of territory, giving them all bloody hell.

As the weeks passed, with his body succumbing to the opiates, he had grown weary, tired of fighting a war in which he had no investment.

Katherine had gone and with her his raison d'être. His world had become a drab grey place, devoid of the joy and colour she had provided. Focusing on and making sense of his predicament had become harder. An increasing part of him welcomed the growing dependency.

Being left undisturbed and having all his basic needs attended to became increasingly acceptable. He could drift back into a happier past. It was comfortable.

Southwell was unaware that the control of his estate had been fully transferred to his two sons. If he had known, his main concern would have been for Emily.

Observing this dark menace of a man, Max Southwell felt a growing apprehension. He smiled grimly, aware o the irony of such a thing. The once influential and formidable academic had been used to making others nervous.

Southwell had never fully trusted Maroc. What sort of name was it anyway, Maroc? The man disturbed him on many levels, yet he could see the attraction. Those blazing blue eyes and a manner that announced to the world he could never be intimidated or ruled.

He felt a grudging respect for this; what would they

call him these days, Alpha male? In a past life and different garb, he had been such a man.

Emily could have had her pick, but she had chosen Maroc. Bloody Maroc! Southwell scrutinised this enigma and, as always, came up with very little. Was he good or bad?

His instincts had always landed firmly on the bad. Maybe not outright evil. Trouble anyway. Trouble that came in a tall, dark, and dangerous package.

Where was his family when he needed them? Where was John, always the level-headed one? Truth be told, he cared little for the cold fish his son had become.

Not for the first time, Southwell wondered which side of the family had contributed to this prissy remote individual that was his eldest son. The man had the soul of an accountant and the moral hypocrisy of a bad priest.

Neither was Southwell much impressed by his youngest son. Malcolm was both weak and greedy, which was a poor mix for any man. But there was always Emily, beautiful Emily.

Since Katherine's death, she was the only reason he hadn't declared total surrender to the dark enemy. Be done with the whole damned business.

Southwell had often reflected on how his children had turned out. Was it nature or nurture? When they were young, he and Kathrine had doted on each child without exception. However, Max Southwell was an authoritarian. A strong character who had expected much of his children.

John was strong-willed and clever, always had been, even as a young boy. Southwell had recognised his son's intelligence. He had tried to encourage it, to channel it in the right direction. But John wanted his successes without the requisite effort.

His son had gained a law degree and had begun training as a solicitor. The curriculum was tough. It required focus and application. To John, the rewards were too far down the line.

Predictably, he had dropped out, deciding that, with money from his father, he could start a property development business with one of his college friends.

Max Southwell had made encouraging noises, but John had read his disappointment. That was when Southwell had first realised his son's growing resentment.

At the time, Southwell had felt overwhelming guilt and sadness. As the years passed, he realised that whatever decisions were taken in those early years, the outcome would have been the same. John, by any definition, was not a good person.

Jill, his youngest child, together with Malcolm, were the weak ones. His wife had protected them from the world. He loved them because they were his own. Yet, as with John, he had failed to hide his disappointment from them.

Southwell recognised the unfairness of it with these two runts of the litter. He had tried to compensate for what he saw as his lacking

The academic in him had tried to encourage them in their education, had hired private tutors, hoping a spark would ignite and burst into a yet undiscovered talent.

The tutors had recognised in Malcolm a love of literature. With monetary inducement from his parents, he eventually gained a Masters in English literature from a red brick university.

For a while, he and Jill had lived at home. Malcolm would apply for impossible positions at universities before giving up completely. With his parents' funding and a massive sense of entitlement, he had lived the life of an educated layabout.

Jill possessed a delicate beauty, growing up to be an attractive young woman. At nineteen, she had married much too soon. The marriage had lasted two years, and she had returned home having acquired bitterness rather than experience.

Then there was Emily. Both he and Katherine had recognised and valued her quiet strength and intelligence. This serious little girl had reached out to her siblings.

She had tried to make things better and easier for them, often acting as a second mother to the others. Her early ambition to be a doctor had never wavered.

Emily was the only person who could influence Maroc. Southwell recalled how his son-in-law would always defer to her in most things.

He felt a flash of the old anger as he recalled the change that had come about in Maroc. It was when he began embarking on his mad capers.

He would take himself away on some bloody mission or whatever he called them, leaving her to imagine the worst. The inconsiderate and foolhardy idiot had no idea how fortunate he was.

'What do you want Maroc, to finally finish me off?'

'Tempting, but no.'

Maroc smiled and reached out for Southwell's wrist. The old man flinched.

'It's alright Max, just going to take your pulse.'

'Doctor Southwell to you. Disrespectful brat.'

'Sure Max.'

Maroc's voice was soft, reassuring, his touch gentle. Southwell sighed, allowing the intrusion. His pulse was taken, with Maroc studiously consulting his watch.

Nurse Price observed his every move from the doorway. Her impression was of a professional who knew what he was doing.

For the first time since she had been assigned to this case, and for a reason, she could not fully comprehend, she felt a sense of rightness. It had been previously absent.

Southwell looked up at the younger man, holding his gaze with surprising steadiness.

'What's in this for you, Maroc?'

He had never used his first name.

Maroc stopped what he was doing, turned and walked out of the room. Southwell heard the front door slam, wondering if he had finally goaded him into leaving. Waiting for the sound of a car engine, he heard the unmistakable sound of the garage door being opened.

Panic came from nowhere, numbing his mind. Months of illness had left him vulnerable and weak. Southwell's period of lucidity was over. It was replaced by irrational fear, a primal need to escape from a terror his confused mind could not define.

He had no idea what this maniac was looking for in the garage, but it would not be good. He had to get away. Get help.

Finding strength born of his growing dread, Max

Southwell crawled from his bed. Finding support on various items of furniture and ignoring the pain, he made his way across the sitting room. Fumbling with the knob, Southwell finally managed to open the door. He stumbled into the hall and lay there, catching his breath.

Emily, he had to reach her. He had to tell her to stop this madman.

He needed help. Where was that damned list?

Finding a number he had highlighted he frantically punched it into the keypad. And waited.

A further five minutes passed before he heard the garage door clanging shut. Moments later, the front door opened. The bloody man was walking towards him.

Peter Maroc was amazed to find Southwell sitting on the hall floor, the telephone and receiver in his lap. The old academic looked terrified as Maroc gently took the receiver, replacing it carefully before placing the phone back on the hall table. What the hell was going on? Where was the bloody nurse?

He stopped and looked down at his father-in-law. When he spoke, his voice was soft.

'Come on Max. Let's get you back to bed.'

Maroc reached for him, and Southwell shrank away, pushing his body into the wall. He placed his hand on the older man's shoulder, and Southwell flinched at his touch.

'It's OK. Max. I'm just going to help you back to bed.'

Maroc picked Southwell up as easily as he would a child and carried him back to his bed. The older man said nothing but Maroc was aware of the tremor in his body.

Without a word of enquiry, he rearranged the pillows and helped Southwell into a comfortable upright position.

'Some tea, Max? Calm you down.'

With childlike meekness, Southwell looked up and nodded.

Maroc found what he needed in the kitchen. He made the tea strong and sweet. Not in a state of shock, perhaps, he knew Southwell was greatly agitated.

He returned carrying two mugs of steaming tea. They drank in silence until Southwell offered up his cup. Maroc took it and placed it on the bedside cabinet.

'What were you doing in my garage, Maroc?'

Southwell's voice, though shaky, still held a challenge. Without answering, Maroc left the bed and walked through to the hall. He returned, and Southwell noticed he had one hand concealed behind his back. He gave a slight start as Maroc propped something against the bedside cabinet.

When Max Southwell turned and looked, he saw his fishing rod and net propped up against the cabinet. He stared dumbly at Maroc, unable to comprehend the reason for this bizarre offering. He waited for an explanation.

'You're a fisherman, a bloody good one I was told."

Maroc's tone was conversational; friendly. Southwell realising the man intended him no immediate harm, reclaimed his belligerence.

'So?'

Maroc continued.

'Still interested in fishing and walking the hills?'

Southwell stared up at him, waiting for the punch line.

'Well, are you?'

'Are you taking the piss, man?'

Southwell's face had gone a bright pink. He tried sitting further up but was too exhausted.

Maroc, not immediately reacting, held Southwell's gaze.

'Not at all, so I'll ask again. Do you want to be out, enjoying life, or are you happy, playing the dying swan?'

Was he missing something? He turned his head and looked up at Maroc.

It was then that Southwell felt something that had long been absent from his life. Curiosity.

'What is this Maroc, some sadistic game?'

'No game Max. Be so kind as to answer the question.'

Both men stared in silence, each waiting for the other to respond. Southwell, because he had no idea what part he played in this act of fools. Maroc, because he needed an answer. Any initial response would be fine. He would know where to take it.

When it came, it was a whisper.

'Don't even know if I want it. Not any more.'

Maroc knew there would be resistance. Knew that Southwell was weak, defeated. The older man had his eyes closed. Maroc could hear his even breathing, and for a moment, it seemed he had drifted off. Then…

'I'm tired Maroc. Nothing left in the tank.'

Maroc hesitated before responding.

'She wouldn't want to see you like this, man.'

At this reference to his wife, Southwell's eyes sprang open. Anger flashed briefly, colouring his pale face. It died before it ignited into a rage. When he next spoke, his voice sounded stronger.

'Fishing and walking? Be serious Maroc, just look at me.'

'Oh, believe me, I'm serious, very serious. I know I can get you up and running. Well at least walking briskly again. At the moment, you're depressed as hell and that's understandable. Your health is in shit order.'

Southwell smiled wanly.

'Is that your medical diagnosis?'

Maroc laid his hand on Southwell's shoulder.

'There's one thing stronger than your body.'

Maroc gently tapped the older man's forehead.

'Once your mind is right, the rest will follow. I promise you.'

Southwell was tiring fast. His eyes closed, he turned his head and spoke quietly.

'So this is all in my head, is it? What does that make you, a hypnotist, Svengali? You're going to persuade me to think myself back on my feet?'

Maroc, glad of any exchange at this early stage, responded.

'No Max, you're going to persuade yourself. Sure, I'll be helping every step of the way. Look, I know there's a large physical component to your condition. That's not going to just disappear. We'll be working on that. Together.'

'So I'm to somehow become happy, ecstatic, and the pain will…just go away? Is that how you see it?"

'Not at first. We have to get your strength back, to reduce the pain, and the inflammation that's causing it. Then, we can work on getting your mind right.'

Maroc was aware that Southwell was tiring. He placed his hand over his and spoke softly.

'If you'll allow it, I know I can help…a lot. I can't

guarantee you'll be skipping over those hills sometime soon.'

He paused.

'I promise you, Max, I'm pretty sure that working together, we can achieve a lot.'

Southwell's eyes remained closed. A full minute passed and Maroc squeezed his shoulder. He wanted to let him sleep, but he needed an answer, a small commitment before allowing the moment to slip away. The eyes fluttered open and focused. Southwell lay quietly, looking up at Maroc. Finally,

'You're serious...about this?'

'I'm serious. Deadly serious.'

'But how and by what means? You're not a doctor. Are you?'

'A doctor? Of course not. Regard me as a healer, if you will. And before you say anything, I'm not talking about faith healing or laying of hands or any of that bloody nonsense.'

'Then how are you going to achieve this...miracle?'

A sly smile.

'How much is this going to cost me, Maroc?'

Maroc walked back to the centre of the room, preparing his answer. He needed to get this right.

Southwell would have to believe success was at least a possibility if the process he intended actioning was to work.

The soldier felt a brief moment of unreality. What the hell was he doing? Why was he committing to this mammoth task? He suspected he knew the answer.

The whole setup with Southwell was wrong. Whatever he thought of the old codger, he did not deserve this ignominious end. He was also Emily's father.

As he had done countless times, he was embarking on a path into the unknown. Doing so without thought of peril or consequence.

Maroc's instincts told him he was doing the right thing. The decent thing. He looked back at Southwell; saw he was more alert. He knew he had to continue while the older man was still awake.

'You know I spent some time both in China and Japan.'

He raised a hand to stop Southwell's anticipated response.

'First, hear me out. I promise to answer any of the questions you're bound to have.'

Southwell waved him on, a somewhat regal gesture. Maroc continued.

'Not all the training I did there had killing and maiming as its main objective. Much of my journey was one of personal growth.'

Maroc paused, anxious not to overtax the older man.

'There were mental as well as physical practises. Many of these have a powerful curative effect. Modern medicine is only now realising the powerful mind and body connection. That the mind has a massive part to play in the healing process.'

'So you do think I...'

Maroc again stopped him and continued.

'That's only a part of what I have in mind. There will be a deal of physical work in readjusting and realigning your body. There will be some pain in effecting a healing process.'

Noticing a slight flinch, he quickly added.

'I said pain, not agony. I'll keep that part to an absolute minimum. I promise.'

A ghost of a smile, his voice so weak, Maroc could barely hear.

'Good of you, old boy.'

CHAPTER 6

Emily Maroc returned exhausted to her small apartment. It was basic but adequate; she had expected much worse. The apartment was situated within the hospital ground and, by regional standards, would have been considered luxurious.

Despite exposure to the hot climate, Emily's face was ghost pale, the colour washed out by the day's demands. She decided on a quick bath before preparing a meal and starting on her patient assessments.

Emily was about to turn on the bath taps when the phone rang. Muttering her frustration, she returned to the sitting room. Picking up the phone, she fell into her only comfortable chair in one fluid motion.

Hearing her father's voice on the line was a surprise. He hardly ever called, his condition making the simplest of actions difficult. At first, his neglect hurt, but later, she became aware of his increasing frailty.

'Darling, thank god. I've been trying to call. This damned phone is all wrong. Stupid codes. Bloody confusing...'

His muddled state did not usually alarm her. This time, however, she detected something more. Her father seemed frightened.

'Slow down, dad, just tell me. Tell me, slowly.'

'It's him, he's here. And Em, I think he means to do something...'

His voice had faded to a low whimper. She could hear his ragged breathing.

Emily had, over the last few months, detected an increasing propensity for drama in him. Southwell's voice would take on a plaintive quality whenever he was upset. This was a universe away from the man she knew.

'Deep breath, dad. Just tell me who you're talking about.'

'Your bloody man, Maroc. He's here and...'

Was he sobbing? Her heart went out to the person she loved most in the world.

'Hey, you."

She chided him softly,

'It can't be that bad. You're talking about Peter, my Peter?

'He means to do me in Emily. He's looking for something in the garage. God knows what. The man's mad. He's bloody dangerous. Christ, he's coming back.'

She heard a soft click at the other end, then nothing.

'Dad, are you there?'

Her hand flew to her face, rubbing vigorously, an action going back to her childhood whenever she was stressed.

Think Emily, just focus and think. Peter, if it is him, is no psycho. Even if he is a little... impulsive. Strike that, a lot impulsive.

She shook her head.

This is bizarre. Is it his illness? He's weak and confused and... No, sod it!

She would call her father back and find out what was really happening. It took her over thirty minutes to work through the area's chaotic telephone system.

After repeated attempts at dialling, Emily finally heard ringing. The phone was answered on the third ring.

'Yes? Who is this?

'Peter, is that you, Peter?'

'Jesus! Emily?'

'What is going on. You're scaring the hell out of dad."

Her anger felt good. It empowered her; gave her room to think. There was an infuriating silence.

'Talk to me, for god's sake. What are you doing at the house, and why is my father so scared?'

'In a nutshell? I'm trying to save his life.'

His voice was calm, measured. He was stating a fact.

'What are you talking about? Are you quite mad?"

'Em, your father will die if left alone in that bloody bed. You know that. I can't just sit back and let it happen.'

She started to speak, but he cut her short.

'What do you want Em? Your father back for a few more decades? I mean as a going concern, not a cabbage.'

'But you don't even like my father.'

She stopped herself, realising it had been an absurd thing to say.

For what seemed an age, Maroc said nothing and, for a moment, she thought they had been disconnected. She continued.

'Can dad hear all this? Is he listening?'

The whole thing had become unreal.

'I don't want him scared to death. I don't want that.'

'He's got those headphone things on. God knows what he's listening to.'

'Have you talked to Gareth Llewellyn, the local G.P.?

There was a short pause.

He's overseeing dad's day-to-day routine. God, Peter, Llewellyn's not an idiot. Let him do what he's good at and leave things be.'

'I've no idea who you're talking about, Emily. There's a nurse Price here.'

It was getting dark outside, the mounting gloom in the small apartment keeping pace with her growing sense of hopelessness. She began again and faltered.

'Em, talk to me.'

'Please Peter, don't do anything that might hurt him. He's my dad.'

Maroc winced at her anguish. He wanted to reach across the distance. Make her pain go away.

'Peter?'

'Listen to me, Em.'

He squeezed his eyes shut, wanting the words to count.

'I'm going to get your father well. Believe that, don't you?'

There was a long pause, then.

'Yes, I believe you... but how? You're not a doctor.'

'I've been around, Emily. Learnt things, good things. Practices that will work on your father if he'll let me.'

His voice became urgent.

'Talk to him. Make him trust me.'

She was genuinely puzzled.

'You mean, from your training? Your Eastern martial arts and things? I just don't know if he's up to it. He's frail Peter.'

'I'm not going to turn the sitting room into a bloody dojo and teach your father karate or Chinese martial arts, Em.'

She sensed his smile. The one he reserved, just for her.

'There's so much more I've learned. So much I can do for Max.

He paused, and she waited for him to continue. Wanting the hope he was offering to be real.

'You've got to trust me, Em. At least give me a chance. You owe it to your father.'

'I trust your intentions... I don't want you to make him worse.'

She heard him sigh. Sensed his frustration.

'He can't be any worse than he is. Without intervention, he's got six months, twelve at the most. Give him a shot at a couple of vigorous decades, eh?'

'And you think these...methods, your practices, can do that?'

She wanted to believe, to believe unreservedly, like a child.

'It's a pretty good bet. A better bet than he has now. Worse case? He stays the same.'

He paused, then,

'Hope to die.'

Hope to die. She began to remember him. His quirky sayings, and what she had called his little Welsh ways. He'd hated that.

She sighed deeply, feeling a ridiculous relief. There could be no basis for this burgeoning hope. But there it was, and with it a lightness she had not felt since before her mother's untimely death. To have her dad back as he was.

Then quietly, cautiously, she spoke.

'All right. But please go slowly. Don't hurt him. Don't you dare hurt him, you bastard.'

Maroc smiled. kissing his finger, he touched it to the receiver.

'Night, Emily.'

Emily Southwell walked away from the telephone with a thousand questions. Could she trust Maroc with her father's wellbeing? His life?

After dating for three years, they had been married for three. She had much to discover about Peter Maroc.

During the early days of their courtship, she had heard stories that had caused her concern. There was never direct evidence of bad character or outright wrongdoing. One thing, however, was pretty clear. Maroc's background and life had been very different from hers.

She wished she could be back home to help sort out this crisis. It was a dire situation that had grown more serious since her departure. At least she could keep a watchful eye on Maroc's great plans for her father.

And what the hell had happened to Dr Llewellyn? She already knew the answer.

Preoccupied with her problems, she returned to the bathroom and turned on the heated water. She began a ritual that had always soothed in the past.

Today something told her, she would need more than scented hot water to assuage her nagging fears and doubts.

She willed the warmth to work its usual magic. Her mind began to drift.

Hearing Peter's voice after all this time had stirred

up memories and feelings she had tried to suppress. The memories were mainly happy, but they hurt the most.

There were moments of regret, of sadness. Hate had never occupied their shared experience. Irritation? She gave an involuntary chuckle, halting the gentle drift into sleep.

They had met in The Garrison. It was the first pub she had visited in London. As a naive undergrad medical student at Guy's and St Thomas', she and her little gang had made it their local.

On her fifth visit, accompanied by some of her edgier med student friends, Maroc had been at the bar with a handful of students from Imperial College.

A couple of her friends knew some of his friends. She had drifted in their wake over to the bar.

Around ten years older than her naive twenty years, he was a mature student reading business studies at Imperial College.

Emily's friends knew him as Maroc. No one seemed sure whether it was his Christian or his surname. Maroc epitomised the worldly and the wicked. A naughty enigma to be experienced at one's peril.

On the surface, he was friendly; easy-going. However, he carried with him an air of detachment. A remoteness that had immediately captured Emily's interest.

She had never possessed the capacity for serious drinking. Her ticket into the inner circle had been a winning combination of quick wit and intelligence. With her fair, ethereal looks, Emily Southwell had no problems being accepted.

She had observed the distance Maroc placed

between himself and the rest of the company. He had turned and looked at her. His smile, while open and friendly, carried a question. – What are we doing here with this lot?

Peter Maroc was not her usual choice in men. Not that she had had much experience. He seemed the quintessence of cool detachment.

Not arrogant, she thought. Maroc gave her the impression that he did not invest too much of himself into anything.

She would admit his dark, Celtic looks and clear blue eyes helped a deal. Yes, he was an older man. For Emily, this only increased her interest. Boys of her age were, well... boys.

Emily had inherited her seriousness from her father. She had been raised in an academic environment where informed discourse had always been encouraged.

Her parents had engendered in her a need for far meatier conversations than her classmates could provide. Yet she could manage crazy as well as the rest. She had the feeling Maroc could provide her with both.

There was something dangerous about the Welshman. The perverseness in her sought to know more.

With the merest of indications, he had nodded at a small table by the window.

Blushing, she had turned to her friends. They had grinned back like loons, their expression telling her to - get on with it.

They had talked. Emily had found Maroc's company comfortable, his faint Welsh accent appealing. He was a distance from anyone she knew, and that difference drew her in.

Earlier in the evening, she had overheard a couple of the girls talking about the tall Welshman. When questioned, they had warned her off. He was not for nice girls like her. The seed had been planted.

Although Maroc had reached his final year at Imperial, unlike her, he was not in the least bit studious. Yet he seemed interested in most things and could talk with impressive authority on several subjects.

Emily had not committed to any political camp. When the conversation did turn to politics, she had been curious about his position. When quizzed about it, he had smiled. She had never got beyond that smile.

They had exchanged numbers. A week passed before he made contact. He suggested he pick her up from her digs and would she spend the weekend with him?

She had voiced concerns about the propriety of such an arrangement. He assured her he had no intention of allowing her into his bed, and what could she be thinking of. His disarming teasing won the day.

The weekend was spent in North Wales, where she had met his parents. The house outside the small village of Beddgelert was a converted Welsh farmhouse set on ten acres of land.

To Emily, this disclosure had been a portent. Her father, a keen walker and fisherman, was a frequent visitor to North Wales. Beddgelert was a village he had often mentioned when describing the tranquillity and sheer beauty of the place. He and her mother had often talked of retiring to the area.

Maroc's paternal grandfather had been Moroccan,

hence the name Maroc. However, both his parents fiercely regarded themselves as Welsh.

It was obvious Maroc had acquired his looks from his mother, Rhian. Emily had been drawn in by the woman's animated nature and warmth. They had quickly become friends.

Maroc senior had required more cultivation. However, by the second day, they had established a bond. It had been mainly based on absurd humour. His son observed their antics with mock frustration.

Owain Maroc was a property developer and owned half a dozen hotels throughout North Wales. At his wife's insistence, he had freed much of his time. Owain had put in place a reliable team of managers.

Strong-willed and self-directing in most areas of his life, his wife's happiness had always been paramount. Whenever this was threatened, he would defer to her wishes. In many ways, Owain reminded Emily of her father.

The young couple had not shared a bedroom. Maroc had announced loftily he would tolerate no smut from a flighty English woman, and what sort of man did she think him anyway. She would occupy the guest bedroom and like it!

At breakfast, there had just been the two of them. Maroc's parents had gone to Llandudno for the day. Partly business, they said. Emily had never been a big breakfast person, so when Maroc suggested the full English, she had declined. He seemed relieved, offering her fresh juice and cereal instead.

His transport for their day out was an old Riley saloon. Maroc had bought it for a song, and he had spent days rebuilding the engine. Emily had refrained from smiling at his evident pride when recounting the undertaking.

Emily had been instructed to bring casual clothing and sensible shoes. There would be walking.

They had driven to the town of Llanberis. The town was the beating heart of British rock climbing and had been the chosen base for the annual meetings of the 1953 Everest team.

It turned out Maroc was an experienced and highly proficient climber. That day he had elected to take her on a relatively gentle outing. They would take the Miner's Track leading to the summit of Mount Snowdon.

Noticing her slight hesitation, he had assured her they would finish the undemanding walk halfway to the summit. They would picnic at a beautiful lake known in Welsh as Llyn Llydaw.

She recalled it had been a near-perfect day with Peter being extra attentive. He had made the journey fun, exaggerating each stage as though it was a Himalayan expedition.

Maroc had packed a picnic which included a bottle of red wine. On reaching the lake, he had spread out a plastic sheet. She had smiled as he produced each picnic item from his rucksack with a flourish.

The first kiss was surprisingly tender. Emily was then duly warned not to take further advantage of a simple country boy and rather pointedly handed a salmon sandwich.

She sighed and sank further into the bath. Would she have continued seeing him had she known the other side of his nature? How his addiction to danger would eventually separate them? She doubted

anything would have dissuaded her on that perfect
day.

CHAPTER 7

After his visit to 'Plas Meurig,' Maroc had made a vow. He would gain control over Max Southwell's affairs. He had faith in his ability to stop, even reverse Southwell's alarming disintegration. Effecting this intervention, however, required full residency at Plas Meurig.

Malcolm was the only member of Max Southwell's family still in the UK. He had reluctantly accepted his role as the executor of his ailing father's estate.

Jill, Malcolm's younger sister, had joined John and Ruth in Perth, Australia. She had longed to escape her failed social life at home, and when John had offered her a job as a low-paid secretary and general dogsbody, she had jumped at the chance.

Peter Maroc had met Malcolm Southwell on several occasions. He had quickly concluded his main drivers were vanity and greed.

Here was a man he could easily influence.

Maroc had phoned his brother-in-law, hinting at a financial arrangement advantageous to both. Initially, Southwell's dislike of Maroc had trumped his greed.

That was before Maroc had talked numbers. There had been a change of heart, and they had arranged to meet at The Blue Cock in Salford, Manchester.

His brother-in-law had to feed his alcohol and gambling addiction somehow. The easy buck had always appealed.

Hardly ever sober, he had found it increasingly easier to rationalise his dalliance with lady luck. Malcolm had started with financial betting. He now harboured the delusion of being a good poker player. He was not.

Malcolm Southwell, M.A, firmly believed his privileged education could trump any strategy the lower orders might present. He ran up debts in some of the roughest dives in Manchester. Generous mates who never refused him a place at the table had suddenly turned nasty. It was time to settle up.

Maroc sat in his car and studied the sketchy street map he had found in his email Inbox. Stanley Street should be just around the corner. Reluctantly parking his Maserati into a tight gap between two cars, he began walking the short distance to the pub. Rounding the next corner, the Blue Cock stood thirty yards on the left.

As he stepped through the pub's well-oiled push doors, he immediately spotted his brother-in-law at the bar. Always skinny, Southwell seemed to have lost even more weight. His creased brown suit looked two sizes too big.

Malcolm's eyes always reminded Maroc of two black raisins. They were now trained on him as he walked to the bar. His brother-in-law looked left and right as though checking for witnesses to the meet. He elected to stay at the bar and not come forward to greet his brother-in-law. It was his idea of power play.

Reminiscent of a schoolboy wearing his older brother's hand-me-downs, Malcolm Southwell attempted casual. He lounged back on the bar, an unlit cigarette stub hanging from his mouth. With his dark greasy hair, the style more suited to a man fifteen years his junior, he looked small and vulnerable.

An initial attempt at cordiality quickly ran out of steam on both sides. Maroc wanted to get down to business, and Southwell was eager to hear what was on offer.

Maroc had previously hinted at a mutually advantageous meeting. It took less than five minutes for Southwell to reveal his desperation.

'Nice as it is to see you, Maroc, we need to get down to the real reason for this visit.'

Maroc realised how easy his job was going to be. He considered halving his offer, then thought against it. He was getting soft.

Malcolm was willing to relinquish his legal position in his father's affairs, trading the only commodity of value he had left. He would hand it over to Peter Maroc, knowing how much it would affect others in his family.

In an attempt at salvaging some dignity, Malcolm had made a token effort at haggling. Realising Maroc would not shift his position, he had capitulated with ill grace. The money would be wired to Malcolm's account. The moment the money transfer was cleared, Maroc would receive the requisite documents.

Peter Maroc had learnt the art of negotiating at a tough school. His ability to read people had often got him out of trouble. On more than one occasion, it had saved his life.

Know your enemy. He considered it an important maxim. Of one thing, he was certain. Malcolm Southwell was now his creature.

Malcolm had secretly welcomed the prospect of freeing himself from his filial duties. All the palaver that went with it was not just tedious, it was time-consuming. It took him away from his other, more pleasant diversions.

Maroc knew there was little chance of Southwell changing his mind. Not with the money in his pocket.

It had been too easy and a clear reflection of his brother-in-law's social and financial descent.

Christ, the man's so bloody vulnerable it's pitiful, Maroc had thought. I can't just leave him here.

He had suggested Southwell leave the pub, try and eat something, looked after himself. Maroc had known desperation, utter hopelessness, a time when he could have done with a friendly word. He had pressed two twenty-pound notes into Malcolm's hand and left him baffled at the unexpected gesture.

Some poker player, you are Malcolm.

Maroc's mood had lightened and he was smiling by the time he'd reached the corner around where he'd parked his car. The Maserati was still there and, at first sight, undamaged. So far, the day had gone well.

CHAPTER 8

Maroc had moved into the bedroom where he and Emily had stayed when visiting Plas Meurig. He had always liked this spacious and airy room with its perfect view of Moel Hebog mountain.

Always a light traveller, Maroc had quickly completed his unpacking. Clothes were put away in cupboards and drawers, his small collection of books laid neatly by his bedside cupboard. Crossing to the window, he looked out, taking in the magnificent scenery. The backdrop to his youth.

Maroc never made a move without his weapon. He felt vulnerable without the comforting heft of the Glock 17. With its polymer outer shell, it could pass undetected through most security checks.

However, he never took that risk, and his gun never left the UK. When abroad, the M.O.D arranged the necessary ordnance.

As for ammunition, his preferred load was the CorBon 90-grain JHP. In the event of it being unavailable, he would fall back on bog-standard 9x19mm Parabellum cartridges.

He checked the gun's ammunition. Pressing the release, he dropped the magazine into his hand. Satisfied, he slammed the mag back in place, returning the weapon to a drawer in his bedside cupboard.

Happy everything was in place, Maroc made his way downstairs where Southwell lay in blissful ignorance of what was to come. Opening the living room door, he entered quietly.

Observing the older man's eyelid movements, Maroc noticed Southwell was in hypnagogia. It was a state where he drifted between sleep and wakefulness. Not a bad thing, Maroc thought. This passive condition would make his initial work with him much easier.

Gently gripping the older man's wrist, he consulted his watch. Southwell's pulse was weak, but not alarmingly so. He felt confident the old boy was salvageable. Perhaps not the best choice of words.

Maroc let go of his arm and Southwell's eyes fluttered open. He slowly focused, taking in his surroundings.

Recognition.

A derisive smile and Max Southwell was back, ready to challenge all suggestions. The old bugger, he thought ruefully. He has no intention of giving me an inch of wriggle room.

'You again.'

Southwell's voice, although weak, still bore his displeasure at seeing his son-in-law.

'You're going to have to trust me here, Max, or do I have to strap you to the bloody bed?'

The older man's smile was wan. This time, however, there was a trace of humour, previously absent.

'I have a choice?'

'Pax for now? Just for a while at least.'

The smile remained. Maroc detected the merest nod of agreement.

He grinned. *The wriggle room. We have lift-off!*

He lowered to a kneeling position by the bed.

'Your circulation. It's pretty sluggish.'

He looked up at Southwell.

'I can employ gentle manipulation and massage. Might kick start it.'

Again, a weak nod. Maroc smiled and winked. His father-in-law closed his eyes and remained quite still.

Believing he had slipped back to sleep, Maroc decided it would be better if the older man was not at full alert for what he had in mind. He was about to continue when Max's eyes sprang open.

'Kick start? What am I, a Harley Davidson?' His eyes closed

As a gentle introduction, Maroc began with a version of Chi Gong massage. He had employed it both on himself and others. It was excellent for stimulating and reviving poor circulation. It could also have a profound effect on the nervous system.

Maroc had great faith in this unorthodox, yet tried and tested approach. More rigorous methods would follow.

This was the start of their journey. Maroc, having witnessed the efficacy of Chi Gong massage, had great faith in this unorthodox, yet tried and tested approach.

Slowly, he would bring this senior citizen back to some semblance of good health. Maroc knew he had to retain absolute belief in the treatment. Self-doubt was contagious and would be quickly transferred to the patient.

The massage started gently, with Maroc first focusing on Max's left forearm. The older man offered no resistance or protest. His eyes shut; he gave the impression of a man in a deep sleep.

Maroc knew such massage and manipulation could overtax a weakened body. He was careful not to overstimulate Southwell's system and, after five minutes of gently flexing and smoothing, he ended the session.

'Not too bad, was it? Not too painful?'

He guessed Southwell was awake and wondered if the old fox would keep up the pretence of being asleep.

'You haven't killed me... yet.'

Maroc grinned as the older man's eyes languidly opened.

It was the beginning of a long process. A method of healing in which Maroc had total faith.

It had been a gift, given to Maroc by less cynical souls than his and, initially, he had harboured some doubts. However, after witnessing some convincing results, his Chinese teachers had finally brought him onside.

This gentle introduction was a safe means of waking both nervous and endocrinal systems. Many massages applied oil to the skin, thus lowering the friction between hand and body. However, employing dry massage was a way of ensuring a more direct and deeper stimulation.

Maroc looked down, realising the older man had drifted into natural sleep. It'll do it every time, he thought. Massage elicited a deep response in the body. This required energy from the recipient and energy had to be replaced. Sleep was a vital necessity.

He patted his father-in-law's arm. Max Southwell stirred slightly, muttering something unintelligible.

'Enough for today,' he said softly. 'Good start.'

Maroc brewed strong tea, settling for the evening. He had brought some books with him which would both entertain and inform him for the first few weeks of his stay. The telephone rang in the hall.

The living room had no phone. That would be John's idea, thought Maroc, done so his father would not be disturbed. He smiled ironically. *It would ensure there was nothing to obstruct your father's gentle drift into oblivion, eh John?*

He wondered whether to answer. He decided against it. If it's important, they can call back. It gave another half dozen rings, then fell silent. He did not want to be disturbed, not this evening.

A lot of thinking to do. A lot to plan. He was happy with the general structure of his programme for Southwell. It would be a while before they would see real progress.

Peter Maroc's expression hardened. Nothing would get in the way of his plans for the older man. He accepted there would be resistance to his new regime. A lot of emotional blackmailing and false concerns from the two sons.

Before settling down with his book, the ex-soldier walked quietly to Southwell's bed. He opened the bedside locker and began a systematic assessment of his patient's medication.

Maroc examined the various vitamins, minerals and IBS tablets prescribed by Dr Llewellyn, nodding as he did so. Looking further into the cupboard, he discovered a couple of boxes of opioid-based painkillers. They had been more recently dated. He examined their strength and recommended dosage.

His expression darkened in annoyance. Apart from

being highly addictive, their continual use would carry Max Southwell unprotestingly into the big sleep.

Maroc looked down at the slumbering man, his face set. Southwell seemed to have settled, his breathing stable. He was determined to get his ward up and moving, even if he had to drag him back to health, screaming and kicking.

Returning to his book, Maroc settled into the old red leather monk's chair. The subject matter was Neuroplasticity.

Western science was achieving results in this area of neuroscience that was groundbreaking. Yet eastern practises had been seeing such outcomes for thousands of years. He had learnt and applied the principles of this new science both to himself and others.

Maroc's experiences in Japan and China had opened his eyes to the power and endless possibilities of the human mind. His first-hand witnessing had been all the proof he needed to become a convert to the old traditions.

The idea of the mind affecting the body and its functioning stretched back thousands of years. Today, simple techniques such as mindfulness meditation were being examined and their effects measured by western science.

Peter Maroc believed in being the Guinea pig in all his experiments or trials. To him, it was clear. The most direct observations of change would be witnessed by the subject.

He was no scientist, his intellectual inquiry having been mainly directed towards Oriental philosophy and its practices.

This had given rise to many heated arguments with his more orthodox and science-based friends. He believed there was nothing better than empirical evidence. His maxim would always be, 'If it works, use it.'

Maroc tried returning to his book. No longer in the mood for reading, he stared at the large open fireplace. He suddenly felt the urge to light a fire using the large logs placed in a neat stack on the slate surround. A fitter and healthier Southwell had both felled and chopped the wood two years earlier. So much had changed.

The process of building and lighting a fire had always satisfied. It was both a primal necessity and a comforting ritual. Rising from the chair, Maroc looked around for paper and found a copy of Country Life. It was three years out of date.

Kneeling on the beech and oak floor just short of the slate surround, he began tearing and scrunching up the paper, placing it into the fireplace. He withdrew from his pocket an oversized Zippo lighter.

Once the paper had ignited, he carefully positioned kindling wood found in an old cardboard box by the logs. As they, in turn, ignited and blazed, he added three sizable logs, making sure not to smother the fragile flames.

Having paid homage to this timeless imperative, Maroc sat back in his seat and sighed his satisfaction. As he stared into the flickering flames, his mind began drifting into slumber.

Running through a ruined city, he was closing in on one of three Serbs who had been firing on their position. It was an arena in which he excelled. A natural hunter, he was never burdened by thoughts of his mortality. Peter Maroc lived these moments in the zone.

No fear of death, not anymore. With nothing to lose, it made him sharper, made him faster.

He rounded the corner of a long corridor. Large wounds in the outside wall let in light, allowing him to see the fleeing figure. It halted, conscious of his proximity, sensing Maroc's tactical advantage. Slowly the lone figure turned, weapon pointed downward, realising its fatal error.

She stood, hair tied in a ponytail, expression frozen between fear and resignation. Each took in the other's position. Maroc, his HK G36 ready to fire; she, waiting like a rabbit caught in headlights.

Shouldering the assault rifle, he stood, taking in her slow recognition of what was. Her eyes fixed firmly on his; she carefully shouldered the AK-74. Briefly, her gaze dropped, then with one last questioning look, she turned and fled. He saw her slim figure rounding the corner, leaving him with too many questions to answer.

With a start, Maroc returned to the here and now. A bead of sweat had begun its journey down his forehead. He fought to calm his inner turmoil and was surprised at how easily he could return to this personal hell.

As an instructor in close protection and hostage retrieval, he was still connected to his dangerous past. It did not come close to being in the midst of it.

Maroc had always been aware of the ambivalent nature of his personality. He valued the rich rewards of a quiet life, yet his alter ego still craved the exhilaration of living life on the edge.

The highs had become a drug and he had acquired the knack of being able to relax amid chaos. Now, he hoped, this addiction was being successfully addressed and overcome.

Strict adherence to a mental and physical regime had brought much order and stability to his life. It had become the defender of his fragile mind. Yet that Judas, his subconscious, still allowed access to the demons ever lurking in his inner shadows.

An ordinary life, once beyond him, was now close to an accepted given. Peter Maroc was grateful for his deliverance. Today, he considered himself a functioning human being. Still a work in progress. Then wasn't everybody?

His mind turned to Charles (Chuck) Turner, ex delta-force and loyal comrade back in the day. Last he'd heard, Turner had taken a whole bar apart, hospitalising two bouncers foolish enough to think they could stop him.

He had ended up in the psychiatric unit of the Chicago General Hospital. As far as Maroc knew, he was still a resident. Other good lads were still struggling with civilian life.

With some irony, he thought of Niels Johansson. A borderline psychopath when in the field. Yet removed from that world he was a prince. Johansson had survived and thrived. Happily married, he was living the good life in Sweden with a woman who adored him.

He and Niels had pushed the limits of danger to the max, had become intoxicated by it. They both missed the close bond, the willingness to die for each other and the balls to prove it time and time again. Rules, authority? They were for others.

They had their differences. Maroc had scruples, big

ones. Johansson, however, was governed by one thing. The mission. Anything was permissible as long as the job got done. For the Norwegian, it was merely a matter of expedience. He regarded himself as a pragmatist.

In the field, Johansson was a mad dog unleashed. An elemental only he, Maroc could control. The body count was certainly lower whenever he was paired with Maroc.

Their mutual respect was total, their bond unbreakable. The friends were a highly effective duo, operating within a patrol of four.

A low whimper from the bed. Maroc rose quickly, walking over to find Southwell muttering softly. The older man moved slightly.

A gentle smile appeared as he approached. Maroc, thinking the smile was for him, realised Southwell was sleeping like a baby. All that was missing was a thumb in his mouth.

CHAPTER 9

The Southwell family in Australia had gathered for a council of war. Now that Max Southwell had been deemed unfit to manage his affairs, John, his oldest child, had appointed himself head of the family. Jill Southwell, his youngest sister, stood facing him.

'What he's doing to dad right now doesn't bear thinking about.'

Ashen-faced, her voice pitched high with tension, Jill was upset.

'After treating Emily so badly, you'd think he would have the decency not to show his face.'

John Southwell cut short her tirade.

'Give it a rest, Jill. You've hardly shown concern in the past. Why start now?'

'And you care about him, I suppose. Do you John?'

John Southwell turned to see his wife entering the large sitting room. Her voice, soft, and sarcastic, still carried an authority that demanded attention.

Ruth came and sat by the unlit fireplace. She looked directly at her husband, her dark eyes boring into him. Turning her head, her gaze alighted on Jill, then back to John, leaving a residue of discomfort on both. If there was a recognised hierarchy in the family, next to John, she was the second in command.

Jill glanced nervously at Ruth before turning back

to her brother, picking up the thread of her argument.

'At least I talk to dad, unlike some.'

Ruth regarded this pretty young woman with her pale blond hair, cut fashionably short. To the older woman, Jill was a perpetually frightened child. Still, the youngest sibling had always been friendly and inclusive of her. Unlike her husband.

John Southwell stood up, casting his eyes over the other two.

'He despises all of us, equally!' His voice was imperious, a general rallying his troops. He paused for effect.

'Except Emily of course, she's the adored one, the special one.'

Ruth reflected on how much John loved the centre stage. He might not be as observably weak as his younger brother, Malcolm, she thought, yet his strength was a facade. The blustering face of a bully.

'I doubt if even Emily likes him. After all, she did kick him out. He's nothing but a lout.'

Jill's voice was quarrelsome, petulant. Being the youngest child, she had always had to fight to be heard by her more forceful siblings. John continued.

'She likes him all right; Emily likes everyone. Don't you realise, she's a bloody saint? A healer and a saint, what a combination. She almost has me convinced.'

The two women stared back at him, each with very different thoughts.

Ruth wondered how she had ended up in such a dysfunctional family. Love had never been a feature of her and John's marriage. He thought her a desiccated prune, devoid of humour and warmth. For her part, she had long seen through his duplicity.

At first, she had been impressed by his air of confidence and authority. That was before he had revealed the mean spirit that lay beneath.

The subject, of course, was Peter Maroc, Emily's estranged husband. He had returned from god knows where threatening their inheritance and thus their future.

'Isn't anyone worried about Em? She's trapped there in all manner of dangers. God's sake!'

Jill was close to tears.

'Sorry, Jill.'

Ruth took a step towards her sister-in-law, putting her arms around her.

'You're right, we should be worried about Emily. God knows what she's going through.'

John shrugged.

'Emily knows how to look after herself. Always has.'

'What possessed that idiot Malcolm to give up his power of attorney? If only I'd taken it on, we wouldn't be in this bloody mess.'

'You weren't in the UK John,'

Ruth's tone was infuriatingly sensible.

'Yes, yes, I know.'

John Southwell hated being corrected by his wife. He looked bleakly at the other two.

'We can't even contact the old man, let alone visit him. That bastard keeps on answering the phone.'

The others murmured their agreement.

Ruth rose from her chair and walked to the centre of the room.

'Surely, we can revoke his arrangement with Malcolm? The agreement between the two can't be legal.'

'Getting things done from this distance is difficult, and Malcolm seems more than happy with the situation. Got to have been something in it for him. Something substantial. There's no way he'd have done it otherwise.'

'But he hates Maroc as much as the rest of us.'

Jill looked around at the others showing her confusion.

'What on earth made him do it?'

John's laugh held little humour.

'God Jill, don't you know anything about your little brother? He has expensive tastes. He's also perpetually broke.'

He shook his head in disbelief at her naivety.

'Do you think Maroc didn't know that? It would have been the first thing he'd have found out about your brother. He's given Malcolm his thirty pieces of silver.'.

CHAPTER 10

Max Southwell was showing slight signs of improvement in both mobility and mental acuity. The daily massage was making a significant impact, both in waking up his system and in helping him relax. Small positive changes at this early stage were encouraging.

Massage is one of the oldest therapies, and Maroc had learnt the art of Chi Gong massage during his stay at the Shaolin temple in central China. The manipulation of muscle and soft tissue removed waste products and improved blood circulation to the tissues. It allowed essential nutrients to reach their desired destination.

Peter Maroc had reached a high degree of competency in this ancient art. Still, there was one big stumbling block.

Massage and manipulation were vital. However, without a further agent to reduce the pain, progress would be slow. And extremely uncomfortable.

It was true, massage produced endorphins, the body's natural discomfort reducers. However, they could not address the inevitable pain resulting from Maroc's programme.

A vital part of Peter Maroc's training was the use of potent herbs and natural products. Maroc was never without a supply and he knew their use in Southwell's recovery would play a vital role in this rescue mission.

His father-in-law had been drifting in and out of an uncomfortable sleep since first light. Between performing his own morning ritual of Chi Gong exercise and deep meditation, Maroc had checked in on him a few times.

Maroc's diet was mainly healthy; mainly vegetarian. On operations, when things got lean, both he and his patrol would resort to anything containing protein. It was best not to recall many of those delights.

Peter Maroc had prepared a tincture of various powerful analgesic herbs for Southwell. He was aware of the dangers of such medication on a weak system. He would start with the lowest strength and gauge their effect on the older man.

'Smells funny. What is it?'

Maroc held the small beaker to his father-in-law's lips.

'This'll kill the pain without killing you.'

Southwell began protesting, and Maroc cut in.

'It's OK Max. I know what I'm doing. Look, the pain medication you're on now are the real killers.'

Southwell grimaced and took a sip. His mouth twisted in disgust.

'Ye gods Maroc, you trying to poison me?'

He narrowed his eyes theatrically,

'After my crown, are you boy?'

Maroc stayed silent, a ghost of a smile on his lips. He raised the beaker.

'Will this convince you?'

He drank some of the liquid and offered the beaker

back, nodding for Southwell to drink. This time, Southwell shrugged and drained the contents.

'Good man. Trust me; that stuff will allow you to get your body moving without the pain you're experiencing now. Just give it a chance, Max. You have nothing to lose.'

Southwell looked up.

'Tell me, why do I trust you, Maroc. Am I mad?'

'Probably, but it's a good madness. You need to trust. Completely. Have complete faith it'll work.'

He grinned.

'Even if it kills you.'

By now, Southwell had his eyes closed, a trace of a smile on his face. He murmured something Maroc failed to catch. He allowed Southwell a full hour of sleep.

The herbs were powerful muscle relaxants. They also had a slight soporific effect. His body, badly in need of rest, Southwell was responding to the soothing medication.

'Time to wake up, Max.' Maroc stood over the bed as Southwell stirred, then grumbled, before becoming fully awake. He took the older man's pulse, nodding his satisfaction.

'Still alive then?'

Southwell's answering expression was sour. Maroc grinned back. He was getting used to the older man's assumed belligerence.

'Try sitting up, Max.

His father-in-law responded immediately, struggling to a sitting position in the bed. Maroc gently eased him forward, adjusting and plumping the supporting pillows.

Maroc stood in silence for a while, then slowly walked away from the bed, his hands together, steeple fingered. A professional deep in thought.

He turned and faced Southwell, his decision made.

'If it's alright with you, Max, I'll start with a brisk massage of your arms and upper body. Then I'll focus on your legs and feet. This time, the process might be a little uncomfortable.'

His father-in-law stared back, considering this. He gave a consensual shrug.

The massage was vigorous and deep. Southwell, grimacing at times, remained stoically silent. After finishing with his feet, Maroc looked up.

'How did that feel?'

'How was it for you?'

An ironic smile. Maroc gave a short bark.

'We'll smoke the cigarettes later. Seriously. Pain? Same or less?'

Southwell decided to be good.

'Yes, less.'

A thoughtful pause.

'In fact, it was considerably less.'

His face registered surprise.

'Good, good.'

Brisk, a physician hearing expected news.

Maroc walked away, returning with one of the smaller armchairs.

'I'll let you have twenty-minute rest, then I'd like you to try sitting in this chair.'

Alarm registered briefly before Soubthwell's features relaxed.

'If you think I'm ready. Doctor.'

'Doctors will kill you. With me, you have a chance.'

'So you keep telling me.'

Maroc decided to leave Southwell. The older man needed to rest. He would require energy for what was to come. Maroc was optimistic.

Knowing the importance of this next step, Maroc realised he needed to start slowly, carefully. This was a pivotal moment. It would be uncomfortable. Too much at this early stage could put the older man off the whole idea.

Southwell seemed fully awake, waiting for his return. Maroc gently manoeuvred him out of the bed until he was seated with both his feet on the thick oriental rug.

The next part would be trickier. It had been some weeks since Southwell had left his bed, not counting his panic dash to the telephone, where adrenaline would have masked much discomfort. Maroc was under no illusion. This next step would be painful.

He helped Southwell to his feet. Using his arm for support, he walked his father-in-law a dozen paces from the bed towards the centre of the living room. After a brief rest, they made the return journey.

Southwell surprised him. He also surprised himself. There were the expected groans, but things went better than either had hoped. Much better.

Finally seated, Southwell looked up at Maroc, his face drawn. Despite looking tired, there was a glimmer of triumph in those intelligent eyes.

Max Southwell was left to recover in his chair while Maroc made his way to the kitchen. He returned, carrying a cup of herb tea which he handed to his ward. Leaving Southwell to his beverage, Maroc returned to the kitchen to prepare a light meal. On his return, he saw Southwell had emptied his cup.

'I'll get you back to bed. A bit of well-earned shut-eye.'

Adjusting the pillows, Maroc noticed a new energy about Southwell. Also, something he had not anticipated so early in his journey. Excitement. The academic had realised he had reached a pivotal point in his recovery.

Southwell became a willing participant in a closely supervised regime. A system of mental and physical exercise.

Maroc provided a diet, both nutritious and varied. The older man was taught various visualisation techniques with increasing periods of meditation. As days extended into weeks, significant things began to happen.

Maroc's patient ceased being the bedridden invalid. Slowly and, at times painfully, Southwell began reclaiming his mobility.

The academic's moods became noticeably brighter, his depression, less debilitating. The once crippling muscular cramps, and the uncomfortable symptoms caused by his irritable bowel syndrome, began to ease.

Maroc was a firm but compassionate taskmaster. For his part, Southwell did all that was required. At times, he would surprise Maroc, showing an unexpected enthusiasm prompted by his progress.

There were times when Maroc had to curb the older man's growing zeal, something he would never have anticipated. They had reached a stage where both contributed equally to the undertaking. The edginess between them had lessened.

Southwell was following a simple but highly

effective routine. By the sixth week, the programme included some gentle Yoga, Chi Gong movements and regular periods of focused meditation.

Maroc had insisted on one hour of intense visualisation to further accelerate his progress. It was to be practised every morning at first light.

'I want to sleep in my own bedroom, Maroc. I'm fully able to walk upstairs. I'll carry this bloody bed up there, on my own if I have to.'

Southwell's tone had lost its petulance. There was now an enthusiasm, previously absent. Maroc turned, a faint smile on his face. He eyed the older man for a moment.

'Did I mention the ice bath treatment? Much favoured by the Scandinavians.'

Southwell looked slightly uncertain.

'I'll phone a mate. With his help, we'll have everything sorted by this afternoon.'

His father-in-law looked startled.

'I'm talking about the bed, man, not the bloody ice bath.'

'Can't just the two of us…?'

'You can supervise. You should be good at that.'

Maroc walked into the kitchen with Southwell's chuckle drifting through.

CHAPTER 11

Edon Berisha was a brutal man raised within a brutal regime. His father, when sober, had spent most of his life working as an enforcer for the Albanian Mafia or Fare.

Their main base was in the hill village of Lazarat, situated in the Gjirokastër County of southern Albania. The area was recognised as the cannabis capital of Eastern Europe.

By the time Edon was eleven, he and his younger brother Burim had lost their mother. Neither brother knew the final cause of her passing, she had always been ill.

In a culture rooted in violence, their mother had been their only source of tender feelings. She had not lived long enough to influence her sons.

Crime had been their only viable career. Their rise through the mafia ranks had been steady. They had quickly recognised it was a culture where success was a function of applied brutality.

Both brothers wanted more. They routinely took from the organisation what they considered their percentage.

Unaware of watchful eyes, their disregard for consequence had grown with their greed. The outcome had been predictable.

Neither brother had an alibi or cover story for the main man. Their father had assumed his paternal role and come to their rescue.

Not over blessed with intelligence, he had an unblemished record and a reputation for blind obedience within the Fare. After making some financial reparations, their father pleaded their case.

Swearing he would repair the damage if it took a lifetime, he awaited the outcome. The young men were allowed to leave with their lives.

A ritual beating was inevitable. Burim was carried off by his father, while older brother Edon staggered behind.

Some within the organisation disagreed with what they considered blatant favouritism. It went against policy. Allowing them to live was not good P.R for the regional boss, the Krye. They were not shy in informing him.

The Krye fully realised he had his bosses to appease. Still, he had made his decision.

Now he wanted the brothers gone. Forgotten.

The father had driven his sons to the north-western village of Vuno, leaving them with a cousin and his family.

That had been three years ago.

The first year found the brothers adapting well to their new life. They laboured in the vineyards, freely offering their muscle to the heavy work. Their uncle had thought his luck had changed. Life for his family was going to become less arduous.

Keeping their true nature in check, the brothers were polite and respectful. Both were grateful for their deliverance.

Gratitude, however, did not rest comfortably with them, and soon they wanted more. They craved the attention and respect they once took for granted.

It was time for a change. Taking the little money their father had given them, and adding it to what they had saved, they moved out.

They had been well treated by their uncle and held no animosity towards him. Disappointed at losing a valuable asset, he realised there was little he could say to change their minds. The parting had been amicable.

At first, the brothers had enjoyed their new freedom. They could sleep when they wanted, for as long as they wanted. Life was good. For two young men with extravagant tastes, it was also expensive.

Having lived their whole life within a dependable though controlling regime, both quickly realised that, in the outside world, indolence had a time limit. A limit governed by their dwindling funds.

Both Edon and Burim were soon to discover the rural area in which they found themselves could never deliver the rewards they needed. The type of enterprises they had in mind called for richer pastures to fund them. It was time for a drastic rethink.

Not political animals, the brothers did possess some global awareness. It was enough to point them firmly towards Western Europe.

When they were in the Fare, they had become aware that the organisation had people active in Western Europe. Edon and Burim had listened to stories told by the more senior members. They had both agreed the United Kingdom afforded the easiest pickings.

They had focused on learning English and everything British, hoping the Krye would eventually notice their suitability. He never had.

Now it was up to them to forge their future. Both the brothers had managed to avoid a criminal record. There was nothing to prevent them from legally entering the country. The paperwork would sort itself out. The brothers were ready for a career move.

There was one impediment. Having saved enough for their passage over to the UK, their limited funds would not be enough to establish them in a first-world country.

The news they were to receive that morning changed everything.

He arrived in his battered Renault 4 van, the father they had expected never to see again. Fitore Berisha was smiling as he stepped out of his vehicle. To both Edon and Burim, this made his entry into their lives the more disturbing. Their father never smiled.

At first, Fitore had been mildly irritated. Having failed to find his sons at his cousin's farm, he had been obliged to track them down to their new quarters. Today, however, nothing could diminish his good humour. His boys had been given another chance, an opportunity to redeem themselves.

The brothers, however, viewed this 'good' news with a degree of dismay. They had grown to enjoy their independent lifestyle.

There would probably be a price to pay for re-acceptance into the fold. They also knew they had little choice in the matter.

The brothers would have to reaffirm their *Besse*, the oath of trust to the *Bajrak*, the executive committee. To refuse would be a direct insult to the Krye, the head of the mafia unit in their district.

The Fere would not tolerate further transgressions. No second chance would be given or expected. Edon and Burim listened resignedly as their father sketched out the pattern of their future.

They would fly to Manchester in the United Kingdom. There, they would meet members of the organisation active in the area. Further orders would be given by the Kryetar, the Krye's lieutenants and head of operations in the UK.

There would be a considerable financial inducement for the upheaval. It gave the illusion of choice, sweetening what the brothers realised was a non-negotiable dictate. Their father, however, was a happy man, his status and bank balance much boosted.

Edon and Burim, having found the flight from Tirana International Airport so far removed from their everyday reality, had forgotten to be afraid. Two excited kids, the flight attendants had exchanged secret smiles. The brothers took delight at, what was for them, the commonplace.

Arrival at Manchester airport found Edon and Burim still in a state of juvenile animation. It had been a step into a new world of modernity and glamour. Never having left their homeland, this had turned into a day of discovery and wonder.

As they walked out of passport control, a small group of grim-looking men awaited their arrival. The leader was craggy-faced and appeared to be in his early sixties.

He was a diminutive man, standing around five feet six inches in height with greying black hair and dark, intelligent eyes. They were trained intently on the brothers.

The other three men screamed, *heavies*. Edon guessed they were not armed, not in this rule-ridden country. Observing them nervously, the young Albanian would think twice before courting their displeasure.

After formal introductions and bone-crushing handshakes, the leader pointed the brothers towards a dark, impressive limousine. Edon, seated beside the driver, peered into the back of the car.

He noticed a further two rows. Each row would sit at least five adults. In his village, this would be called a bus.

Sinking into the comfortable leather seats, the brothers exchanged smiles. If this was a taste of things to come, they would manage it very nicely.

The drive lasted twenty-five, maybe thirty minutes.

As they travelled along the M60 motorway, Edon and Burim looked out at their new country. They observed a more affluent landscape, where the opportunities would be more rewarding.

Arriving on the outskirts of Salford, the limousine headed towards Broughton Park. They made a final turn into one of the more desirable roads in the park. Old Hall Road.

The house was large, ultra-modern and tasteless. The drive leading to it was tree-lined and impressively long. To the brothers, it was palatial.

They followed the others through a solid oak front door, finding themselves in a spacious reception hall. They had arrived at the wolf's lair.

The Kryetar led the way to an enormous sitting room. Edon noticed that one wall was made of glass and looked onto the grounds at the front of the house.

Indicated to sit, they both sank into an oversized leather settee. There was no doubting it was the home of a very wealthy man.

The Kryetar launched into the day's business. There was a job to do; the job was urgent, and it involved the new arrivals. Both brothers focused their full attention on the small man standing in the centre of the room.

They were to abduct and deliver someone important to the organisation. Yes, this person was a UK citizen and yes, he was still in the country. His residence was less than two hours drive away.

Tonight, they would be allowed to rest, to enjoy what this rich country had to offer. The brothers could, within reason, have whatever they needed for their comfort.

Tonight, they would stay with the Kryetar. There was to be a party. A party with plenty of beautiful and willing women.

Edon and Burim were determined not to spoil things with an ill-considered response. Say nothing. Just nod and smile. It was the best way.

They had, however, some homework to do. An attractive woman in her late thirties entered the room. Without speaking, she handed the Kryetar a buff-coloured folder and left. The small man tapped the folder with a thick forefinger.

'You study all that is contained in here until you know everything about this man. His daily routine, where he eats, the drinking places he visits, everything. Understood?'

The brothers nodded dutifully, determined to keep their council. They exchanged glances, conveying nothing besides sibling solidarity. There was a lot to learn and much reason to be prudent.

Their bedroom was vast. Having been informed this would not be their permanent residence, they still considered it a good sign of things to come.

Edon opened a large wardrobe. Inside, he found a jacket and a pair of matching trousers. Two silk shirts hung next to them. The quality was superior to anything he had worn back home.

Everything was exactly his size. He gestured to his brother that he should open the remaining wardrobe. Burim was similarly impressed with the offerings inside. If this was an indicator of their new life, the trade-off for their independence might just be worthwhile.

Both showered and dressed at their leisure, luxuriating in the fragrance of expensive toiletry. Predictably, a full change of underclothes had been provided.

Edon was determined that this second chance would be fully exploited. They would make every effort to fit into this new life. Looking over at Burim, he was sure his younger brother would view things in the same way.

Fully dressed, Edon lowered himself into one of the comfortable chairs in the room. The folder lay where he had placed it on the walnut coffee table.

He now reached out and opened it. The content was not extensive.

Edon extracted a couple of photocopied maps, together with an A4 sheet of written information. There was also a large white envelope.

Edon opened the unsealed envelope carefully and

slid out a black and white print. He examined it, unsure of what he was supposed to see. Looking back at him was the face of Peter Maroc.

CHAPTER 12

Peter Maroc, escaping cabin fever, left the house and walked the quarter of a mile to the village. Max Southwell would be fine for a couple of hours. Maroc was just a phone call away.

A balmy summer day and life was good. Maroc felt things were going well at the house with Southwell's progress giving him reasons to be optimistic.

The man was sixty-six years old, and would not be winning medals. Neither would he be suffering an untimely and ignominious death.

On entering the *Prince Llewellyn*, the aroma of ale greeted him like a dissolute friend. Maroc was by no means a boozer. Although, as a younger man, he'd had his moments.

He was, however, a discerning beer man. This ruled out most of the drinking establishments in the area.

The Prince pulled a good pint. Not always as quiet as he'd have liked, the company was usually diverting.

The Edwards brothers had already taken their position at the bar. He headed for the only empty stool next to the two. Quiet men around his age, Maroc had known them forever.

He gave a casual wave to some young local girls. One of them gave him the glad eye. He smiled, shaking his head as he approached the bar.

'Peter. Long time.'

The eldest by a year, Arwyn Edwards was a gentle giant. Maroc remembered he had once played prop for a prominent rugby league team in the North West. The teasing from his union mates had never stopped.

Both he and his younger brother Aled had studied engineering at Manchester University and now ran their successful consultancy business on the outskirts of the North Wales city of Bangor.

Aled, a marginally slimmer version of his brother, grinned at Maroc.

'Thought you were dead, you bastard.'

'Good to be back, mate. What're you having?'

Both men waved their empty glasses, and Maroc caught the landlord's eye.

'Three pints of best, please Arthur. To the top this time.'

An old joke; it still evoked a smile and a rude gesture. Arthur Evans liked Maroc. Had always liked him since he had been a slim, wiry, slightly under-aged drinker at his pub.

'Been serving queen and country Peter?'

Arthur lifted his head from his pint pulling duty.

'Gets more than the queen's shilling this boy.'

Aled had always been impressed by Maroc's SAS status and had always pumped him for tales of daring-do.

Maroc still had no idea how his military standing had spread around the village. His diffidence in discussing it had added to the mystique, the glamour. Not quite a local legend, he was quietly respected by most of the younger men.

An hour passed quickly, as happens when fuelled

by good company. Maroc checked his watch. Usually happy with a couple of pints, he contemplated a third.

He was still staring into his near-empty glass, gauging his mood, when he heard the discordant sound of voices raised in anger. They were coming from outside.

The two brothers immediately rose from their barstools, their curiosity aroused by the commotion. Arwyn gave Maroc a questioning look.

Maroc jerked his head towards the pub entrance and made his way outside. The Edwards plus a handful of other regulars closely followed.

Fifty yards up the road, they could see the source of the commotion. A tall, thickset man, almost obscured by a small ring of people, was bellowing at someone.

As Maroc approached, he saw the object of this tirade was a short skinny individual of around fifty. The man, obviously frightened, seemed to be remonstrating with the aggressor.

Maroc walked up to the small crowd. The man's companion had his arm around his terrified victim's throat. He was roughly turned and made to face his interrogator.

Aled Edwards, the first to reach the scene, quickly identified the target of the attack as one of the bar staff at The Saracen's Head. By the time Maroc and Arwyn had caught up, the big man was stabbing a finger into the bar worker's face.

'I give you twenty pounds. Twenty!' He held up two thick fingers.

Aled stepped forward, but Maroc quickly pulled him back.

'OK Aled, I'll sort it.'

A token protest and Alex shrugged. Hell, he was not a fighter. Well, not anymore. He stepped back, giving his friend centre stage.

Maroc had his first clear look at the two men.

Eastern European features, with closely shaved heads. They did not evoke happy memories. The one holding the barman was a couple of inches taller than his companion. Both over six feet of lean muscle, they would have intimidated most.

'Let him go; there's a good man.'

The taller of the two gave no response. His companion, still pinning the unfortunate man to his chest, was more reactive. Without turning, he growled at Maroc.

'Go away bastard. Mind your business.'

Maroc tapped him on the shoulder and waited. Letting go of the small barman, the man spun around and threw a wild swing at Maroc's head.

Maroc was ready and easily deflected the blow with his left arm. He quickly stepped in, and with his right palm, Maroc delivered an explosive shove to his attacker's chest.

The thug was propelled backwards and, managing to stay on his feet, came to a halt a few feet away. He seemed to consider his position, surprised by his lack of success.

Then, without warning, the man rushed forward, his face a contorted mask of hate. Twisting his body at the last moment, he launched a high kick at Maroc's head.

In a street fight where drink often fuelled tempers, Maroc would have grabbed the leg and yanked, tipping the man on his backside. It was enough to end most scraps and with the least damage.

This, however, was vicious. It was meant to injure.

In a flowing arc, Maroc's left forearm parried the raised leg. He stepped in close, his right fist slamming forward and down into the man's groin.

As his attacker's knees buckled, Maroc continued his forward momentum, following up with a sharp palm strike to his opponent's right shoulder.

The man staggered backwards, ending in a sitting position on the ground. He clutched at his groin, his face reflecting his agony.

A part of Maroc's mind cooly assessed the action. *Fast for a brawler. Bloody fast.*

Maroc was in full fighting mode, his mind and body in synergy. It was at times like these he felt alive.

He was a battle-hardened combatant and had trained beyond the adrenaline surge level of most fighters.

A cry of pain caused him to turn around. The taller of the two thugs had the small barman in a painful arm lock.

Maroc detested bullying in any form, and this had to end. He growled at the big man.

'Let him go. Now!'

The bully turned his head at the intrusion; and froze. He remained that way, an expression of surprise on his face. This was not the reaction Maroc had expected.

Aware he had the time, Maroc returned his attention to the man's fallen comrade. He still sat in the middle of the road with both hands cupped his groin.

Sensing Maroc's attention, he slowly climbed to

his feet. The SAS man waited. However, the bully just stood where he was. Maroc detected a look of recognition on his face. Turning to his friend, he spoke rapidly, his voice urgent.

Both men looked at him guardedly. Maroc was both intrigued and baffled at this change in mood.

He looked directly at the taller of the two.

'An apology is in order, gentlemen.'

The man sneered and spat at the Welshman's feet.

'Zhduku, little man.'

This was accompanied by a clarifying gesture. A middle finger pointing straight up.

He relinquished his hold on the terrified barman, pushing him away with contemptuous indifference.

He turned to his suffering friend and barked an order:

Shkojme. Tani!'

Albanians, this was a surprise. Maroc would have guessed maybe Poles, even Russians.

'Need any help, Peter?' Alex and his brother were enjoying the drama. Maroc waved them back.

'No problem here, Aled. Nothing I can't handle anyway.'

Maroc now identified the badly shaken barman as Dave Morris. The man skirted around the two men, seeking refuge behind his rescuer.

'All that because they thought I'd short-changed them.'

His voice shook badly.

'You okay, David?'

The barman nodded at Maroc.

'Yeah, just about.'

'How did all this kick-off?'

'He gave me a tenner. When I gave change, he insisted he'd handed over twenty. He got nasty. Grabbed me and hauled me over the counter.'

'I meant, how did it end up outside?'

'I left the pub to get help. Things were well out of hand, and no one was helping. Bastards followed me.'

Maroc turned to face the Albanians, but they were walking away. He decided to let it go.

After making sure David Morris could manage, Maroc walked back to where his friends stood waiting. The brothers were grinning from ear to ear.

Aled stepped forward, his hand extended.

'My hero.'

Maroc shook the proffered hand, delivering a gentle cuff to his friend's cheek with his left.

'Think I will have that third pint, mate.'

He looked back at the Albanians. The tallest was helping his still suffering companion. The man turned and glared murderously at Maroc, furious at the public humiliation.

'What was all that about?'

Maroc shrugged.

'Misunderstanding that got out of hand, Arwyn? You tell me?'

The incident was over. Forgotten. Peter Maroc had no idea that this would be a prelude to what Johansson would later call a shit storm.

CHAPTER 13

Maroc found Southwell reclining on the chesterfield, his eyes half-closed. A book lay open on his lap. On hearing Maroc, he sat up, placing the book on the floor.

'Good book?'

Southwell gave a dismissive wave. 'Nothing a yokel like you would understand.'

Maroc walked over and picked up the book.

'The Ladybird's Guide to Philosophy? Anything eventful happened while I was away?'

Southwell, trying not to smile, turned to face his son-in-law.

'Will Roberts, the plumber chap. He hasn't long left. Calls himself a hydro engineer nowadays.'

'What did he want? Anything needing fixing? Bloody old gossip.'

'Just checking the boiler in the cellar. Annual thing.'

Southwell struggled with his house slippers, and Maroc bent down to help. The older man stood up, giving his son-in-law a keen look.

Maroc could sense there was something on his mind. Something he was dying to tell him.

'What bit of tattle has he been peddling?' He looked directly at Southwell.

'Can't imagine what. I get the feeling that something's afoot.'

'Afoot?' Southwell grinned broadly.

'Heard you had a bit of bother in the village this morning, Sherlock.'

Southwell, tired of being confined, welcomed any diversion from the repetitive norm. He waited expectantly.

Maroc took off his jacket and shoes with exaggerated care. Reaching for the house slippers he had found in his room, he put them on. Southwell lost patience.

'Come on man, give me the lowdown.'

Maroc, shaking his head, sank into the Monk chair. He looked over at Southwell.

'Ye gods, that man's worse than the North Wales Chronicle.'

'So?'

Southwell was eager.

'Some foreign types in the village I heard.'

'That's right. No idea who they were. Certainly not local.'

Southwell sat down again, nodding sagely.

'I'd like to say, young people of today, but it was always thus. Every generation has its thugs and bullies. I've put a few on the deck myself.'

Maroc looked up sharply. Southwell was grinning.

'With help from individuals like yourself, of course.'

'Of course. Get the ruffians to do your dirty work. Anyway, I doubt if they'll be back.'

Maroc noticed Southwell was wearing the black tracksuit he had bought him.

'How did you get on with the breathing exercise I showed you?'

'The deep abdominal breathing? Tried it this

morning.'

'And?'

'And it made me dizzy. At first anyway, but I persisted.'

He looked up at Maroc. 'What's it meant to do for me anyway.'

Maroc walked over to the coffee table and picked up a book. He gave Southwell a reproving look.

'This was your required reading for today. You haven't looked at it, have you?'

The older man shrugged, then continued airily.

'I thought I'd crack on with the practical side first, then fill in with the theory.'

'I'll tell you anyway, Max. It's meant to do a couple of things. Firstly, it's an effective way of fully oxygenating your body. Also, those lung muscles could do with the exercise, and deep breathing will do just that.'

Southwell nodded.

'I certainly feel more relaxed. After the dizziness that is.'

Maroc rifled through the book and stopped at a page.

'Have a read of this chapter later, it may clarify a few things. The relaxation part is due to the movement of the diaphragm massaging your solar plexus. Anyway, read it for yourself.'

Maroc nodded at the tracksuit. What else have you been up to?

'Tried those basic Yoga moves you showed me yesterday. I find sitting upright on the mat bloody hard. So I propped myself against the wall.'

He pointed to a wall space near the bay window.

'Found if I did that, I could do the one where you

stretch your hands towards your feet. Ye gods, that hurts.'

'Good idea. I see you're taking things seriously, thinking things through.'

Southwell stood up and walked to the large bay window. He stood there for a moment staring out. Maroc sensed his sudden change of mood.

'Still miss her like hell, Maroc. Sometimes feel like...' His voice trailed away.

Maroc, not expecting this, realised he should have. He, more than anyone, should have understood the pain of such a loss would not simply vanish overnight.

He thought of Emily, how her absence from his life tore him apart. Christ, she was still alive. At least there was hope. Katherine would never return.

This was the start of a long journey for the older man. There was a lot of healing to be done. A lot of adjusting to a new way of living.

'You're bound to, Max. She was a diamond. Don't need to tell you she'd be proud of your efforts. Happy you're having another crack at life.'

Max gave a sad smile.

'Jesus, Maroc...'

'I know mate. She'll never leave you. Not for real.'

Southwell looked down. He nodded slowly.

Maroc stood up abruptly, the quick movement startling the older man.

'Fancy a walk around the garden later? Let's say after dinner.'

'You mean, go outside?'

Maroc nodded. 'Yes, why not? I think you're ready, don't you?'

Southwell looked up, his expression revealing a hint

of panic.

'You think that's wise? I mean...

'Nothing strenuous. A gentle walk in the garden, not bloody Mount Snowdon.'

As Southwell walked from the window, Maroc noticed the change in his demeanour. It was as though someone had thrown a switch. A switch that had reanimated the old warrior.

'Yes. Yes by god! Why not.'

The two men faced each other. Maroc placed his hand on Southwell's shoulder. He spoke softly.

'That's more like it.'

Maroc turned and walked through into the kitchen. Southwell picked up a book. It had been staring accusingly at him from the coffee table. His son-in-law called out.

'Fancy a brew?'

'Wouldn't say no. How about some bog-standard workman's tea for a change? Strong, no sugar.'

'Coming up. You eaten yet?'

'Apart from that green swamp water? Oh, had a slice of toast and marmalade.'

Maroc called from the kitchen.

'Wholemeal bread, I hope?'

Southwell grinned to himself.

'Of course.'

'Liar. Anyway, good to treat yourself once in a while. It's not an easy regime, Max but stay with it. At least until you're up and running. Then you can eat whatever you like. Within reason of course.'

'Of course.'

Maroc came through with two large, steaming mugs of tea. Placing them on the table and taking one himself, he resettled into the comfortable monk chair. He looked at Southwell.

'You're getting stronger. How's the pain when you're exercising? Do you remember the breathing technique I showed you?'

'Breathe through the pain. Stay with the pain. Become one with the bloody pain. Yes, I'm doing it all, just as you said.'

'It helps?'

'I believe it does. I'll keep using it.'

It was Maroc's turn to become animated.

'Look, you know it's a process. A slow and sometimes painful one. The tinctures I give you will help. Help a lot.'

He paused briefly, considering his next words.

'We're cracking this, Max, be in no doubt. Working as a team, we'll get you back to where you want to be. Where the people who care about you want you to be.

'That include you, Maroc?' Southwell wore a sardonic smile.

'Don't be bloody stupid, man. I'm in this for the cash.'

The older man threw back his head and laughed. For the first time in a long time, the laughter was real. It came from a good place.

CHAPTER 14

Dinner was a simple affair. Maroc had prepared a pulse casserole, announcing it as his 'signature dish.' Southwell muttered a comment that Maroc failed to catch. However, he recognised the sentiment.

'Fancy a coffee?'

His father-in-law looked up in surprise from an empty plate.

'Is that allowed, under this... regime of yours?'

'Why not. Your system's getting more robust. I think you can take coffee. By the way, how is the old bowel today?'

Southwell's hand went to his belly, rubbing it absently.

'Not as many trips to the bathroom.'

He patted his stomach.

'You know? I don't think it's quite as swollen. You think this whole thing you're putting me through will cure the IBS?'

'If you mean that irritable bugger Southwell. No cure for that.'

Maroc smiled his apology.

'The aim of this whole thing I'm putting you through, as you phrase it, is to normalise your physiology, optimise the body systems. That includes your digestive tract. And yes, there's a good chance of it curing your IBS. If you stick at it.'

Southwell was slightly irked at his commitment being in doubt.

'Every intention of doing so, old man. Every intention. Now, how about that walk you promised?'

Maroc glanced through the window. Spring had arrived sedately, its entry assuaging the harsh memories of winter. He had smelt its freshness on the morning air earlier, on his way to the village. He nodded.

Max Southwell was wrapped up like a parcel. Thanks to the stretching exercises Maroc had incorporated into his regime, Southwell's movements had improved. They had become less painful.

Still, he found it challenging addressing the various buttons and fastenings.

'These bloody fingers. They feel like sausages.'

'They'll improve as your circulation improves. Stop fretting, man. The great plan will take care of everything.'

He grinned, as Southwell stood like a child refugee from the second world war. All he needed was a label attached to his coat.

Maroc ran up the stairs to his bedroom. He had left his mobile on the small desk opposite his bed. Quickly, he keyed in and sent a couple of short, urgent texts, one to a friend in Germany, the other to Bill Gordon.

Walking into the living room, he could sense his father-in-law's new energy, his impatience. Southwell punched his fist into his palm.

'What are we waiting for?'

Maroc smiled and reached for the door. Stepping aside, he allowed Southwell to exit.

Once outside, Maroc noticed Southwell's reaction. It had been over a year since he had seen the garden. Turning to Maroc, he began speaking. He stopped and, swaying slightly, reached out for support. Maroc quickly placed a hand on his shoulder, steadying him.

'This fresh air can be intoxicating, Max.'

He offered his arm.

Southwell nodded his agreement. He cast his eyes around the garden

'Doesn't take long for mother nature to reclaim her dominance.'

He shook his head sadly, and then, remembering the purpose of the evening, he accepted Maroc's arm.

Like men from an earlier time, they continued in amiable companionship. Southwell was quiet, and Maroc noticed a tear on the older man's cheek.

He said nothing, honouring his inconsolable loss. Platitudes about time being a healer would be inappropriate.

'She loved this place, spent hours on her knees planting things, digging things up. She used to laugh at my lack of knowledge. Never could tell a flower from a bloody weed.'

He shook his head ruefully.

'Still can't.'

Maroc let him talk, allowing him to get the poisons of grief out of his system. He understood the healing power of sharing.

He remembered the selfless friends. They had listened to his drunken outpourings, minding his distress until he could.

Later, his embarrassed apologies would be met with restorative savagery.

'Always knew you were a boring bastard, Maroc.'

They continued walking and Southwell turned to him.

'You probably think I'm a pathetic old fart?'

His smile was uncertain.

'Of course, Max. Always have.'

Maroc squeezed his arm. They continued towards the front gate.

Southwell paused, remembering why he and Katherine could never walk away from this place. He gazed with fresh appreciation as the light began to fade. It conferred its silver greyness upon hills and meadows. Wooded valleys returned to their secret dark.

He sighed deeply, contentment and sadness vying for dominance. That evening, there would be no winner.

CHAPTER 15

John Southwell was in urgent conversation on his office phone.'

For god's sake, Malcolm, you must know someone who'd be willing to do it. You run with some shady types.'

He listened to his younger brother's indignant reply before cutting him short.

'I'm prepared to speculate five thou. It'll be money well spent if we get that meddling bastard off the scene.'

He paused, listening and nodding.

'I know... I said I know it's a risk, but it's one worth taking, don't you think?'

He continued to listen, his patience wearing thin.

'They turned it down? Did they by god? OK, then, get someone else.'

John allowed his brother to answer. Eyes rolling, he cut in.

'Fine, I don't care what nationality, Malcolm. Albanians? Why not if they're willing to do the job. Are they capable, I mean in your opinion?'

He nodded to the voice at the other end, his expression pained.

He had known Malcolm would be difficult, and not because of any moral scruples. Whenever financial gain was a possibility, his brother could always be relied on to lay aside his moral compass.

The brothers had an impressive flair for ethical escapology. Both were equally expert at rationalising themselves free of guilt or feelings of wrongdoing.

'You have their number? Contact them, and I'll wire you the money. Yes, today. You'll have it within a couple of hours. Yes, fine, an extra five hundred for expenses? Yes, Malcolm, I understand it'll take some organising. That's why you're the man for the job.'

He immediately regretted the last remark. His younger brother may be weak and greedy, but he was far from dumb. He waited for the reaction.

'No, Malcolm, I mean it. I wouldn't have involved you if I didn't mean it. Yes, OK, I'll get online now. It'll be with you in a couple of hours.'

Expelling a sigh, John Southwell replaced the receiver and leaned back into his office chair. He was not a man to waste time on emotions, negative or otherwise.

His feelings for Maroc had never been an issue. He had never given it much thought. It was not about feelings. He was an accountant, and Peter Maroc was an unnecessary financial impediment. An extra expense on his ledger. It was that simple.

The phone rang again, stirring him from his reverie. To his surprise, it was Emily. She was the only member of the family he had time for. To say he loved her would have been, as they say, a stretch.

'What a lovely surprise. How are things in darkest Africa?' He listened, this time with more patience.

'I know you're worried, we all are. Yes, I fully understand; you're practically a prisoner in that bloody hospital. But don't fret, Em. Things are moving here.'

He paused, allowing her to answer. 'I mean on the legal side. I think we can wrest power of attorney from Maroc. Yes, legitimately, what else would I mean?'

'Emily, you there?'

John Southwell frowned his irritation at the growing static. The line went dead.

Another ring. John picked up immediately.

'John? Can you hear this?'

It was Emily. This time the static was not so loud

'Yes, Em, it's clearer. As I was saying, we can regain control. Still not certain how Maroc managed to get it in the first place.' He paused.

'But I can hazard a guess. No, everything will be above board and legal.'

John knew Emily was too smart to fall for a serious deviation from the truth. She had always been able to read him, to read all of them.

Proving anything, however, was another matter. John Southwell gave a deep sigh as he replaced the receiver.

Attention to detail was crucial. There could be no paper trails. If Emily was to find out what he and his brother were planning...

Since childhood, John Southwell had always found talking to Emily vaguely disturbing. His sister had the knack of somehow accessing the better part of his nature, the part he had long regarded as a hindrance.

He leaned back in his chair, allowing his mind to deliberate on what was happening. He had to believe he was doing all of this for the family. Yes, he thought, for the general good. Confronting scruples was, for

John, unfamiliar territory. His sister had a lot to answer for.

Being alone in the building they rented for their struggling enterprise. John decided to use the office shower. It was something he did when the rest of the staff and family members had gone home. It avoided a lot of awkward questions from Ruth.

He followed his shower with a wet shave. Padding to his locker, he retrieved clean underclothes and a fresh shirt.

John Southwell looked in the cloakroom mirror. Happy with what he saw, he made his way to the shared parking area behind the office block. There, his five-year-old black BMW 3 series stood waiting.

Pulling out of the car park, he felt the tension in his body slowly release its grip. He swung the BMW onto the highway and headed towards the red-light district of Perth City.

He was confident Cherry, the petite Thai girl employed by the Sweet Ending massage parlour, thought of him as more than a client. Much more. His hands tightened on the steering wheel as he anticipated a time when he did not have to budget for such recreations.

CHAPTER 16

Peter Maroc had awakened early and was out of bed by five a.m. He looked through his bedroom window. The dawn light would not appear for another hour.

He loved this time of stillness and quiet, where the day had yet to find its full voice. It steadied him; gave him time to think and plan.

Southwell was getting there. He needed at least another week before he was ready for a serious walk. The man was raring to go. Maroc could sympathise.

His father-in-law had made impressive progress towards full recovery. His input had been nothing short of heroic, earning him Maroc's respect and, to his surprise, a grudging affection.

Maroc had witnessed the discomfort he'd endured. Each step towards mobility had been a battle, hard-won.

No longer the prissy academic, Southwell had emerged from the shadows, a warrior.

After sitting in quiet meditation for twenty minutes, Maroc showered and dressed. He had planned a reasonable journey. Given Southwell's walking pace, it should take perhaps two hours.

Opening the bedroom door and not wishing to disturb the older man, he quietly descended the two flights of stairs leading to the front hall. A line of light shone from under the living room door. Surprised, he continued until he reached it. Hesitantly, he turned the doorknob and stepped through.

Southwell was kneeling in the Burmese position on a large cushion on the floor. His eyes were closed in meditation.

Good man, Maroc thought. Bloody good man.

Trying not to disturb him, he made his way to the adjoining kitchen.

'Up early, Maroc. You in training for something?'

Maroc turned and smiled.

'I'm impressed by your dedication. I wasn't sure whether Buddhist practises conflicted with your Christian faith.'

'Jesus and Presley will be around years after the Buddha's been long forgotten.'

Maroc gave him a quizzical look and, shaking his head, continued to the kitchen.

'Tea or coffee?'

'Green tea please, grasshopper.'

Southwell carefully rose from his meditation cushion and stood silently for a moment. Then, performing a couple of yoga stretches, he finished with deep abdominal breathing.

'What's on the cards today?'

Maroc came out of the kitchen carrying a mug of tea and a glass of green tea.

'Fancy a walk somewhere local? Nothing too strenuous.'

'Fine. When will I be ready for that fishing trip I've been promised?'

'Can you hold out for another week? I promise it'll be worth it.'

'Yea, suppose so.' Not exactly grumpy, but close.

'Really,' said Maroc. 'You're coming on well, but since we'll be camping over a couple of nights, I'd rather make sure.'

Southwell's eyes lit up.

'You never mentioned camping.'

'We don't have to if you're not up to it.' The teasing had become a game; two men cooped together for close to six months. It was lubricant. They weren't exactly buddies, not yet. However, things could have been a deal edgier.

'Camping is good.'

Maroc smirked.

'Christ, you going American on me?'

Southwell smiled. Drawing the blasphemy card each time Maroc transgressed would not work. He was yet to find malice in the man.

Southwell had thought long and hard about their relationship. It was still a stretch to call him a friend. Too many rumours still circulated about Peter Maroc, although most had originated from his son, John...

'We'll set off straight after breakfast then. The cereal will do me.'

Maroc, returning to the kitchen, grunted his agreement. He emerged carrying a tall tumbler filled with a dark green liquid. He handed it to Southwell.

A few months ago, this offering would have been accepted with ill grace. Now, it had become part of the regime. Max Southwell had abandoned many of his doubts, his bedroom mirror providing all the proof he needed of his progress.

'Not bran again, old boy. Something less scouring. Weetabix, perhaps?'

'In the kitchen, go help yourself.'

Southwell rose from his chair, making his way to the kitchen, mumbling something about 'staff today.' Maroc could hear his tuneless humming as he prepared his cereal.

The two walked up the gentle slope leading away from the large Victorian manor house that was Plas Meurig. They could have been father and son, out for an early morning stroll.

Southwell looked relaxed and healthy. He was happy to be alive on this shiny new day. The weather could not have been better. He was eager to put his revitalised body to the test.

They walked up a short steep hill, the path turning into a narrow lane. The lane continued for a hundred yards before bending to the right. Houses were replaced by trees and open country.

They had gone less than half a mile, and Southwell paused, hands-on-hips. A man pleased with himself. Not out of breath, he felt he had plenty left in the tank.

This role of the pupil was a liberating experience; it afforded him freedom from having to be in charge.

From their elevated position, Southwell looked down, taking in the distance from the village. The term *newborn* came to mind. Surprising himself, he did not squirm from the sobriquet.

Was he becoming, what was the term, mellow? He liked the sound of that, though doubted the expression was current.

'You OK, Max?'

Maroc looked abstractedly at the morning sky, giving the impression the question was one of courtesy rather than concern. He'd heeded Emily's warning to go easy on her father. He had also chosen not to make this apparent to Southwell.

Maroc led the way; a loose stone wall on his left gently climbed into the wooded hills above. They had walked upwards in silence for close to a mile when Southwell turned to his son-in-law.

Max Southwell considered himself a straight talker. Some would call him blunt to the point of rudeness. Yet he felt oddly ashamed of what he had to say to this man.

'Straight up, Maroc. What are you after? What do you hope to get out of all this?'

Maroc stopped abruptly. As he turned to face him, Southwell noted his expression of surprise. His voice, calm, he looked directly at his father-in-law.

'Until proven otherwise, you'll have to accept I'm doing it to stop you checking out before your time. It would be a useful life wasted.'

'And I'm supposed to accept that at face value? I mean, all the work you've put in, the dedication, the time you've spent. When am I getting the bill?'

Maroc said nothing, looking back, his expression unreadable.

Southwell, having started, felt compelled to give voice to the suspicions and doubts that had been stewing inside him for months. He needed answers from this enigmatic man. He continued.

'My family and friends might call it stretching trust to its limit.'

'You believe them, Max? What does your gut tell you? You think I'm after money, simple as that?'

'Nothing simple about you, Maroc. If it's your game, it won't be simple.'

Why was he talking like this when he could see no dark motive? He thought of the miracle of the last few months.

Maroc made no reply. He stood looking into the distance as though his mind was on other things. Finally, shaking his head, he turned and continued walking.

Southwell thought he detected disappointment in his son-in-law's face. He was not surprised at how bad that made him feel.

He mentally shrugged and continued following the path. As the terrain changed, he experienced his old trepidation. The trail took them along a narrow ridge, a sheer drop of around fifty feet to the left.

Never comfortable with heights, he was conscious of his vulnerability, with Maroc a mere step behind. If the joke had always been on him, this would be a good place for the punch line.

As if on cue, Southwell's boot caught on an exposed root. He stumbled and immediately felt a steadying grip on his right arm. He looked back at Maroc, who winked and smiled reassuringly.

'You're not the fall guy here, Max.'

Southwell felt relief sweep through him. He felt like laughing and crying. God all mighty, who was writing this script?

CHAPTER 17

According to the general buzz, the crisis was over. The announcement had confirmed this, and there was optimism in the little camp. Emily could only hope the Quarantine would be lifted. She should know more in the next few hours.

It was never wise to accept anything at face value. In this part of the world, the truth was one of expedience, presented to fit the current agenda. Identifying it was a game Emily and her colleagues played daily.

There were no new cases. With the remaining patients stable, the authorities had accepted the findings of the hospital medics.

This happy state had been further endorsed by the visiting W.H.O officials. They had taken a week to reach their findings. Their team had been allowed to return to Europe the following day.

It was a good sign; Emily could go home. She knew, however, that the military in the area could reverse any decision on a whim. She would remain optimistic.

Emily had spoken to her father as often as the telephone system in this beleaguered country would allow. She was pleased with his recovery.

Her mind turned to Maroc. Was he doing it out of compassion? All that work for a man with whom he had never connected? She struggled to see it.

Was he, as John suggested, just an assassin with a game plan. Funny way of killing someone.

Another motive perhaps, one not yet apparent...? Then it struck her. God, was he trying to win her back? She found she liked the idea. But would she end up with the Maroc of old? The absent husband whose life required endless peril to have meaning?

Emily thought her day had earned her a hot bath. Closing the door of the small bathroom usually triggered a soothing response. It allowed the busy doctor to enjoy one of the simple pleasures of solitude.

Wearily, Emily allowed her body to slip into the soapy warmth. She lay back with her eyes closed.

Today, her perverse mind seemed determined to create a buzzing halo of conflicting thoughts, making it hard for her to settle.

Maroc had taught Emily a simple mind trick she had always found effective. She waited for the familiar ritual to perform its minor miracle.

Her mind fought back briefly, before finally slipping beneath the blanket of unconsciousness.

Emily Southwell woke with a start. Disorientated, she took in her surroundings.

When not in her own bed, Emily would often awaken into uncertainty. This period of confusion was disturbing though brief.

Maroc would laugh, calling it her morning muddle. She thought it strange, how so many things in her day referenced her absent husband.

Her brief slumber failed to yield answers to her many questions. Her body shivered briefly. She blamed the chilled bathwater.

Emily dried herself and dressed quickly. Today, she was not concerned with impressing.

There was to be a meeting at eight that evening. It would be held in the small reception area of the hospital building. She expected there to be around a dozen concerned people.

Emily checked herself in the narrow wardrobe mirror and nodded her satisfaction. She took a small, well-thumbed notebook from the bedside table. *Record everything. You can never be too informed.*

Her father's voice. She smiled.

Opening the door, she stepped with cautious optimism into the courtyard outside her apartment. The evening air still carried much of the day's heat. At this hour, it was at least tolerable.

It was a short walk to the main building. Emily took her time, drawing in and savouring the sounds and smells of this dangerous, exotic place.

The Swedish couple had already arrived. Inger was her favourite person, her only confidante in this sorry place. Tall and slim, with short white-blond hair, Emily secretly thought her the perfect cliche for Scandinavian womanhood.

Conflict in North-Eastern Nigeria had raged for over six years, resulting in the displacement of over two million people. Warring factions had damaged most of the medical facilities, with many health workers being either killed or abducted.

The stark statistics had finally been the final clincher in her decision-making. She would not remain in her safe bubble while people died in their hundreds.

Close to four million individuals were left with

limited or no access to the most basic health services. Emily Southwell had made up her mind to align herself with the most effective organisation operating in the area.

The World Health Organisation had worked tirelessly to help alleviate the situation. This was no British or European hospital, and things remained challenging and dangerous. Emily had anticipated and accepted the difficulties.

Three people emerged from behind double doors leading to the wards and operating theatres. Two wore heavily decorated and braided military uniforms. The third she recognised as the country's chief medical officer.

Emily was impressed by this diminutive man. Modest to the point of self-effacement, Amadi Abebe was Ethiopian-born. He had received his education at Cambridge University. From there, he had moved to a leading London teaching hospital. Abebe was considered one of the good guys.

She knew how much he hated public speaking, being more at ease in a one-to-one setting. The small group hushed, each person eagerly awaiting good news. Clearing his throat, the C.M.O began speaking.

'As you might have heard, and with thanks to all the excellent work done by all.'

He nodded in the direction of his audience.

'The situation has stabilised and is no longer at crisis level. We received a visit from officials of the World Health Organisation who were allowed into the area. Their conclusion...'

He paused and smiled broadly.

'And mine also. The situation is under control. A

decision has been reached that movement in and out of the area will no longer be restricted.'

He looked up, his eyes sweeping the group. 'Those of you who wish to leave are free to do so.'

There was an immediate release of excitable chatter together with muted laughter. The tall Swede reached out to Emily, embracing her warmly. Inger understood her friend's situation; knew how desperate Emily was to return home to her father.

They both promised to keep in touch. These were not empty platitudes. The two had formed a deep and lasting bond, and the promises would be kept.

Emily reminded her they would have at least another week together. Inger and her husband made it clear they would be very available for at least one good leaving party.

With another week remaining before she departed the country, Emily knew her situation was still fraught and that things could change hourly.

The political stability in the region was fragile, with warring factions in the militia fighting for regional dominance. Who could say that another group entering the area would not be far worse than the present lot?

Each team member knew that each day could bring danger to their small community. The hospital staff were always at the whims and vagaries of the soldiers. Often drunk and undisciplined, they could be unpredictable, even violent.

The female personnel had taken to barring their apartment doors in the evenings. With stories of assault and even rape on single female staff members, they were not taking chances. Emily had, on occasion, been the object of unwanted attention.

The hell with that, she thought. It comes with the territory. She owed her colleagues the extra week.

CHAPTER 18

Southwell was recuperating well. The overall improvement was steady, becoming more apparent each day. He was also becoming more demanding, wanting to do more; achieve more.

Maroc needed a break; twenty-four hours would do it. He marvelled at his father-in-law's overall attitude. Over the last few months, he had seen the man becoming increasingly committed to the programme.

Southwell was engaged in a visualisation exercise. Maroc had found it useful in his own advancement. He had recommended Southwell try it.

The old scholar was applying this mental practice to everything he thought needed changing.

The improvement in Southwell's moods had become apparent. So had the advances in his physical well-being.

The older man's reliance on prescription drugs had been observably reduced. The potions provided by Maroc still helped with the pain. His need for them, however, had lessened.

There were mornings when Maroc almost wished for a return of the Southwell of old. Grumpy and belligerent.

Peter Maroc liked his mornings quiet. It was a time he considered sacred when he would engage in his meditative practices.

The space it gave both energised and centred him. Still, Maroc would never deny that childlike enthusiasm.

Maroc smiled, seeing the sixty-six-year-old so utterly engaged in what he would have considered hippie bullshit a few months before.

'Glasshopper, come back to us.'

Maroc smiled at the mispronunciation, courtesy of David Carradine's TV series, Kung Fu. The programme had proven a surprising diversion. Southwell had not only found it hugely entertaining but, in its showy way, instructive.

Practices such as meditation, mindfulness, Chi Gong, and Thai Chi. All had been introduced by Maroc within the context of neuroscience.

The ancient practices had finally been vindicated after years of ridicule and being branded pseudoscience.

Southwell was impressed by the research on the efficacy of such practices as meditation and visualisation. He had come to realise it was not all bullshit.

'I've been thinking of taking a day's break, Max. I'm talking twenty-four hours, no more. Mrs Loyd-Edwards can pop in and keep an eye on you while I'm gone. I'll make sure she gives you both the prescriptive medication and the remedies I've provided.'

Over the last four months, the formidable nurse Price had gradually reduced her hours. A month ago, she announced her decision to discontinue her position at Plas Meurig.

Price had seen how, under her guidance, Maroc was

coping well. She now felt confident he could be left alone with her patient. Maroc had been effusive in praise of her invaluable instruction.

When it came to Southwell's recovery, he had come to realise they were on the same page. Price was on the side of the angles and had not been comfortable with her ward's obvious decline.

Maroc's appearance introduced an approach that made professional sense. Max Southwell needed movement, exercise and fresh air. At first, she had been unsure of the herbal tonics. Given the way her patient had responded, her doubts had quickly vanished.

Southwell rose slowly, considering Maroc's announcement.

'Not a problem, Maroc. It'll be nice to have some time to myself; do a bit of reading. Perhaps make a restart on my book. The world awaits its publication.'

'Seriously. You'd be OK with it?'

'I said yes.'

Southwell smiled.

'Stop worrying about me, man. You need a break. When you get back, we can plan a trip together. You think?'

'I've got a few plans for us. Yes, definitely. It can be part of your recovery.'

Gwen Lloyd-Edwards was one of the few people Southwell could get on with. Down to earth, with an intellect that more than matched his, she was also their nearest neighbour.

Having been in academia most of her life and a past principal of a private girl's school, she was no mental slouch. The two held strong, often opposing views on just about everything.

'She'll keep you entertained. Quite a brain that one.'
The older man had picked up a book. He looked up.
'Yes, she's bright enough.'
In Southwell's world, that was a huge compliment.

Maroco planned to reconnect with some of his climbing mates in Llanberis. A few could always be found at a popular climber's cafe in town. It would be his first call.

The Llanberis pass possessed a stark and unforgiving beauty. It had never failed to impress him. Guiding his Maserati around the snaking road down to the town, his heart rate quickened in anticipation of the day.

Today, he was in the mood to tackle some advanced slate routes. The Dinorwig slate quarries, situated on the far side of the large Peris lake offered some challenging problems. The climbing there had never disappointed.

Today, his luck was in. Entering the café, Maroc nodded to the owner. He ordered a pint mug of tea and, on making his way to a table by the window, he was spotted.

Dave Thomas and Michael Moore had not long sat down. They had arrived in Llanberis that morning and were considering various climbing options.

Maroc joined them at their table and, after the usual banter, turned the conversation to climbing. Neither man had a programme for the day. When Maroc suggested Dinorwig, they had agreed. It was an excellent choice.

Both were based in the midlands. Dave, originally from Llanberis, had moved down there with his girlfriend. Michael, born and brought up in Duddeston, was a true Brummie.

At five foot nine in height, the blond Englishman was the shortest of the trio. He was also the strongest. Michael possessed a build that was both powerful and flexible.

Welsh climbing had much to offer them. The travelling time was reasonable; the climbs technically challenging. Maroc considered his day to be developing well.

Michael left for the bathroom, and the two Welshmen reverted to their native tongue. To do otherwise would have seemed unnatural.

Dave, a physical training instructor, worked with several large companies in and around the midlands. A tall, lean man with cropped, auburn hair, he was also a superb athlete.

He had taken to climbing like the proverbial duck to water. Whenever they met, their main topics of conversation were a given. Climbing and Dave's impossible love life.

Dave had always been tactful when it came to his friend's private life. He approached the subject diffidently, asking whether Maroc was still making trips abroad. Maroc's evasive responses had him changing the subject back to a topic he was always comfortable with. His own love life.

'A real looker, Peter. With the brains to go with it.'

Maroc chose not to go for the low-hanging fruit. Dave could be sensitive when it came to matters of the heart, something many of his less considerate mates exploited to the full.

Michael's return abruptly ended a riveting story starring Dave and his girl and a very public park bench.

As anticipated, the climbing was superb, the chosen routes taking all three to the limit of their technical abilities. Their fitness levels had always been on par.

Dave and Michael equalled Maroc in both skill and courage, with the SAS man extending his lead through sheer recklessness. The Englishman, always excellent company, had, hands down, won the banter award.

Maroc held back on the beer, a decision he would later be thankful for. Still, he considered the evening a great success. He was a happy man, glad to be back on home ground, relaxing to the musicality of his language.

The evening came to an end, and Maroc was persuaded to bunk down at Dave's parents. Dave and Michael would stay in the house, and he could have the medium-sized caravan permanently parked in the small back garden. It was an arrangement that suited all.

Peter Maroc did not regard himself as reclusive. He enjoyed his occasional immersion into good conversation and banter. Maroc would emerge feeling both energised and happier.

Now, it was time to kick back and enjoy some quiet reflection. He had brought with him an expensive sleeping bag. And a book.

Maroc looked over the small caravan. He had slept in less forgiving places.

His repeated attempts at the reading were soon abandoned. The effects of the day's exertions quietly coaxed his mind into a natural sleep.

His drinking that evening had been deliberately restrained. To Maroc, the trade-off was to not lose most of the following day. His careless younger self would have laughed at his caution.

Maroc quickly sank into a hypnagogic state, where lucid dreaming and hallucinations are possible. Entering this realm of endless possibilities, he immediately recognised both time and location.

The Serbian sniper's Zastava M76 would spit out a second round. He would not repeat his mistake. This time it would be a headshot.

Terror always takes its own sweet time, and Maroc's mind turned inward. He sought refuge in the stillness he could always find. He waited.

A splash of red, closely followed by a sharp spitting sound. The sniper rolled to one side, his Zastava swivelling skywards.

It had been a busy day for Tony Ashley. Thankfully, the little Yorkshireman had found a gap in his sniper duties.

A movement at eight o'clock. Maroc saw the girl. She was squeezed snugly against what remained of an arched doorway.

The ponytail flicked. She had spotted Tony's position. Seeing her at this distance, he noted the hard beauty of her face. As she lined him in her sights, he recognised her.

Tony had not clocked her, he was pretty sure of that. So was she.

He tried sitting up. The smoulder in his side burst into full flame.

'Sentiment has no place in war.' Yes, yes Niels, you bloody Norwegian sage. A bit late now.

She cocked her head, the ponytail flicking. Bizarrely, she reminded him of uncle George's West Highland Terrier, but with less emotion.

Maroc saw recognition in her narrowing eyes as she lifted her head from the weapon. He also knew his HK G36

lay uselessly out of reach.
A ghost of a smile. She turned and melted into the
ruins.

CHAPTER 19

Max Southwell awakened that morning, more alive than he had been in years. He felt like a child allowed a special treat for his industry. He was about to put his newly found vigour to the test.

He rose from his bed and looked out through the wide window of his reclaimed bedroom. Today's dawn held a long-withheld promise, and he knew it would be a special day. He welcomed it with a short prayer to a neglected god.

Showering quickly, he chose an outfit appropriate for the day's activity and made his way to the living room. Southwell could hear Maroc in the kitchen. He wondered about joining him when his son-in-law emerged bearing steaming cups.

'Tea this morning Max. With extra caffeine. Get the old ticker kick-started, eh?'

Manoeuvring around Southwell, he placed the hot mugs on one of the cork mats on Southwell's oak bureau.

'Careful with the furniture Maroc. I realise you're not bloody house trained.'

They started breakfast with cereal. It was followed by toast and some suspect marmalade Maroc had found in one of Southwell's kitchen cupboards.

Both were keen to get going. Maroc checked the

older man's clothing, paying close attention to his footwear. He nodded his approval.

'You'll do.'

As they left the house, each carried a small rucksack, the content having been judiciously packed the previous evening. Maroc had carefully prepared each item, with Southwell conferring final approval.

They set off from the village just after first light. The day was yet to be unwrapped with both men anticipating its rich content.

Maroc had decided on a local destination. A place they had both frequented and loved. Heading north on the A498 out of Beddgelert, they arrived at a junction where they turned right onto the A4086. Soon, they approached the hamlet of Capel Curig, taking a left onto the A5.

They continued for four miles alongside a narrow river that ran with the road to their left. Both men rested comfortably in the moment, appreciative spectators to the increasingly mountainous terrain.

As the road bent gently to the left, mount Tryfan revealed itself to them. Crowned by twin pillars, it brooded in lofty majesty above the waters of Lake Ogwen.

The lake was to their right, and they followed it to its furthest end. Here, Maroc slowed the Maserati before turning left into the parking area by the Ogwen Valley Mountain Rescue Post.

'Up for a bit of adventure?' Maroc's expression held a spark of mischief. It ignited in the older man.

'Hope you can keep up, Maroc. This boy's on fire.'

His grin widening, Maroc opened the car door. Both men had rediscovered their love of undergraduate humour, never missing an opportunity to indulge.

Southwell had been shown a portal to a new dimension of possibilities. He would step through it like a lion, and he would roar.

Passing the rescue post, they continued up and onto a stony path leading towards Idwal lake and the dramatically named Devil's Kitchen.

Southwell, encouraged by the bright warmth of the day, breathed in the clean mountain air. Today, he would brave the stark beauty that had first drawn him to this magical place.

As they continued up the gentle gradient, a muted splendour painted itself around them. Maroc deliberately maintained the leisurely pace, keeping a vigilant eye on his companion. Southwell seemed to be coping well, but gently does it, he thought.

The lake appeared before them, a tarnished silver platter in the morning light. It had been too long since Max Southwell's last visit. He was not disappointed.

They stood by the calm water, united in quiet reverence to an ancient devotion.

'Always the simple things'

Southwell turned to his companion. His face held a trace of sadness.

Maroc gave a slight nod, preserving the sacred silence. Both were conscious of the transient nature of such moments, making them the more precious.

CHAPTER 20

It had been a few weeks since his outing with Southwell, and Peter Maroc had been keen to return to his adventure playground. He was increasingly able to leave Southwell on his own or in the company of the erudite Mrs Lloyd-Edwards.

As much as he enjoyed the older man's company, it was good to be treading the same path on his own. He had pushed himself in Llanberis, encouraged to excel by his fellow climbers. It was an experience that had reconnected him with his passion.

He relished the physical challenges the mountains had to offer. Today, however, would be gentler, defined by nostalgia, not adrenaline.

Max had been fine about it. He had encouraged him to go. Maroc wondered if the old boy was being unselfish or if there was an increasing appeal for gentler company.

He somehow doubted the latter. There had only been eighteen months since Katherine's passing.

As he trod the stony path to the lake, the mountains hailed his return. A deeper part of him echoed their calling, and he was reminded of the first lines of a Welsh poem:

Aros mae'r mynyddau mawr
Rhuo trostynt mae y gwynt

The great mountains remain
The wind roars above them

Again, he felt the ancientness of this land, his connection with it, a blessing. The Carneddau mountain range loomed ahead. Old friends, he would visit another day.

By the time he approached Idwal lake, Maroc had made his decision. He would free climb the Idwal slabs.

The slabs rose above the lake to the south and would present Maroc with few difficulties. On reaching the top, he would make his way back to Mount Tryfan. Then a steep descent to the main road running alongside lake Ogwen.

For Peter Maroc, it was an undemanding climb. He felt comfortable attempting it without protective gear in place. The slabs had been his first introduction to climbing. At age thirteen, there had been born a lasting passion.

Standing at the base of the slabs, he looked up and examined his options. He chose a relatively easy climb. The route had been named Hope in the guidebooks. There was also a Faith and a Charity.

It would be a trip down memory lane when Maroc could relax; allow his body to flow. He hoped the experience would forge a connection across time with the thirteen-year-old Peter.

He felt the privilege of being able to enjoy such experiences and thought of comrades less fortunate. Maroc's mind turned to Southwell, impressed at the old warrior's progress.

On reaching the top, Maroc sat in silence and remembered. Perhaps not having captured the euphoria of that first ascent, the experience was still a poignant reminder of his youth. He offered a silent salute to his younger self.

Back in those potent days when hopes soared untethered, anything had been possible. He wished it were as true today?

He decided against the walk to mount Tryfan. Instead, he chose the more direct scramble route down. It would take him back close to his starting point.

On his climb down, he paused, turning to look at the cwm. Once more, he marvelled at its tranquillity. He felt unready to end the experience and decided to walk around the small lake.

It was, in this place, he had first felt a sense of the numinous. The experience had been deeply personal. It had helped direct his life.

He had never shared it. Not even with Emily.

Maroc had never embraced conventional religion and was comfortable with where he was on his journey. Over the years, he had come to accept there was a spiritual dimension to reality.

Maroc walked the rocky path back to the road, feeling pleasantly tired. He dug into his jacket pocket for the ignition key, giving scant notice to the brown Ford van next to the Maserati. Maroc bent to open the door of the low-slung car.

A loud pop and he was hit by a thousand stinging bees. His body went rigid. It convulsed, then went rigid again. Maroc lost control of the major muscles and could do nothing to stop himself from falling.

The taser was kept tight against his spine, the pain relentless as the high voltage assaulted his body. A vicious blow delivered to the back of his head opened up a merciful void of velvet blackness.

Maroc experienced a brief sense of falling and waited for the pain of landing. It never came.

Swimming through the dark waves of an alien ocean, he felt peaceful, safe.

The two burly figures wore black ski masks. They bundled his unresisting body through the side door of the van.

Peter Maroc desperately clung to the last vestige of a warm consciousness. Inside the van, all that changed.

The blows, delivered with a short-weighted club, rained down on his head. Meant to incapacitate, not kill, their delivery was measured. Later they would need him to talk.

His captors, however, had not finished with him and their attention shifted to his body. It was personal, their actions directed by rage. He had made them look like fools outside the tavern, and now he would pay.

Maroc was defenceless, unable to regain control of his arms and legs. He was incapable of putting up the most basic resistance as the pair continued their onslaught.

It was happening somewhere else, to someone else. His mind shielded itself from the brutality as his world became dimmer and darker.

As the nondescript van swung out of the car park, a casual observer would observe no indication of wrongdoing. A silver Maserati, the driver's door open with the owner inexplicably absent. Unusual, but nothing to be alarmed about.

CHAPTER 21

Max Southwell was worried. Peter Maroc was undeniably a punctual animal, reliable even. The bloody man had arranged to be back no later than seven. It was now eight-thirty.

still light, everything about the day gave the impression of normalcy. This rationale gave Southwell little comfort. Maroc should have appeared by now.

Another searching look through the sitting room window. The garden gate looked back in sympathetic silence. Nothing. Not a bloody sign of the man.

Southwell sighed. God, he was behaving like a fretting wife waiting for her drunken husband to return from the pub.

Another hour passed. Southwell played back his last exchange with Maroc.

He strained to remember. Maroc had told him he would be back shortly after six. They would take an evening stroll to the village pub. The drinks would be on Maroc. He was certain. Almost.

Southwell glanced at the firm round *safu* on which he sat and practised his meditation. He had come to associate the round black cushion with peace and liberation from worry. Today, he badly needed those benefits.

He lowered his body to the safu. Assuming a

familiar posture, he closed his eyes and made a valiant attempt at letting go of the chatter in his head.

A few minutes into the practice, Southwell realised he was getting nowhere. He abandoned the endeavour and returned to the window.

Come on man, where the hell are you?

Southwell was an orderly man. Not evident in all areas of his life, the trait had served him well during his career in academia. His student life predated personal computers. There was, however, one lesson he had learnt. It was the value of having quick access to information.

Opening the top drawer of his bureau, he found his thick address book. He quickly located a number Maroc had given him and phoned the Ogwen Valley Mountain Rescue post.

What if it was all in his head? Max Southwell would have some explaining to do.

Maroc was a well-known figure within the North Wales climbing community. It included the rescue people. After what seemed an age, he heard a man's voice.

'Ogwen Mountain Rescue, how can I help?'

Southwell dived straight in.

'I'm a friend of Peter Maroc. You seen him in your neck of the woods today?'

There was no hesitation.

'Saw him come in on his own. We had a chat. Long story short, he was planning on doing some easy climbing on the slabs. He had no ropes or gear with him. I took him up on that. Well, you know Peter, he said he'd be fine. Been climbing em since he was a nipper.'

Southwell cut in, trying hard to hide his impatience.

'So, has he come back from the climb?'

'That's the funny thing. His car's still here. Driver door open. No sign of your man anywhere. Bloody odd.'

'How long ago was that. I mean when you found the car?'

A short pause.

'I spotted it over two hours ago. No idea when Peter returned to the car. Like I said, odd.'

To Southwell, this news solved nothing, leaving him more worried. Maroc had returned safely from the climb. A relief. But why should he then have left his car with the door open? As the man said. 'Bloody odd.'

'Hello? You still there?'

Southwell snapped out of his musings.

'Sorry, yes, still here.'

What to do? Should the local police be informed, or was that too precipitous? He made his decision.

'Give him another hour. If he's not back, phone the local bobbies in Bethesda.'

There was a pause at the other end.

'You think it's that serious? After all, he's a grown man and... it's only been a few hours.'

Southwell had made up his mind. Later, when Maroc was safely back, he could bollock him all he wanted.

'Yes, I do. This doesn't feel right. Can you do that for me?'

'Will do. Give us your number and I'll call back either way.'

Thanking the man, Southwell ended the call. He could feel the onset of panic. Where the hell could

Maroc have gone? This was not right. Not bloody right at all.

He could not just sit around waiting, like a nervous groom at the altar. Maroc had previously mentioned some business with the Edwards brothers. They were down at the pub most evenings.

He knew it was a long shot, but what was the alternative? Sit and do nothing? The brothers might know something of his arrangements going forward. He would look for anything that would explain Maroc's uncharacteristic behaviour.

Southwell put on a light jacket and hat. He considered his walking stick and dismissed the idea.

He was in luck. Arwyn Edwards was leaving The Prince. He waved to the younger man.

This was going to be bloody awkward.

'You'll probably think I'm daft, Arwyn. Did Peter mention any plans he had for today?'

Arwyn gave him a blank look. Southwell continued quickly.

'He left for a spot of climbing around the Ogwen valley this morning'

'Never mentioned a thing to me, Mr Southwell. What's the problem? You're as white as a sheet.'

'He hasn't returned, Arwyn. His car is still in the car park near Ogwen lake. Passenger door wide open. It's been there for close to three hours. At least.'

'Who told you? The rescue?'

'Yes. They're phoning back in an hour or so. I'll have to get back to the house. Didn't give them my mobile number.'

Southwell smiled weakly.

'Want some company? I'll come over to the house

with you. See what we can find out.'

Edwards laid his large hand on Southwell's shoulder.

The older man nodded, the potential gravity of the situation becoming more real with the sharing. The abandoned car, its door open. A missing driver. He could conceive of no logical explanation. This worried him.

Max Southwell required logic in his life. Things should make sense.

CHAPTER 22

The brown Ford van had been travelling south for over two hours. An inspection of the van's exterior would reveal nothing remarkable. It was what it was. An old, unmarked brown van.

Maroc lay in the back of the van on old carpets. The carpets were incidental, not meant for his comfort.

He had received further beatings as he lay unconscious. It was part prudence and part malice.

His abductors needed Maroc alive, at least until they had reached their destination in Albania.

The brothers were aware of the man's capabilities and knew they had to keep him passive. However, they could not keep beating him into unconsciousness each time he revived.

At first, Maroc had been tied and gagged. It allowed them to extract due payment for the humiliation of their first encounter.

This was fine as long as he remained concealed inside the van. To take him outside and risk him being seen was not an option. This problem had been anticipated.

They had purchased a small supply of Diprivan, a general anaesthetic and sedation drug, through their contact in Manchester. It would render the recipient passive for hours when injected into the system.

It meant Maroc could be transported by wheelchair as a sleeping invalid. Not a perfect plan but one that would ensure Maroc would be delivered to his destination and able to answer questions.

Peter Maroc returned to consciousness in confusion and growing alarm. His eyes opened to a world of suffocating blackness. He thought he had gone blind or was entombed within a place where light could not reach?

As his eyes adjusted, he noticed the weak daylight as it seeped into the van's interior between the badly fitting doors. Relief swept through him, pushing back his growing dread.

Maroc had been temporarily blinded by a stun grenade when on ops in Kosovo. His vision had taken hours to recover, and the experience had left him badly shaken. He still retained a morbid fear of total darkness.

His first attempts at moving brought agony, forcing his awareness to return to its dark refuge. As time passed, his efforts became more informed, more cautious.

Maroc became aware of being bound and gagged. The next revelation came gradually. When it arrived, it shocked him.

He was a man without a name, without a story. Much of his memory had been wiped clean.

He had drifted into an uneasy slumber when Edon, the taller of the brothers, entered the van. The big man had sat on him while administering the Diprivan. The Albanian was no medic. The procedure had been bloody painful.

The effect was almost immediate. A warm blanket

of numbness allowed his mind to escape, leaving his tormented body in another place.

Spectres from the past invaded a present that fought their intrusion. Maroc hated his impotence, his inability to resist. Dragged helplessly into a realm of dread, he had no voice with which to shout his protest.

He was thrust into a familiar nightmare.

Tony should have been there, would have been there if the bloody op had gone to plan.

Maroc held one certainty. If he was still inside, the diminutive Englishman would not be abandoned.

He was first through the door, Johanson a trot behind. The flashbang he'd lobbed into the room would give them a tactical margin. Its 300,000 candlepower, together with the 160 decibels of sheer bloody noise, would have had Zeus covering his ears.

The wiry little sniper was more than a comrade in arms. Together, they'd been to hell and beyond. Had fought their way out of dozens of tight spots, always against ridiculous odds. Damn it all, Tony should have been waiting for them at the RV point.

His mate was missing. That would not do. He might still be in the building that had previously held the American hostage. A building they'd previously been lucky to get out of alive.

The bloody job was done. The American was now on his way to the Chechen, Russian border. They had bundled him into the back seat of a car. A perfect extraction with no losses. It had to be.

At first, Maroc could see little through the smoke and dust kicked up by the flashbang. He looked for movement, his HK MP5 sweeping each corner of the large room.

Johansson pushed past him, making his way to the

far-left corner. Maroc could make out a desk covered in debris from the blast. A desk his friend was now savagely dragging to one side.

A figure was slumped in the corner, the head a mass of scarlet. His mind rejecting an unacceptable truth, Maroc joined the kneeling Norwegian. Johansson shook his head, and for the first time, the Welshman saw him cry.

His mind exploded at the sight of his friend. His face was bloody, most of the right side, blown away. Maroc could barely recognise him. This wasn't how it should be.

Johansson's voice sounded strange.

'Back of the head. Execution style. Bastards!'

The words barely registered as he held the lifeless body to him. When he released him, Tony would be fine. He knew it. The little bugger was indestructible.

He was pulled to his feet, led away from the horror. His friend was talking to him, consoling him. Consoling himself.

Johansson's words trailed behind him, the fading tail of a dark comet.

He awoke to the present, but his mind was not yet ready. He sought and found comfort in the drug-induced stupor. Peter Maroc slept.

CHAPTER 23

The brothers had a plan. They would take the ferry from Fishguard, arriving at Rosslare harbour on the southeast coast of Ireland. From there, they would drive to a nearby private airstrip. An old but serviceable Cessna T-210L would then fly them most of the way to their destination.

All was arranged. The transport had been paid for in kind. A favour for services rendered.

They would take off under cover of darkness, their destination southern Italy. From there, an Italian fishing boat would ferry them into Albania.

The drug had done its work, and Maroc lay still and compliant, not having moved from where they had left him. Their Diprivan contact had provided a collapsible wheelchair that the brothers had quickly erected. Between them, they managed to squeeze an unprotesting Maroc into it.

Edon secured him to the wheelchair with a belt around his chest. The belt was then threaded around the back of the seat. The arrangement would ensure he would not slide forward. His arms were similarly secured to the chair, making his position more stable. A blanket concealed this arrangement. The Diprivan would hopefully do the rest.

The boat journey went without incident. No one

took much notice of the man in a wheelchair. The exception came when two old dears began fussing over their patient. The brothers had offered a limited explanation.

'Very ill.'

Further enquiries turned them into dumb foreigners, shrugging and gesturing their lack of comprehension.

Once off the boat, Edon produced three Albanian passports. Maroc travelled under the name of Besmir Cela. Roughly translated, it meant good faith. The irony had not been intentional.

Passport control proved straightforward. There was an enquiry concerning the invalid's fitness to travel. The brothers had given their assurance they would be with their ward the whole time. They were over the first serious hurdle.

Once safely back in the van, Maroc was unstrapped from the wheelchair and laid on the vehicle floor. A further shot of Diprivan would ensure an easier journey for all.

The ride from the ferry took under half an hour. The lush scenery of rural Southern Ireland passed by unappreciated. Edon finally stopped the vehicle outside the small brick building at the edge of the strip. The brothers leapt out, eager to get their prisoner onto the plane.

The pilot ran a one-man operation. Well, mostly. He could always call on the services of a couple of local mechanics when the workload demanded it.

These men had never required explanations for work done. Both had witnessed the consequences of overt curiosity.

The money was good. It was none of their business.

A man of few words Connor (Con) Byrne had serviced the IRA during the troubles. Work was scarce, and he had taken what was available.

Never a curious man, Byrne needed nothing more than basic information from a client. It had always suited both parties.

Byrne emerged from the building carrying a small holdall. He was a short man with thinning grey hair. His ordinariness belied his many talents. It was also an asset.

The six-seater Cessna was warming up on the tarmac. The Irishman greeted them with a nod and a grunt, he led them to the waiting aircraft.

The Albanians respected the man's professionalism, and also his verbal brevity. Reliability was rare in their line of work. This quality alone made Byrne a valuable asset.

'Dead or alive?'

Burne's delivery was deadpan.

'Alive, of course. What you thinking?'

Burim did not possess his older brother's social savvy. His inability to read people and situations had, in the past, landed him in trouble.

'All the same to me. Just can't stand the smell of carrion.'

Not fully comprehending, Burim was happy to nod and smile. His brother said nothing, his focus mainly on getting Maroc into the plane as quickly as possible.

The airstrip was in a remote location. Still, there was always the chance of curious eyes making things awkward.

The three made light work of lifting their human

cargo into the aircraft, where he was securely strapped into one of the passenger seats. After some final checks, Byrne executed a surprisingly smooth take-off.

The brothers exchanged glances, relieved at having reached this far into their journey without incident. The next challenge would be flying over the UK and continental Europe into Italy. Once over Italy, they would travel south, landing at Brindisi. From there, a friendly fishing boat would carry them over the Adriatic sea into the port of Vlore in Albania.

The opiate worked well, with Maroc remaining in a fugue state for most of the trip. Byrne seemed unconcerned, giving the impression the whole thing was normal. Nothing to worry about.

The Irishman hummed tunelessly. Edon and Berisha failed to catch his buoyant mood. Already on edge, the constant humming made them agitated.

They crossed the Irish Sea, and their flight path took them over the English Channel. Byrne responded calmly to enquiries from UK traffic control. By this time, the Albanians were nodding off, soothed by the steady hum of the engines.

On Entering French air space, the brothers woke to the sound of conversation and radio static. The Irishman surprised them by responding in French. They had no idea how fluent he was, but evidently, fluent enough.

As they listened, it became apparent from the tone of the conversation that the flight had been expected. No red flags were being raised.

To Byrne's relief, the brothers resumed their slumber. Agitated passengers pissed him off, though he would never let it be known.

Three and a half hours later found them flying over Italy. This time the language of communication was English. Everything went smoothly with the traffic controller clearly on good terms with the Irishman.

Continuing their flight southeast towards the heel of Italy, the brothers, now fully awake, had begun to relax. It would seem their trust in Byrne had been well placed. The man may be taciturn, but he knew his job.

Having never flown in a small aircraft, the brothers anticipated the landing with trepidation. Byrne sensed their increased agitation. He did not take it as a slur on his competence.

He would be glad to see the back of this sorry pair. His third passenger had been as good as gold. He almost felt sorry for the poor bastard.

The touchdown at Salento airport was textbook. The Albanians became visibly happier, even remarking on the glorious weather. Byrne returned their cheery comments. It was easier that way.

As the Irishman taxied his plane off the runway, the brothers turned their attention to the hostage. They need not have worried. Maroc, sitting unmoving, his eyes closed, would not be a problem.

Salento airport at Brindisi was bathed in sunlight. Connor Byrne emerged from the plane, leaving the two Albanians with their cargo.

He drank in the sweet, warm air, relieved to be away from their limited conversation. He loved Italy, especially the south, and was familiar with the small airport.

Two officials emerged from the building, greeting him like an old friend. To Byrne, Italian people were much like the Irish. Warm and friendly, as long as you didn't cross them. They even worshipped the same god.

They entered the airport building, and Byrne noticed the Italian carabinieri armed with their Beretta 12S subs. They looked tough, self-assured. Coppers! Same wherever you go, Byrne thought. Cocky bastards!

The paperwork completed and the formalities over, the small procession emerged from the airport. Once outside, Byrne approached a waiting taxi, motioning the Albanians to wait. After a conversation involving many hand gestures from both sides, he waved to the brothers.

To the relief of all, the taxi could accommodate a wheelchair. The driver was helpful and, emerging from his cab, opened a sliding side door. A small ramp was dropped, and Maroc was pushed into place inside the spacious cab.

The taxi driver did most of the talking. Byrne, grunting and nodding, gave the impression he understood.

They arrived at the harbour in minutes. Byrne paid the driver, and the process with Maroc was repeated in reverse.

Facilities in the port itself were limited. Byrne, however, seemed to know his way around. Soon, they were sitting outside a pretty little cafe, with Maroc parked close to their small table.

Edon stood and walked over to the wheelchair. Lifting one of Maroc's eyelids, he grunted his satisfaction. The man was still heavily sedated. He would not be a problem.

The conversation was stilted but civil. Edon

enquired if this was a trip Byrne made often.

'I come here now and then. Holidays and the like.'

The Irishman, irritatingly non-committal, gave them no clue about his regular activities. They asked about the boat and its captain. Again, the response was both brief and sketchy.

Further attempts at extracting information were met by the same infuriating diffidence. They gave up, finally accepting their need-to-know status.

After a light meal, washed down by a couple of bottles of the local beer, the group made their way to the boat. Guido, the captain, could have come from central casting. Sporting a well-distressed cap, he would not have seemed out of place on a film set.

A short, stocky figure, he greeted the Albanians with the airy wave of a man comfortable in his habitat. Turning, he led the way up the gangplank, calling out.

'Come on board, gentlemen.'

Tourists would have found his accent charming.

His age could have been anywhere from forty to sixty. His movements, whether through infirmity or inclination, were slow and deliberate. He walked with the fluid rolling motion of a seasoned sailor. The brothers exchanged smiles.

The next part of the journey would be a little more pleasant. A little more convivial. Both shook Byrne by the hand and formally thank him. There was no denying the man's professionalism. Perhaps a future asset?

Connor Byrne concluded his business and left by the gangplank. He waved to the captain, then, as an afterthought, nodded to the two Albanians.

CHAPTER 24

Guido was pleasant enough, and at first, they had enjoyed his genial chatter. He was the complete opposite of Byrne. However, his garrulous nature quickly became irksome.

Not used to such social demands, they had sought their own company. They had found refuge at the prow of the vessel. Here, the brothers could relax and not have to laugh at the captain's endless amusing tales.

Travelling by boat was still a new adventure. Neither seemed prone to seasickness and, left to their own devices, they were finding the experience enjoyable.

Maroc had been locked in one of the smaller cabins below. Soon after the boat had set off from Brindisi, a further shot of Diprivan had been administered.

The suppliers of the powerful narcotic had warned the brothers to use it sparingly. He had carefully explained how its excessive use could adversely affect memory functions.

Peter Maroc's world had become one of shadows and echoes, where emotions seemed curiously absent. The warrior was away. What remained behind carried no memory of the previous dweller.

It was inevitable. Guido walked his sailor's walk towards them, a steaming cup of black coffee in each hand. Their luck had run out.

'I hope you have not been too bored on your own.'

His concern seemed genuine, prompting a twinge of guilt.

Edon came up with the best he could think of.

'We did not want to be in your way. You're a busy man, captain.'

Guido smiled hugely, waving his hand in modest agreement.

'I can always find time for special guests.'

Over coffee, fortified by a little brandy, the three spent an hour discussing the comparative merits of their homelands.

Guido's narrative skill was seductive, his description of places and people both poetic and vivid. In comparison, their lesser talent rendered Albania a rather pedestrian destination.

The journey took over seven hours. On sighting land, the brothers were reminded of the seriousness of their assignment. Rather reluctantly, they made their way below deck.

Their hostage had not moved, the rhythm of his breathing signifying a man in a deep sleep. Burim suggested another shot of Diprivan. His older brother, recalling the caution of their Manchester suppliers, shook his head.

'He's fine. I'll give it to him in, maybe the next three, four hours.'

This decision was to prove a grave error.

Maroc's returning awareness, though lacking identity, did possess one deadly quality. Purpose.

He could not respond to a name, yet he sensed within himself a potent discipline. One that, in the past, had served him well.

The wheelchair was lifted and manoeuvred onto the deck. The occupant gave no protest, no resistance. Unnoticed, an almost imperceptible flush of pink had crept into the deathlike pallor. The Albanians had grown careless.

Guido seemed sorry to see them go. They had prefered his company to the Irishman. However, the brothers were relieved to be left to their own devices.

They were on home ground. Edon and Burim could already taste the rewards of a job well done.

They turned one last time to the colourful Guido. Both parties waved and smiled, with the captain swaying back up the gangplank.

The brothers made their way to the designated pickup point. Their transport was already waiting for them. Edon looked glumly at the transit-size van, similar to the one they had used to travel from North Wales to Ireland.

As they approached the vehicle, they noticed someone in the driving seat. The van had come with a chauffeur.

Edon gripped the wheelchair and shot his brother an expectant look. Between them, they manoeuvred both the chair and its occupant through the open back doors.

The driver was a gangly youth and a member of the Fare. Edon vaguely recognised him.

The youth immediately adopted a familiarity the older brother found annoying. His constant chattering irritated, only ceasing when he noticed their lack of interest.

The brothers had always enjoyed authority and

respect within the organisation. This fool presented himself as an equal.

The brothers exchanged a meaningful look. The mild insult would be addressed and sorted after Maroc's safe delivery.

Maroc could feel a steady return of his powers. His obdurate mind still veiled his identity and past, but he would fight that battle another day.

For now, nothing would divert energy from his purpose. To escape from his captors.

Peter Maroc was held by the one supporting belt, causing his upper body to slump forward. To an observer, the SAS trooper presented no immediate threat.

Edon gave him one final look. He closed the van door, satisfied with what he saw.

The Fare had organised a flight from a small airstrip just outside Vlore. They would travel south-east to Lazarat. However, this arrangement had been compromised and subsequently discarded.

The revised plan was to continue east in the van on the SH100 before joining the E853 southward to Lazarat. To Edon's relief, the driver would leave them in Vlore where he would conduct further business for the Fare.

A further ten minutes of driving saw them parting with their annoying companion. Edon parked the van in front of a small Bistro. They would enjoy a light meal and a beer before continuing their three-hour journey to Lazarat.

Maroc gathered his strength. He realised his window of opportunity was shrinking fast. It was time to act.

Fully aware of the need to employ all his powers, he focused his breathing, driving energy to every part of his body.

His Chinese instructors had taught him well. Maroc had no memory of where this knowledge had come from, but his body had internalised the training. He waited.

The brothers had finished their meal and sat at one of the small tables outside. They had allowed themselves the indulgence of one beer apiece. Arriving at Fare headquarters in a state of even mild intoxication would be pushing their luck.

Edon and Burim shared their vision of a successful career within the Fare. They had messed up in the past. The mistake would not be repeated.

Both had observed and envied the indulgences of more senior Fare members. A few more kudos under their belt, and such a lifestyle could be theirs.

Unlocking the back of the van, they found what they had expected. Maroc remained slumped forward in the wheelchair. Edon observed him with contempt. *No longer so tough Mr SAS*, he thought.

To the brothers, he appeared as helpless as a baby. Happy with this reversal of power, they had relocked the doors and set off on their journey.

The outskirts of Vlore were quite beautiful. To their left and right, fields of olive trees extended into the distance. Edon inhaled deeply, taking in the familiar aroma of his native land. His brother's voice interrupted this simple pleasure.

Burim wanted to relieve himself. Again.

His older brother, rolling his eyes, pulled the van over. At times, his brother could be a big child.

It had been hours since Maroc had received his medication. Edon was taking no chances, not when they were this close to delivering the dangerous bastard.

Walking back to the van, he fumbled for the right key. He unlocked the back door and opened it.

Edon saw the wheelchair standing against the left wall of the van. It was empty. The leather belt lay on the floor in front of it.

From the darkness of the interior, Maroc emerged like a raging bull. Leaping from the van, he head-butted the large Albanian in the stomach.

Edon, driven backwards and badly winded, tried to regain his balance. He was struggling to breathe as he attempted to rise to his feet.

That was when Maroc delivered a short, vicious punch to the point of his jaw, snapping his head back. The big Albanian fell backwards, landing hard.

Following him down, Maroc struck another solid blow to his forehead. Edon was vaguely aware of a strong pair of hands tightening around his throat.

The world around him began withdrawing. His mind struggled to understand what was happening.

A voice was calling him from far away. Over and over. He was comfortable where he was. He wished the voice would stop.

Was it Burim? What did his idiot younger brother want now? The voice seemed distant, muffled. He tried to make out the words.

'Edon. Wake up. We've got to get this bastard back into the van.'

He stared blankly at the shadowy figure above him, thinking it was still Peter Maroc. The voice emerged at full volume, blasting his ears. Why was his brother shouting?

Things came back slowly. A jumble of images and sounds. Where was the British pig? He would kill him.

Burim half lifted, half dragged his brother to his feet. Still cursing, Edon looked wildly around. Maroc lay on his back a foot away to his right.

On his return to the van, Burim had heard the commotion. He was still in the field zipping up his pants when he saw the attack on his brother.

The younger man had looked around for a weapon. A stone, twice the size of his fist, had presented itself. It lay just by the gate. Picking it up, he had vaulted over the gate and moved towards the waring men.

Burim Berisha had no intention of fighting fair, or in fact, fighting at all. He had aimed at Maroc's head, bringing the stone down hard. The damage to their asset had become a secondary consideration.

One blow was enough. The Brit had collapsed on top of his brother and was still. Burim, using his boot, had rolled Maroc's lifeless body off an agitated Edon.

On his feet, Edon swayed and, reaching out, used his brother's shoulder to steady himself. He stood with his eyes closed. Burim spoke.

'You OK big brother?'

The words triggered something dark in the big Albanian. Edon went crazy. Pushing his brother out of his way, he staggered towards Maroc. The Brit had not moved. His face was tinged an unhealthy yellow, and Burim prayed he was not dead.

Usually the sensible one, Edon was now beyond reach. He began kicking and punching at Maroc's defenceless body. His actions were clumsy, uncoordinated and failed to inflict the intended injuries.

Burim pulled at him in panic, and Edon staggered backwards, flinging away the restraining arm. Cursing, he lumbered forward, his rage still burning bright. Maroc's head, now matted with blood, had become a thing of hatred. He, Edon Berisha, would kill that head.

The bloodied stone Burim had used to strike Maroc now lay next to the SAS man's unmoving body. The younger brother scooped it up, and seeing no other way to prevent what he knew would be a costly murder, he struck. As though a switch had been thrown, Edon froze.

A man in a dream, he touched his bleeding cheek, unable to comprehend or believe. Blankly, he looked up.

'You were killing him, brother. We need him alive.'

Voices from the field snapped them back to reality. Three men were approaching, one carrying a shotgun. The taller of the three called out.

It was more of a howl than discernible words. The meaning, however, was unmistakable.

'Get him back in the van. Now!'

Burim, for the first time, found himself in charge. Things were happening too fast. Edon took his brother's lead, still groggy from the double assault.

The three farmworkers had seen enough. This was no ordinary fight between angry men. Seeing the brothers lifting Maroc's lifeless body into the van, the shotgun carrier discharged his weapon into the air.

The effect on the brothers was instantaneous as an inherent need to survive took charge of their actions.

Dropping Maroc's lifeless body, they scrambled around to the front of the van.

The cries became louder, nearer. A predictable fumble with the ignition key, and the engine roared like an angry beast. A head appeared at the driver's window. A shotgun barrel was pointed at Edon's face.

The Mafia man knew it took a lot to kill in cold blood. He ignored the weapon.

To stay and fight three men, with one of them armed, had not been an option. The brothers knew fighting was always a gamble. Today, they did not like the odds.

The old diesel engine howled its indignation as they made their escape down the road. There was silence between the two until Edon spoke.

'We're dead brother. You know that.'

CHAPTER 25

A slow climb towards a distant light. Maroc's mind recoiled against the pain. It beat him back, and he retreated into the comforting darkness. He tried and failed to define its boundaries. Its intensity, however, was not in doubt.

The hunters who had intervened on his behalf had carried his bloodied body into the field. After much arguing and deliberation, they had decided on a course of action. The stranger was trouble. They would leave him for others to find.

The dull amber of his consciousness became a momentary flame. His vision cleared, and Maroc willed himself to focus.

He took in the ancient hay wagon that would not have been out of place in a Constable painting. The effort drained him. He felt himself falling away.

Maroc fought the growing weakness; his world became shadowy, less real. The last thing to reach his failing senses was the distant sound of voices.

Time and space were uncertain notions as he resurfaced from a place where both were ill-defined. Maroc, struggling to focus, read one thing from the steady jolting to his body. He was moving.

To an observer, Peter Maroc was still out of the game. It was a game he knew well, though he could not explain how. Somewhere in his past, he had learnt the art of playing dead. His instincts told him, this time, there would be no tactical advantage.

His body hurt with immobilising intensity. Maroc bit down hard on his hand, drawing blood as he traded the pain with a pain he could accept.

His captors were talking. He recognised the cadence. A Slavic tongue. He felt threatened; afraid, but failed to find a reason for his fear.

Gather as much Intel as possible, and store it. Wait for an opportunity.

When captured, however bad things look, never think you're going to die. Always plan your next move. How do I get out of this? What's my escape route? Think, think, think. Do not roll over and die.

Where the hell did that come from?

His mind began to drift.

Find the stillness inside, a refuge from all suffering. Focus on it. Be it. A softer voice.

Maroc recognised neither but sensed the wisdom of the latter. He had found his escape, his path away from pain.

Again, he slept.

He woke to the sound of early birdsong. He was in some kind of dwelling.

A tiny window admitted a pale light. He struggled to identify his surroundings.

His bedding was firm, basic. A rough blanket that may have covered him lay on the floor to his right.

Maroc braced himself against the wave of agony. This time its impact did not overwhelm. It was something he could manage.

Voices approached. Russian? No, not quite, but

Slavic, yes. He would wait.

A door, not evident in the gloom, opened slowly. He strained to better see the hesitant figure framed in the morning half-light.

Maroc's right hand followed a habit of its own. It groped under the makeshift pillow for a weapon. There was nothing.

A woman of indeterminate age stepped inside. Her movements were cautious, hesitant.

He pushed his body to a sitting position, instantly regretting the sudden movement. He winced, a sob escaping through clenched teeth.

The woman came towards him, her words reaching ahead of her. Soft, kind, they were meant to calm. Not what he'd expected. He looked beyond her and saw the man.

He hung back, waiting inside the doorway, affording him time to settle, to trust. The man entered, approaching Maroc in the same cautious manner.

The ex-soldier tried to make him out. A bearded face emerged from the early gloom. He was a foot taller than the woman.

In his late thirties, he looked solid; dependable. There was no threat in his demeanour. Maroc fell back on the bed and waited.

'Amerikan?' The woman looked at him then knelt. He noticed she held a small basket, partially covered by a cloth. Removing the cloth, she revealed light round bread. She then produced a small thermos flask.

'Amerikan?'

This time, it was the man who spoke. Maroc's mind raced to find an answer.

'Not American.'

Both looked blank.

'American, no.'

This time he shook his head in the negative.

'Ah, Anglisht.'

The woman again. He smiled weakly and nodded. And wished he hadn't. His head exploded, forcing him to close his eyes.

When he opened them, the woman was smiling. She reached for the flask, handing it to the man. Again she dipped into the basket, producing a small white bowl.

The man unscrewed the flask as if not used to such a task. He poured some of its contents into the bowl.

'Hani Kete.'

The man's voice was lighter than he had expected.

'Ha! Ha!'

He pointed to his mouth.

A spoon was produced and dipped into what he imagined was broth or soup. Maroc hesitated, and she continued.

'Jani me fasule'

She dipped the spoon into the bowl, holding it to his face.

'Supe me bathe?'

A question? Or a description of the soup. Maroc guessed it was both.

He nodded and opened his mouth. His primordial brain told him he needed food. It was a directive that outranked his pain.

As the smell of hot soup assailed his nostrils, Peter Maroc realised he was famished.

She carefully paced his eating, the man nodding his approval at every mouthful. He was a baby again. Or a bloody invalid.

Realisation came. These two were not his captors. For the moment, he was safe in this small room in... god knows where. Eastern Europe somewhere? Jesus, he could be on a movie set filming a bizarre version of The Nativity. He smiled, and his new hosts smiled back their encouragement.

The man reached out, patting his shoulder gently. He pointed to himself. 'Une jam Bekim. Bekim Ahmeti.'

He kept nodding encouragingly. Maroc realised it was his turn to answer.

His mind was blank, and he pointed to himself, shaking his head. They were puzzled. He tapped at his temple, then gingerly, he shrugged with shoulders and hands.

A moment of baffled silence. The woman was the first to comprehend. She spoke to her companion. He shook his head, his expression sad.

'Ah. 'Asnje kujtim.' He nodded his understanding and sympathy.

Maroc had refuted his amnesia. Having declared it openly, he felt trapped by its undeniability.

The nothingness frightened him, and he felt the pressure of what lay beyond it. That secret truth would push and push until it ruptured his reality. Until he was crushed by its recognition.

He fought to remember. Anything, any small bloody detail.

They felt his agitation, his fear, and they understood. Fear recognised no geographic boundaries. It did not discriminate between rich and poor.

The woman spoke softly as he ate, her gentle voice

stemming his panic, soothing his fears. Somehow, Maroc managed to finish his meal.

The flask was empty and Bekim, smiling broadly, tipped it over to reveal this triumph. The woman went to a cupboard, producing another pillow.

He was gently lifted forward, the pillow carefully positioned. They lowered him down with equal care.

'Fle tani.'

Again the nodding encouragement.

'Gjume.'

Seeing no response from their guest, she repeated.

'Gjume?'

With hands together, supporting her head, her eyes closed and her meaning became clear. Maroc nodded.

'Gjume'.

Sleep arrived quickly. It did not come alone.

Separated from his patrol, the sense of exposure and vulnerability chilled him like cold mountain mist. He had no memory of losing his Heckler and Koch G36. The weapon had somehow vanished in his frantic flight from an unknown foe.

He forced himself to think, to remember. They were looking for him, and they would find him. He tried not to dwell on his fate when it came. It would not be good. It would not be good.

Scanning his new surroundings, he tried and failed to find a familiar landmark. This place was alien, somewhere and something he was not a part of.

He acknowledged his inherent sense of isolation. The feeling of abandonment that had become the subtext of his life.

One thing was undeniable. He was the enemy, the outsider. The one to be eliminated. No warm reunion, no returning to the fold. Not this time.

He had always known it would happen. Just like this. An inglorious ending to a wasted life.

'Peter.' He turned and saw her standing on the far side of a raging river. How had he failed to notice the torrent now separating them? She waved and smiled as she had always done, then stepped into the angry surge.

The strong current took her, sweeping her downstream. Away from him. He tried to see her, could not see her…

He was being shaken, pulled away. Pushing against strong hands he shouted his protest, knowing he could not leave her in that place.

'Sir, sir, please become awaking.'

A face not recognised looked fearfully at him.

'Dream, bad dream Sir.

Maroc was back in the small room. He tried to form the words. To make them understand, but could not. They were not listening to him.

They let him settle, affording him space to calm his agitation. Slowly, he began to understand, and with the understanding came relief. It poured through him like the torrent he had left behind.

Maroc fought the tears. He was too weak to stop them.

The small group stood watching in silence. They allowed him to settle, to bleed out whatever anguish tormented him.

'Sir, my name is Ardit. I speak good English. We talk now?'

Maroc looked up at the man, his face tear-stained, distraught.

'I don't… I can't remember.'

'Yes, yes, I know, I understand. Your head…'

His hand waved vaguely around his own head.

He felt an overwhelming urge to laugh, to yell out. He checked the impulse. He was certain that once he started, he would never stop.

Ardit turned his attention to the two people standing in respectful silence behind him.

'You know this people.'

It was a statement.

Maroc nodded. He felt a wave of nausea and waited for it to pass. I know them. They have been... kind.'

'Yes, kind people. Friends. Me also.

He smiled then. A brown-toothed smile that was both open and friendly.

'Where am I?'

He smiled his apology, abashed at the banality of his question. Ye gods, he was in a B movie.

'You are in the farm of Mr Berisha and Mrs Berisha.'

'Where is that'

He knew he could never show rudeness to these people. He had to be patient. His questions would be answered. Eventually.

'Near Vuno.' Little town, no... small village.

'What country is this?'

Maroc could see the question surprised him. Ardit hesitated before continuing.

The answer, when it came, was courteously given. There was also a hint of pride.

'Albania. You are in the country of Albania.'

Maroc tried not to react. After all, he knew it wasn't Wiltshire, he could understand their bloody English.

He smiled at his bad humour. Again, they generously smiled back.

CHAPTER 26

The interpreter was still there when he awakened. He had no idea how much time had passed. Although in a deal of pain, Maroc could now stand unaided.

Determined to test his legs, he tentatively walked to the front door. Opening it, he stepped outside.

Having been confined to the family's cramped front parlour, it felt good to be standing with the sun on his face. Taking a deep breath, he savoured the warm summer fragrances.

Ardit Berisha joined him. A mild man, he viewed his guest with some trepidation. Maroc was from another world. Something told him it was one of intrigue and death.

He looked up at the troubled stranger, guessing he was not an evil man. He had met evil men. Men who would take your life without a second thought. Ardit also knew he would be glad to see him away from his village. Out of their very ordinary lives.

'My friend, can you now remember anything about who you are?'

Maroc turned to the diminutive Albanian, his expression providing the answer. He shook his head silently.

Ardit's face brightened.

'I have an idea Mr, Sir.'

Maroc held up his hand.

'Call me James. For now.'

The man's face broke into a huge smile.

'Like James Bond. In the movies?'

Maroc smiled back.

'Yes, like James Bond. In the movies.'

'I have idea for you, James. When you are stronger, when you are more ready, I will contact the British Embassy. Perhaps they will know who you are, what your name is. Yes?'

'Sounds like a plan.'

Ardit looked blank. '

Yes. It's a good idea. Thank you, Ardit.'

The interpreter looked pleased. He needed to impress their good intentions on this man. They were working in his interest. They were his friends.

In truth, it was part friendship, part appeasement. He feared that this man could bring disruption to the quiet life of his community.

The days passed pleasantly, with Maroc being well cared for by the Ahmetis. These were kind people, good people, he thought. He felt guilty for bringing nothing to the table. Guilty that they shared their meagre provisions, and gave of their time. A time that could be better spent tending to their affairs and needs.

When Maroc tried helping with the household chores, he was shooed away by Mrs Ahmetis. She treated all who ventured into her domain with the same gentle resistance.

As he grew stronger, he offered his services to her husband. He, in turn, had given him easy tasks. Maroc would fetch tools when needed but was not allowed to use them, being told he should not overtax his recovering body. When he insisted, he was sent to collect eggs from the three hen houses.

The gentle life relaxed his mind, leading it away from discursive thinking. He smiled, doubting he would ever become a man of the soil.

It was early, around eight o clock, when the two men came to visit. Maroc was outside doing some light work, enjoying the pleasures of physical labour.

Accompanying the men was the interpreter, Ardit. He looked apprehensive. Maroc felt a tightness in his gut. A willingness to fight whatever threat they presented. The reaction disturbed him, causing him to once again question his former identity.

As they drew nearer, he could see these were not men from the village. Both wore dark, well-tailored suits. The way they carried themselves made him nervous. They screamed government. He wondered which government. And which department of that government.

They were fifty yards away. At a guess, Maroc would have said Western Europeans. Remembering the last conversation with the interpreter, they could be either Brits or Americans.

This could be good or bad. Although obliged to wait and find out, Maroc was not required to like it.

On their approach, Maroc noticed that both were athletically built. CIA, MI6? He thought not. They lacked the menace that set such men apart. But how would he know that? Another question to add to his growing list.

He was getting ahead of himself. Maroc decided he would reserve judgement. He waited as they entered the front yard.

It was the interpreter who spoke first. He was nervous and in obvious awe of the men.

'Sir. James. These gentlemen are British officials and would be pleased to speak with you.'

Close up, Maroc could see they were more Harrow than Harvard. Their haircuts did not look American and neither, on closer contact, did they smell like Americans.

The first man extended his hand, and Maroc shook it. The handshake was firm but lacked the machismo grip of the action hero.

Probably admin, he thought.

So nice to meet you. I'm Mainwaring'

Public school?

The smile, however, seemed genuine if a little practised. Maroc began.

'Gentlemen, how can I help?'

An inappropriate response considering they were more likely here to help him. He tried again.

'British embassy?'

'Consulate, actually.'

Definitely public school?

'Right. Shall we go in and talk?'

The interpreter smiled nervously as he welcomed the newcomers into the small living room come kitchen.

'Mr and Mrs Ahmetis are not here at the moment, but I am sure it would be fine for us to talk inside. Would you like something to drink? Tea perhaps?'

Inside, the second man introduced himself as Armstrong. Once more, hands were shaken.

They sat around the small dining table, the interpreter busying himself with brewing the tea.

All was amicable and civilised. Very British. Maroc suppressed a smile.

'As a British subject, which remains to be verified.'

Here Mainwaring gave an apologetic shrug.

'I believe you could do with some assistance?'

He continued hesitantly.

'I also believe you have a spot of memory trouble?'

Maroc smiled inwardly.

Masters of the understatement. You had to love the English.

'I have no idea who I am or much else about my identity. Yes, gentlemen, you could say I have a memory problem.'

Justin Mainwaring seemed to be in charge. Glancing at his colleague, who had in the meantime produced a small notebook and was busy scribbling, he continued.

'We're here to help in any way we can. But obviously, we will have to go through our data. Try to ascertain your identity, you understand.'

It was a statement, not a question.

'Of course. And I shall cooperate as much as I'm able. Trouble is, there's very little I can give you.'

'There's not a lot we require you to do. You certainly sound British, and, I'm guessing you might be forces. You look like an army man.'

He smiled, then gave a short laugh.

'And you seem to have been in the wars.'

Maroc shrugged his agreement.

'What will you do, take a photo? Perhaps shoot it over so they can ID it from military records? Facial recognition sort of stuff?'

Mainwaring looked up sharply.

'You seem to have some knowledge of procedures.

But of course, you would have no memory as to why that is.'

Maroc caught the mild scepticism.

His reply showed his irritation.

'I don't. I've no recollection of anything further back other than when these good people found me.'

He hesitated, needing to be accurate.

'There's a vague memory of a scuffle. A fight with someone.'

Mainwaring gave him a searching look. He nodded and smile in tacit apology.

'Actually, it should be straightforward. A simple photo should do the trick. Well, several photos from different angles, for a more complete picture, so to speak. As for the rest, height, weight and so on, we can fill in the blanks as we go along.'

He treated Maroc to one of his broad grins.

'Don't look so worried. Someone is bound to know who you are. You have quite a distinctive face.'

CHAPTER 27

Finally satisfied they could glean nothing further from Maroc, the officials rose and made to leave.

'I wouldn't worry too much, sir.'

Mainwaring nodded to Armstrong, who was delving into a shoulder bag. The man produced a small, expensive-looking digital camera.

'We'll send over a few mugshots. Scotland Yard will have you on file if you've been listed as missing'.

Mainwaring was handed the camera. After taking several shots from different angles, he seemed satisfied they had everything.

'If you are or have been in the forces, you'll be in one of their files.'

Seeing the doubt in Maroc's face, he smiled encouragingly.

'Don't worry, old chap, someone somewhere will be missing you.'

Their departure left him with a feeling of relief mixed with apprehension. He was to find the truth about himself. Was that what he wanted, or would he prefer his safe world of not knowing?

Maroc finished a few light duties around the farm and decided to retire indoors. More tired than he had expected to be, he had dozed off. Maroc woke at the sound of voices outside and decided to investigate.

He rose from what had been designated by the Ahmetis as his chair. A bout of unexpected dizziness caused him to abruptly sit down. He felt hot, sweaty.

Only last night, Maroc had congratulated himself on his recovery. In some pain and by no means back to his full powers, he had felt he was making good progress.

He owed the Ahmetis some decent work and was painfully conscious his contributions to date were paltry.

Memories from a previous existence may have been erased or at least blocked. His preferences and predilections, however, remained hardwired. Peter Maroc was not indolent, that much he knew; it did not agree with him. His core persona seemingly loved the freedom of self-determination, of being his own man.

Ariana had searched for her new ward in all the more obvious places. Slightly puzzled, she had quizzed her husband, Bekim.

He had looked up at her from his work and shrugged. In response, she had shaken her head.

Men!

It was time to eat. Returning to the house, she was surprised at finding Maroc asleep in his chair. It was not like him. Ariana approached the foreigner cautiously.

She noticed his breathing. Heavy; ragged. This was not right. She placed a hand on his forehead, and her face registered alarm. The man was burning up.

Over the next twelve hours, Maroc's condition worsened. He would wake up, mumbling words in his native tongue, before lapsing into either sleep or unconsciousness.

Ariana, clucking like the proverbial mother hen, ordered the men to stop gawping. To rally around and bloody well help.

Bekim, aided by one of his sons, helped turn Maroc's chair into a makeshift bed. There were no extra beds in this small household. They did their best, making sure he was warm and comfortable. Bekim wished his wife would not fuss so.

Women!

Maroc's fever seemed to be worsening, despite the regular application of cold towels to his forehead. Ariana watched over him, monitoring his every movement, listening with growing alarm to his erratic breathing.

It would cost money to bring in a doctor, money they could ill afford. As had always existed in poorer communities, there were alternative healers. Ariana Ahmetis, nodding to herself, decided on her next port of call.

How Lule obtained her medicines was a mystery. A mystery no one was interested in solving. She was a raw-boned woman in her late fifties and carried her permanent scowl like a badge of office.

Responding to no other, her name meant 'flower.' None had dared question her on its origins.

Lule's skills as a midwife were never in doubt. Neither was her ability to bring about some spectacular recoveries in her patients. Not all put up with her abrasive ways, but her reputation had been hard-earned, backed by good results.

Lule had more than earned the respect of the community. Able to read and write, she brought more to the table than the old cures and manipulations taught her by her mother.

The authorities had never questioned her source of pharmaceuticals. The health services in the area were already overburdened. Lule was allowed to operate unimpeded, protected by the laws of expedience and necessity.

On hearing from Ariana that Maroc was a westerner, possibly British, Lule decided to adjust her fees northwards. Ariana would have none of it. She had informed the healer it was the Ahmeti family footing the bill.

Lule had looked down and, spreading her hands in a gesture of surrender, had nodded her agreement. She would come to the house within the hour.

Lule arrived as promised and went straight to Maroc. She had registered that he was barely conscious, his breathing uneven and noisy.

After examining his eyes, she had requested to see his tongue. It had been tricky, but with Ariana's help, she somehow managed it. Finally, she had taken the tall westerner's pulse.

Maroc, in obvious distress, drifted in and out of consciousness. He had been calmed by the soothing voice of either Lule or Ariana.

Any qualified physician worth his or her salt would have recognised the early stages of pneumonia. Lule's hands-on experience was extensive. It had made her as astute as any doctor when it came to a prognosis.

Dipping into a distressed Gladstone bag, she produced a stethoscope. Lule put the stethoscope to her ears and opened Maroc's shirt. There was much listening, followed by judicious tapping. Maroc was vaguely aware of someone helping him and remained mostly amenable to her ministering.

Finally, having completed her diagnosis, she stood up. The stethoscope was put away.

After a quick rummage in the Gladstone, Lule produced a small paper bag which she handed to Ariana Ahmeti. The dark green leaves contained within were to be boiled in a measure of water, the resulting tincture to be given to the patient.

The healer was about to leave when Ariana halted her with a questioning look. Her instincts told her Maroc's condition was serious. She needed more reassurance from this woman.

'They will make him more comfortable, help him sleep.'

'Will he get better with...' Ariana gestured at the herbs.

Lule, pausing at the door, beckoned Ariana to join her.

'He will need antibiotics. They cost more...'

Dismayed, Ariana bowed her head. The healer continued.

'In your case, I have some left from my last purchase. They are a few weeks out of date, but...'

'Are they any good? Will they work on him?'

'Yes, I'm sure they will be fine. No extra charge for you, Mrs Ahmeti. You and your husband are old clients.'

Patting Lule's hand, Ariana thanked her. The transaction was over; the Ahmetis would be given the usual week to pay. It was now in the hands of the man upstairs.

The following morning Ariana Ahmeti walked to Lule's place and collected the antibiotics. The healer would visit in a few days. Unless, of course, there was a downward turn in her patient's condition.

As Ariana left, Lule wondered why the Ahmeti family would spend time and money on an outsider, a foreigner at that. After all, charity began at home.

A part of her responded to their altruism, their simple goodness. She gave an inward shrug. It was none of her business.

Ariana had made herself a makeshift bed on the living room floor. The arrangement would allow her to respond to changes in Maroc's condition. She had experienced a few nights of broken sleep.

His toilet needs were discreetly attended to by the eldest son, also named Bekim.

Often woken by his shouts, both in English and a second language she thought to be German, Ariana Ahmeti remained unwavering in her duty of care.

Maroc possessed extraordinary resilience. Partly the result of good genes, he had also developed a body trained beyond the capacity of most men.

The combination had worked in his favour, and the following days had seen him responding steadily to the medication.

The breakthrough had come four days after receiving the antibiotics. Maroc was able to sit up and take a little soup. Not having eaten in days, he was ravenous. Ariana's smile had widened when he had requested a little more.

On seeing Maroc's remarkably rapid recovery, the whole family were, in equal measure, both gladdened and relieved. While their patience and kindness were infinite, their financial resources were far from that.

The following morning, Maroc insisted on

standing. Ariana had tutted and fussed, conveying to her patient it was far too soon. After a couple of false starts, he managed to stand. An hour later, Maroc walked a few paces. The son Bekim stood by, ready to catch him if he stumbled.

Peter Maroc made steady gains in strength and mobility. When Ariana found him sitting outside the cottage in the morning sun, she gave a token protest.

Maroc could see how delighted she was. He swore he would pay them back for their unstinting kindness and compassion.

The following day saw the return of the consul officials. It amused the ex-soldier how they always travelled in pairs. He considered it a waste of manpower. Perhaps, in this backwater post, they had little else to do except take short excursions. He wondered if they brought sandwiches.

The one called Mainwaring waved a greeting as they strolled up the slight incline to the cottage. He felt a growing tension and tried to relax. Any signs of nervousness might be misinterpreted.

Mainwaring ran his hand through his thick black hair. He was a handsome man in his early forties. His less garrulous companion, a burly sandy-haired man in his mid-fifties, nodded and smiled.

At least I'm not under arrest.

'May we go inside?'

Maroc led both men inside, waving them to the same table. He suggested tea. Mainwaring requested a glass of water, his companion nodding he would have the same.

'Any luck?'

Maroc felt obliged to ask.

'It's good news.'

Sensing that Maroc was still tense, he continued.

'Really, nothing to be worried about. Your name is Peter Maroc. No middle name.'

He looked up before continuing.

'It would seem you have been in the wars.'

His face remained serious. Maroc waited.

'A captain in Her Majesty's Special Air Service, no less.'

He looked up at Maroc, taking in the full measure of the man.

'You have an impressive service record, Mr Maroc. Afghanistan, Iraq. You've operated extensively within Eastern Europe and seen action in Kosovo, and more recently, Crimea.'

He paused and added significantly.

'As well as this very country of Albania. You then left the regiment and worked a year as a close protection officer for MI5. Recently, you've been self-employed, using your training as a freelancer.'

'You mean a mercenary?'

'Mainly as a training instructor, training bodyguards. Yes, you have been involved in operations where your skills have been paid for.'

Mainwaring looked up and noted the concern on Maroc's face. He added quickly.

'Nothing bad, Mr Maroc. It would seem you've been working for the good guys.'

'You can tell the difference?'

'I'm a patriot, Maroc. Of course, I can tell the difference.'

Mainwaring ameliorated the comment with one of his trademark grins.

'As far as the British government is concerned, you are whiter than white. It's quite obvious you have made enemies. Whoever set about you intended causing you serious harm.'

'That's one thing I've gathered, Mr Mainwaring. Someone wants me removed from the game.'

For a moment, Mainwaring was thoughtful. He continued.

'Normally, we would insist on an immediate and thorough debriefing at the consulate, followed by further questioning in the UK. As things stand, debriefing would yield little to nothing.

He gave Maroc a concerned look.

'Until you've recovered enough of that memory of yours, I doubt if you could give us anything of value.'

Maroc was mildly surprised at being accepted back into the fold so easily. He supposed Mainwaring had a point. Still...

He had a name, Peter Maroc. It part dispelled his feelings of displacement since regaining consciousness at the Ahmeti household.

He was a real person with real, if yet undiscovered, connections. As for the rest? That would take some processing.

As though it had just occurred to him, Maroc looked at Mainwaring.

'How do you propose I get out of this country? I've no means of getting to the nearest town, let alone back to Britain. How am I to pay my way?'

'You're forgetting, Mr Maroc, you are now officially a bona fide British subject. Fully paid up. You have no criminal record, nothing to prevent you from re-entering the UK.'

Before Maroc could speak, Mainwaring held up his hand.

'Furthermore, you are entitled to our assistance in getting there. That includes taking care of your travelling expenses plus a deal more.'

Mainwaring stopped and looked directly at Maroc.

'You're a distinguished soldier, Peter. A bit of a war hero.'

Maroc sat for a moment, absorbing this last piece of information. He had a rather silly grin on his face.

CHAPTER 28

Peter Maroc sat aboard a British Airways plane a half-hour out of Albanian airspace. He was still processing all that had happened over the last week.

The consulate officials had handed him back his life in a slim manila folder. He had read it, and nothing it contained resonated at the conscious level. His life remained an enigma.

Sometimes he felt if he could reach out in the right direction, he might snatch some truths from a parallel reality. He suspected his nightmares and flashbacks might be grotesque parodies of such truths. But how was he to make sense of their cryptic nature?

Mainwaring had been patient. He had questioned him more like a counsellor than a government official.

Maroc had grown to like the man.

There were additions to his nightly lineup of terrors. The familiar demons still visited, but now there were other dreams, different dreams. Not as frightening, they still disturbed.

The face of a woman. At times smiling, then disapproving. Familiar? Maybe. He thought so.

When he had focused harder, tried to assign a name, an identity, she would fade like morning mist. Her leaving always left him empty.

One question still troubled him. Why had all

the information given him not yielded a single recollection? Was it possible to live a lifetime and forget so much?

The consulate had given him an address. He looked at it now. A house name and a small town in North Wales. Again, he wondered what he would find at the end of his journey. Who he would find?

The reasoning part of his mind raged against this wall of nothingness. He refused to accept that such a natural act as remembering was, for him, so bloody impossible.

He was in the SAS so he must have army mates. Could they, even at this minute, be looking for him? Jesus H Christ, someone, somewhere, must be looking for him.

Arrival at Heathrow airport presented the usual tedium of disembarking. It began with the usual game of 'Spot the luggage' on the carousel. Maroc was travelling light.

Mr Ahmeti had packed everything into a medium-sized suitcase. He had insisted.

The farewell had been a sad one, with even the stoic Bekim senior a little damp-eyed. Maroc had promised to return and had meant it.

He, once again, vowed their unstinting kindness would be fully rewarded. Maroc owed them his life.

A passport had been sent from the UK. All documentation had been arranged by the consulate. Mainwaring had been true to his word. A week after their last meeting and he had been good to go.

Inside the consulate, Maroc had been allowed access to a computer. He had used it to find suitable accommodation in the UK.

Peter Maroc was not yet ready for company, polite or otherwise. His fragile psyche would inform his choice of dwelling.

His destination was an address in the small town of Llanberis, situated among the Welsh mountains. He had searched for climber's cabins within the area.

It took a while before he found one situated on the side of a hill above the town. Cheap and functional, it fitted the bill. Mainwaring had given him a funny look.

'Are you sure, Peter? It seems rather...basic.'

The transaction was completed online, with Mainwaring sanctioning another two hundred pounds of spending money. The consul official had come to admire this unusual man.

Mainwaring found his army record impressive and was slightly in awe of it. He found Maroc's faint Welsh lilt pleasant, and in the tough SAS soldier, he recognised an intelligent and cultured man.

Maroc's connecting flight was to John Lennon Airport, Liverpool. He was directed to the right desk and finally handed a boarding pass. Maroc noted his flight was due for take-off in twenty minutes. Grabbing a quick coffee from a vending machine, he was surprised at how good it was.

His flight was with British Airways. Navigating his way smoothly through the system, part of his mind noted how comfortable he was with airports and the whole business of air travel.

He was waved through passport control, his one piece of luggage failing to elicit even mild interest from customs control. Not that he was hiding anything.

Maroc made his way to the Hertz offices, where a previously booked vehicle was waiting. Picking up the keys to the modest Ford Focus, a company man escorted him to the car.

There followed a laborious explanation on how he would examine the vehicle for existing marks or damage before handing it over. Within an hour of landing, he was out of the airport, driving his way towards the M56 and North Wales.

According to his onboard sat-nav, the eighty-seven point six-mile journey would take one and three-quarter hours. How precise, he thought, and how irrelevant. He would enjoy the freedom of driving; enjoy being on his own, free from the constraints of both time and social expectations. King of the road!

Where did that come from? He threw back his head and laughed until his eyes teared. Whatever he had gone through, he had survived. He'd bloody well made it. Home and dry!

CHAPTER 29

Max Southwell had chronicled his last four months with Peter Maroc. He had carefully noted each event, each triumph on his path out of a dark world of pain.

Emily had been amazed at his transformation. Gone was the man she had left on her departure to Africa. Southwell stood restored, the father she had known. Healthy and self-assured.

She recalled how miserable he had been a year ago. Her mother's death had left him feeling empty, questioning his raison d'etre. Emily had been witness to his perverse determination to give up and die.

She remembered how it had affected her. How it had filled her with guilt at what she later came to regard as her selfish abandonment.

And to what end? To follow her mission? Shouldn't he have been her first concern?

Later, trapped in a health centre in Africa, Emily had become increasingly alarmed by news of his continuing deterioration. It had begun with complaints of tiredness and aching muscles. Each passing day marked a decrease in his mobility and general functionality.

Within weeks, he was experiencing chronic muscular pain and fatigue. Even a short walk around his beloved garden exhausted him. Her brothers had intervened and insisted on putting in place a support structure designed to accommodate his failing health.

On her arrival in North Wales, Emily's first call was to the Gwynedd hospital just outside of the city of Bangor. She would have the orthodox version of her father's condition.

The specialist in charge of Max Southwell's progress was a Mr Edwards. She was immediately impressed by the man's calm, assured manner. Recognising her medical background, he had explained his involvement in her father's case.

Edwards was a man in his mid-forties with closely cropped grey hair. Quite early in their conversation, the specialist had struck her as someone with a quiet sense of purpose and little ego.

He admitted to being perplexed by the manner and rate of Southwell's recovery. The whole thing had baffled him. It still did.

Early into the conversation, she found that Edwards was not a devotee of alternative therapy. He admitted it could be used as a way of maintaining general health. Even here, he remained sceptical.

The mystery of Southwell's journey back to health remained an enigma. Despite it being mainly good news, it had left Edwards feeling uneasy.

There were too many questions unanswered. How was the older man able to dispense with the prescribed opiates? The pain would have been unbearable.

Edwards had his suspicions, and, at first, these had troubled him deeply. However, the orthodox physician was also a pragmatist. Today, Southwell was a going concern, and that outranked most other considerations. The specialist could have wagged the moral, even legal finger at Peter Maroc. He had chosen not to.

It became clear to Emily that Edwards liked Maroc; trusted him to do the right thing. Not that he had known the full nature of the man's methods, what magic he had employed to reduce Southwell's pain.

He had been impressed at seeing the results this maverick had achieved by electing to ignore his prescribed programme. The man had accomplished seemingly impossible results.

If Edwards had to guess the main ingredients for this minor miracle, he would say that Maroc had somehow accessed Southwell's cussedness and used it well. However, this would not have given him the whole story.

As the conversation progressed, Emily could see that Edwards was a man who inhabited the real world. A world where, in rare cases, results trumped strict medical standards. This had been one such case.

Edwards had not been there to regularly monitor Southwell's progress. The specialist admitted that his decision had been reached post-event. It had been solely based on her father's remarkable transformation.

The big reveal came when he was told by a rather smug Southwell that the bloody poisons, he and Doctor Llewellyn had prescribed had played no part in his recovery.

Emily drove back to Llanberis. Rather than returning straight home, she elected to shop in town. She would catch a quick coffee at her favourite place.

Emily exited the café and all but collided with... Peter Maroc.

The shock of seeing her husband back in the town they had both chosen as their home floored her. God, it had been so long.

His reappearance engendered a range of emotions, the overriding one being anger. Anger at how he had suddenly appeared in her father's life, only to exit it as quickly. He had left the older man feeling both bewildered and hurt.

Yet, when she showed that anger in front of the small café, he seemed confused. Why? His reactions made no sense. The bastard should know the reason for her irritation.

At first, Maroc parried with his trademark wit, and as usual, it had made her smile. But, today, there was much wrong with her husband. Something about him alarmed and worried her.

As he began turning away, his earlier cocky defiance to her questions had vanished. What replaced it troubled her.

Peter Maroc had always possessed a good sense of dress. Now, he looked like he had made bad choices at a charity shop. As the shock of seeing him subsided, Emily began noticing other changes.

It wasn't just his clothes, she thought. Her husband looked ill. He had lost weight and his face, although tanned, had a gauntness that shocked her.

She called him, and he stopped and turned, wary under her questioning gaze. Gone was the supremely confident bastard she had known and loved. The man standing before her bore the edgy nervousness of a cornered animal.

Emily thought of her father. Why had Peter deserted him? Why, after doing such sterling work in bringing him back from the brink? Where the hell had he been for the last two months? She studied him now and was shocked at what she saw. He was frightened of her.

A flicker of his fear leapt between them, entering her like a charge. She felt a shift; something primal responding to his pain.

Maroc wanted to run. This woman expected much, and he had no answers to give. He fought to tear down the wall which kept him from the truth. He needed and feared it in equal measure.

As panic rose to further paralyse his struggling mind, he fought to remain calm. *Focus, man, focus!*

She kept her gaze on him and in that endless moment, he was certain she could see every sin he had committed.

What could he offer her? His instincts told him he was not a good man. Not in a way good men are known in the world. Spectres from his darkness whispered of brutality and death.

Nothing!

He knew he had to get away. Return to his lair in the mountains. No more questions. Not yet.

'I have to go.'

A stark statement. He made to leave.

'Wait. We have to talk.'

This new Maroc, with his ill-concealed fear, disturbed and pained her. Again, he tried to speak.

'Nothing...'

He shook his head.

She crossed the dividing gulf, consumed with the need to restore him to a wholeness she could recognise. Holding him, she whispered meaningless sounds. She felt his trembling and tightened her embrace.

For a time, they remained this way, and she ignored the passers-by who offered curious glances. Then, linking her arm through his, she gave a gentle tug.

'You're coming home with me?'

She saw his panic, saw him fight it. He resisted her pulling, and they stopped.

'I have an address, the name of a house.'

Reaching into an inner pocket, he withdrew a folded piece of paper, handing it to her.

Emily glanced at it and smiled.

'At least we're on the same page. Come on.'

Something in him yielded. He took her proffered hand. As they walked, she made a decision not to question him further. She had always been able to make him laugh. Thumbing his awful jacket, she quipped.

'You always were a snazzy dresser, Peter.'

An uncertain smile. Encouraging.

Where had he been? More pertinent, where was he now. It had become clear he had no idea who she was, though she sensed his awareness of her at a deeper level. Her question was out before she had time to think.

'How did you get here?'

His answer was vague.

'I've been staying up there.'

Seeing her confusion, he continued.

'In a cabin. It's up in the mountains.'

'Peter, do you know who I am?'

Her previous vow had been abandoned, and Emily needed to hear his answer.

He looked down, fearful of what he would reveal, knowing it would hurt her. She watched him closely, seeing the answer. She also saw how much her knowing pained him.

'It's all right. There'll be plenty of time for us to talk.' Taking his arm, she pulled him in. No more questions. There would be time for words. Space was what he needed now. And a good meal by the looks of him.

The house was made up of three terrace houses converted into one sizable accommodation. It was spacious and comfortable inside. In another life, they had both fallen in love with it.

Emily left him sitting in a room he should have recognised; felt comfortable in. Familiar surroundings might work their magic. They might help break through the wall that barred Peter Maroc from his old life.

Minutes later, Emily emerged from the kitchen, carrying two mugs of strong tea. She wondered for a moment if his preferences had changed. Whether there was any of the old Peter left.

'Still like it strong, a hint of milk? No sugar He took the tea and sipped. He nodded.

'It's fine. Thanks.'

What to say next, do next?

'Are you hungry? I can make you something to eat.'

'Later. Maybe.'

He sensed her uncertainty.

'Thanks, this is great for now.'

He hesitated. Then...

'How long have you...we lived here?'

A recognition. An admission of a possibility.

'We bought the house six years ago. You lived here for three.'

'We were happy?'

Looking up, he seemed wary, nervous about saying the wrong thing.

'At first, very. It was three years ago, Peter. There was fault on both sides.'

'Were we...?'

'Married? Yes, five years ago.'

'Did I do something...?'

He searched carefully for the right words.

'Nothing bad. We just wanted different things.'

She wanted to add that it would be all right now. That she would accept him for who he was.

Her feelings had not changed, had never changed even back then. Despite her insistence that they separate.

This woman...Emily was his wife. He had no recollection of history. Nothing where his mind could take hold. Yet he recognised a familiarity. The rightness of her. She joined him on the large settee.

Her closeness reached him like a cool fire, lessening the burden he carried for sins not remembered. With it came the fear of losing, of returning to his disconnection.

Her questions had stopped, and she had replaced them with unspoken kindness. A warmth, strangely familiar.

Maroc pinched his arm, willing it to be real. He had grown to hate the awakenings into emptiness. The disappointment of countless dawns.

As time passed, his sleeping improved. His surrender became easier. Sleep was no longer the gateway to a realm of demons that had him waking in dread.

The first night he had occupied the guest bedroom, but after, she had led him to her bed, their bed. No demands or expectations. She was a warm presence, a comforting exceeding all he had imagined.

Later, they came together. At first, a gentle recognition. As the trust grew, she encouraged and accepted his fierce hunger, answering and matching it with her neglected needs.

The days turned over like playing cards, each a surprise, an enchantment of normalcy.

Peter Maroc lay beside his sleeping wife and wondered at this new beginning.

Is this how life is meant to be? If so, why did I leave for such a poor facsimile?

Maroc made a vow. He would not question this new reality; he would be the best he could be. He owed her that. And more.

CHAPTER 30

He took in the serious profile, wondering why he had ever allowed the marriage to fail. Sensing she was being watched, Emily Maroc looked up to find her husband leaning on the door frame which led to the kitchen. He gave her a cheeky grin.

'You look like a schoolmistress. All studious and serious.'

'Peter. I'm reading a bloody book. And stop staring or I'll brain you.'

The easy banter had emerged over the last couple of weeks. It had now been a month since his return, and they had grown comfortable with each other. The awkward phase had left without either noticing its passing.

Her doctor's practice was in the town of Caernarfon, her heavy workload reflecting the demands on workers in today's health service.

Today belonged to them. All of it. They would be spontaneous and yield to their impulses. This was their second honeymoon. She smiled at the cliché and did not care.

Maroc was getting stronger. The wolfish look, still evident, was softening. Emily thought; if he carries on with this sedentary lifestyle, will he end up a comfy bum? Somehow she doubted it.

His memory or lack of it had still not improved. Occasionally, he would point out to her a view or a person he thought looked familiar, turning to read her reaction. She would smile her encouragement.

Today, they planned a visit to Caernarfon. A place with much history, the town had started as a Roman settlement. The Romans had known it as Segontium.

On her arrival here with Maroc, she had not been impressed with this down at heel corner of Wales where time and tourism seemed to have passed by. Within a few years, the town had grown into an attractive and interesting draw for both locals and tourists.

Today, it offered a good choice of coffee shops and thriving bistros. Even a couple of very decent restaurants. Some of the pubs were excellent social gathering places, catering for all age groups.

As in most towns, there were suspect watering holes that Maroc neutrally described as... interesting. She would have employed a less flattering term.

Anyway, Emily thought, today was special. Her father, after pestering her to see Maroc since his return, was meeting up with them in town.

She had felt bad at having kept him away. A month did seem a long time, but Emily needed to make sure Maroc was ready. Max was hurt. She would make it up to him.

The plan was to meet up at one of the town's landmark pubs. *The Black Boy* had evolved much from its origins as a spit and sawdust tavern. Now a comfortable venue to eat and drink, it had become their favourite place.

Maroc had discovered he could understand and

speak Welsh. She saw how much it meant to him.

However, it was a currency he could not stop spending. She had found herself having to drag him away from bemused strangers who had quickly become 'friends.'

As they walked down the narrow street to the pub, she caught a glimpse of Max's back as he entered the pub.

'There's dad.'

She had made a move to call him. Maroc held her back.

'Let him go in. He can get the first round.'

She nudged him in the ribs.

'You be nice to my daddy, you bastard. You saved his life. In some cultures, that means you're obliged to serve him. Forever!'

'Not in my bloody culture.'

He grinned happily, and she knew, although he had no recollection of her father, that Maroc was beyond curious.

They entered the pub, and Max, who was standing at the bar, turned to face them. His eyes shone on seeing Maroc.

'Grasshopper, you have returned.'

Then, Peter Maroc's world grew dark, and he thought he would faint. He closed his eyes so he could fight the vertigo that threatened to topple him.

He had no way of knowing how long he had stood like this. Carefully he opened his eyes, and everything was in change.

Southwell's face had become two. Then, slowly, as though through a correcting lense, it became the face he had always known. A face he had unknowingly missed.

His legs betrayed him, and Emily took her husband's elbow, steadying him until she was sure he could stand.

The recognition, when it came, was complete. It was a force that punched through his wall of unknowing. It robbed him of speech, and he could do nothing except gaze at what had always been, yet hidden.

Maroc seemed to recover, and instinct made Emily step away. She sensed the change and was anxious not to hinder a process before it was fully realised. Made permanent.

Tears sprang unbidden. Maroc wiped away the wetness with a quick brush of his hand as he took in the man standing before him. His voice was steadier than it had a right to be.

'Bugger me, didn't I use to know you?'

To an observer, they were two men meeting. Southwell, stepped forward, embracing Maroc, his face unreadable to all but Emily. She had seen that emptiness when all was taken from him. When such extremes had no face.

This time the reason differed. The look was the same.

Maroc needed to see her, this wraith that had haunted his nights and days. She had been the flicker at the edge of his vision, both in and out of his dreams. He wanted to turn, to know that she was real.

Emily stepped forward, her arms embracing the two most important people in her life. They stood like that, his hand seeking, then capturing hers in final recognition.

CHAPTER 31

The Black Boy was filling up. Emily found a table in a room less crowded and bought more drinks. The conversation was kept light and current, with Max providing amusing vignettes of the goings-on in and around Beddgelert.

As the evening progressed, Emily and Max witnessed a further breaking down of Maroc's mental barrier. Conscious of the delicacy of such a process, they recognised the wisdom of restraint.

This would be an afternoon of reconnection rather than a fact-finding exercise. Father and daughter were happy to welcome Maroc back into the fold, and today they would accept him completely. No questions asked.

Maroc remarked on how well Max looked and gave him an appraising look.

'Still practising, Max?'

It was a reference to the meditation practice that had been so pivotal in Southwell's recovery.

'Twice a day, at least twenty minutes per session.'

'Impressive. You seem happier, more relaxed.'

Max slapped Maroc on the shoulder.

'OK, I look great, Emily looks great. You look bloody awful. Let's talk about the important stuff. When are you taking me on this long overdue fishing trip you promised?'

'I did?'

Maroc rubbed his chin as though considering.

'Let me think. Did I talk about a fishing trip?'

'Yes, you bloody well did. And, that included camping. A camping, fishing trip.'

Emily nodded her agreement, smiling broadly.

'You did, Peter. Can't back down now.'

Rising from her stool, she flicked a strand of blond hair from her face.

Maroc looked at her enquiringly.

'Another drink, anyone?'

She waved an empty glass.

'I'm off to the bar. Let you make your man plans.'

Today, Emily had a one-drink policy. As a student, she had had a few wild nights and had blushed at each retelling by Maroc. The sod would never let her forget.

It had made her the obvious candidate for driving on occasions like this. It suited everyone.

Both men ordered another beer. It had been decided that Emily would drive them back to Llanberis, leaving Max's car to be picked up the following morning.

'It's like an avalanche in my brain, Max. Things keep crashing in. A bit overwhelming.'

His smile was unsure, relief eclipsing his fear.

'Good, good. Let it happen naturally'

Southwell's tone implied it was no big deal.

'Anyway, remember the fifty quid I lent you just before you disappeared?'

Maroc, looking up quickly, saw his father-in-law grinning like a loon. He shook his head.

'Only fifty. Oh well, if you're happy with fifty...'

Southwell thumped the table, smiling broadly.

'A trip out will do us both good. Fresh air, exercise, the works. How's Emily taking it? You two seem back together. An item, I believe it's called.'

Maroc became serious.

'Never stopped loving her. You know that.'

'Nor her you, my boy. That's why I was always so angry with you. You were a bloody fool, Maroc. Leaving my daughter for weeks on end to go traipsing off on your... missions.'

'It's coming back slowly. Need time to process everything that's pouring through.'

Maroc smiled.

'Cut me some slack, man.'

Southwell held up his hand.

'Let's leave it for now. Plenty of time to evaluate the past.'

The grin returned.

'I can bollock you later.'

The drive back to Llanberis was short. Both men were quiet, each enjoying the other's company. Emily kept up an easy flow of conversation, filling Max in on what she and Maroc had been doing since his return.

It was good having both her husband and her father at Bryn Awel. A long time since the three had occupied the same space. Emily was happy.

Secretly, she embraced a quiet optimism for the future. Her contented smile did not go unnoticed by the others.

Maroc viewed his relationship with Emily through the fresh lens of his new perspective. He agreed with Max that he had been a bloody fool for leaving her on her own.

'What's the weather going to be like tomorrow,

Em?'

Emily turned to her father.

'Fine for the rest of the week, dad, if you can believe them. Why do you ask?

Southwell looked at Maroc.

'Ideal opportunity for that fishing trip, Peter. I'm at a loose end. How are you fixed?'

Not ready for this, Maroc looked over at Emily.

'Don't break the habit of a lifetime by consulting me, Peter.'

He frowned, and her face broke into a smile.

'Go on. Dad will be there to see you don't get into trouble.'

It was agreed. They would head for the secluded beauty of Cwm Idwal and camp by the lake. Maroc expanded his plan for the outing.

'A little lake fishing, then head back to the main road where we can try the river Marddwr.'

Marddwr was the name given to a stretch of the Ogwen river that meandered down the valley towards the town of Bethesda. It translated as 'dead water.'

The lake would be difficult fishing, but, according to Maroc, Marddwr should reward them with a few small trout.

While her father's excitement was expected, Emily was both surprised and pleased at how happy Maroc seemed. She looked at the others.

'This calls for a drink?'

Maroc raised an arm theatrically.

'Woman, my special malt. Now!'

She rolled her eyes, hiding her delight at how good things were between the two men. How things had changed. Not that long ago, they were hardly on speaking terms.

It was getting late, and Southwell was assigned his usual bedroom. It contained some of his books and personal possessions. Since Maroc's departure from the marriage, he had come to view it as his second home.

Southwell woke early and was downstairs before Maroc. He and Emily were breakfasting when he finally emerged. They looked up at him, smiling at some private joke.

Seeing how openly happy they were, Maroc reflected on how much of it was due to his return. He vowed he would do his uttermost to deserve their affection.

Maroc had woken up at around four to the echoes of a dream he failed to recall. He had settled into a more restful slumber, waking up late but surprisingly refreshed.

Max was eating porridge, but the real surprise was the empty glass of Maroc's special green pond water.

The old bastard's still staying with the regime, he thought.

Good man!

Maroc sat opposite his father-in-law.

Nudging the empty glass, he looked innocently at Southwell.

'Any of that good stuff left?'

Max gave him a sour look.

'What time do you want to set off, Max?'

Southwell became visibly animated.

'I'll take my rod this time. What about camping gear? Rucksacks, sleeping bags, and the like?'

Maroc stood, a piece of toast in his hand.

'Got everything, so you don't have to lift a finger.'

Preparing would take under half an hour as he had everything they would need for the trip, packed and ready for the off. It had been something he had done ever since he had discovered climbing. Packing another unit for Southwell had taken little extra work.

The car loaded, the day theirs, Emily had waved them off at eight sharp. She was not comfortable with the situation, still nervous at what had happened to Maroc.

Emily wondered if Maroc had a gun in his first aid box. It would not surprise her.

They were two grinning teenagers in an open-topped roadster enjoying the day. Max had insisted he was robust enough to have the top down, and Maroc had agreed. Thirty minutes later, they pulled into the same small car park outside the mountain rescue centre.

'No Albanians?'

Max was in satirical mode. Maroc shrugged.

'This time, I'm ready for the bastards. Anyway, I've got you to watch my back.'

Max bowed with his hands together in the Buddhist gassho.

'The pupil has become the master as the gentle breeze bends the mighty oak.'

Seeing Maroc's baffled look, he shrugged.

'Don't ask me. You're the one who's into this heathen horseshit.'

They unpacked the car, his father-in-law taking the smaller rucksack. Maroc looked forward to an enjoyable couple of days, knowing that Southwell was more than fit for the trip and everything would be fine.

Still, you can't be too careful, he thought, patting the comforting bulge on the left side of his jacket.

The short walk from the main road to lake Idwal was as pleasant as on their last visit. Even more so since, on that previous visit, Southwell had been a work in progress.

Maroc sorted out the sleeping arrangements while Southwell set up the double burner gas stove. The tent was soon up, the equipment and sleeping bags arranged neatly inside.

'Two bog standards coming up.'

Southwell walked carefully, bearing giant-sized mugs of tea. Maroc had remembered to bring a couple of folding canvas chairs. He quickly set these up around a small folding table, just in time for Southwell to park the mugs.

'Hungry, Maroc?'

'Will be later, Max. We'll get this down us, then I'm for a bit of a stretch on the slabs. Fancy coming over to watch?'

Maroc had his climbing pumps in one hand and his safety harness in the other.

'Might even join you. Reckon I'm fit enough?

Maroc patted the older man on the shoulders.

'Give it a few weeks, and I'll take you up Tryfan. There's a climb called Milestone Buttress. It has a very interesting chimney pitch.'

Southwell looked doubtful.

'You serious? If you are, for the love of God, don't mention any of it to Emily.'

Maroc nodded and grinned.

'Commit to some serious strength exercise, a bit more cardio, and we'll climb it.'

Satisfied, Southwell checked his rucksack. He decided to stuff a paperback book into one of the pockets.

'We off then?'

They reached the southern side of the lake, arriving at the base of the Idwal Slabs. Maroc stepped into his harness. Sitting with his back to the rock face, he squeezed his feet into the tight climbing pumps.

Today would be a day of leisurely climbing, starting with a technically easy ascent to seventy feet. He would then decide how the rest of the climb would unfold.

Southwell, producing his paperback, found himself a convenient rock. Carefully positioning his rucksack, he made himself comfortable. Sensing that Maroc was waiting for him to say something, he looked up.

'Off you go. Try not to break your bloody neck.'

'Be down before you know it, Max.'

He grinned.

'And no, not by the quickest route.'

Not wanting to leave Southwell waiting too long, Maroc decided to shorten his intended route. He ascended the first pitch before traversing right onto a second and continuing up. Keeping well within his limits, the activity soothed and relaxed him.

Southwell looked up from his reading as his son-in-law joined him on the ground. Maroc removed his harness and grinned down at him.

'Fancy a stroll back to base camp for a bite to eat before the fishing? Nothing too strenuous. Perhaps when we next visit, we could scramble up the Devil's Kitchen.'

Maroc pointed to the western side of the cwm,

looking cautiously at Southwell.

'Taking it easy, of course.'

Arriving back at the tent, they decided on a light meal. A chicken pie that Emily had prepared, followed by a bottle of beer apiece.

'We'll take a couple of extra bottles with us. I'm sure the fish won't mind.'

Talking and walking, the time passed pleasantly. Fishing was one of the treats Southwell had been looking forward to while convalescing. A fair caster of the rod, he was giving Maroc a run for his money.

Lake Idwal had yielded nothing, and, after a couple of hours, they had given up. Walking down towards the main road and the Marddwr part of the river Ogwen, both Maroc and Southwell were relaxing into the day.

They could not have suspected their every move was being closely observed through two pairs of powerful binoculars.

CHAPTER 32

Edon and Burim Berisha knew they had to employ their full creativity to emerge unscathed from their meeting with the Krye.

The brothers stood nervously before the oversized desk in his private office. Edon made a halting start.

'Things did not go as planned. We were forced to kill the man, Maroc.'

The Krye cut him short with an impatient wave of his hand. He was momentarily silent, and the brothers braced themselves for the inevitable explosion.

When he spoke, his voice was unexpectedly low and soft. The menace it held, however, was not lost on either man.

'Killed? Your job was to bring him back. Alive. How in the name of God did you allow this to happen? You realise the information he carried in his head was worth a fortune to us?'

His eyes bore into Edon's as he continued in the same sinister tone.

'You have made me look an idiot.'

The Krye walked from behind his desk to stand facing the younger brother. Burim began speaking and received a hard slap to his face.

He staggered backwards, more from shock than pain. The formidable little man turned to Edon while the dazed Burim regained his composure. The younger brother tentatively stepped forward, assuming his position beside his older brother.

They remained, heads bowed like naughty schoolchildren hoping whatever their fate, it would be quick, if not painless. Their boss returned to his desk and began writing. Then, picking up his desk telephone, he spoke rapidly. His voice was low and urgent, and the brothers strained to hear.

On replacing the receiver, the small man looked up. When he spoke, his voice had lost its menace. It had assumed a brisk, business-like manner.

'Now, tell me how this happened. From the beginning.'

Burim began speaking, but his brother placed a hand on his arm. He knew what transpired in the next few minutes could mean life or death. What he would say would be mainly true. It would just not be the whole truth.

'Yes sir, Peter Maroc is dead. It was a mistake, an accident. He had regained consciousness in the van. He fought like a madman.'

The Krye's response cut him like a whip.

'You did not check his condition? Make sure he was sedated?'

Edon looked up nervously at the Krye. He continued, in his plea for understanding, his voice trembling with the fear of retribution.

'When I checked on him, he seemed unconscious. Like he had been through most of the journey.'

'But he wasn't unconscious, was he? He was very much conscious. You have not answered my question. How did you end up killing him?'

The Krye's tone reflected his barely contained fury. They had the desired effect on the big Albanian.

Edon spoke in a breathy staccato, his words tumbling out of him as he pleaded for his life.

'He had to be stopped, or he would have killed me. It was self-defence. Me or Maroc.'

Burim was dismayed at seeing his big brother begging like a girl. Would he have behaved better? He already knew the answer to that question.

'How was he disposed of?'

The question had been anticipated, and the brothers had a ready answer.

'We cut him up and fed his body to the pigs. My friend in the area has a pig farm.'

'Is this friend reliable or another loose end we have to take care of?'

Edon knew he had to assure the Krye that they were on their own when Maroc's body parts were offered as pig fodder.

'He would give us part-time work on his farm. He trusted us. We were often left on our own when he was away on business. That day, we were the only ones there. No one saw us.'

Fear gripped him by the throat. He hoped the Krye would not interpret his nervousness as guilt. He also hoped he was not a reader of minds.

Both men were sweating as they left the Krye's office. Burim found the nearest staff toilet, where he promptly parted with most of his stomach content. Edon, not much calmer, managed to control the same impulse.

For the moment, the pressure was off. Still, they recognised this was but a reprieve. They would return

226

to Vlore and find Peter Maroc. They would wait for their opportunity and kill the British pig.

Their boss, however, had other plans for them. The Krye had concluded a brief but pointed conversation with Berisha senior. He had explained how his sons had squandered an ideal opportunity to retrieve the stolen money and drugs. Berisha had pleaded for his sons to be given one last chance, once again using his exemplary record with the Fare as a lever.

Eventually, the Krye had come around. He recognised there had been no deliberate intention to deprive the organisation of their asset. However, his son's idiotic incompetence could still harm his reputation.

Ever since their previous transgression, Berisha had worked diligently for the organisation in an attempt to make up for their mistake. The Krye had again taken into consideration his unstinting loyalty and dedication to the cause.

The Mafia boss sat alone in his office. He was still fuming. He had waited a long time to lay his hands on at least one of the British bastards who had embarrassed him on that fateful evening.

Still, there were two more thieving pigs out there. Two more opportunities to retrieve what was rightly theirs. They went under the name of Mark Fisher and Niels Johansson.

This information had been extracted from the unfortunate Albanian special forces traitor in their midst. The Krye's smile held no humour as he recalled the man's hard-gained confession.

Dushku had held out longer than most, longer than anyone who had gone through his 'special' interrogation process. Finally broken, the man never offered excuses or pleaded for his life.

Brave, yes. An idiot, undoubtedly. Why suffer such agony? Everyone talked in the end.

The Krye believed Niels Johansson to be in his home country of Norway or with his family in Sweden. He would be a difficult extraction whatever Scandinavian country he was in. He had finally decided on Mark Fisher as the easier option.

He shook his head in disbelief. It seemed he was surrounded by bunglers. First Blandford and now Maroc. Both were killed in what should have been a simple extraction.

He would, despite everything, send the two idiots back to the UK. There were two reasons for his decision. Their father had been a stalwart of the organisation for many years and did not deserve the pain of losing two sons. The man had given him a cogent argument regarding his sons' culpability or lack of it.

Secondly, disposing of any of his men reflected badly on him. On how he ran his operation.

Returning to the UK would provide them with an opportunity. A chance to finally get rid of the evidence that was Peter Maroc.

This time, they would make sure the SAS man's death would not be a lie.

The Kryetar back in Manchester would have been informed of their poor performance within the organisation. Edon hoped it would not result in the man giving them all the shit jobs.

The brothers had cultivated some resourceful people while in the UK. They had deliberately hidden their valuable connections in the Greater Manchester area from the organisation.

There was a ceiling to the money they could earn working for the Kryetar. Edon had an alternative career planned for them both. It was a career that did not involve the Fare. Edon Berisha was a great believer in free enterprise.

CHAPTER 33

On their arrival at Manchester airport, Edon and Burim were met by a solitary foot soldier. How their status had diminished.

Edon eyed his brother and shrugged. They would have to do better. They would also have to create their own destiny in this land of opportunity.

Both brothers knew there was some risk of the Fare's UK branch hearing of Maroc's continuing existence. It was a matter of luck that the bloody man chose to live in such a remote part of the country.

Then there was the other consideration. Maroc could be looking for them. The man had worked and may still be working for the intelligence community. He would have access to intel concerning the Fare's activities.

The solution to their problem was obvious. To make sure this threat was removed as quickly as possible.

Maroc's routine was already being closely monitored by Edon's new British friends. The knowledge gave the Albanian the comforting impression of being in control.

There was one other fly in the ointment. Maroc's brother-in-law, Malcolm Southwell. The pathetic little man had paid them for disposing of Maroc. This had amused them since Maroc had already been picked as a target for abduction by the Fare.

The brothers had no compunction in keeping this quiet and taking Southwell's money. This money would come in useful, allowing them to put it towards the extra muscle needed to eliminate Maroc.

Edon knew a second attempt on the SAS man would not be without its problems. Maroc would be prepared and waiting.

The Albanian was confident that this time he and his brother would have the advantage of surprise. He doubted Maroc would be expecting anything to happen soon. Then again, they were dealing with a tricky bastard.

This was their last chance at making good with the organisation. With two strikes against them, a third would not be tolerated. Their father's good record would not buy them further leniency.

The brothers were aware of their precarious position within the Fare. They expected, at least initially, to be under scrutiny. They would be as good as gold, at least until the Kryetar began trusting them again. After that? They would certainly need some latitude to take care of the Maroc threat.

Edon knew they required at least three days free of Fare business. Within that timeframe, they could execute a plan that would ensure their continuing safety within the organisation.

Malcolm Southwell would be disposed of first. The man had a loose tongue. He was already bragging to his cronies of his connections with some 'heavy Albanians.'

Edon and Burim had become aware of the Fare's deep involvement with the many forms of gambling in the UK. They could not afford the chance of the Kryetar coming across Malcolm Southwell.

If the organisation discovered they had transacted to eliminate Maroc, the game would be up. After all, the man was supposed to be dead. Southwell had to be silenced.

Edon had no intention of dying from a bullet to the back of the head, courtesy of the Fare. With both Maroc and Southwell dead, there would no longer be evidence of their blundering.

Killing Maroc would require more surveillance and planning. The execution would be tricky. This time, they would bring along some extra muscle.

The Wilson brothers, Don and Jimmy, were old-school heavies. They came from a respectable working-class background. However, their parents' attempts at instilling good, honest values had failed miserably.

Early in their teens, they had concluded honest work was for mugs. The brothers had no intention of following in their father's footsteps. At first, it had been small stuff. Shoplifting and opportunistic thievery.

There were two years between them. Don was the eldest and, at least, another decade older in maturity. Don Wilson was the architect and planner of their nefarious activities, and Jimmy was a faithful and enthusiastic follower.

When Don took his brother to see a movie based on the lives of London gangsters Reggie and Ronnie Kray, everything changed. Sitting in the small cinema, they had discovered their role models.

With the passing years, their crimes grew more serious, more violent. Still using the Krays to inform their lives, they had joined a boxing club. There they had found malcontent young men of their age.

Don Wilson had painted a picture of easy gain for little effort. To this end, he had utilised his hard man charisma, together with his talent for rhetoric.

The brothers had contacted a handful of shady car dealers in the Manchester area. The dealers had a ready clientele base, hungry for high-end cars.

At first, the newly formed gang enjoyed the inherent thrill of their new career. Vehicle alarms, however, were becoming increasingly sophisticated and harder to circumvent.

Breaking into expensive cars had gradually evolved into a techno skill. A skill the brothers had no interest in acquiring. The gang had been disbanded, and both Don and Jimmy were forced to discover a different modus operandi if the business was to continue.

They had found it easier and safer to hang around upmarket hotel entrances. While more time-consuming, they could be sure of a careless owner leaving keys in a vehicle for the short time needed to complete some errand. This simple lapse was all the brothers needed.

Soon, they were able to drive flash cars of their own. This alone symbolised their brand of lifestyle.

It proved an irresistible lure for jobless men barely managing on basic living allowances. It meant the brothers had an easy source of recruitment.

For a couple of years, both men were happy to orchestrate their new business model from a safe distance, allowing their foot soldiers to take the risks. Car thieving, however, was never going to be enough to fund their growing extravagances.

One enterprise had long appealed to both men. To

date, they had lacked the boldness to enter it. However, with an increase in manpower came increased confidence.

While the protection racket was well covered by older, more established gangs, there were still areas of greater Manchester with gaps in the market. The brothers had stepped in.

At first, they employed threats to achieve their client's compliance. In the rare cases where cooperation was withheld, they would provide their targets with a preview of a bleak and unprofitable future. The majority eventually paid up.

When Edon and Burim turned up, looking for muscle, Jimmy was affronted. To him, they were cheeky foreign bastards. Don had persuaded his younger brother to hear them out. He had long been aware of a Mafia-style organisation operating in and around the Manchester area.

Neither brother had mentioned their mafia connections. Don, however, had drawn his conclusions. Based on this tenuous inference, he had painted for his brother a bright image of the future. They were about to go big.

The Wilson brother's office in Prestwich, North Manchester, was impressive. It showcased how far they had come since their youthful entry into the world of crime.

The Albanians were satisfied they were dealing with an established firm. They would employ them in their pursuit of Peter Maroc.

That first encounter had taken place a little over three weeks before. Edon had given the Wilsons all the information they had possessed on Peter Maroc. Most of it had been from the two mafioso's previous visit to North Wales.

What was needed now was an update on his daily activities. When and where would he be at his most vulnerable. There was also a matter of weaponry.

Unlike in the old country, the Fare in the UK had a policy of never allowing its members to carry arms. Unless the situation necessitated it.

On that second visit, the Wilsons had made a show of welcoming them back. Don showed the brothers into their inner sanctum, where the men were poured a generous measure of decent malt whisky and settled into comfortable chairs.

Respect was vital to both parties. The Albanians, recently starved of that commodity, succumbed to its illusory comfort.

The Wilson brothers provided the two Albanians with a detailed report on Maroc's activities and movements. It included comprehensive lists and diagrams of the area.

The report lay on the desk in front of the brothers.

Edon, whose English had advanced the most, quickly scanned the document and was pleased by its thoroughness and attention to detail.

Edon's thoughts returned to Maroc. The elite soldier was not as clever as he thought. Peter Maroc had been spotted in some remote places, often by himself. Sometimes he would be in the company of a much older man,

The big Albanian smiled. The idiot had a brand of confidence that would get him killed.

When the time was right, they would capitalise on his foolishness, ending the threat to their security within the Fare. But first, there was the equally pressing, albeit easier task of disposing of the other nuisance, Malcolm Southwell. That lesser task had been handed to the Wilsons.

The Mancunian brothers had offered to extend their services to the disposal of Peter Maroc. Edon had politely declined. They would deal with the final matter themselves. It was personal. A matter of honour.

Don had nodded his understanding before turning to Jimmy. His younger brother grinned and nodded sagely.

CHAPTER 34

Malcolm Southwell was feeling quite chirpy. He had money in his pocket, and for the moment, the constant dread of tomorrow had been removed. His recent financial deliverance gave him some leeway, an edge he intended to keep.

A lot had happened since Maroc's visit, good things. Southwell had even taken the man's advice and slowed down on the booze. He thought about that.

Maroc was a bit of an enigma; he had acted as though he cared. Malcolm had his doubts. Given what he and John had in mind for Mr SAS, thinking ill of him was the easier option.

His pace quickened. He looked forward to a relaxing hot bath on returning to the flat. He reflected on his present living quarters, its drabness. Life was so bloody unfair.

He had started life with hopes of a brilliant and affluent future. A world in which he presented as a respected and admired man of affairs.

His mood lightened, as his mind shifted to a time when Maroc would no longer feature in his father's life. With that thought came the same nagging questions. What was in it for the bloody man? Where was the payoff?

Nurse Price seemed pleased with the way Maroc was helping his father. The silly cow had even endorsed his method of treatment.

Did Maroc intend to ingratiate himself with their father by somehow restoring him to health? Then, when the older man was deemed compos mentis, he would favour Peter Maroc in his will?

To Malcolm, it sounded a rather tiresome way of acquiring wealth. It was also damned hard work.

Looking on the brighter side, Maroc, never having got on with the old man, might be planning something more sinister for their father. Now, that would suit very nicely.

Without Maroc's support, his father would soon give up his preposterous fight. The old bastard would revisit his melancholy and maudlin self-pity. His health would deteriorate, and hopefully, he would never recover.

Did he resent his father that much, or was it John's influence? Malcolm realised the old bugger had long ceased liking either of his sons. It had not always been so.

He still remembered his father's warmth, his humour. However, as both he and John grew into men, he had grown to disapprove of their emerging deviousness. They, in their turn, had lost all affection for him.

Both boys knew and accepted the relationship or lack of it. Emily had been his father's favourite as far back as Malcolm could remember, with her younger sister a tolerated second.

Malcolm Southwell thought of his sister Emily, and, not for the first time, tried to dislike her. Beautiful, considerate Emily, who loved everyone. Even him. Christ, even John. He felt a deep fondness for the one warm constant in his life and failed to summon even the slightest resentment.

Turning the corner to his apartment, Malcolm Southwell returned to his reverie of changing fortunes. A fortune that would cause a certain lady to view him through a different lens.

He had already cast a few casual allusions to an expected inheritance. Mainly when in earshot of the vivacious barmaid of The Blue Cock; a certain Lucy Cromwell.

When serving him, Lucy had been civil, nothing more. Of late, her neutral manner seemed to have changed. Her usual reserve had been softened by the occasional coy smile. She had complimented him on his new suit, even reaching for his wrist to better admire his Rolex Submariner.

'Makes you look manly, Malcolm, stainless steel. Prefer it to gold myself. Gold's too showy I always think.'

He'd smiled, accepting the compliment easily. A man of the world, he was used to such approval.

He had failed to disclose that for the princely sum of fifty pounds, you could get a decent copy of any expensive watch. Perhaps he should have chosen the Breitling?

On further visits to The Blue Cock, Malcolm's legend had further evolved. There were hints of an ancestral home. A Bentley which was 'badly in need of a run.'

His father's terminal illness was something he stoically coped with. It was sad. He would soon have the added burden of having to manage a large part of his father's inheritance.

The ploy had not yielded immediate results. Mild

desperation had spawned the oblique mention of a business trip abroad in search of commercial premises. Lucy had become increasingly receptive. They had become an item.

Eager to prove herself Southwell's equal and thus worthy of elevated status, Lucy Cromwell declared her credentials. She was the direct descendant of the great man himself, Oliver Cromwell.

Southwell had been suitably impressed, indicating the revelation had come as no surprise. He had always recognised a certain air of nobility about her.

His mood buoyant, he all but skipped up the stairs to his second-floor apartment. First a hot bath. Plenty of fragrances and bubbles. He would recline in warm comfort and dream of the evening ahead.

Malcolm Southwell knew his luck was turning. He could feel it. He always went with his feelings, his gut instinct.

Glowing from the hot bath, the world seemed a kinder place. A place where a man of his calibre would be fittingly rewarded. By the gods, he was not about to allow anything to stand in his way.

His thoughts returned to Peter Maroc. Maroc the usurper, who had imagined he could outmanoeuvre the combined cerebral clout of the Southwell brothers. Some hope, little man.

The Southwell brethren. Now, that had a ring to it. It was biblical; powerful. Maroc was about to find out how powerful. His walk quickened and his smile had become slightly manic.

Before setting out, Malcolm had made arrangements with Lucy. They would meet at 'their club.' Having only once been there together, he realised this regard to be rather fanciful.

So what? They were in love. It was allowed.

The Siberia was a small nightclub, not long opened. He felt comfortable there. Safe. Run by Eastern Europeans, Russians he thought, both he and Lucy considered it quite exotic.

At nine-thirty, the bright daylight softened into a summer evening, Malcolm Southwell turned right into the quiet little street. He noticed the discreet neon sign glowing above the club's entrance. His pulse quickened.

Malcolm gave scant notice to the sound of a vehicle pulling up behind him. His thoughts lay ahead. Taking Lucy into his arms, the perfect couple glided into the first slow waltz...

He was unaware of the two men wearing black balaclavas stepping out of a dark colour Mercedes. The duo closed in on the smaller man with practised stealth. Vicious blows from a weighted club were delivered to the back of Southwell's head. The perpetrators knew their craft and how to apply it with devastating effect.

Mercifully, their savagery never registered. Nor did Malcolm Southwell feel the further blows and kicks to his head and body.

He lay face down in the road, his head at an awkward angle off the pavement's edge. There had been no significant last thoughts. More a summer evening, rushing headlong into an endless night.

CHAPTER 35

Emily found it difficult to believe the change. Watching Maroc with her father was a near surreal experience. The banter was spontaneous and natural. Old friends, making up for lost time.

Gone were the suspicions and resentments. They had been replaced by a comfortable trust and, yes, humour. She tried not to show her amazement. Her complete delight.

Tea was a light salad followed by fruit and yoghurt. No complaint, her father not even pulling a face.

They were on their coffee when the phone rang. Emily smiled and, excusing herself, rose from the table.

'Are you sure you have the right number?'

More silence, then.

'Oh my god. How bad is he?'

By now, both men were paying attention. Emily's face was ashen, and Maroc saw her hand shaking, hardly able to hold the receiver. He rose to join her. Gently taking the receiver from her, he enquired.

'This is Peter Maroc, Emily Maroc's husband. Could you tell me what this is about?'

It was his turn to be shocked. Maroc looked over at Max. His father-in-law's face was showing increasing alarm.

'Let me take down the details.'

He turned to Emily, his hand extended. She reached under him, opened a drawer in the telephone table, and handed Maroc a small yellow pad and pen.

Maroc thanked the voice at the other end as he scribbled down some details. Replacing the receiver, he found Max Southwell on his feet.

'What the hell's happened? Emily?

Turning to Maroc

'Peter?'

'It's Malcolm, dad. He's been attacked and...'

Her voice broke.

'It's not looking good, Max,' said Maroc. 'He's alive, so there's hope.'

'But it's bad?'

Southwell was on his feet, his face ashen.

'How bad Maroc, for God's sake, will he pull through?'

'That's all they can tell us.'

Maroc stood helpless, unable to supply the glimmer of hope they yearned.

'We can travel up to Manchester today. Now. He's in the Salford Royal. We'll take Emily's car if that's OK. I'll drive.'

Emily reached into her bag, taking out her car keys. She handed them to Maroc, her tear-filled eyes burning into his.

They drove for a whole hour in almost complete silence. On reaching the M56 motorway heading to Manchester, Max broke the silence.

'You think it could be a case of mistaken identity? Where would Malcolm go to get attacked by anyone? It's not the sort of world he inhabits. Is it?'

Southwell looked at Maroc, his eyes pleading for confirmation. This was some terrible clerical error. A mix-up with the hospital files. It had to be.

Keeping his eyes on the road, Maroc considered his answer. He knew the older man needed some hope to cling to.

'It's possible, Max. Let's keep the faith, eh?'

Arriving at the Salford Royal in Royal Stott Lane, they parked in the central car park. Emily and Max wore grim expressions. Maroc was not one of Malcolm's greatest admirers, his main concern was how this crisis would affect his two companions.

Maroc led the way through the main entrance to the Hope Building. Making his way to the front desk, he gave the receptionist Malcolm's details, given to him by the member of staff who had first contacted them.

The receptionist was taking forever. Max Southwell's nerves were stretched to their limit. Emily, familiar with the system, remained sympathetically patient.

The middle-aged woman eventually found Malcolm Southwell's details, and picking up the phone, she called the relevant department. Still holding the receiver, she turned to Maroc.

'Mr. Southwell is at present in the critical care unit. Mr Wood, the specialist in charge of his case, will be down to see you shortly.'

She delivered the message with the right amount of professional sympathy.

'Is there a place where we could get coffee or tea?'

Maroc's main concern was for his father-in-law, whose pallor alarmed him. He had to get the man to a seat. Get him something to drink.

Southwell sat at a table in the small hospital cafeteria, and Maroc, without consulting him, ordered his father-in-law a coffee. Emily asked for tea.

When his coffee arrived, Southwell made no effort to drink. He took a few gulps on Maroc's insistence before pushing his cup away.

Within minutes Mr Wood appeared. Maroc thought he looked remarkably like his bank manager in Germany. He was a short, neat man, in his late fifties, with dark greying hair, cut unfashionably short. He carried a clipboard in his left hand and seemed to be studying it intensely.

Wood looked up, his intelligent grey eyes taking in the dejected trio. Maroc immediately sensed the man's awkwardness and braced himself for the bad news.

'Malcolm has serious head trauma.'

He paused and looked at all three in turn before continuing sombrely.

'He also has severe internal injuries.'

Wood allowed genuine sympathy to reach his face as he surveyed them in silence. He gave them time for the bad news to sink in.

'It seems he was badly beaten up and left in the road. If he does live…'

He paused, struggling to find the right words.

'Well…, he has suffered severe head injuries and might not regain consciousness.'

He looked directly at Southwell.

'He's in a bad way. A very bad way.'

Tears rolled down Emily's cheeks. Southwell's face was like stone. He sat in silence.

'Would it be possible to see him?'

Emily's voice was flat, emotionless.

Wood glanced at his clipboard, reluctant to meet her eyes. When he finally looked up, he addressed all three.

'Malcolm is on life support. The brain damage has resulted in him not being able to breathe without assistance. As I said, he's unconscious. There's a chance he may not recover.'

He turned, gesturing with his free hand for them to follow.

'But, of course you may see him.'

It was as bad as Maroc had expected. Having seen many injuries in his line of work, he did not need a doctor's degree to reach his conclusion. Malcolm Southwell would not be coming back from this.

Wired up to several monitors, he looked small, vulnerable. His head was heavily bandaged, and Maroc felt a twinge of pity. Poor bastard didn't deserve this.

Emily and Max were propping each other up, and Maroc quickly pulled out chairs from a stack in the corner of the room. Both father and daughter knew Malcolm would not be coming home. The grim knowledge placed them beyond tears.

Maroc could do nothing, and he hated this unaccustomed helplessness. He placed his hand on Emily's shoulder.

'I'll leave you for a while, love. I won't be far. You can get me on my mobile if you need me sooner.'

Emily reached back, laying her hand over his. Squeezing Southwell's shoulder, Maroc reluctantly left them.

His feelings were ambivalent. He felt like a hypocrite in front of the others. On his own, he could be more honest.

There was not much to like about Malcolm Southwell. Self-absorbed and unbelievably shallow, his greed had led him into some dark places.

Maroc gave a long sigh. It was mainly for his two companions. He knew he could not feel what they felt.

He had his theory. Malcolm had most likely failed to use the money to pay off his gambling debts. His creditors would have offered him a choice. Pay or you pay with your life. The final message had been delivered.

As Maroc made his way to the main entrance, he felt a growing sense of unease. In his world, this extra perception had protected him countless times. He trusted it.

At first, it was a visceral thing. A warning, before his other senses began gathering data from his surroundings, adding flesh to the alert.

As Maroc approached the large double doors, he spotted the two men. They were loitering immediately outside the main entrance.

To most, they would pass as visiting relatives grabbing some fresh air. Maroc immediately had a bad feeling about them. He could be mistaken. He knew, however, that in such scenarios, his judgment was rarely wrong.

They were looking directly at him, and he held their gaze. One of the men turned quickly away, his abrupt action betraying both.

The glass door had enabled Maroc to take in some detail. Powerfully built, they were the heavies from a thriller movie. He examined the remaining man, catching him in profile. He took in the badly broken nose; the strong jaw. Maroc was about a dozen feet from the doors when the man decided to follow his companion.

Both men were dark-haired and swarthy. Foreign? Their features and skin tone suggested homegrown. Could they have been responsible for Malcolm's beating?

There had to be some connection. Yet today, it was he, Peter Maroc, who was the focus of their attention. Interesting.

Into which part of his complex life did they fit? He would find out.

Opening the main exit door, he quickly approached the men. They were about twenty yards into the car park and now stood with their backs to him. On hearing his approach, both men spun round. They looked startled.

'Got a light, mate?'

Maroc addressed the taller one who, after a nervous glance at his companion, reached into his pocket. He produced a lighter.

'Shit, I've just remembered, I've given up. I intend to live a long and healthy life.

He looked at the shorter one.

'Know what I mean?'

Before either could recover, he continued.

'You visiting someone? Perhaps in the intensive care ward?'

'You trying to be funny, mate?'

The shorter one turned on him, giving him the full mean look. His companion tugged at his arm.

'Let's go, Al. Just another weirdo.'

Al hesitated, still in aggressive mode. Maroc could see the man's reluctance to back down. His need to save face.

'Let's go. Now!'

The man called Al hissed at Maroc.

'You're one lucky bastard.'

With that, he turned and followed his more prudent friend. Maroc stood, looking at their retreating backs, a grim smile on his face. Interesting day so far.

Realising he had been gone a while, Maroc returned to the spacious reception area. He felt he could use another coffee. Perhaps something stronger.

Maroc found Emily and her father where he had left them. They were both adamant in their decision to stay. They would spend the night, either inside the hospital or somewhere nearby. Maroc agreed, and after a discussion with the ward sister, they came to an arrangement.

Emily would not leave her brother's bedside. She would sleep in a chair if need be. The sister assured her she would be provided with a comfortable reclining chair for the purpose. Southwell and Maroc would find a motel nearby.

Four hours later, Emily and Southwell were still by Malcolm's bedside. Maroc had returned from an aimless walk around the hospital grounds. All three now sat in silence, prisoners of their troubling thoughts.

The heart monitor gave an alarming high-pitched whistle. Emily rose quickly from her seat, desperately looking towards the door for help. The response was immediate, a nurse entered, checking both Malcolm and the noisy monitor.

Mr Wood, whom Maroc thought must have been

waiting for this event, appeared within seconds. The nurse pulled a screen around Malcolm's bed, and both she and the surgeon disappeared from view. Before Emily could stop him, Southwell decided to follow them inside, desperate for answers.

The small specialist had his hands full, and a nurse led a distressed Southwell out of the screened area. Emily took charge, suggesting all three vacate the cramped ward.

They stood, huddled together in the corridor. No one spoke, and Maroc extended his arm around the other two.

They were eventually noticed by a male nurse. Smiling sympathetically, he suggested they would be more comfortable sitting down in a nearby waiting room.

At first, Emily refused to leave her place by the ward door, wishing to remain close to her brother. The nurse promised that all three would be immediately alerted if Malcolm's condition worsened. She yielded to his suggestion.

The nurse led them a short distance before ushering them into a small waiting room. They were offered hot drinks. This time, all three accepted gratefully.

An hour passed with Southwell wanting to look for the specialist. Emily snapped back into professional mode, suggesting they waited a bit longer.

Wood appeared, looking solemn. Emily and Max were on their feet. At first, the specialist said nothing. Maroc was about to tell him to get on with it when he spoke.

'He went a couple of minutes ago. I'm deeply sorry

for your loss.'

Emily and Max froze, then turned to each other for comfort. Wood hovered before turning to Maroc.

'I'm afraid I have to leave you. Take as much time as you need. I'll be in my office for the next fifteen minutes when...'

He nodded his head towards Emily and Max.

Maroc nodded back, thanking him as he left. He turned to the others, placing both arms around them in a gentle embrace. They stood unmoving for some time, a doleful huddle in the centre of the small room.

Driving out of Salford, towards central Manchester, the man called Al turned to his companion and smiled nervously.

'Remember what we said. Just stick to the story.'

They had agreed it would not be in their interest to reveal that their target had engaged with them.

Instead, they would report a good outcome. Peter Maroc had been found. Their job was done for the day. They could go home.

Using his mobile, Al alerted the second team. He provided them with full details on both Maroc and his vehicle. The information should lead them to their man's base. After that, it would be up to their superiors to give further instructions.

CHAPTER 36

The conversation was predictably sparse on the drive back to Wales. Emily sat in the front seat beside Maroc. She kept her eyes fixed on the road ahead as though she were the driver. Her tears had stopped. Maroc found this harder to handle.

He checked on Southwell in the rear-view mirror. His face was ashen, his eyes fixed in a thousand-yard stare out of the side window. Maroc sighed. It would take a lot of time and care to reverse this new trauma.

The Black Mercedes had been following them the textbook three cars behind. He had spotted the tail a quarter of a mile out of the hospital car park. No surprise there.

Maroc had no real idea who was after him or of their motive. What other enemies did he have in the UK? The smart money would be on the Albanian mafia. He would be a fool in thinking the Fare was going to forget about him.

He thought of the bizarre sequence of events. They had got him, and they had lost him. Would this be another attempt at a snatch? If so, then Mark Fisher and Niels Johansson would be equally targeted.

Maroc had no doubt the Albanian and UK Fare would have a record of all members of the SAS team who had struck at the heart o their Lazarat drug operation.

If what was happening was Fare directed, he doubted if the occupants of the Merc would try anything today. Their brief would be to check on his routine, then pass the intel back to their masters.

Maroc was convinced he alone was the target. Johansson and Fisher would only be considered in the event of a failure to obtain what they needed from him.

He had no way of knowing the response within the organisation to the brother's bungling or of their attempt to cover their tracks.

He was convinced that the real action was to come, the time frame being anyone's guess. Maroc reckoned it would be soon. Two days, three days tops.

They finally reached Llanberis and found it cloaked in comforting darkness. The small town felt more like a haven than ever.

As they approached the house, Maroc spotted the Merc seventy yards up the narrow road. *Predictable bastards*, he thought. It would, however, be a mistake to believe he was dealing with amateurs. A fatal one.

Maroc helped his father-in-law out of the car. With Emily leading the way, he decided the baggage could be dealt with later. Southwell made his way to the front gate, moving like a sleepwalker.

Maroc did not attempt conversation. He realised the man needed some space for his grief.

He followed Southwell through the open front door, closing it behind him. While Emily was joined by her father in the living room, Maroc stood in the hallway, allowing them time to settle.

His anger, when it arrived, surprised him in its intensity. He was damned if he would allow interlopers to invade this refuge he had so recently reclaimed.

This was his domain, and these were his people. He would defend them.

It was time to gather his forces. Niels Johansson, he knew, would drop everything and be with him within a day. Like Maroc, he would be packed and ready.

They were two peas from the same pod when it came to all things military. However, Peter Maroc lacked the Norwegian's detached expedience when addressing certain life and death positions. He was glad of the distinction.

Mark Fisher and Bill Gordon would understand the significance of what was happening. They would not hesitate in joining him.

Dave Blandford was the only missing member of the Lazarat quartet. He would be sorely missed. Maroc decided he would need Fisher as the marksman if things escalated.

Fisher was in the UK. and would be eager to re-engage with the Fare. News of Dave's murder had affected him deeply. They had been mates. There was a score to settle.

Maroc thought of the women in his friend's lives. Jean Gordon would not be happy. As a soldier's wife, she knew it went with the territory. But Bill was no longer a member of any army.

Johansson was afforded more latitude. Or so he said.

He was never sure with Fisher. His private life was...complicated.

As for his position, the less Emily knew, the better. Prudence as well as consideration suggested he leave her and Max alone. He could make the right noises, but he could not take away their pain.

In any case, he needed time to think. His instincts screamed a clear warning. This threat was real.

In the event of a firefight, Maroc knew it would be conducted away from the town. Away from any witnesses. Whoever was after him, of one thing he was certain. They would choose somewhere remote to strike.

On his side, the team would have to agree on the necessary ordnance. The weaponry would have to include the L129A1 Sharpshooter rifle.

The rifle had a folding bipod stand at the business end and featured an extendable stock. Its accuracy over mid-range distances had been battle-tested. It was also a weapon Fisher was familiar with. Considering what he had in mind, it was the perfect tool.

His training allowed him to see the broader picture. He knew the safety of his family was not an immediate concern.

This lot was strictly surveillance. He was not certain, never certain. Still, Peter Maroc was pretty sure it was just him they were after.

If it was the Fare, targeting him, it would be a matter of expedience, not revenge. The organisation, after all, was a business, however illegal.

They would want him alive. Also, they would use their people, not hire from the UK. No, it was not the Fare.

If he were a betting man, he knew where he'd place his money. Maroc was becoming increasingly confident the whole operation had been initiated by the two bastards who had attempted his extraction. The Albanian brothers were getting rid of a loose end.

After the debacle leading to his escape, they could hardly have returned to the Fare and confessed to their bungling. He remembered snatches of their conversation and knew the organisation needed something from him.

With most of his memory restored, he knew what that something was. The location of the drugs and cash his team had relieved them of.

The brothers or their hired guns would wait until he was isolated. Somewhere remote. Their agenda differed from that of the Fare since they needed nothing from him. If they were to succeed, Peter Maroc would not emerge alive.

Maroc joined Emily and Max in the living room. Once again, he realised there was nothing he could do, nothing he could say that would make it easier for them.

Outside in the street, dangerous people wished them harm. This was no game played by civilised people. Maroc knew he had unwittingly brought the fight home to his family, and he needed to act. He needed to identify the occupants of the black Mercedes.

Nodding briefly to Emily, Maroc gestured towards the door to the hallway. When she followed him into the hall, he turned to his wife.

'I won't be long, Em.'

Taking the stairs two at a time he walked quickly to the front bedroom. Using only the hall light, he worked in semi-darkness. Opening the bottom drawer of the chest of drawers, he took out his dSLR camera with the Astroscope night vision module attachment.

Maroc had recently bought the expensive

Astroscope lens arrangement in Germany. With it, he was able to capture identifiable photos in low light conditions.

Crossing the small bedroom, he reached the window overlooking the road. He saw the Merc was still parked in the same spot.

Outside, the light had not completely gone, and he could just make out the two occupants. Judging by the distance and the poor light, he conjectured he could open the window without being noticed.

Maroc adjusted the camera focus, bringing the driver and his passenger into sharp relief. Pressing and holding the shutter, he took a dozen shots. When he had finished, he carefully closed the bedroom window.

He examined the results on the small camera screen. The photos would not win prizes. Still, they were good enough. He would recognise the pair if he saw them again.

Maroc returned downstairs where he found Emily trying to tempt her father with some homemade soup. Max was seated by the fireside, staring listlessly into the flames. He seemed hardly conscious of her efforts.

'Is there anything I can do, Em?'

He saw how drained she looked; they both looked.

'Why don't you guys retire for the night? OK, you might not sleep but at least you can rest better lying down.'

It was kindly meant, but she knew him better than he knew himself.

'Get yourself to the boozer, husband. You've earned it.'

She gave a wan smile. He took her in his arms, realising how lucky he was.

'See you later, Max.'

Southwell lifted his head and gave a small wave. There was the ghost of a smile.

Exiting the house, Maroc ignored the black car. He felt relatively safe as he walked away from the vehicle. Continuing up the narrow road, he took a left turn which would take him to a favourite pub in town.

Tonight, Peter Maroc would allow himself some time with his friends. Tomorrow, he would let the enemy come to him. He patted his jacket and smiled grimly. You could never be too careful.

CHAPTER 37

Malcolm's death had affected John. Perhaps more than even he'd expected. He felt no sadness for the loss of a younger brother, not in the way the others felt it. An intelligent man, he possessed sufficient self-awareness to recognise this.

Never one for deep self-analysis, he found no reason to correct his behaviour just to assuage the feelings of others. For monitory or strategic gain? Well, that was different.

He would miss the benchmark Malcolm had brought to his life. As a constant disappointment to his father, John could look at his brother and recognise someone further down the scale of achievements. He knew this in no way elevated his status. However, it was some consolation.

He thought of how he would conduct himself in response to this...tragedy. Those who knew him would not be fooled by an outward display of grieving.

Southwell would elect solemnity over sorrow. For briefer acquaintances, the distinction would go unnoticed.

He would have to travel to the UK. Bloody inconvenient, but there was never the right time. However, when life handed you a lemon, etc... Ever the opportunist, he would apply himself; find the advantage in this reversal. It was something he was good at.

John Southwell was aware of how each member of the family would react according to his or her nature. Both sisters would feel the loss.

His brother, Malcolm had always recognised the inherent vulnerability in his younger sister, Jill. She had looked up to him; made him feel valued. In turn, he had become her buffer, a shield against all hurts. Emily, without doubt, the strongest of them all, had loved Malcolm unconditionally.

Emily. He must contact her. This would be difficult, bloody difficult. She had always been able to see through his artifice, his lies. He must get it over and done with. *God sakes, come on man, just do it!*

John was hoping she wouldn't answer, that he could leave it for another time. On hearing her voice, his mind went blank. Failing to get his words out, he willed himself to speak. Then...

'John, is that you?'

He realised his name had appeared on her phone. He had to answer.

'Emily? Awful news. The hospital just rang. They had my number from Malcolm's mobile. This is a massive loss to all of us.'

This was Emily he was talking to. He struggled to continue.

One interminable hour later he replaced the receiver. He stood for a while, cringing at the recollection. Talking to Emily forced him to see his true face. With her, there was nowhere to hide.

After the ritual of comforting had come the inevitable question. Who could have done such a terrible thing? John Southwell, usually the first to offer his informed opinion, had no suggestions. None that would satisfy his intelligent sister.

Her tearful goodbye echoing in his head, he found himself shaking. He looked around his office for the bottle of Jack Daniels. He badly needed a drink.

John Southwell had his theories. The mob had run out of patience; made their final collection. A jealous husband or partner had exacted his revenge. He favoured the former.

His little brother had been playing games with the devil. He had thought himself fireproof. Living a delusional life, Malcolm had failed to recognise the simple law of karma. Actions have consequences. Now he was dead.

Southwell was keenly aware of how a police investigation could reveal damning evidence that could lead to his door. If the plot to eliminate Maroc were to come to light, it would be the end of him.

Malcolm had failed to listen to his frequent cautions regarding his lifestyle and the company he kept. Of course, there would be an investigation. His mind replayed every phone conversation he'd had with his brother.

He wondered if Malcolm had kept diaries or made notes that would put both of them in the frame. For now, it was all he could do. Wonder. And worry.

One piece of good news was Maroc's sudden and mysterious disappearance. Malcolm's hired hands had done their job. The whole thing had cost a packet, but he was determined to view it as an investment for the future. He wondered if there would be a future for him, as a free man.

Malcolm had reported a substantial change in his father's health. No longer the bedridden invalid, Max Southwell was now beyond John's reach. His depressed state was a thing of the past. The old bastard had been restored to his insufferable self.

Malcolm, why the hell did you have to be so weak? I'd have bailed you out myself. You only had to ask.

Southwell knew this was a lie; would only have been true if he had the gift of anticipation. Like his younger brother, it was another quality he lacked.

This was all Maroc's doing. Not for the first time, Southwell hoped his brother-in-law's demise had been both painful and protracted.

A lot to think about. Much planning to do. John Southwell had to cover his tracks.

The next calls would be to his co-directors. His wife Ruth and his sister Jill. His younger sister, still tearful at the loss of the only significant male in her life would present no problem. Ruth would not be so easy to influence.

His wife was a cold and distant woman. She was more than a match for Southwell. His wish was to journey to Wales on his own. To get away, if only for a few weeks.

His attempts at reasoning, that it would be cheaper for him to travel alone got him nowhere. When he had suggested the business would suffer without her to oversee it, she had laughed in his face.

Southwell rang Qantas, booking two business class tickets. He made a mental note for it to feature as a necessary business expense on his tax returns.

He needed something to calm his frayed nerves. His gaze returned to the bottle on his desk. He thought better of it. Less mind-dulling relaxation could be found with the lovely Cherry. Would she be available at such short notice? He dialled Sweet Endings.

His thoughts turned to Ruth. A dark-haired stair rod of a woman, he wondered if there had ever been an attraction between them. Spending so much time in her company was not something he anticipated with relish. God knows why she wanted to come. Probably to keep him out of trouble.

He had found, early in their relationship, that the woman had never shown signs of enjoying his company. Yet they had married. His mind travelled back to those early days.

Ruth's family had wealth, and John was always looking for seed money for his many projects. When she had hinted at approaching her father for an investment in his business, her appeal had skyrocketed. Twelve years on, found himself financially tied to the bloody woman.

Back in his office, Southwell gloomily considered the next few days. His favourite lady had not been available at the massage parlour and he had decided to save his money. He dreaded the long flight to Manchester.

Ruth was a woman who had little talent or use for small talk. He supposed there would be some diversion in his laptop and book. He sighed deeply, his gaze once again drifting to the bottle on his desk.

CHAPTER 38

Maroc was on the phone with Niels Johansson. He could hear his wife Eva in the background.

'Give him my love.'

Johansson laughed.

'She might change her mind when she finds out why you called.'

Maroc shook his head and grinned hugely.

'Never, mate.'

Eva had a soft spot for Maroc. She hated it when her husband was away on ops. In this, she was like most of the wives in his exclusive circle.

Eva trusted Maroc to take care of him. That had always made him smile. As if a man like Johansson needed taking care of.

Well, that was not exactly true. The mad Norwegian did need him there if only to minimise the body count.

'Heard about Dave, so you can count me in. Any opportunity to get back at those bastards. I tell you, Maroc, they are dead.'

Always a way with words, Maroc thought. He also knew his words could be backed by deadly action.

'How soon can you get over, Niels? Sooner the better for me.'

'See you tomorrow, sometime in the evening.

Where do you live now, Peter? You are like a bloody Gypsy. Here, there. Bloody everywhere!'

'I'm back with Emily in the same house in Llanberis. Do you remember that town in the mountains? The one with the good pubs?'

The question was rhetorical. Johansson had made quite an impact on the locals.

'Same house? I remember the long house.'

'Yes, the same house. I'll text you the address.'

'It's not a problem, Maroc. I remember my way there. No worries.'

He paused.

'Everything OK with Emily? She still loves you?'

Maroc gave an obscene reply. He heard Eva in the background.

'I'm listening to you, Peter. Bad boy!'

He grinned and blushed. He hardly ever swore. And never in the company of women.

'Niels, this one has to be called in. We need it sanctioned by the MOD.'

It was as Maroc had anticipated. Johansson started protesting indignantly. Maroc pointed out that their chances of acquiring and using serious ordnance on British soil would be the quickest way to a prison sentence. And, how the hell could they justify a firefight in their backyard?

'They'll want to send in an armed police response unit to the scene. They'll just get in the bloody way, Peter.'

Maroc stopped him.

'Don't think they will this time, mate. This was always our operation. We know better than anyone what we're up against. Anyway, the MOD needs all loose ends neatly tied. They're viewing it as a continuation of our operation in Albania. The job's practically sanctioned already.'

'How do you know all this?

'Bill Gordon has some connections at Sterling Lines. He's had the nod from the Director Special Forces. That's all I know. The powers that be were not happy about my abduction. They reasoned that the Fare won't let this rest until they get their cash and narcotics back. Not to mention some payback.'

'The DSF himself is giving us a clear run?'

'I believe he is on this one. They need to be kept in the loop all the way. Anyway, Niels, if any of the bastards are killed, or injured, we'll need someone to sort it. Cart them off. What would we do with them?'

'I could tell you, Peter, but you probably wouldn't like it.'

Maroc's next call was to Mark Fisher. Fisher was immediately up for it. Maroc had anticipated this, however, he felt he had to clarify things to his friend.

'You understand mate, this one's a freebie.'

The statement was unnecessary and potentially an affront. Fisher, however, took no offence.

'Understood, Peter. This has to be put to bed. Not just for Dave, but all our sakes. We have families.'

Bill Gordon had expected the call. Both he and Maroc had known the Albanian Mafia would not allow the raid on their compound in Lazarat to go unanswered. They had lost money and property. They had also lost face.

Maroc had known of Gordon's friendship with the Director Special Forces. He knew the two had a history but had never questioned the Scotsman.

The SAS patrol that had originally carried out the raid in Lazarat would be the best choice in dealing with further incidents on UK soil. Furthermore, Peter Maroc had first-hand knowledge of the combat area.

Gordon and Maroc were considered a safe pair of hands. They could be trusted to contain the situation. The operation would be a sanctioned one. All the ordnance to be supplied by Hereford.

While Maroc was relieved to have everyone on board, he would not have expected less of his comrades. They were the best of the best.

He knew the coming week would bring its inherent dangers. As with any armed encounter, there was always the risk some might not make it. He prayed there would be no fatalities. At least not on their side.

Niels Johansson breezed in the following evening. He smiled hugely on seeing Maroc, stepping forward and giving him one of his bear hugs.

In civvy street, the SAS man was as safe as a pistol without a firing pin. It would be hard to find a more affable companion.

Women found him charming; quite sweet. In truth, Johansson was all of those things. Men got on well with him, finding him very much a man's man without being intimidating. He could be pushed further than most without reacting.

In the field, it was different. Efficient; sometimes ruthless, his decisions and actions were governed by expediency rather than morality. Maroc trusted him with his life and often had. It had worked both ways.

Neither Emily nor Max Southwell was in any mood to socialise. Aware of this, Johansson had moderated his usual exuberance. His sympathy was sincere, and both father and daughter recognised and appreciated its genuineness.

Maroc was conscious of the strain on Emily and her father to keep up the small talk. He had suggested he and Johansson find a pub. There, they could talk and plan.

The Norwegian had fallen in love with Welsh pubs. Although singing in such establishments had been restricted in the late seventies and early eighties, this ruling had always been at the discretion of the landlord.

Johansson, a surprisingly good baritone, had in the past, delighted the locals with a few offerings in Norsk. This evening, however, would be given to more serious matters. They had a lot to discuss if their counteraction was to succeed.

Emily and Southwell received a highly edited version of what had happened to Maroc during his absence. When things became more settled, less threatening, he could be more honest.

Johansson's visit was presented as that of a concerned friend, checking in on his buddy. Neither Emily nor Southwell possessed the energy to query this.

First light saw both men heading to Hereford in Johansson's hired four-track. An early pick-up meant less curious eyes. There was also a lot of setting up needed before the others arrived.

The armoury at SAS headquarters, Credenhill had been informed of their requirements. Bill Gordon had sorted the preliminaries. This would make the procedure that much quicker. Both Maroc and Johansson were known faces and Maroc did not anticipate a problem.

Johansson suggested night vision goggles and body armour. Maroc had already included them on his list. The Norwegian had largely approved the list but requested a change of handguns.

Maroc respected that each man had his weapon of choice, and Johansson favoured the Sig Sauer P226 semi-automatic pistol. It was a popular choice, with its fifteen-round magazine. Maroc had carried it when on his last mission in Albania.

Throughout his service, Maroc's first choice had always been the lighter Glock 17. It felt good in his hand. To Johansson, the polymer-framed Glock would always be a plastic toy. To each his own.

Maroc insisted on three assault rifles. He and Johansson agreed on the German-made HK G36. The rifles would be essential if they were to be effective at a distance. They assumed the opposition would be similarly equipped.

Handguns were more concealable when it came to taking prisoners. It made the process less visible to enquiring eyes during their transportation. The powers that be had specified capture rather than kill.

It was not exactly a black op, where the government would refute all knowledge or accountability. However, it was made clear there would be a limit to their support if things went badly wrong. The two men drove home in silence.

With the death of David Blandford, each man on the team had to rethink his life. They had been SAS, and death was a part of their day-to-day reality.

However, Blandford had been a friend, known to their wives; their families. There would be pressure from their partners.

Eva Johansson had, at first, given her husband an ultimatum. He was to grow up and face his responsibilities. Or else!

Johansson had explained the necessity of this last mission to his wife. The enemy had left them with little choice. The four friends could not have trouble brought to their door. Place their families at risk.

She had understood, as he knew she would. Still, Johansson had been warned.

Maroc had been affected by his brutal treatment at the hands of the Albanian brothers. On his return to Wales, there had been a sea change in his attitude towards his family; his life.

He acknowledged he could no longer get away with being an active combatant. However, this threat was different. It could involve people he loved. It needed sorting.

Despite their respective epiphanies and sombre declarations, neither Maroc nor Johansson had outgrown their laddish needs for adventure.

Total honesty would have them admit that their regret at being selfish bastards was always retrospective. When they were in the thick of it, it was a game of cowboys and Indians. They loved it.

CHAPTER 39

The surveillance team relayed their report to their bosses in Manchester. They remained unaware of having been spotted and identified by Maroc.

Going as planned. Target returned to N Wales. More details on location and movement to follow.

Don Wilson received the report with some satisfaction. He would pass the news to his clients. He had no problem working with foreigners as long as they showed professionalism.

The Albanian brothers had convinced him they knew what they were doing. He did not have to like them.

Wilson picked up the phone and contacted the surveillance team in Llanberis. He relayed his instructions in a clear, non-ambiguous manner that even the slowest of his employees could understand.

'Book yourself into a hotel, keep on his tail. I want to know who he meets and where he goes. And for god's sake, try to blend in. Get as much info as you can on this Maroc. Call me if you find anything unusual, is that clear?'

After the call, George, the youngest of the men, could not hide his delight as he turned to his companion.

'Blend in? We can do that. It'll be great being a

tourist for a couple of days. Oh yes, I can live with that!'

He was tall and gangly; his straggly pale blond hair fell forward, obscuring part of his thin face. He looked like an unhealthy teenager.

'Bout time we had a holiday. A holiday in bloody Wales. Weather's right for it. This job's going to be a doddle.'

His companion, older by a couple of years, grinned his agreement. He was short and powerfully built. Well-groomed, with professionally cut short auburn hair, he was the more sensible of the two. They laughed like kids, enjoying their treat, confident the job would go well.

Maroc had the feeling the tails would soon be leaving the refuge of their car. It would be an ideal opportunity to drop a little disinformation their way.

To Maroc and Johansson, these clowns were far from great field operators. Their inexperience would be put to good use.

The mood in the house remained unchanged, with Maroc feeling helpless in the face of such grief. He and Johansson had decided to back off; give Max and Emily some space.

With father and daughter operating on remote, their attempt at lightening the mood would not only be ill-advised but could be misconstrued. The two soldiers would leave the house.

Maroc and Johansson would put themselves out in the open where they could be seen and, more importantly, heard. Maroc had informed Johansson of his intent with 'Laurel and Hardy.' It would be an opportunity to wrong-foot the opposition.

A friendly pub, serving good beer, *The Heights*

was arguably the best place in town. Whenever the Norwegian had visited, drinking had been mandatory. Both he and Maroc would usually start and end at The Heights Hotel.

On ops, it was a different story. Both men were professionals, serving with arguably the most professional unit on earth. To Johansson, excessive drinking and work were mutually exclusive. Maroc agreed.

The weather was the warmest it had been all year. The friends decided that a walk around the small town would be both pleasant and productive. Maroc was determined to discover more about the two visitors. He had to know the reason for their being on his home turf.

To Maroc, the tourist trade was a growing annoyance. The town had always been a popular centre for climbers and serious walkers. This had always been fine with him.

Over the last few years, especially on weekends, the place had begun attracting a less serious element. Had he become a snob, or was he just getting old?

Within twenty minutes of walking, Johansson had spotted pale blond and thin. When he looked in his direction, the man, made a production of looking into a shop window. It was going to plan.

Maroc suggested taking a stroll to the shore of the beautiful lake Padarn, which lay on the northeastern part of town. On walking the short distance, they toyed with the idea of hiring one of the rowing boats moored at the furthest end of the lake. It was tempting, but perhaps for another day. This was work, after all.

They decided to drop into one of the small cafes. It would be an opportunity to see what their tail would do. Would he follow them in, amuse them with his studied nonchalance?

They ordered coffee, and after fifteen minutes of sipping and chatting, there was still no sign of their pallid friend. They decided to give him another five minutes.

The five minutes expired, and he had still not appeared. Maroc and Johansson paid and left.

Maroc spotted the second man on the other side of the road. The photographs he had taken were clear enough to identify him with little room for doubt.

The man immediately averted his gaze. Taking out his mobile phone, he treated them to a convincing display of casual conversation, complete with laughter.

Maroc smiled. *Another star is born,* he thought.

The SAS man checked his watch. He decided it was time for a real drink. It was also time to see how dumb these two out-of-towners were. As they walked back to The Heights, Maroc and Johansson rehearsed their pub act. They both found it hard not to laugh out loud.

They would enact a scene of a couple of friends planning a pleasant day out. Maroc was confident they would come. He was banking on it.

Could anyone be that stupid? Peter Maroc guessed these two might well be.

Johansson suggested they sit at the bar. He settled onto the high stool and ordered the beers. Less than five minutes had passed before the bar-room door opened.

Both tails arrived and made straight for the bar,

sitting within feet of the soldiers. Showtime!

'You want some great local fishing? I know just the spot, and I can do better than that. I'll take you there. Day after tomorrow.'

Niels took his cue.

'What about equipment. I've brought nothing with me. Not even a rod.'

'Not a problem. I'll have everything you need. Rod, net, a bag with all the gear. And as many flies, as you want.'

'So, are we fishing river or lake?'

'Lake. Right up in the mountains from the A4086. We'll make a start from Pen y Pass. Park opposite the hotel. That'll get us on to the Miner's Path.'

He spelt each name carefully.

'A bit of a trek from the road, but hell, we're young!'

Johansson was getting into his role, laughing at Maroc's weak joke.

'What's this lake called. Something I can pronounce?'

'Llyn Llydaw.'

Maroc spelt it out carefully. He could see the burly one furiously writing on a beer mat. His partner, sitting next to Maroc had his phone on the bar no more than a couple of feet away. Maroc guessed he had it on voice record.

He had to smile. The man was a pro.

Both he and Johansson knew the whole setup went beyond corny. But hell, they were not performing for the Oscars. He looked over at Johansson, and both tried hard not to corpse.

Maroc had given the men everything they would need to report back to whoever sent them. Mancunian accents? Most definitely. It was too early to draw solid conclusions from this.

Finally, their drinking buddies decided they had heard enough. They had the time, day and place; even how to get there. They were happy. The tails finished their drinks, exiting without a sideways glance.

'Is the fishing that good?'

For some reason, Johansson was curious.

'How the hell should I know? It's bloody cold, I can vouch for that.'

'Peter, you're a mad bastard.'

Laughing like idiots, Maroc ordered the next round. He turned to face Johansson and added meaningfully.

'It's also very out of the way.'

They had identified the kill zone. It was now a matter of setting up and waiting.

CHAPTER 40

Back in their hotel room, George, the blond Mancunian was complaining about his mattress. His bulkier companion, Simon, signalled him to be silent. He was on the phone with the Manchester office.

Simon was surprised when Jimmy Wilson picked up. Don had been away on business on the day of their departure from Manchester. He had expected the older brother, to have returned to the office by now.

His brother Jimmy had made all the arrangements for the surveillance job. However, it was understood Don would take up the case as soon as he got back.

Jimmy seemed on edge, cagey. Something was not quite right.

'You sure they're not onto you? I mean, perfectly bloody sure?'

'You mean Maroc and his mate?'

'Who the hell else would I mean for Chrissakes!'

'They haven't a clue Mr Wilson. We blended in, just like you… I mean your brother said.'

'Well, you make bloody sure you keep it that way. You tooled up?'

'Always, boss.'

One thing Simon had picked up on. Jimmy Wilson liked to be called boss.'

'Got my Beretta 9 mm. George brought the SA 80

from the storeroom, just as you suggested. That's in the boot of the car. It's well hidden. No worries.'

Neither Simon nor George had a clue as to why Jimmy Wilson insisted they carry. Especially a serious weapon like the SA80. After all, this was meant to be a surveillance job.

'A scope! Have you got a scope for the rifle?'

Simon nodded, then realised he had to speak.

'Yea, boss. Rifle plus scope.'

Wilson's tone became conspiratorial.

'Listen, Simon. The Albanians want to off Maroc themselves. Fair doos. I sympathise and all that. If we can do the job for them, it'll be a feather in our cap. Know what I mean?'

This was a completely different ball game. It was taking things to another level and Simon was not happy.

'Boss, Mr Donald definitely...'

'Just do what you're bloody told. I want you to off Maroc. If his mate is with him, you do em both. Right?'

There was a noticeable pause before Simon responded.

'Understood, boss.'

Jimmy Wilson could tell Simon was unhappy. He also knew the change of orders went directly against what had been arranged. Their lads would find the target. The Albanian brothers would do the wet work.

He was sick of being the little brother. Whatever the Albanians had decided with his brother, it stood to reason they'd appreciate the job being done for them. Why wouldn't they? Anyway, wet work came at an extra cost. A win-win all around.

Jimmy continued.

'Did I mention the bonus? Couple of grand each if you do the job and cap the two.'

Simon looked at his partner, who was nodding like an idiot. He shrugged, realising he had no choice if he wanted to continue breathing.

'OK, boss. If we can get them on their own, we'll do the job.'

'Good boy. But be bloody careful. You're not dealing with the local bobbies. This Maroc's a tricky bastard. They both are.'

The phone went dead. This was Jimmy Wilson's way of ending a conversation with the hired hand.

Turning to George, Simon began voicing his reservations. This change of plan was rash. What was being asked went way beyond their skillset.

Looking at his less cerebral partner, he knew he would be wasting his breath. Simon had seen that dreamy look before. George was already spending the bonus.

When shooters were involved, things became unpredictable. Dammit, he had to say something before things got out of hand.

'Georgie.'

George's head jerked up.

'Told you not to call me that. I'm not a bloody kid.'

'Sorry, mate... George. We should wait for Don to return to the office and take this up with him. Could even get him on his mobile, though I don't like doing that, it being just for emergencies.'

'This isn't a bloody emergency though? We've been handed two grand. Each! Let's not bugger this up by going through Don. Anyway, he can't say anything seeing as it's his brother that put us up to it.'

Simon looked up, considering his partner's perspective, wanting to see sense in it. After all, two grand was two grand. Anyway, by contacting Don, they might end up pissing off both brothers.

CHAPTER 41

Bill Gordon was on the phone first thing. 'How are things progressing, mate?'

'Niels is already here. We have a couple of shadows in town, Bill. Mancunian accents.'

'You think the Fare's sent them?'

Maroc considered this.

'It's not like the Fare to contract out when it comes to sensitive internal matters. Sure, if they needed specialist talent for a job or they were looking for a supplier.'

He paused.

'On the other hand, the Fare might hire Brits when operating in rural North Wales. My money is still on the Albanian brothers, sending out eyes and ears. They wouldn't come themselves. They'd stand out like a sore thumb.'

'So, who else have you pissed off?'

Maroc considered.

'No idea, Bill, unless there's a jealous husband somewhere.'

Gordon chuckled. 'Come off it. You haven't looked at another woman since Emily.'

His tone became serious.

'So, you reckon you're pretty safe, I mean, for now. These boys aren't the hit squad?'

'Pretty certain their recce, and bad at it. Anyway, the Fare would want me alive. Same with Mark and Niels.'

'And the brothers?'

Maroc was silent for a moment.

'I'm wondering what they'd have told their bosses when they got back to Lazarat.'

'What are you saying mate?'

'If the Fare believed I'd got away from those two idiots, they'd have put the word out. It wouldn't have taken them long to find me in Vlore. After all, the British consul found me easily enough.'

'Wasn't that through a friend of the family you were with?'

'Yes, the interpreter. But the Fare has ears everywhere. I can't believe, as a foreigner, I could have stayed there as long as I did without being noticed.'

Gordon was thinking, trying to process what Maroc had told him.

'Let's get this clear. You reckon the Fare thinks you're dead. That the brothers told them they'd killed you?

'It's a thought, Bill. It would be viewed as less of a blunder than admitting I'd escaped and able to warn off the others in the patrol.'

Bill Gordon paused.

'It's a fair theory, Peter. If it is the brothers, then we could be looking at a hit.'

'Bloody confusing, I know. If the Fare knew I was still alive, they'd be toast. So, it could be a hit. My guess is they'd want that pleasure for themselves.'

'So, we're back to the two tails being just that. A recce crew.'

Maroc nodded.

'That's my gut feeling. They don't look that dangerous.'

'But they could be. So it means you being bloody careful'

Maroc heard the tension in his friend's voice. They both knew another death would be unacceptable.

Emily seemed better, but Max was still inconsolable. To him, Malcolm had been the runt of the litter. He should have done more to protect him. Showed him more affection.

Maroc looked at his father-in-law, knowing what he was going through. Southwell had told him enough about his children and his perceived guilt at how they had developed as individuals.

Loss was one thing. Loss, combined with such guilt would be a bitch to overcome. Maroc knew from personal experience. No amount of reasoning from him would change that.

Give it time, Maroc thought. *Everything is dulled by time, eventually.*

Emily had become aware she was neglecting her house guest. For his part, Johansson felt nothing but sympathy and admiration for this beautiful woman. However, conveying it in the right manner would always be tricky.

When Maroc suggested he and Johansson got out of their way, perhaps do a bit of fishing, she busied herself in the kitchen, making a small hamper of food. The men knew better than to protest.

His wife was that rare mix of matriarch and warrior. If Emily had a weakness, it was Peter Maroc. She had, in the past, made the error of allowing him the freedom to exercise his dangerous passions.

She had been comfortable with the climbing, knowing he worked within strict margins of safety. The soldiering to god knew where had been much harder to accept.

Despite her objections, he would always justify his actions, promising her this would be his last op. Worn out by the stress of never knowing he would return, she had finally thrown him out.

In all other respects, Maroc had been a good and loving husband. However, she had deemed the missions, jobs or whatever the hell he called them, to be unforgivable indulgences.

She had called him a selfish, uncaring bastard. His large bonuses that were hers to spend as she liked, meant nothing. Emily had made it clear that she needed a husband, not a generous acquaintance.

The love between them had never waned. Her resentment, however, had grown to a point where she had ordered him to go. It was over. No, she no longer felt anything for him. Not a damn thing. She just wanted him out.

By eight in the morning, he and Johansson were loading the Maserati in preparation for the drive to Cwm Idwal. There they would try their hand at some lake fishing.

Maroc thought back to a few days ago. How he had been there with Southwell. A lot had happened since then.

They were on their way up the daunting Llanberis pass road when Maroc glanced at his rear-view mirror. He turned to Johansson.

'We've got company.'

Johansson flipped down his sun visor and adjusted the vanity mirror.

'Why are they still here. They've got everything they needed.'

Maroc nodded his agreement.

'Unless there's been a change of plan. I'm not sure I like this. You carrying?'

Johansson nodded.

'You can never be too careful.'

Maroc grinned. It was their mantra.

The winding road became a steep descent, a metal barrier shielding them from a steep drop to the right. The black Merc was staying well back. At the bottom, they turned left onto the A 4086 towards the small hamlet of Capel Curig. Maroc checked his mirror as he drove.

They were a good hundred yards away from where they had turned when the Merc finally appeared. It maintained the same distance behind them. They entered Capel Curig before turning left onto the A5 road to their destination.

'I don't like this, Peter.'

Johansson's hand went inside his jacket.

'They have all the info. Why the hell are they following us now?'

His eyes switched from the visor mirror to Maroc.

'What do you want to do?'

Maroc glanced in his rear-view mirror.

'Let's just carry on and see where this takes us.'

'If it's a hit, I wonder what they're carrying.'

Maroc said nothing. The road continued with lake Ogwen on their right. Today, the lake was as still as a millpond. Mount Tryfan loomed to their left.

'OK, we're just about there. Let's see if Laurel and Hardy follow us into the parking lot.'

Johansson had his head out of the car window. Craning his neck, he looked back up the road.

'They've dropped back about three hundred meters.'

Maroc swung left into the Mountain Rescue parking area and waited. There was no sign of the Merc. Johansson climbed out and looked back up the road.

Using his Mini Pentax binoculars, he could just see the Merc parked on the lake side of the road. It was almost obscured by a small blue van.

'They've stopped by the side of the lake. It's a couple of hundred meters away Peter.'

'OK, if they want a target, I'll give them one.'

Johansson threw him a questioning look.

'I've got a flak jacket with SAPI plate inserts. It's in the back of the car. We were testing them out when I was working in West Germany a few months ago.'

Maroc opened the small boot.

'I took one as a souvenir.'

He took out the khaki flak jacket.

'They'll stop a high-velocity round, allegedly.'

'What? What?'

Johansson looked at Maroc as if he'd lost his mind.

'You crazy, Peter?'

Maroc gave his friend an impatient look. He reached into the boot for his fly rod.

'Are we going fishing or not?'

Johansson continued to look at Maroc, wondering what else he would produce from the car boot. Maroc, lifting his head, snapped at the Norwegian.

'Let's get going, man. We'll head straight for the lake

and set up there. We can talk as we go.'

He trotted off and Johansson took one last look at the Black Merc. Shaking his head, he reluctantly followed the Welshman.

'We'll take the path through the little gully to the right of the main stone path.' He pointed up, leading the way. 'It's a slightly quicker route to the lake. I know where we can set up.'

'Set up with what, for god's sake? All I have is my Sig. We may be up against scoped rifles.'

'Trust me, I have a cunning plan.'

'Jesus Peter, this isn't funny.'

Maroc turned around and faced his friend.

'We're not up against combat soldiers, Niels. Sure, they can fire weapons, but you've seen them. A real firefight would scare them shitless. My guess is, these boys are fine when the odds are well in their favour.'

'And this isn't one of those times? If they've got rifles...'

He let the rest of the sentence hang in the air.

'As I said. I have a plan. I'll wear the body armour and you can set up just behind the wall. The one with the wooden stile over it.'

'I have a Sig Sauer 9mm Peter. Like your Glock, an effective hitting distance of what? 50 meters? What bloody use is that?'

Johansson shook his head. He trusted his friend. Had good cause to trust him. Most of Maroc's tactics in the field were solid, sometimes brilliant. There were other times when both had survived through a smile from the gods.

'The jacket could pass as a fishing jacket. I'll set up my rod and stuff by the lake.'

'Brilliant, my friend. Why don't you tie yourself to a post and make like a billy goat?'

Maroc grinned and made bleating noises.

'You can spot them with the binos. The first sign of a rifle being set up, you empty your mag at them. Seriously, I can't see them staying around for more.'

Maroc reached into his jacket.

'If you run out, then use this.'

He unholstered his Glock 17, offering it to Johansson.

The Norwegian shook his head.

'I always carry two spare mags.'

He looked directly at his friend.

'I have a feeling, this is not going to be our finest hour.'

'It'll be a doddle.'

Maroc waved and started down to the lake. He kept level with the wall, leaving Johansson to climb over it. Maroc knew his friend was not as apprehensive as he made out. They had been in far worse shit and survived. They were two elite soldiers against amateurs. What could go wrong?

The ground sloped gently down to the lake, and he could no longer see Johansson. The tails would probably follow the main stone path, approaching them from the north.

He looked around for other walkers or climbers in the area. It was still relatively early and the place was deserted. He prayed it remained so. At least for the next hour.

Twenty minutes passed. Maroc had finished putting his rod together when, in his peripheral vision, he spotted a movement fifty yards to his left, on the north side of the lake.

Two figures appeared over the rise. Although Maroc did not indicate having seen them, they quickly retreated. He was right between Johansson and the opposition.

Feeling exposed, Maroc was aware he was placing a lot of trust in the Norwegian, hoping his friend would react in time. Watch his back, as he had always done.

Another arena and they would have a better plan. A better kill zone backed up by better weapons. Two handguns did not cut it.

Still, this was a tourist beauty spot, not a war zone. The plan had been cobbled together at the last minute to fit the purpose. Not ideal.

Another five minutes passed; nothing! He had to turn around.

A marshy knoll behind him, no more than fifty yards away. He spotted the unmistakable silhouette of a shooter, the rifle barrel aimed in his direction. Maroc experienced an overwhelming sense of Deja vu.

A confusion of explosions. Half a dozen rapid shots from a semi-auto, followed immediately by a single rifle crack. The fishing bag to his left leapt into the air.

Maroc dropped hard to the ground, his left-hand grazing against something sharp. Another six to eight single shots in rapid succession, followed by a yelp of pain.

Pushing both hands hard against the ground, he sprang upright and ran south towards the wall where Johansson should be waiting.

He heard voices raised in anger above him and to his left. Ignoring them, he powered his legs and ran towards the only safe place.

Cover lay ten yards away, and he did not slow down as he approached the small stone wall.

Half vaulting, half scrambling, he was over. He saw his friend further up, still holding his semi-auto. He had stopped firing.

Maroc, still crouching, trotted towards the Norwegian. Johansson turned to him.

'Started shooting as soon as I saw the rifle in position. Sorry, Peter. The bastard got one off. My shot obviously threw him.'

Maroc looked at his friend in disbelief.

'Obviously? There was nothing less bloody obvious!'

Johansson looked at Maroc, grinning.

'You're still here, aren't you? Still breathing?'

Maroc ignored the comment.

'You hit him. I heard a yell.'

'Nothing serious. They're running off.'

The two men were about seventy yards away. One was carrying a rifle.

The other was holding a hand to the side of his head. Maroc thought he could see a ribbon of scarlet trickling down the man's hand.

He gave the Norwegian a quizzical look.

Johansson shrugged, only slightly embarrassed.

'That was an accurate piece of shooting. No real harm done, and no dead bodies all over the place. Look.'

Johansson pointed. Maroc could see walkers making their way to the lake.

He patted the Norwegian on the shoulder.

'I'll get my fly rod and gear. Let's give the bastards time to get clear.'

He nodded his head at the approaching walkers. 'We can't afford a public firefight.'

By the time they reached the car park, there was no sign of the black Mercedes.

CHAPTER 42

Mark Fisher arrived at Maroc and Emily's house early the following morning. Gordon rolled up an hour later in his spacious Range Rover.

The arms were transferred from Johansson's four-track to Bill Gordon's vehicle. An observer would have seen canvas bags along with a few boxes being loaded on board, nothing that would alarm the neighbours.

It was a half-hour drive to the Scotsman's place. Here they could be assured of privacy, away from curious eyes.

All four were gathered around the large desk in Gordon's office. They were discussing the plans for the weekend fishing trip. It was only two days away. A lot to arrange if things were to go to plan.

Bill Gordon had brought out a large Ordnance Survey map of the area. It covered Llydaw lake and the surrounding area. Now the opposition had revealed itself, both Johansson and Fisher doubted another attempt was imminent.

The enemy, whoever they were, had received a bloody nose. They would not be eager to re-engage anytime soon.

Gordon and Maroc took a different view. If the Albanian pair was behind all this, they would think Maroc and his trigger-happy SAS friend were satisfied they had scared off further attempts on their lives. At least for a while. It would be the ideal time for a further strike.

They argued back and forth until it was decided the fishing exercise was at least worth a punt. They should keep to the date and place as fed to the idiots in the pub. If no one turned up, they would have had a pleasant trip out to the mountains and lakes of Snowdonia.

Finally, Johansson stated his disappointment regarding the last encounter at Idwal lake. It should have been the Albanian pair, not a couple of hapless Brits. Those sorry Mafia bastards would never have left the kill zone alive.

Maroc had not mentioned Malcolm Southwell's death to either Gordon or Fisher. There had been more immediate things to discuss. He would now bring his friends up to speed.

On being told of Southwell's death, Mark Fisher had inquired if it could have involved their Mafia friends.

'I don't think so, mate. I gave him the money. He should have used it to pay off his gambling debts. A more obvious explanation is that he failed to do the sensible thing.'

Maroc shook his head.

'You do not piss those people off without consequences.'

Fisher doubted that anybody could be that dumb or short-sighted. He nodded his agreement.

'As you said, Peter, Malcolm was bricking himself when you saw him in Manchester. Those guys were breathing down his neck.'

Maroc nodded.

'It's just an idea, Mark. I agree it would take a complete idiot to push lady luck that far. Mind you, the jury is still out on Malcolm's common sense.

Maroc spread his hands.

'I don't know who the hell else would do it. A jealous husband? Bit of a stretch but not impossible.'

Bill Gordon showed little reaction to the news. He had heard Maroc speak of Malcolm and had not been impressed. However, he had decided to keep his own counsel.

Johansson had also been unusually silent. He looked at Maroc.

'I know Malcolm meant little to you, mate, but he was Emily's brother, Max's son. After we sort these bastards out and we still don't have the answer, how about a trip to Salford. You mentioned a pub and a girlfriend. We can find out soon enough who he owed money to.'

Maroc smiled his gratitude. 'I've been considering the trip. Be good to have company.'

'You might need some. Whoever they are, they're vicious bastards.'

In an uncharacteristic gesture, Johansson placed his hand on Maroc's shoulder.

'There's a hell of a lot happening, my friend. Don't take things on by yourself. Anyway, a trip to Manchester? Got to be good.'

Gordon and Fisher were quick to add their support. Johansson grinned at them.

'We already have one Norwegian and one Welshman? Any more, and it would not be a fair fight.'

This was followed by the expected groans. Johansson grinned and gestured to the others.

'Let's get this stuff sorted.'

The four friends walked over to Bill Gordon's extensive double garage. Inside they had taken everything out and arranged it on the concrete floor.

It was a matter of picking out what was needed, with a nod to personal preference. Maroc suggested each member take what they felt was the best fit for them.

It had been decided. Mark Fisher would carry the L129A1 scoped rifle. Perhaps not the best shot in the regiment, he had proven his worth with the weapon on a few missions.

Snipers were invaluable in a war zone. They could effectively change outcomes. Maroc would never forget the Serbian incident and how his mate Tony's intervention had saved his life.

While in the regiment, Fisher had been a designated marksman and not a sniper. It was an important distinction. Still, with the L129A1 Sharpshooter in his hands, he could be the icing on the cake in this little encounter.

There would not be a repeat of Cwm Idwal, where Maroc had chanced his luck. They had all agreed he had been rash in taking such a risk, even against amateurs.

All four of them would be at the Pen y Pass parking lot one hour before time. By the time the opposition arrived, they would have taken up positions in the hills above the lake. There was a good chance the Albanian pair would be backed up by Brits.

Fisher and Johansson still argued their viewpoint. It was way too soon for a second attack.

Maroc, however, stuck to his theory. The Albanians would be convinced he and Johansson would be the surprised party in this encounter.

He smiled grimly.

It would be a bloody shame if they didn't turn up. They would have a welcome in the hillsides they would never forget.

The plan was straightforward. When the Albanians reached the lake, they would find two sets of fishing gear set up. The rods would be placed upright in their stands, easily spotted from a distance.

Hopefully, they would conclude that Maroc and his friend had left to relieve themselves. Whatever thinking they did beyond that would come too late.

With the possible exception of Johansson, none were comfortable with cold killing. The Norwegian though not quite a psychopath, acceded to a simpler logic. Whatever was the best fit for the job. Do it.

The other three had drawn the ground rules. If possible, they would keep the body count to zero. Or near.

If the opposition came heavily armed, or in greater numbers, the rules would be changed. The bastards would then be fair game.

As Johansson put it:

'Those mothers would have shot Maroc in the back. Lucky for us, we had a plan.'

He looked at Maroc, who waited for the punch line.

'A shit plan. He was fortunate I'm such a good shot.'

They all laughed, including Maroc.

CHAPTER 43

His face was stone, unreadable, yet his rage was a palpable presence in the room. Edon Berisha faced Don Wilson in the gangster's main office.

Not usually bothered by bluster, threatening or otherwise, Wilson was affected by this foreigner's smouldering resentment.

'We had an agreement. I and my brother thought we are dealing with professional people, not stupid thugs. The man Maroc was to be dealt with by us. No one else.'

Wilson would not usually have accepted such effrontery. The man's attitude was inappropriate. To him, it came down to respect. However, he was firstly a pragmatist and recognised the long-term benefits of appeasement.

The Albanian continued his rant.

'The instructions were simple. Send a couple of men to the hospital. Keep an eye on visitors for Malcolm Southwell. If Peter Maroc turned up, inform the other team. They would then follow him back home. Who could fail to understand?'

The simple answer was his dumb brother, Jimmy. He fully recognised the impulse that drove his little brother to rescind his orders. He needed to prove he was capable. That he also was a leader of men.

Whenever Jimmy had tried to improvise in the past, things had gone badly wrong. It had never deterred him.

Edon's voice was low, menacing. The rage had been contained, transmuted into cold fury.

'We have paid good money for your work for us. You were told very clear. We would take over and deal with the man Maroc. This is how we do things. Do you understand?'

Anyone else and Don Wilson would have driven a meaty fist through the man's face. With commendable restraint, he contained his impulse. The Albanians were paying more than decent money for what should have been a simple job.

Wilson held reasonable expectations there would be more lucrative contracts down the line from the Albanian mafia. In the meantime, this foreign scumbag had to be placated, cultivated even. Sometimes he hated his job.

The gang boss held out his hand, palm forward, indicating the man pause his tirade; that he wished to be heard.

'This is a misunderstanding by one of my men. He will be dealt with.'

The Albanian, still furious, started to speak.

'Severely,'

Wilson added with emphasis.

'How does that help me? My brother? Now he has knowledge we are coming after him. This is a matter of honour. We wish to deal with this… this bastard of a man personally.'

'And you will, Edon. You'll have another chance to do the job right. I understand he may be more ready for you next time. That's why we, I mean my company, will provide you with four of my best people.'

He saw the incomprehension in Berisha's eyes and clarified.

'We will give you help. Four good men with guns. That ought to do it.'

Edon Berisha paused, then.

'This is not how we planned. We will not pay for the men you give'

Wilson smiled, offering the man a near regal wave of agreement. Shit, he was going overboard for this bastard.

Berisha was quiet, outwardly giving Wilson's offer serious consideration. In truth, he had made his decision to accept. With four more men, the job would be less tricky with less personal danger.

To hell with honour. He was learning to do business the western way.

Giving the impression of a man pained by a moral dilemma, the Albanian accepted the offer.

'I want your men to listen and obey what I say.'

Again Wilson answered with a gesture. The crisis was over. They had an agreement. Jimmy had cost the firm money. That would be sorted later.

Having shown Berisha out, Donald sat in his office. Was he losing his grip, his authority? He was far from happy at having to risk his men with no immediate returns. However, if he and Jimmy could hitch their waggon to the Albanian mafia, it could just be worth it.

What to do about Jimmy? He was becoming more unpredictable, more of a liability. If one of his foot soldiers had behaved in such a manner, the consequences for him would be less than good.

But Jimmy was family. They'd built the operation together, admittedly with him doing most of the heavy lifting.

Don Wilson sighed deeply. *Jimmy, Jimmy!* He knew he had nowhere to go with this one. His brother would have one more chance to make good. After that? Well, after that, Jimmy's future would be in his own hands.

The Albanians had never encroached on their patch. Their interests must have overlapped at some point, but it had never been a problem. Whether this was due to good manners on their part, Don had no idea. He knew one thing. He and Jimmy would never knowingly piss off the Albanian Mafia.

One thing did not add up. Made him uncomfortable. Why did the Mafia send these two to do business? Don had never been introduced to their operational head in Manchester. Had no real knowledge of how these people went about things. However, he had the feeling this protocol was all wrong.

CHAPTER 44

Don Wilson's knowledge of the armed forces was sketchy at best. In his line of work, you were bound to attract some ex-forces types. He was certain of one thing. You did not get into the SAS without having met some serious standards.

This Maroc was no ordinary thug. He and his mate had outmanoeuvred his men. They had made them look stupid, leaving one with a badly damaged ear. His lads were not to blame, they had just followed orders. Jimmy's orders.

Eliminating Maroc would not be easy. Their first attempt had resulted in complete embarrassment. The man would be even better prepared the next time, perhaps bringing in more of his SAS buddies. Wilson would need at least four of his lads to back up the Albanians.

The element of surprise would be their main ally. Maroc would not expect another attack so soon. Knowledge was everything, and Don had that knowledge. He knew Maroc and his mate were planning a fishing trip. Knew the exact location, the exact time.

A dark cloud of doubt cast a momentary shadow over his optimism. Had all this been a little too easy, or had the Welshman unwittingly revealed vital information that could get him killed? Jeez, he wished the eastern Europeans had never walked into his office.

Perhaps he was overthinking things. He shrugged the thoughts away, returning his attention to the map on his desk. It showed the exact location where the hit would take place. This time Maroc and co would be the surprised party.

For the Albanian brothers, the job was personal. They had initially planned to hunt and kill their man without outside help.

Wilson had no way of knowing their skill level. To pitch themselves against the SAS, they would have had to be bloody good. He doubted they were.

Don Wilson was confident that, with the extra manpower from him, the brothers would stand a good chance of taking down the Special Forces trooper.

Bloody North Wales was a backwater. Having to chase Maroc and his mate up and down the Welsh mountains was not Donald's intention.

There should be enough hiding places where his men could set themselves up and take out both Maroc and his mate without breaking a sweat. If Maroc did bring a couple of extra guns, they would also be easy targets.

Wilson dialled the Albanian's mobile number. It was answered immediately. He tried to keep his voice as level as possible as he outlined a rough plan to a somewhat morose Edon Berisha.

They would arrive early at the Pen y Pass car park. From there, they would walk the direct route to the lake and set themselves up in strategic positions in the hills. Then, using scoped rifles, they could pick the opposition off without engaging them in close combat.

Edon thought the plan a reasonably sound one, given there would be six of them against Maroc and his friend. This time, it was hard to see what could go wrong.

Edon Berisha was getting more and more frustrated by the stupid laws of his new country. They were for girls, not men.

Neither he nor his brother possessed a weapon. The Fare was not in the habit of allowing its members to walk around armed in this rule-obsessed country.

The decree was simple. The supplying of weapons would be sanctioned when the need arose. When a job warranted it. This deficit would be addressed by their new English friends.

The date and site of the operation were already determined by that fool Maroc. This was one fishing trip he would not enjoy.

CHAPTER 45

The task was sanctioned at government level, with the SAS allowed to deal with the two Albanians and whoever else they brought into the fight. Action on British soil had substantial restrictions, especially when its citizens were involved.

Every effort would be made to avoid casualties, especially among the Wilson gang. They were less fussy about the Albanians. However, their brief was clear, capture rather than kill.

A plan which involved termination with extreme prejudice would be deemed unacceptable. The SAS operation was no longer a private one where the four troopers could dictate the rules of engagement. Where life and death were decided by the gods of wars.

Niels Johansson was not happy at the MOD being informed. Now they would have to play nice. He found the idea...restrictive.

The bastards had killed one of their own. The ground rules had already been determined by the enemy. Maroc knew his Norwegian friend better than anyone. He would have to be vigilant; make sure Johansson was kept in check.

Both Bill Gordon and Maroc were privately relieved it was now official. Or at least legitimised.

Gordon could be ruthless, but he did not need the consequences of having to operate outside the law.

There was another advantage to official authorisation. If there were casualties, a government backup team would arrive to clean up.

Full endorsement had been given, and Maroc had submitted their combat plan to the intelligence services. They had agreed that the operation would go ahead with nothing changed. The time and place would remain the same.

MI6, and the Director Special Forces, were keen to put an end to this continued fallout from the Albanian operation. It was becoming an embarrassment.

No one within the intelligence community had anticipated the discovery by the Fare of the Albanian special forces mole inside their camp. It resulted in the revealing of all four SAS members involved in the operation.

The SAS had done its usual thorough job in disrupting the Fare. It had been a near textbook operation.

The Fare had wanted the return of what was taken from them that night. David Blandford was their first attempt at a snatch.

Something had gone wrong, and Dave had died. Maroc had been the second abduction. He had been luckier and had managed to escape.

It remained uncertain whether the Fare was behind the attack on Maroc and Johansson at Lake Idwal. For his part, Maroc had become more certain that his two incompetent abductors, keen to eliminate a loose end, had re-entered the arena. The government could not afford to lose more good men, especially on British soil.

The walk to the lake was upbeat, with Johansson providing most of the humour. All four were confident their special forces training and combat experience would make them more than a match for whatever came their way.

It was true that the enemy could never be underestimated. However, they would enter the encounter with total commitment. Defeat was not or could ever be a consideration. This mindset had made the SAS the best of the best.

The opposition had 'overheard' Maroc and Johansson giving their arrival time at the lake as ten a.m. He guessed they would come at least an hour earlier, and set themselves up above the lake at around nine a.m.

Maroc and his team had agreed to be in position an hour before the opposition arrived. This placed their own arrival time at eight in the morning. To allow for a broader margin of error, Gordon had suggested seven-thirty.

Given the data, it was difficult coming up with a more accurate projection. This arrangement, however, would give them more than an hour to set up.

They arrived at Pen y Pass, the point at which they would take the well-travelled Miner's track leading to the lake. The path carried on beyond their destination, continuing to the peak of Mount Snowdon.

The weapons were carried in four separate canvas holdalls. Each man wore state-of-the-art PPSS body armour. The walk was moderate, even for the ordinary hiker. Having undergone and passed SAS selection, each man could have run the distance carrying four times the burden.

They had chosen the north side of the lake. It was the best place to set up an ambush. Here the land rose sharply above the lake, affording good cover behind rocky outcrops. They would dictate where the opposition would end up.

Two fishing rods would be propped up by the water's edge, giving the impression the two SAS pals had arrived earlier and had wandered off.

Mark would take his position high in the hills above the lake. There, he would set up the L129A1 Sharpshooter rifle. The other three would occupy positions below him, advantageously placed above the enemy.

If they took the bait, the Albanian brothers, including whatever reinforcement they would bring, would climb towards the rocky outcrops to take up their positions above the fishing rods. Maroc and his men would intercept them before this could happen.

As in most ambushes, a few assumptions had been made. Still, everyone had agreed it remained a reasonable projection. They would wait and see how things played out.

Ten minutes before nine, Johansson nudged Maroc. He pointed southward to a group of people on the path. They were coming towards the lake. The Norwegian grabbed his pair of high mag binoculars, training them on the approaching party.

'It's them. Looks like they've invited a few friends to the party. I can see seven people, including the brothers Grimm.'

'Given our advantage, some additional guests won't matter.' Maroc sounded as confident as he felt. They had a positional advantage plus the element of surprise. A bit of luck, and this could be bloodless. He signalled Mark Fisher, alerting him to what was happening. Fisher waved back his acknowledgement.

Each member of the patrol knew what their initial action would be. Whatever followed would be governed by the opposition's response. As the group approached, the troopers fell silent and did what they were good at. They waited, and they watched.

There could not afford collateral damage. Maroc and Johansson had been lucky in their engagement with the two Mancunians at Cwm Idwal. Maroc prayed for equal luck here and that no hapless walkers would be caught up in the encounter.

As the opposition drew nearer, Maroc was able to identify the Albanian brothers amongst the group. Like his own team, they carried their weapons in canvas bags. The four watched and waited.

Edon was the first to spot the fishing tackle. He looked around at the others.

'They have arrived before us.'

One of the Wilson gang, a short, bald, heavily built man, looked and shrugged.

'Could be anyone's stuff. This is a bloody lake after all. People fish on it.'

Edon nodded.

'It is them. I feel it. Maybe they gone for a piss.'

He pointed towards a rocky outcrop above and in line with the fishing equipment.

'We set up in the rocks above this point. Then we wait. If it is someone else, we wait for Maroc and his friend to arrive and, as you say, do the business.'

The bald man shook his head.

'Look, mate. If there's someone else here, then we

call the whole thing off. Nobody said anything about killing civilians.'

'OK, but we still wait and see who comes back to this.'

He waved vaguely in the direction of the fishing rods.

'Let's get up there before someone comes.'

The man nodded, turning to the others.

'Right lads, you heard what he said. We'll get the weapons sorted when we're up there.'

Listening, Maroc grinned, shaking his head in near disbelief. This was going to be too easy. It was *How to walk into an ambush 101.*

There was no need to instruct the others. Maroc's team would make their move as soon as the gang reached a point just below their position. Before the bastards could unpack their weapons.

Wilson's men were dressed and booted in walking gear. The Albanians wore casual jackets and jeans. Both brothers wore expensive trainers.

The team watched their slow upward progress towards a position to the right of their own. Still, they waited.

They were twenty yards away when Maroc gave the signal. His three friends stood up. Each had his HK G36 assault rifle unwaveringly trained on the group.

Edon Berisha's jaw dropped, his swarthy features devoid of expression. For Peter Maroc, this moment was one to be savoured.

There was a sudden movement. Burim, the younger brother had produced a handgun from inside his jacket. Before the troopers could move, he had fired.

A fraction of a second later, they heard a rifle

crack. It was the unmistakable sound of Mark Fisher's L129A1 Sharpshooter.

The Albanian flew backwards. He lay still on the ground, his gun a few feet from his outstretched hand. The whole incident had taken around three seconds.

All three SAS men kept their weapons trained steadily on the men below.

'Anyone hit?'

Bill Gordon took a quick look at his two friends.

'Went past my right ear, Bill.'

Maroc grinned. Johansson gave his friend a concerned look.

Bill Gordon waved for Mark to join them. Wilson's men seemed rooted to the spot while Edon crouched over his brother, attempting to staunch the blood coming from the wound in his shoulder. Maroc barked at him.

'Stand up and kick the gun away.'

The Albanian looked up with cold hatred in his dark eyes. As though wounded himself, he slowly got to his feet.

'I said, kick the gun away.'

The big Albanian looked confused. Looking down, he viewed the weapon as if for the first time. He kicked the gun a few feet away whilst glaring at his nemesis, Peter Maroc.

Mark Fisher joined them, his rifle packed away in a canvas bag. In his hand was a Glock 17.

He looked down at the wounded Albanian.

'Nasty. Just managed to snap one off.'

Good one, Mark. The bastard made his choice.'

Bill Gordon winked at his friend. Worried he had not reacted quickly enough, Fisher gave Gordon a tight smile. He reached into his belt pouch and took out a satellite phone.

The Thuraya XT-PRO DUAL was about the same size as the average household handphone. It was invaluable in dead spots.

He handed it to Maroc, together with a small booklet.

'Want to call this one in, Peter?'

Maroc thumbed through the booklet and then called his superiors on a designated number. Speaking rapidly, he gave a detailed account of the situation. There was a pause at the other end, then.

'How bad?'

Maroc looked at one of Wilson's men, who was attending to the wounded Albanian

'How bad is it?'

'Shoulder. Passed right through. He'll live.'

All the fight had left the Mancunians. They hung around as if waiting for a bus. Maroc relayed the information, adding his suggestions.

The reply came back. Abrupt to the point of rudeness.

'We'll arrange a heli from RAF Valley.'

Maroc began explaining his position when the voice cut in.

'Yes, we know how to find you, Maroc.'

They waited forty-five minutes for the RAF rescue helicopter to fly in from the Isle of Anglesey. Maroc always carried a first aid kit as part of his equipment. Making his way down, he knelt by the wounded Albanian.

The younger man, realising he was not going to die, looked up at Maroc. The look of fear was gone. In its place was an expression of complete bewilderment. He had tried to kill this man. Now Maroc was helping him. Using pads and bandages, he managed to stem the flow of blood oozing from Burim's shoulder before administering a shot of morphine. This left the Albanian in a more comfortable state. Maroc thought he deserved less.

The team bagged their assault rifles. This left them with handguns to guard their prisoners. Fisher and Johansson searched each gang member for weapons. Those found were similarly bagged, ready to be carried down to the waiting vehicle at Pen y Pass.

With handguns concealed, the four-man patrol watched as the red and white rescue heli landed on the gravelled shore of the lake. The rescue boys looked curious but said nothing. They had been briefed.

This was a matter of national security. No questions. Just do your job. They showed their usual professionalism, and the patient was stretchered and onboard within minutes.

Burim entered the craft wearing a light oxygen mask. He had an IV line in his right arm, running to a clear plastic bag held by the medic.

The helicopter rose to around fifty feet. Banking sharply, it flew northward towards the valley rim, its destination the Gwynedd Hospital at Bangor.

As soon as it was out of sight, Maroc and his team drew their concealed weapons. There was no need to level them at their prisoners. Wilson's boys looked more bored than threatening. Even Edon Berisha had lost the will to fight.

Maroc signalled them, and they started walking down towards the rough track skirting the lake. The same track that had got them to this point would now lead them back to the main road at Pen y Pass.

Berisha gave a last show of rebellion. He glared at Maroc, his dark eyes flashing him a look of pure poison. The SAS man would have none of it. Taking a step towards him he gave Berisha a sharp shove which had the Albanian staggering backwards.

The big man managed to keep his balance. His dignity did not fare as well. Knowing he was beaten, he muttered angrily in his mother tongue, before turning away, dropping into line with the rest of the gang.

On reaching the main road at Pen y Pass, four range rovers, windows tinted, waited silently in the car park. Four armed policemen emerged from the first. They took over from the SAS patrol, herding the prisoners into the third and fourth vehicles. The small convoy left immediately.

The one remaining vehicle stood silently. Maroc was staring at it curiously when the driver's door opened. A man in civilian clothing stepped out. He strolled casually towards Maroc and his team.

Johansson hissed in Maroc's ear.

'Bloody spook.'

The man was rangy and moved like an athlete. He was good-looking and tanned, his blond hair cut short. He gifted Maroc with an easy smile. Maroc smiled back.

'Tucker. Heard you were still in Eastern Europe.'

'Peter Maroc.'

He extended his hand, his smile broadening.

'Heard you were dead.'

A full debriefing would follow, but Maroc knew Tucker would be registering most of what was said on his compact recording device. Maroc believed the man went to bed with the bloody thing. Nothing wrong with that, he thought. I've slept with my Glock for years.

They had met during the Russian military intervention by proxy in The Republic of Crimea. Both had been on covert operations in that country. Tucker was dependable. Tough as old boots. They had become friends.

The tension on the return journey was relieved by the usual robust humour. Maroc was ribbed mercilessly for having a spook friend.

Bill Gordon grinned as he looked over at Maroc.

'You had a bit of a close shave, Peter. But apart from the shooting Mr president, did you enjoy the ride?'

They laughed at that. Maroc affected a hurt expression.

They all agreed on one thing. It had been the easiest encounter to date, or, as Fisher called it.

'A bloody doddle.'

CHAPTER 46

Bill Gordon and Mark Fisher would be going home that day. Gordon had a demanding business to run. His wife Jean had reached her tolerance limit and had made serious noises.

She would rather be on her own than sit at home worrying about him. Fisher had people who required his presence.

All four friends were aware they had reached a place where life's focus required some serious adjustments. Dressed in men's bodies they would comport themselves as men; put away their bows and arrows. Their friendships would always be accessible; a safe and constant refuge.

Maroc and Johansson returned to Bryn Awel to find John Southwell in the living room with Max and Emily. All three turned to face them as they entered.

Something was wrong. Emily's face was ashen. She looked up at him, and Maroc had never seen such an absence of warmth in her grey-blue eyes. Her father looked flushed and angry, his mouth a grim line.

Maroc turned to his brother-in-law. John's expression was more hostile than usual. Behind the hostility, however, there was something else. He thought he detected a hint of triumph. What was the bastard up to?

He gave his wife a questioning look. To his dismay, Emily avoided his eyes, and, bowing her head, she stared pointedly at the floor.

Maroc turned to Max Southwell.

'What's going on, Max?

There was a bark of incredulity from John.

'You've been unmasked, Maroc. That's what's going on.'

Maroc turned to look at him. He was smirking like a schoolboy.

'What?'

Confused, he turned to his father-in-law.

Max Southwell looked at the man he had come to trust. He started to speak and faltered. Southwell tried again when John cut in.

'You've got a nerve, I'll give you that. We'd all like to hear your version of what happened to Malcolm.'

'*My* version? What the hell does that mean?'

Maroc turned to Emily.

'Em, can you tell me what all this is about?'

Emily still had her head lowered and, at first, refused to meet his eyes. Finally, with effort, she looked up at him.

'John has reason to believe you had something to do with Malcolm's death.'

A blank look from Maroc prompted her to continue.

'Well do you, I need to know?'

Maroc had never witnessed such an absence of warmth or feeling in her voice. That time when they were together, when she had told him they were through, to leave the house, it had not been like this.

At least then, there had been anger, some show of

passion. At a loss, he turned to Max, half expecting Southwell to burst out laughing, shouting, *'gotcha!'*

But this was no joke, and Max was not smiling. The two mainstays in his life had placed him firmly on the outside.

John's opinion meant nothing to Maroc. His support or lack of it was an irrelevance. The man was a snake.

There followed a moment of uneasy silence. Max broke the spell.

'Where on earth did you dig up this claptrap from, John. There's no mystery surrounding Malcolm's death. He mixed with the wrong types. Fell foul of them. Your brother was consorting with gangsters and casino owners. Loan sharks, for god's sake.'

Johansson moved restlessly in the doorway. He knew better than most people; Maroc was incapable of murdering in cold blood.

This man, Malcolm, had been attacked, probably from behind. By cowards. To the Norwegian, it was enough evidence to rule out Peter Maroc as a suspect.

'You think I could do this, Em? Kill your brother? Really?'

He was dismayed and saddened by her lack of response. Maroc needed to see and hear her declaration of his innocence. Her angry defence of him.

Her voice was so low he could barely hear her.

'I don't know, Peter. There are so many versions of you.'

Emily looked lost and miserable. She shook her head.

'I don't know who you are. You keep on changing'

Her voice trailed off, ending in a sob.

'Well, I bloody well do.'

Max Southwell had come to life. He looked at both his children.

'What the hell is happening here?'

He turned his full gaze to John, who was still glaring triumphantly at Maroc.

'John, you're my son. And I love you.'

The last part was said with less conviction.

'But I wouldn't trust you as far as I could throw you. There, I've said it.'

John Southwell was not surprised, nor was he particularly affected by his father's outburst. He had been outed for his lies and deceit too often by the man. However, he decided to look hurt. Mildly shocked.

'It's a damned shame. You should have heard my brother's take on Maroc.'

He looked over at Emily.

'How much your husband scared him.'

John turned and stared coldly at the man who stood in the way of his inheritance. His future.

'He's fooled all of you, you know? Now he has the keys to the kingdom. What he's always been after.'

Johansson sensed a sudden tension in his friend. He placed a calming hand on his shoulder while recognising the irony of this role reversal.

Maroc knew better than to react to the nonsense laid at his door. That would be playing into John's hands. But Emily? He was stunned and wounded by her lack of faith.

A part of him sympathised; could recognise her dilemma. How could she know him when he hardly knew himself? What a bloody mess.

Max Southwell continued.

'A year ago, I'd have bought your story, John. A lot

has happened since then.'

He turned to Maroc.

'Back then, I would not have given Maroc time of day. I thought him an arrogant fool of a man. Dangerous even.'

He looked at his daughter.

'Em? He saved my bloody life. You of all people know that.'

'No doubt he persuaded you to change your will. In gratitude, maybe?'

John's voice dripped sarcasm.

'Keep your wits about you from now on. That's my advice. Do you think you're safe with Maroc? Emily? Father? He's a murderer. It means nothing to him, killing another human being. It's been his job for years and I bet he's bloody good at it.'

Maroc was certain that John did not believe any of the bullshit he was espousing. It was pure verbiage meant to seed doubt and suspicion.

It was a way of regaining what John imagined he'd lost. The intent was to remove him, Peter Maroc, from the inheritance equation.

Maroc looked at his wife. The uncertainty in her eyes wounded more than a bullet ever could. He turned abruptly, pushing his way past Johansson and into the hallway.

The Norwegian stood at the entrance to the living room. An uninvited guest at a party.

Maroc had run up the stairs with no explanation to his friend. For a full two minutes, nobody moved. Johansson, feeling deeply uncomfortable, no longer wished to be part of this sad tableau. Confused, he turned to leave through the door when Maroc came down the stairs carrying a large holdall.

'Let's get out of here, amigo.'

As the two friends reached the door, there was a cry of protest from Max Southwell. Maroc heard his anguish and stopped. He walked back into the living room.

Cupping Max's head in one large hand, he pulled his father-in-law to him, kissing him lightly on the forehead. He turned and left without a backward glance.

Outside, he turned to Johansson, who was hurrying to keep up.

'I can't stay, Niels. You saw the way she looks at me. We'll head back to the cabin. Then you can help me plan my future.'

'This is crap, Maroc. She knows you better than that. Give her time, man. Her brother's dead. She's all over the place.'

He groped for a more convincing argument.

'She's a woman, Maroc. They're all crazy.'

'Maybe.'

Maroc patted his friend's shoulder.

'For now, let's take the two cars and drive to an off-licence. I feel like getting reacquainted with my friend, Jack.'

Johansson gave him a blank look.

'Daniels?'

Maroc made a drinking gesture.

CHAPTER 47

The evening had meandered towards morning through a numbing haze of alcohol and nostalgia. Maroc and Johansson had quaffed the Jack Daniels along with a couple of packs of beer each. Late morning found Maroc searching the small cabin for alcohol-free analgesics.

Johansson was still asleep, his snoring starting to irritate. Maroc nudged him with a socked foot, managing not to fall over in the process.

An hour and several cups of strong tea later, the two friends stood outside the small cabin above the town. Johansson was shaking his head in disbelief.

'You say you lived in this dog kennel?'

Maroc looked at his friend.

'Jeez, Niels, I've been in worse shitholes. Often with you for company.'

Johansson grunted and grinned at his friend. It was true. In their line of work, they had crashed down in some dire places.

'Yea, right. So what now. You two ever going to kiss and make up?'

Maroc drew a long breath, shaking his head, more to clear the mental fog than in response. He turned around, making for the cabin door.

'Let's go in and review my options. You OK with

sticking around for another week?'

'Nothing urgent calling me back.'

Maroc looked seriously at his friend.

'Except for saving your marriage?'

It was Johansson's turn to sigh.

'Another week won't make a difference. I can always lie about the length of the operation.'

After yesterday's departure from Bryn Awel, Maroc had managed to buy a few provisions in addition to the medicinal alcohol. He fished out two bowls and some cereal and milk. Neither he nor Johansson could face a fried breakfast.

'If John Southwell's accusation is to be answered, I'll have to discover the truth about his little brother. Who killed him and why.'

'Hell, Peter, given he was such a little shit, it could have been anybody. As your father-in-law said, it was probably someone he owed money to.'

Maroc nodded his agreement.

'I've been thinking of going over to Salford. There's a pub where Malcolm and I met. He had a thing about the barmaid there. Think they were an item for a while.'

'Worth a try. Will we be carrying?'

Maroc nodded.

'We could kick up all sorts of shit. If they can beat a man to death over a debt...'

Johansson grunted his accord.

'I did a bit of homework on our boy. There's a nightclub he frequented in the centre of Manchester, *The Mogambo*. Been there for years. Word on the street, it was taken over by a couple of London hard men. That would be around a year ago. They have a Blackjack table. They also run a nightly poker game in one of the back rooms.'

He looked at Johansson.

I'm taking the Glock. We could stash a couple of G36s in the car. No such thing as too much firepower.'

'Assault rifles? Seems like overkill. Will we need them if we're carrying handguns?'

Maroc nodded.

'I think they're worth including.'

He looked at his friend who still looked doubtful.

'OK, maybe I'm being over-cautious. I just thought, better safe than sorry.'

Johansson's expression became serious.

'This isn't a sanctioned job, Peter. We can't afford to escalate a private matter into a full-blown firefight.'

'My guess is they won't be needed. You're right, it needs to be low key and we'll do our best to keep it that way. But we're going into unknown territory. Let's find out who we're dealing with before we go in light-handed.'

The Norwegian shook his head ruefully.

'Sometimes, Peter, I think you're crazier than me.'

CHAPTER 48

Emily Maroc's mind was in turmoil. The doubts of earlier years had returned. Uninvited guests, they had infected her trust like a virulent pathogen.

Why am I even thinking this way?

She had reaffirmed her love, their love. Hadn't she? The man who had appeared from nowhere was an innocent. A blank canvas on which she had drawn their shared future. With time and love, she had brought him back. He had not denied her.

Capable of cold-blooded murder. Her brother's scathing charges had changed all that. They had redefined her husband, and in doing so, had left her world a bleaker place. A world filled with suspicion and fear.

She felt the pain of guilt because she could no longer see him clearly. The good man had left, leaving her with, what? She sat back and let her mind drift back to their early life together.

Emily would never know what he was capable of in defence of the Realm. She had always accepted this. To her, it was an unknown country, one she refused to explore and one he would never reveal.

To kill a defenceless civilian for gain? To deny her of a brother she loved? The murder had been a heinous act, the work of a coward.

She could not, would not recognise Maroc dressed as a coward. Then why had she not defended him? Stopped him from leaving?

The other voice, the unkind one, spoke. If Maroc thought there was some gain in being in her father's favours, to what length would he go to acquire it?

It occurred to her that Peter had no affection for the men in her family. He recognised in John what they all did. In her younger brother, Malcolm, he saw a weak and greedy opportunist.

Was his newfound friendship with her father a sham? A ploy towards the gain of a further end?

Perhaps Malcolm had discovered something about her husband. Something Peter did not want him to disclose to the others.

It all returned to the one question that frightened her. Could Maroc kill a civilian he had no affection for, who could thwart his purpose? Could he do such a thing if it served him?

Her mind could not settle, and she longed for the simple contentment of the last few weeks. She recalled her happy amazement when observing Maroc and her father together. All three reunited in impossible closeness.

Could he be so duplicitous? Was there a cold and predatory face he hid from the world?

According to John, Maroc had nursed their father back to health in furtherance of some heinous plan. He would gain Southwell's trust; persuade him to change his will, citing him as a major benefactor. Emily recalled her brother's certainty.

Her father would have none of it. He had recognised the John of old and had called him out. Had her father been right to trust his instincts? Was he seeing things as they truly were?

And yet a part of her had accepted the enormous charges John had levelled against Peter. A part of her she now despised.

The Southwell family was already dealing with the pain of Malcolm's death. John had now brought further suffering to their door. Her brother was dead, murdered, and she could not wholly ignore such damning accusations.

She envied her father's loyalty. He had never thought of Peter as a materialistic or acquisitive man. If anything, the opposite had been true. Her father had found his independence, his unwillingness to accept help exasperating.

She recalled how Peter had rejected his offer of assistance in buying Bryn Awel. It was their first home together. Her father had called her husband proud and pig-headed.

A gentle knock on the living room door. Her father's manner was hesitant as he entered the room.

'Em, I have something you must see. Peter asked me to keep this quiet. At least until there was a need to show it.'

Emily had not noticed his briefcase. Now Southwell delved into it producing a buff-coloured document. He handed it to her.

'Read this, darling, it might clarify a few things. Clear up this whole bloody mess.'

Her father's last will and testimony had been drawn up by a firm of solicitors in Caernarfon. Emily took the document and carefully read through the will.

She saw her father had added a codicil. It stated

that, in the event of his death, no part of his inheritance would pass to Peter Maroc. She looked up at her father.

'When was this drawn?'

'The day we went out to Cwm Idwal. He insisted we visit my solicitor in Caernarfon. You can see I've signed it. It's also been witnessed.'

Southwell looked hard at his daughter.

'Emily, that's all the proof I need. The man's not interested in money unless he can dig it out of the ground with his own bloody hands.'

His gaze went to the window, looking at nothing in particular. He smiled. A man remembering something good.

Southwell looked back at his daughter.

'If he means to be rid of me, then how is it I felt, no, feel safe with him? Is he that duplicitous? Is he that bloody good an actor?'

His voice softened.

'Ask yourself. When did he change into the person John describes?'

Emily was momentarily silent, rereading the document. Maroc had made it impossible for him to inherit from her father. She looked up at him, her face brighter.

'I remember, he was adamant he wouldn't accept your help when buying this place. Anyway, we're forgetting something. Maroc is an only child. His parents, when they died, left him a substantial inheritance.'

She gathered pace, the words tumbling out, her face flushed with this new realisation.

'I never got involved in his financial affairs. I

wasn't interested. But, I remember, a few weeks after we moved into Bryn Awel, he instructed his father's business manager to realise all his assets in the hotel business. Peter didn't want the hassle of running a half dozen hotels. I remember telling you, dad.'

Southwell got to his feet and took his daughter's hand.

'I've always known Peter wasn't your usual soldier of fortune. That he did what he did... for the kicks or some other bloody reason.'

'Come on, dad you never trusted him in the past. You used to tell me to be careful around him.'

Southwell nodded his agreement.

'There's no doubt your husband is a dangerous man. That's what I felt, and that's what I feared about him.'

He hesitated before adding.

'By the way, into which account did he deposit his money?'

She gave him a blank look.

'Oh, yes, I see what you mean. He put it into my account. I've never even thought about it.'

'Exactly, darling. Nothing about Peter points at him being a money grabber. John's my son, Em, every bit as much as you're my daughter, but that boy has always had his agenda. And it's not always been an ethical one.'

Emily sat, still clutching the document. She liked the way her father now referred to Maroc as Peter. She looked directly at him.

'So, it comes down to who we believe. John or Peter. I hate myself for it, but I'm still left wondering if his recent trauma has changed him. Made him capable of killing. I mean, you do hear of such things.'

Southwell shook his head.

'From what I've observed, it could even have knocked some bloody sense into him. Surely, you can't doubt his feelings for you?'

Emily stood up, her face deeply flushed.

'Damn it all, I wish John had never come here with his accusations.'

She looked at her father.

'Have I killed what we had, dad? Is there a way back?' have I… what did Peter use to say?'

Her father grinned.

'Pissed on the chips?'

Max Southwell smiled at his favourite child.

'Don't be so bloody daft. Click your fingers; that's all you have to do. That boy will always be mad about you.'

CHAPTER 49

The decision to involve Bill Gordon and Mark Fisher in the Manchester trip was revisited. Both agreed it was best to leave them out.

The trip to Salford would be a recce. They would glean as much intel as possible on Malcolm Southwell's activities before taking action. Johansson was happy to join Maroc.

Both men recognised they were going into the unknown. They had no idea what an encounter with the owners of the Mogambo Club would lead to.

Johansson spent ten minutes on the phone with his wife. Maroc had left him to it. The Norwegian finally ended the call and looked over at his friend. He grinned and patted the 9 mm Sig in his jacket pocket.

'Let's do this!'

It was evening before they drove into the centre of Salford. Maroc had not forgotten his way to 'The Blue Cock.' He parked the Maserati in the small parking space at the back of the pub.

As they entered, the Norwegian turned to his friend.

'Christ man, what a dive.'

'It's not that bad, Niels. This isn't bloody Scandinavia, where everything is covered in Dettol.'

Johansson gave Maroc a quizzical look, then

grunted. They walked directly to the long bar and ordered their drinks. Today was not a day for drinking spirits; they needed to keep a clear head. Besides, they were still suffering the effects of the previous evening.

They ordered two halves of bitter. Maroc looked up and down the bar before asking the barman.

'Lucy not here today?'

The young man serving them looked at his watch.

'She won't be in till seven. You know her?'

'We've met. More a friend of a friend.'

Maroc kept his tone casual, conveying it would not be a problem if she failed to turn up.

Maroc looked at his watch. It was six-thirty. They had decided to remain seated at the bar. This way, it would be a more natural encounter when she did turn up.

Lucy arrived just before seven. The same barman caught their attention and nodded towards the front entrance. Maroc turned and saw a dark-haired girl in her late twenties coming toward them.

Around five-seven in height, she would have been slightly shorter than Malcolm. He vaguely recalled seeing her on his last visit. Maroc thought she could have gone easier on the makeup. Still, he could see why his brother-in-law had found her appealing.

'She's here.'

Maroc looked at Johansson.

'Give her time to settle in. Don't want it to look as though we're stalking the girl.'

A few minutes later, Lucy appeared at the bar. Maroc waited until she was free before signalling he needed a refill. She came over immediately.

'What was it, then?'

She pointed at his empty glass.

'Two pints of best, please. Lucy is it…?'

She looked up quickly, her dark eyes guarded.

'I knew Malcolm. Malcolm Southwell? I believe you were friends'

Maroc was relieved when she gave him a bright smile.

'I thought you looked familiar. You were in here with Malcolm a few months ago. Never forget a face, me.'

She hesitated before continuing.

'He was attacked not far from here? Never recovered from it, poor lamb. They got him to hospital, but he died.'

For a moment, her eyes lost their sparkle. Her face crumpled, and Maroc thought she was going to cry. He tried to determine whether the sadness was genuine. He concluded it was.

Maroc, looking sombre, nodded in agreement.

'Chance of a quick chat when you're less busy?

Before she could answer, the young male barman who had served them earlier called out.

'Luce, you're needed.'

He pointed to customers at the other end of the bar.

Lucy excused herself.

'If you gentlemen are around later, I get a break at eight. Only ten minutes. We could have a chat then. Away from the bar.'

She stared pointedly at her fellow worker.

'Nice lad.'

She smiled.

'Bit nosey.'

Maroc and Johansson nodded their understanding.

They decided to chance a further half of bitter each.

Both took their drinks to a table by the window. As promised, Lucy joined them within the hour, taking a seat directly opposite Maroc. She had brought a soft drink which she placed in front of her.

'I do remember you. Thought to myself, nice looking fella.'

This was said without coyness. Maroc was warming to this girl. She was OK.

'You're making me blush, Lucy.'

He flashed his trademark roguish smile. Johansson, groaning inwardly, did not comment. In truth, he appreciated a fellow pro at work.

'As you can imagine, his family would like some justice. As I'm sure would you. So we're trying to find out who his acquaintances were. Especially the more recent ones.'

Lucy smiled into his eyes.

'I do like your accent. Posh. Bit foreign.

'He's a Welshman. That makes him foreign around here.'

Johansson grinned at her.

She continued, blushing slightly.

'He often had a few of his gambling mates with him. They seemed all right. You know, regular fellas.'

Her face darkened.

'There were these others. A couple of foreigners.

She paused and smiled at him.

'Not foreign like you. You know? Russian accents'

'Russian?'

Johansson seemed surprised. He looked over at Maroc with dawning comprehension.

'You mean, Eastern Europeans?'

Lucy shrugged.

'I suppose. You know. White, not coloured, but with thick accents.'

Maroc described the two Albanian brothers. She nodded enthusiastically, glad to be contributing.

'Yes. That's them, definitely.'

She continued.

'Poor Malcolm. He was convinced they could help him get rich. How did he put it? Something about getting rid of a roadblock to his inheritance.'

She smiled sadly before continuing.

'Always going to hit the big time that one. If it wasn't the gambling, it would be some wild talk about claiming his birthright by removing an imp... something.'

'Impediment?'

Maroc offered helpfully.

'Yes, impediment. Definitely. I'm going to get rid of an impediment he would say. These blokes are going to help me.'

It was almost time for Lucy to continue her shift. Maroc pressed two twenty-pound notes into her hands.

'That's for spending your break with us, Lucy. Maybe we can arrange a little more from Malcolm's family.'

He cringed at his indelicacy.

She smiled a good-natured smile, not in the least offended.

'Oh, I wasn't with Malcolm for his money. I must admit, he did impress me at first. What with his nice car and talk of inheriting a small fortune. But I soon realised that's all it was. Talk. His flash Rolex was fake.

My brother has one just like it.'

Her face took on a sweet sadness.

'He was nice to me, Mr Maroc. I liked him. I liked him a lot.'

CHAPTER 50

She had to know the truth. That last message her brother claimed to have received from Malcolm still echoed in her mind. *I think he means to kill me, John.*

Why would John lie? That would be monstrous.

Reading her father's enhanced will had initiated a liberating process in Emily. She had been in a state of emotional inertia, held fast by doubt. Now, she was able to think clearer. Or, as Peter would put it, more like a man.

Emily envied her father's faith in her husband. He had grown close to Peter; discovered something good in him.

Thinking clearer than she had done in days, she found John's take on her husband's plans and motives too convoluted and contradictory. Why would anyone save a man's life and then... Emily found it impossible to imagine anyone being that evil.

The guilt hit hard. Peter felt betrayed. She had seen it in his eyes, in his angry reaction at her lack of faith.

She had failed to defend him, leaving him no choice but to take himself away, taking his hurt with him. He had packed his bags. Left her.

He's a killer. Means nothing to him, killing another human being. Peter Maroc was a soldier. Soldiers killed in battle.

Emily had no knowledge of him in that context. She knew him only as a gentle man.

Despite the emerging clarity, two voices still vied for dominance. One had to be silenced. Her sanity depended on it. She would phone John. She would see if there was any legitimacy to his story.

John Southwell had finished unpacking his luggage at Llys Meurig. He was still angry at his father's refusal to accept his condemnation of Maroc.

The phone rang for the third time in the hallway. He sighed wearily as he made his way down, his mind still echoing his vexation.

That bastard, Maroc, had made an impression on the old man. But for his father to place his trust in an outsider over his flesh and blood? That was unforgivable.

John had never had a problem with hypocrisy. The convenient dichotomy in his thinking was something he could easily live with.

He picked up the phone, and Emily's voice cut in before he could say a word. Dispensing with the niceties, she came straight to the point.

'I have to ask you, John, have you any tangible proof you received that phone call from Malcolm?'

He was momentarily taken aback.

'What sort of proof do you need, Em? Other than my word.'

Her response cracked like a whip.

'Stop the bullshit, brother, you know exactly what I mean. Recordings. Something more substantial than your word.'

John caught the sarcasm. The hurt he felt took him by surprise.

'Steady Em, let's take this a step at a time.'

'Don't patronise me, John. I need hard evidence if you're making such monstrous accusations. Your bloody word as a... gentleman just won't cut it.'

John Southwell could not remember his sister being so angry. And the sarcasm? Where the hell had that come from? He considered falling back on wounded dignity. He thought better of it.

'Well, there was someone in the office with me when Malcolm made the call. He could back up everything I said.'

His mind working hard, he continued.

'It wasn't just the one time, Em. Malcolm was always saying how much Maroc scared him. I'm telling you, he was terrified of the man.'

There was a long pause before Emily spoke.

'Why then would Peter insist on having a codicil added to dad's will if his motives are as you say? Why place such an obstacle in his own path?'

'Codicil? What are you talking about?

Emily took a deep breath.

'Maroc practically dragged dad to the family solicitors in Caernarfon. He had him add an addition to the will, ensuring he'd never inherit a penny from the estate.'

'I'm no legal expert, Em. But if dad has already included Maroc in his will, any such document could be circumvented.'

'And you're certain of that?'

'As I said, I'm not an expert. But I'm pretty certain Maroc could get around it.'

He paused.

'When the time came.'

Emily came off the phone, her mind in turmoil. John's words had taken the shine off her newfound hope, and she hated him for it.

Feeling the need for a drink, she made straight for the elegant drinks cabinet to the left of the bay window. Opening it, she looked for the single malt, a drink Maroc had introduced her to.

Her mind travelled back to a spring afternoon in Llandudno, where Maroc had spotted the cabinet in one of the old antique shops in town.

'An essential piece of kit for the country gentleman.'

They had both laughed at his affected delivery.

She found what she was looking for and carried the bottle back with her. Pouring herself a large measure of Maroc's favourite *Laphroaig* single malt, she tipped the glass to her lips.

The ten-year-old scotch immediately warmed, its smoky flavour lingering on her palate. She leaned back and closed her eyes, allowing the alcohol to work its magic. God, she was tired.

CHAPTER 51

The Mogambo was situated off Market street in central Manchester. Maroc remembered his uncle George mentioning it in stories of his younger days on the Manchester scene. He described it as a place where you could relax without fear of bother. Maroc wondered if that would be the case today.

They parked their car in the small car park behind the club and walked around the building to the front door.

'Why are these clubs always so bloody dark?' Johansson looked warily left and right.

'Relax, Niels, don't be so edgy. They wouldn't know who we were anyway.'

'They're about to find out.'

The Norwegian gave a humourless smile.

'Not like you to be on edge, mate.'

Maroc eyed his friend.

'Don't like going up against civilians. Give me soldiers any day. At least you know they're out to kill you.'

Maroc grinned. He gave his friend a gentle push towards the entrance doors.

The Mogambo seemed all a small nightclub should be. Relaxed and friendly. Maroc looked hard for a more sinister element. Nothing leapt out at him.

The place was starting to fill up, and there were two couples on the small dance floor. They made their way to the bar at the far end of the large lounge. After ordering a couple of small beers, served by a barman who looked well past his prime, they stood around taking in the flavour of the place.

Johansson cut to the chase.

'Who runs this place?'

If there was to be any action, he wanted to get on with it.

They received the classic response.

'Who wants to know.'

'A friend of a friend.'

Maroc stared hard at the old man.

'Play nice, eh mate? We're not here to cause trouble.'

'You coppers?

'Not a chance'

'So, who's in charge?'

'It's run by a couple of brothers. The O'Connells. They've been running it for a year now. It's a respectable place, let me tell you. Nice clientele.'

He stared pointedly at both men. *Until now.* No mind-reading required.

'They in?'

Maroc arched his brows expectantly.

The barman gestured with his head, his expression still sour.

'They'll be in the back office.'

They finished their beers and began walking to the right of the bar. Maroc could see an entrance covered by a beaded curtain.

Pushing aside the curtains, he found himself in a dimly lit passage. A bulky man, his head closely shaved, exited from a door on the left. He wore a black tunic and trousers. Everything about him said, bouncer.

Johansson stepped around Maroc, and before the man had time to close the velvet-lined door, the Norwegian shoved him sharply in the chest, causing him to stumble back through the entrance. Maroc followed the pair closely.

All three ended up in a large office. Maroc scanned the room in one sweep. Well lit and tastefully furnished, it could have belonged to the CEO of a successful company.

Two men stood in conversation behind a massive antique desk. One, tall and lean and in his early fifties, had closely cropped silver hair. The other was a slightly younger clone.

Both were dressed in well-cut black suits. On hearing the commotion, both men looked up in alarm.

Embarrassed at being caught unawares, the bouncer recovered and lumbered towards Johansson, his large hands reaching out for the Norwegian. A bark from the older man stopped him in his tracks.

'Let the gentlemen be and wait outside.'

Then in a gentler tone which surprised both Johansson and Maroc.

'It's all right, Billy, close the door and give us some privacy, there's a good lad.'

Faithful to his Irish roots, the Londoner's voice carried the faintest hint of brogue. The bouncer gave Johansson a final once over before exiting, closing the door softly behind him.

Maroc and Johansson stood in the centre of the room, facing the massive desk.

'Mr O'Connell?'

Maroc's eyes moved from one man to the other.

'And you would be Peter Maroc?'

The older of the men smiled, opening a drawer in the large desk. Both soldiers reached inside their jackets.

'That won't be necessary. The deadliest thing in this drawer is a paper clip.'

The man chuckled at his own humour.

Maroc and Johansson kept their hands inside their jackets, pinning both men with their eyes. The older of the two carefully withdrew what looked like a photo print. He placed it on the desk.

'By the way, I'm Michael or Micky. This is my younger brother Al. And you would be...?'

Johansson remained momentarily speechless, taken aback by the unexpected formality.

'Niels Johansson.'

Conscious of the brevity of his response, he added, 'At your service.'

He finished with the hint of a bow.

'You don't need the hardware, gentlemen. You're in no danger here.'

Al O'Connell's voice was lighter than his brother's, the Irish flavour a little stronger.

The Londoner was stating what was, and Maroc chose to believe him. The trust would endure as long as he could see both their hands. He removed his hand from inside his jacket. Johansson reluctantly followed suit.

Michael O'Connell pushed the print forward, allowing both men a view. Looking up at them was a head and shoulders print of Peter Maroc.

The Welshman looked up and shrugged. O'Connell had known his name, so the print came as no great surprise. Johansson, however, was surprised, but his face gave nothing away.

Maroc nodded at the print. Choosing to go along with the goodwill, he smiled.

'You gentlemen have us at a disadvantage. It would be good if you were to bring us up to speed.'

O'Connell looked thoughtful. He gave both men a searching look. Finally stepping from behind the desk, he extended his hand.

'Good to be discussing matters with a more enlightened section of society Mr Maroc.'

'Maroc's fine.'

Johansson would not be left out of this rather bizarre exchange.

'You may call me Niels.'

His smile more than matched Maroc's

'Maroc, Niels, your visit was not entirely unexpected, although the timing caught us out. Then I would have expected nothing less. Not from members of her Majesty's Special Air Service.'

Johansson's demeanour became slightly more challenging. He kept his tone light.

'You know a hell of a lot about us. We know practically nothing about you.'

Maroc picked up the print. He turned it over, searching for anything that could tell him where it came from.

'I take it this wasn't delivered by my publicity agent?'

'No, it came from a more personal source. You may be able to kill two birds with your visit.'

'Not meaning to be rude, but could you come to the point? I've already had two attempts on my life. It's becoming rather tedious.'

Maroc looked directly at O'Connell.

'Let's make one thing clear, Maroc. Nobody in my organisation gets hired out for... what do you call it? Wet work?'

'You're saying you had no hand in Malcolm Southwell's death.'

It was a statement.

Al O'Connell walked over to an old but highly polished wooden filing cabinet standing against the far side office wall. Raising a hand to placate Johansson's sudden wariness, he opened a drawer and carefully removed a blue folder.

Looking back at his two visitors, he held up the folder.

'Our dealings with Mr Malcolm Southwell.'

He returned to the desk, placing the folder on it.

Maroc waited, sensing he may be nearer to getting some answers concerning more than just Malcolm. Michael O'Connell took over from his younger brother.

'Malcolm Southwell owed us money.'

He looked up at both men.

'Not serious money. Certainly not the sort of money people get killed for.

We have a strict policy of placing a cap on borrowing. Things are more manageable that way.'

He gave Maroc a level look.

'They don't get out of hand.'

O'Connell turned the opened folder towards Maroc.

'As you see here, the debt was honoured. Paid in full. Book closed.'

'No unpaid interest?'

'Interest would have been deducted from the capital borrowed. No, Maroc, he owed us nothing. Even if he did, there would be no way he would have ended up...'

O'Connell's hand gesture was clear.

'It would be a shoddy way of conducting business. People would soon stop dealing with us.'

O'Connell sat on the corner of his desk and looked at his two guests before continuing.

'Anyway, we don't deal in violence, it's against the law. We may be from the smoke, gentlemen, but we're not the Kray brothers.'

Maroc checked his body language. He decided to believe the Londoner.

'Was it Malcolm who gave you the print?'

A brief nod.

'Indeed, yes. He made us an offer which we could refuse.'

Maroc's eyebrows shot up.

'Malcolm requested a hit on me?'

He looked in disbelief at Michael O'Connell.

'Needless to say, we turned him down. Kept on pestering us. He finally got the message when we threatened to boot him out of the club. After that, he stopped asking.'

He looked at his younger brother, who nodded his agreement.

Maroc shook his head, finding this news hard to accept.

'Well, someone had a couple of pops at me. A few of the jokers were from a Manchester gang.'

'May I make one thing clear.

O'Connell held Maroc's gaze his expression hardening.

'We don't have a gang. Not in the way you understand the word. We run a few clubs, and those clubs include the opportunity for a flutter. That's it.'

His tone was emphatic. Final.

Maroc nodded.

'I believe you, Michael.'

Michael O'Connell relaxed visibly. He came around the desk to join Maroc and Johansson.

'There is a probable candidate in the Manchester area. The Wilson gang. Run by two brothers, Don and Jimmy Wilson. However, I have my doubts they would bother with cheapskates like Southwell.'

O'Connell was smiling. He looked over at his brother.

'Tell him, Al. Tell Maroc how much he's worth dead.'

Al O'Connell chuckled.

'He offered five grand for you, Maroc. I mean, no self-respecting hitman would kill a cat for that price.'

Johansson shook his head in disbelief. He looked at his friend and grinned.

'Five grand? Tempting offer.'

Maroc was serious.

'What do you know about the Albanian mafia in and around the Manchester area? More specifically, two brothers who may be operating independently.'

Michael looked sharply at his brother. Maroc realised he was on the right track.

'They came in here a couple of times. At the same time as Southwell. Rubbish poker players.'

He ran a hand over his cropped head.

'The older of the two. Edam?'

'Edon'

Maroc corrected him.

'Edon. That's right. Big ugly bastard. He inquired if we had any work for them, implying nothing was off the menu.'

'They knew Malcolm?'

'Not as far as I know. Well, not when they first came in and Malcolm was here. The second time was different, they became as thick as thieves. Quite quickly in fact. That's what puzzled me, there was no common ground there. Southwell was well-spoken. Educated even. He was also a snob, so it was surprising they got on so well.'

'Unless they had some business interests in common.

Maroc looked pointedly at Johansson. Michael replied.

'Never thought of it.'

'If he'd approached them with the same contract he offered us, the Albanians would have jumped at it. They seemed up for anything.'

'For five grand?'

Johansson seemed unconvinced. Maroc added.

'Don't forget, those bastards had me marked down anyway. Malcolm's money would have been an unearned bonus.'

He looked at his friend. Johansson shrugged, accepting the possibility. Maroc smiled sympathetically, shaking his head.

'Poor Malcolm.'

'We may also have found his killers.'

'You think they killed him?'

Al O'Connell seemed surprised.

'They seemed the best of mates.'

Maroc nodded.

'From what you say, it could be a friendship based around a common purpose. Can't see those two befriending anyone unless it was to their advantage. Malcolm may have requested their services, having been turned down by you.'

Maroc waited for their take. Al O'Connell looked unconvinced.

'But why kill him? Even people like that need a motive.'

Maroc nodded his agreement.

'Malcolm, being a greedy little sod, might have held back on paying them for work done. It could be several reasons why they fell out.'

'You're right.'

Micky crossed the room to the drinks cabinet.

'Doesn't matter now anyway. He's dead. Sad little bugger.'

He brought over glasses and a bottle.

'You fellas drink scotch?'

'Is the Pope Polish?'

Maroc winced at Johansson's lack of Catholic knowledge.

'No, he's not.'

Micky O'Connell looked sternly at Johansson. Seeing the deflated look on the Norwegian's face, he burst out laughing.

'I'll take that as a yes.'

He poured four generous measures of Glenfiddich sixteen-year-old malt.

The toast was to a better future for all. Not a bad sentiment thought Maroc. They left the brothers as

friends, promising to keep in touch. It had been a day
of unexpected outcomes.

CHAPTER 52

Maroc had a good idea why the Albanian brothers wanted him dead. However, he had no intention of giving the O'Connell brothers too much information. There was much concerning the Fare that came under the Official Secrets Act.

Maroc should have been delivered alive to the Fare's headquarters in Lazarat. The brothers had failed, and he had escaped.

The Krye in Lazarat would not have been pleased. He had been denied an opportunity to extract information from Peter Maroc. Information concerning the whereabouts of his stolen drugs and money. Maroc knew how the Albanian Mafia dealt with such ineptitude.

It would have better served the brothers to report Maroc as having died trying to escape. Alive, he could alert the other British troopers in the patrol to be on their guard against a similar abduction.

For the Krye, it was a matter of saving face. He would have been perceived as incompetent by others seeking his prestigious position.

The job had been straightforward. Abduct Maroc and bring him in for interrogation. The Fare would not have seen Maroc's death as the best outcome. However, it was better than the SAS man being at large and alerting his comrades.

If the Krye was to discover Maroc's escape to freedom, the brothers would pay dearly for such an embarrassment. Edon and Burim needed to make their story a reality.

Peter Maroc had to disappear. This time, he could not return.

As he and Johansson began their journey back to North Wales, Maroc thought of John Southwell's complicity in the plot to kill him. The Southwell brothers had a mission. To secure all of Max Southwell's inheritance. He was the fly in the ointment.

Maroc smiled at the irony. The hit on him was already in place. Their planning and scheming had been unnecessary.

Proving John's involvement could be tricky. Maroc was certain of the man's guilt. His suggestion to the family that Malcolm was scared of his brother-in-law was an obvious lie. For Maroc, there would be no advantage in Malcolm's demise.

If John could manufacture such nonsense to alienate him from the rest of the family, what else would he be prepared to do?

The Albanian brothers would be Maroc's perfect witnesses, but why should they help him. They would have to admit their association with Malcolm and their complicity in his subsequent murder. That they would never do.

When Maroc's continuing existence came to light, and this information was to reach the Fare, their future would be bleak to non-existent.

The hospital had given all of Malcolm's personal

effects to his next of kin in a plastic bag. Maroc remembered Emily taking it from one of the nurses.

There was also Malcolm's flat in Salford...Then it came to him. Malcolm could have a diary, a mobile phone. There had to be something to incriminate John at Malcolm's flat. Prove his involvement.

Johansson had dozed off when Maroc gave a loud whoop. The Norwegian woke with a start, wondering if his friend had taken leave of his senses.

'Jesus, you crazy Maroc?'

Maroc glanced at his watch.

'We're going back, Niels. We can make it to the 'Blue Cock' before Lucy finishes her shift.'

Fully awake, Johansson stared at his friend.

'What the hell for, man? You've got everything you came for.'

'Not everything, Niels. Not by a long shot.'

Fortunately, they had only just got onto the M56 Motorway, and Maroc drove until he reached the next junction. Taking it, he pointed the Maserati north, back towards Salford.

As they drove, Maroc explained his reasons for going back to a groggy and rather reluctant Johansson.

It was ten by the time they reached the Blue Cock, and the car park was in darkness. Making for the entrance, Maroc hoped Lucy would still be there and free to talk. Entering the pub, he saw her. She was busy serving a customer, her expression serious and focused.

Once again, Maroc could appreciate Malcolm's attraction to this good-hearted girl. Had he lived, she might have helped him forget the pretentious fancies that had led to his death.

Surprised at seeing them a second time that day, she gestured to her young colleague to take over. They sat at the same table, and she immediately joined them.

Maroc briefly explained his reason for the return visit. Lucy replied she had never seen Malcolm using a diary.

'Yes, he had a mobile phone, but that would have been with him when he...'

She had faltered, and Maroc had laid a hand over hers.

He asked her gently if she could give him Malcolm's address in Salford.

'His father wants a few mementoes.'

He hated the lie.

'I can help you there, Mr Maroc. I can give you the key to his place. Shan't be needing it. Not anymore.'

She fished around inside a small handbag and withdrew a set of two keys on a silver key ring.

Maroc reached over and kissed her cheek. Johansson began following suit. He hesitated and thought better of it. Maroc smiled, impressed by his friend's unexpected sensitivity.

They emerged from the Blue Cock around ten thirty, deciding to leave the car where it was. The directions Lucy had given were straightforward. Malcolm's flat was a hundred yards away.

'At least we don't have to break into the bloody place.'

Johansson was keen to get going. The day had been a long one.

The flat was on the second floor of a three-storey Victorian terrace house. One key fitted the tall black-painted front door. Maroc opened it, and the men found themselves in a spacious hall.

Johansson groped for a light switch. He managed to find one on the left wall just inside the entrance.

At first, Maroc failed to identify the faint smell as they stood inside the hall. He decided on boiled cabbage, laced with disinfectant. The floor was a period diamond black and white.

A slightly worn Persian rug covered most of it. The walls could have had the original wallpaper coated with numerous layers of dark cream paint. A hat stand stood rather pointlessly to the right near the door.

The stairs were to the left, a dozen feet inside the hall. Maroc took the steps with Johansson close behind.

They came to a short corridor. The door to the apartment was on the right.

The second key was a fit. Maroc stepped inside into a large and comfortable lounge. It appeared Malcolm had used some of his money to good advantage. The furnishing and fittings looked brand new.

Johansson began searching the lounge while Maroc went through to the single bedroom. Nothing jumped out at him. The large bedroom was surprisingly tidy, as was the whole flat.

To the left of the double bed was a wooden cabinet. On top sat a modern reading lamp and a couple of ballpoint pens. The top drawer had a lock. However, when he pulled at the neat brass knob, the drawer opened smoothly.

Bingo! Inside the drawer was a brown leather notebook. He opened it. It was what he had hoped for. A page-a-day diary. The year was current, and Maroc flicked through the pages, speed reading as he went along.

He came to a page where Malcolm mentioned an outing with Lucy. Maroc smiled. The language was that of a fourteen-year-old boy out on his first date.

The Blue Cock had a few mentions, including his meeting with Maroc. Malcolm's description of him was less than flattering. *An uncouth Welshman with ambitions above his station.*

Maroc laughed out loud at the archaic language. Malcolm certainly was old school.

Johansson entered the room.

'What's so funny?'

He walked over to the bed and peered over Maroc's shoulder at the diary.

'I've been mentioned in dispatches.'

Maroc read out John's comments.

'Seems about right. You are a peasant, Maroc. No argument.'

Maroc grinned and made a rude gesture. He continued reading while his partner looked around the rest of the bedroom.

'I think we've got what we wanted.'

He stood up from the bed.

'I'm taking this. We can go through it when we get back.'

Johansson was preoccupied, rummaging through a magazine rack.

'Shouldn't we keep looking? We're here now. We might as well.'

Maroc nodded.

'I agree. Can't have too much evidence.'

He raised the diary.

'I think this is going to nail the bastard. There might also be something on Malcolm's phone. Text messages to and from John.'

This time Maroc took the living room while Johansson conducted a more thorough search of the bedroom. The bathroom yielded nothing. That left the small second bedroom. Looking in, they found it to be practically empty. They continued searching for another hour. Finally, deciding the flat had given up all its secrets, it was time to make the journey back.

With Maroc driving, Johansson asked if he could go through the diary. Maroc nodded.

'Anything which connects the Southwell brothers to the Albanians, mate. Also, any references to phone conversations with his brother.'

'You mentioned a mobile phone. Did you say Emily's got it?'

Maroc nodded.

'Yes, she was given it in the hospital,'

'Providing the evidence from the diary is strong enough, I can approach her for the phone. By the way, not a word to Max about this. The knowledge would crush him.'

'But it's bound to come out when the cops hear about it. Wouldn't it be better coming from you?'

Maroc, taking his eyes off the road, looked at his friend.

'I'm not reporting any of this. It stays with the family. Malcolm's dead. You can't prosecute a dead man.'

Johansson grunted.

'That leaves John. You can't let that slimy bastard get away with it.'

Maroc was silent for a while.

'He won't. I'll sort him, so he retracts his accusations. I'll also make sure my dear brother-in-law stays in Australia for a hell of a long time.

'He could disappear. For longer'

Johansson had an expression Maroc was only too familiar with.

'Leave him to me, Niels. Let's not visit more grief on the family. He gets to live. But by Christ, it'll be on my terms.'

CHAPTER 53

Max Southwell reflected on the brief time he had spent with his daughter. A period of ridiculous contrast and emotional roller coasting. Now it was time to return home.

His reunion with Emily and Maroc had been everything he could have wished for. The three of them together again. John's visit had ruined everything.

It had robbed them of all they had reclaimed. And now, Max Southwell was obliged to spend the next few days with his least favourite child and his sour wife.

Ruth Southwell was the ice queen personified. A remote woman devoid of passion, she would sit in his living room in complete silence. As far as Max could see, she neither sought nor needed the company of others.

Spending time with the pair was a grim prospect. He was shocked by his lack of affection for his eldest son. The accusations he'd laid at Maroc's door were false. He would stake his life on it. A life he now owed to his son-in-law.

Ye gods, he thought. Even if it turns out Maroc is the devil incarnate, the happiness of the last few months more than made up for it.

His heart informed him Maroc was no killer.

Reckless, hard-headed, and a bloody fool, the man could cause emotional mayhem. That he committed a greed-motivated murder? And in such a cowardly manner? No, he would not accept that.

After a tender goodbye to Emily, he drove home to Plas Meurig. On his way to Beddgelert, he would stop in a quiet lay-by above the lovely Llyn Gwynant. There he would meditate.

The practice had helped coax his mind away from the bleak darkness of depression. It had also increased his mental resilience, making him able to recover quicker from emotional trauma. Silently, he acknowledged another debt to Peter Maroc.

By the time he had reached Beddgelert, he was calmer, more prepared to tackle his strong-willed son. He opened the front door with trepidation.

Entering the living room, he came upon his daughter-in-law. Ruth greeted him with a broad smile. An unexpected, surreal experience. What would he next encounter? John, kissing him on the cheek?

'John's gone to the pub. Went about an hour ago. I've made you something to eat.'

Southwell detected the aroma of cooking coming from his kitchen.

'I hope you don't mind me using your kitchen.'

He was momentarily taken aback by her mildness and surprisingly amiable demeanour. This was new territory. Realising he had not answered, he responded with equal good humour.

'Not at all, Ruth. You're family, so feel free to treat the place as home. Whatever you've prepared, it smells good.'

Her answering smile held a trace of mischief.

'Wait until you've tasted it.'

Humour too. Where was this going?

He mentally admonished himself.

Give the woman a break. Respond to what is, not what you think it should be.

The voice was Maroc's. The bloody man was in his head.

'I believe you're eating healthier nowadays. Not a bad thing either. I've prepared a vegetarian quiche. Hope that's OK?'

'Ruth, that sounds perfect. You shouldn't have gone to the trouble. Must admit though, I'm famished.'

She retreated to the kitchen, and he could hear the sound of her preparations. Emerging with a tray, she asked.

'Table or a tray on your knee?'

I'll sit at the table, thanks. Fancy some tea? I'll make it.'

Placing the tray on the table, she smiled.

'That would be lovely, but do let me make it. Best eat while it's hot.'

Max Southwell considered he might have entered an alternative reality. Could he have been mistaken about this woman? It had been over two years since he had last seen the couple. Could the taciturn person he remembered have changed that much? She left him, returning to the kitchen.

The quiche was surprisingly good, the potatoes and vegetables tasty and well prepared. Fifteen minutes passed before she returned with the tea.

'Thought I'd leave you in peace. Nothing gives me indigestion quicker than having to entertain someone while I'm eating.'

Southwell smiled his appreciation.

'That was lovely, Ruth. Thanks.'

She poured the tea in silence. It was not an uncomfortable one. Still, Southwell had the feeling there was something on her mind. Something she needed to say.

'Tell me if you don't want to discuss the matter, Max.'

Her manner was diffident. An outsider offering an opinion that might be considered intrusive.

He gave her an encouraging smile, and she continued.

'Do you think Maroc had anything to do with Malcolm's death?'

It took him by surprise, leaving him needing time to gather his thoughts. Finally, he looked up at her.

'No, Ruth. I do not.'

It was an emphatic response that harboured no doubts.

She remained quiet for a few moments. Then in a voice so low, he could barely hear.

'I tend to agree with you.'

'You do?'

He failed to contain his surprise.

'You don't think John has a point?'

She looked at him squarely.

'You and I may not see eye to eye on many things, Max. However, I'm far from comfortable with accusations so easily levelled.'

She paused to gather her thoughts.

'Maroc, working that hard on getting you back to health whilst planning your death? I can't quite see it. I'm not denying that people are complex, but Maroc is no psychopath.'

Ruth stopped, giving her father-in-law time to respond. He indicated for her to continue.

'Neither do I believe him capable of killing Malcolm in cold blood.'

She looked hesitantly at Southwell.

'I'm not clever and witty with words. I prefer to stand back and consider situations before making wild allegations. What's been happening over the last few days is... wrong.' Her voice dropped to a whisper. 'Monstrous.'

Southwell had never seen Ruth so garrulous or so emphatic in her convictions. He had always found it difficult to engage her in conversation and never one in which she revealed herself.

Could he have been wrong about this woman? Perhaps her proximity to his son had cast her in an unfavourable light. He had heard of reflected glory but reflected infamy? The academic in him deliberated on whether such a phenomenon existed.

He was momentarily lost for words. Could he believe Ruth, or was this some game of double bluff concocted with her husband?

'What makes John so sure of Maroc's guilt?

The question caught her unawares.

'I've given up trying to second guess my husband. He works to *his* agenda.'

For a moment, she looked lost, forlorn.

'It's hard to get close to him.'

He sensed her pain and felt an unexpected sympathy for a daughter-in-law he may have misjudged. He smiled at her now.

'Forget tea. I think we could both do with

something stronger.'

Southwell went to the drinks cabinet. Taking out his best malt, he poured two glasses, handing one to Ruth.

'To truth.'

He reflected for a moment.

'And a new start.'

She smiled and raised her glass.

'A new start.'

She took a deep gulp, spluttering and smiling as the strong spirit hit her throat.

An hour later, John Southwell returned. He found his father sitting on his own in the living room.

'Ruth about?'

Max looked up.

'She went for a walk. Clear her head.'

John saw the bottle and the two empty glasses on the table.

'You two been celebrating?'

His tone carried its familiar sarcasm, knowing it would irritate.

Rising from his chair, Max Southwell walked over to his son.

'John, we need to talk.'

'I believe you said your piece at Emily's. It's obvious Maroc's done a number on you.'

His father shook his head.

'He saved my life, if that's what you mean. I find it hard to believe he has some twisted agenda. Some nefarious get rich scheme.'

'Then why, if the man's such a bloody saint, was Malcolm so scared of him? Scared for his life, he said.'

Southwell gave his son a searching look.

'Did he, John? You have some evidence to back these accusations?'

'What do you mean by that?'

Max Southwell had grown tired of John's divisive games. They had brought nothing but misery and discord to the family.

He looked directly at his son.

'What I'm asking, what we would all like to know, is quite straightforward. Can you back this nonsense up with hard evidence? Until you do I'd be obliged if you kept your own counsel concerning your brother's death.'

John shifted uncomfortably under his father's gaze.

'Your own son's word not good enough for you? You prefer the word of a trained killer?'

He was about to continue, then seemed to falter. He looked uneasily at his father.

'Has Ruth said anything? Have you two been having a cosy chat behind my back?'

'She's a better woman than you deserve, John. And yes, she has her opinions.'

'I bet she has. Opinions which, no doubt, you accept.'

Max Southwell gave a weary smile.

'You seemed to have planted doubts in Emily's mind. You've left her not knowing what to believe. Doesn't it bother you you've managed to split her and Peter?'

'Peter? So he's Peter now. Is that the way you see it? My god, father, I'm trying to look out for her. Can't any of you see that? She's in danger from that man. You all are.'

Max Southwell shook his head in exasperation.

'Let's just leave it at that, John. I believe you return home in a couple of days. Until then, we'll be civil to each other.'

He added without a trace of humour.

'Even if it kills us.'

CHAPTER 54

Maroc parked the Maserati in town, and both men climbed up to the cabin. On their journey back from Salford, Johansson had been making careful notes. The dates and times of each of Malcolm's incriminating entries were recorded.

Maroc sensed his excitement but insisted they could better discuss it over coffee when they got back. He had discovered an ancient percolator in a cupboard when he'd first arrived. Badly in need of cleaning, Maroc soon had it serviceable.

Standards became basic when the two holed up together. A comfortable slovenliness, as Maroc had once put it.

'Milk in your coffee?'

Maroc hovered the bottle of Jack Daniels over his friend's cup.

Johansson grinned and nodded. He placed Malcolm's diary and his own notebook on the old wooden bench that served as a table. Maroc pulled out a chair and joined him. He pushed the fortified coffee over, and Johansson got down to business.

'Now, let's see what we've got so far.'

Consulting his notebook, the Norwegian opened Malcolm's diary to the relevant date page. He read aloud.

Approached Michael O'Connell yesterday evening re Maroc. He refused to take on the job. Thought it highly amusing that I would ask.

Johansson looked up, and Maroc shrugged.

'Close, but not conclusive. John would say he was referring to something quite different.'

'Like what, for god's sake? What else could he mean?'

Maroc looked at his friend's notes.

'Not enough, Niels. John could say Malcolm had tried to hire the O'Connells for protection. From me.'

Johansson shrugged.

'I Suppose. Anyway, there's more. A hell of a lot more.'

'Read on, dear friend.'

Maroc waved his hand expansively, his mood lifting at the prospect of nailing John Southwell. Johansson smiled, sensing his friend's emergence from his gloom.

'This was written a week later.'

Talked again, this time to Al O'Connell. He said he'd talk to his brother, and they would both get back to me. Later that evening, I was approached by both brothers and warned that if I brought the subject up again, I'd be banned from the club. Arrogant Irish bastards.

Again Maroc shook his head.

'Unless Malcolm expressly mentions a hit on me, then, John can explain it away. One good thing. This is consistent with what the O'Connells were saying. At least they were telling the truth.'

'Agreed. But it gets better, my friend. Much better. This is what he wrote after his next visit to the Mogambo.'

The Mogambo is getting quite cosmopolitan. This

evening we were joined by two Albanians. Brothers, as it turned out.

Having seen me talking to the O'Connells, they asked if I was in the nightclub business and if I had any work for them. When I asked what sort of work they did, they said they would do anything that pays.

I offered the same five thousand pounds for the same job. At first, they were diffident, saying it wasn't enough. After I showed a photo of Maroc, they seemed to come around to the idea.

Since I needed a professional job, I asked if they'd killed anyone before for money. They assured me the job would not be a problem. I had the impression the whole thing amused them, which seemed strange.

Maroc smiled, slapping Johansson on his back.

'We're halfway there, Niels. Now we need proof of John's involvement.'

The Norwegian pointed to his notebook.

'It's all in here, Peter. Everything you need, and more.'

He bent over his notes and was about to speak when Maroc held up his hand to stop him.

'Let's have another drink and something to eat. I can't take all this excitement in one sitting.'

His friend shrugged, grinning tolerantly. Turning from the table, he bent down and rummaged in Maroc's provisions cupboard.

'OK, I'll prepare an omelette while you do the potatoes. 'We'll drink and cook.'

Johansson, seeing Maroc reaching for the JD, shook his head disapprovingly.

'Don't be a Philistine, Peter. We'll open the bottle of five-year-old Merlot we bought yesterday.'

They ate, and they laughed as they had always laughed together. Maroc's mood was elevated by a new optimism. He could now envisage a path back to his family. John Southwell would lose this game.

Proof of his innocence would gain him little unless it was made known. Max did not need to know, but others did. One of them was his wife.

In the past, Maroc's honour had been a personal matter. It had always been his affair and his only. He cared nothing for the opinion of others. To him, his honour could never be tarnished by the fetid breath of slander.

Yet, he knew all this was changing. His good name and its retention were central to both Emily and Max. Their opinion of him had come to matter.

Peter Maroc understood he was losing his independence and, to his surprise, realised he did not care.

He would fight to regain the one precious thing he had lost. Emily required proof of his innocence; his lack of involvement in her brother's death.

On reflection, he did not blame her, could not blame her for not knowing his true face. His past actions had often been selfish, and he was prepared to settle his debts.

After clearing the table, they returned to the diary and Johansson's notes. There was one final thing Maroc needed. Proof of John Southwell's participation in the plot to kill him.

What the diary revealed so far made Peter Maroc a happy man. Far from running scared, Malcolm had been complicit in planning his death.

John would interpret his brother's writings to suit

his cause. He would say they were actions taken by his brother, in defence of his safety, and did not involve him.

When Maroc revealed his thoughts to his friend, Johansson smiled.

'Wait till you read this.'

Maroc felt a frisson of excitement.

'OK, Niels. Don't keep me in suspense. What else have you found?'

The Norwegian turned the diary to a page two days following Malcolm's conversation with the Albanians. He smiled as he read.

Everything seems to be running to plan. Edon and his brother have agreed on a date for the job. With Maroc out of the way, John and I can get everything back on track. Without Maroc's support, together with the grief from his death, the old bastard will hopefully give up the ghost. Then all we have to do is wait.

Johansson held his hand up before his friend could comment.

'There's more of the same, except better.'

John makes me nervous. He says he has no intention of waiting for dad to just fade away slowly. Even talking of ways and means to accelerate the process.

I want no part of it. Too risky. Given the old man's list of underlying complaints, and without Maroc to pull him through, I can't see him lasting long anyway.

Again, Maroc was about to comment. Johansson, however, was on a roll.

'That's not all of it, Peter. There's more on brother John. Enough to nail the bastard. Have a look at this.'

Guided by Johansson, Maroc read several entries covering Malcolm's long-distance phone conversations with his older brother. Twenty minutes later, Maroc concluded he had enough on John Southwell to put him away for a very long time.

It was time to celebrate. They finished the Merlot and brought out two six-packs of John Smiths bitter. The rest of the Jack Daniels would complete a successful day. A hangover in the name of a good cause could always be coped with.

CHAPTER 55

It was six-thirty a.m, and John Southwell had carried the last of their luggage, placing it in the car boot. He and Ruth would drive to Liverpool Airport. From Liverpool, they would fly to Heathrow where they would take the afternoon flight to Perth.

John was still seething from the confrontation with his father. Thanks to his damned brother-in-law, Max Southwell remained healthy, and with Maroc's aid, would continue getting stronger and harder to influence. His dreams of financial independence were evaporating like morning mist.

John, however, was not yet ready to throw in the towel. Maroc had escaped two attempts on his life. Would he expect a third? With John orchestrating operations, the outcome would be different. This time, he would hire real professionals, not Eastern European peasants.

He stole a glance at his wife. She and Max seemed to have reached an understanding. While not being the best of pals, they had been more than civil with each other. What the hell was going on there?

He was losing his grip on things. With Malcolm gone, it would be difficult to hire from the UK. He might be better off using his contacts back home. Also a hell of a lot more expensive. He would find the money somehow.

As a last resort, he would go cap in hand to Ruth with some cock and bull story about needing the extra financing. His mind shrank at the thought of being subjected to her interrogation.

Their early start found the A498 from Beddgelert devoid of traffic. The narrow road snaked its way through the wild countryside. As they passed the tranquil lake Dinas to their right, John Southwell felt his tension starting to ease, and he willed his mind to forget the unpleasant confrontations of the last few days.

They had been driving around ten minutes when the larger Lake Gwynant appeared to their left. Its beauty that morning, however, was wasted on him.

Southwell noticed that the road ahead appeared to be blocked by a silver Range Rover. He sighed. The last thing he needed was to miss his Liverpool flight.

Giving a couple of short blasts on the horn, Southwell waited for the vehicle to move. Nothing happened, so he gave another longer blast. He waited for a reaction. There was still no movement from inside the Range Rover.

He thought he could see an outline of the occupant through the heavily tinted windows. What was the bloody driver waiting for? Perhaps he or she was ill. Perhaps the vehicle had been abandoned for some reason.

He turned to his wife.

'Wait here while I find out what the hell is going on.'

Ruth Southwell sighed, maintaining her usual silence. Stepping out of the car, Southwell covered the dozen or so yards to the four-by-four.

He reached the driver's side and was about to knock on the window when the door abruptly opened. It hit him squarely in the chest, causing him to stumble backwards.

Before he had time to recover, a tall man stepped out of the driving seat, closing the door behind him. The man turned and, without warning, grabbed Southwell by the lapels.

Spinning him around, the man slammed his body against the vehicle door. Winded and alarmed, John Southwell looked up into the grim face of Peter Maroc.

Niels Johansson had, by this time, stepped out from the passenger side of the four-track and walked briskly over to Southwell's car. Opening the passenger door, he encountered a cowering Ruth Southwell.

Johansson presented the terrified woman with his most charming smile.

'It's all right, Mrs Southwell, nobody's going to get hurt.'

Ruth Southwell looked up at Johansson, her mind desperately trying to process what was happening.

'My friend just wants to discuss something with your husband. It's nothing serious.'

His voice was soft and encouraging. He stepped back from the car door, demonstrating he was no threat.

'You'll soon be on your way to the airport.'

Ruth's expression turned from terror to fear, then finally to utter confusion.

'That's Maroc. Peter Maroc! What does he want with John?'

The terror returned.

'Is that a gun he's holding to my husband's head?'

'Don't worry, Mrs Southwell. I doubt if it's even loaded. I'm sure it's not. Your husband is in no danger.

Ruth Southwell was, however, very worried.

'But it's a gun, for pity's sakes. I need to know what is happening.'

She looked up at Johansson, her eyes bright with anger. The fear was still there but now it was suppressed by her outrage.

'As you know, your husband has been making some accusations. He's saying Peter killed his brother Malcolm. My friend is... setting the records straight. When he's done, you can both continue on your journey.'

'What has my husband done? He would hardly kill his own brother.'

Johansson gave her a searching look.

'Now, why would you say that?'

He paused, pondering the point.

'It's an interesting idea.

'That's a monstrous thing to say.'

He noticed her indignation lacked the expected conviction.

Johansson's voice was gentle. Both he and Maroc guessed this woman was not a part of John Southwell's circle of one. Psychopaths were good at keeping secrets.

'Are you sure of that, Mrs Southwell? John is capable of many things.'

Pressing the Glock hard into Southwell's cheek, Maroc snarled at the terrified man.

'From now on, think of me as your worst nightmare, Johny boy.'

Fear constricting his larynx, Southwell's voice was

pitched high.

'You're a madman, Maroc. You should be in a bloody cage.'

'You'd better believe it, Southwell.'

Maroc paused, slightly easing his grip on the man.

'I've got something here I'm certain you'll be interested in.'

With his free hand, Maroc reached into one of the large pockets of his outdoor jacket and pulled out Malcolm's diary.

'This little book has enough information to put you away for a long time, you scheming bastard.'

Southwell struggled to turn his head.

'What bullshit are you trying now? You're the one who's going to jail.'

Maroc noticed the man was getting braver. He tapped the side of Southwell's head with the pistol. Not hard enough to damage. Enough to focus his attention.

'If you think this is a game, you're in serious shit, my friend.'

Maroc brought his mouth to Southwell's ear. His voice took on a menacing tone.

'You think I won't put a bullet through your temple? Is that it? Think you're safe? You underestimate people, John. Little snots like you always do.'

Maroc hauled a now cowed Southwell away from the car.

'See my friend over there? I love the guy, but he's a bloody psycho. Compared to him, I'm a boy scout. He's begged me to give him five minutes alone with you. You know, I think I'll do just that.'

Johansson walked around the car and got into the driving seat beside Ruth Southwell. She seemed less frightened, and he was glad.

He noticed the engine was still running. Putting the car into gear, he drove it into the small parking area to the left of the road and switched off the engine.

'Stay here, Mrs Southwell.'

She looked up, and Johansson noticed the doubts had returned. He spoke gently.

'Stop worrying. Nobody's going to get hurt today.'

Maroc ordered Southwell into the passenger seat of Johansson's hired four by four. Diary in one hand, gun in the other, he was ready to reveal the weight of evidence against the Southwell brothers. He placed the diary into the cowering man's hands.

Reading Malcolm's entries, Southwell silently cursed his younger brother. It was what he had feared all along.

Despite being repeatedly told not to record anything incriminating, Malcolm had chosen to disregard his advice. He had left a paper trail.

Looking increasingly resentful, John Southwell was compelled to continue reading. Realising the extent of the evidence against him, he remained silent. The bluster had gone. Maroc witnessed the crumbling of a persona carefully cultivated over decades.

His voice icy, Maroc continued.

'This is what's going to happen. You return to Australia and stay there, or at least stay away from this country for the foreseeable future. You tell Max your own story, you're good at that. Anyway, I doubt if he'll miss you much. You haven't exactly been the ideal son.'

Southwell began to protest. Maroc raised his gun until it was level with his eyes.

'You listen, or it ends here for both you and Ruth.

Your father needn't know of your murderous schemes. He's suffered enough. Emily, on the other hand, will get to know everything.'

Southwell, forced to listen, could do nothing. He stared sullenly through the windscreen, seeing a bleaker future than he had hoped for.

Maroc continued.

When your father dies a natural death, you'll inherit your share. Any deviation from this and you go away for a long time. Your father gets to know all the facts, and you inherit nothing.'

Once again, the Glock was pressed hard against Southwell's cheek. He leaned over, making direct eye contact with his brother-in-law.

His voice, cold with a rage not feigned, Maroc delivered his last message to John Southwell.

'Any move against me or mine, and you will die. Do not doubt that. I shall come for you, and I shall kill you.'

Leaning over the terrified man, he opened the passenger door.

'Your wife will be spared all knowledge of your activities. That's for her benefit, not yours.'

The ex-SAS man's expression was feral. His voice, a snarl.

'Now sod off before I change my mind.'

As he stepped out of the vehicle, Southwell muttered something from under his breath. Maroc raised the gun, and the man's schoolboy scowl vanished.

Thoroughly cowed, Southwell slammed the car door, his action done more to shield himself than out of consideration. He ran to his car.

Johansson had been waiting by the other car. Southwell passed him, his head deliberately turned away. The Norwegian smiled. His friend had delivered his message.

Johansson found Maroc in the passenger seat, and he took his place behind the wheel. For a long moment, they looked at each other with Maroc retaining his fierce expression.

The mirth, when it came, broke through like water from a bursting dam. They laughed until tears wet their cheeks.

Victory and vindication, both tasted equally good. Maroc looked at his friend.

'What now?'

Johansson considered the question.

'Now, we find an old woman in town, and we mug her. After all, Peter, you have a reputation to keep.'

CHAPTER 56

Still smiling, Johansson, engaged first gear of the four-by-four. He looked enquiringly at his friend

Maroc shrugged.

'Let's go to the cabin, and look at what we've got, Niels.'

His face became serious.

'The evidence against Southwell has to be kept from Max. After what he's been through, it would break him'

Entering the town of Llanberis, Johansson parked the hired four-by-four on the same side road as Maroc's Maserati. They decided to top up on provisions before returning to the cabin.

On reaching the High Street, Maroc saw Emily entering an outdoor clothing stall. He placed a restraining hand on Johansson's arm.

'Leave it for the moment, Niels. I need to collect my thoughts before I talk to Emily.'

Johansson shrugged and nodded.

'You'll have to talk to her at some point, my friend. At least show her the diary. Make things right between you two.'

Maroc nodded.

'Oh, believe me, I mean to. Just not yet. Let's get some stuff from the supermarket and head up to my cave.'

'Dog kennel,'

Johansson corrected.

They opened a fresh bottle of Jack Daniels. Maroc poured two glasses, raising his in a toast.

'To a successful couple of days. And to you, Niels. Thanks, mate, I couldn't have done it without you.'

Johansson blew him a kiss before raising his glass.

'Skal.'

Maroc smiled at his friend.

'Skal.'

They downed the whisky and slammed their empty glasses onto the bench.

'More tea, vicar?'

Maroc hovered the bottle over his friend's empty glass. Johansson grinned and nodded.

'No more after this, Peter. Let's get this business out of the way first.'

This was not the time to get wasted. There was too much to discuss. Johansson began.

'The Albanian brothers. What's going to happen there? Any word from the top?'

'Nothing yet. They'll be dealt with by the Home Office rather than Scotland Yard. I'm pretty certain the Albanian authorities will be informed, and they'll be deported.'

Maroc shook his head.

'I wouldn't rate their chances in an Albanian prison. The Fare can't allow them to live. Not if they're to maintain control of business.'

Johansson shrugged.

'I've no sympathy for those animals. Not after what they did to you. What about the Fare? The Albanian government has to be seen taking some action against them.'

'I'm no political expert, Niels. I can see the Fare in Lazarat being paid a visit by the Albanian authorities. A few arrests maybe. Whether the charges will stick is another matter. The Fare has influence all the way up to government level.'

Maroc sighed wearily.

'There's no guarantee the bastards won't still be after us.

Johansson shrugged.

'Life is dangerous. What about the Manchester gang? The Wilson mob?'

'Since they had no agenda other than profit, that'll be a matter for Scotland Yard. They'll be arrested and tried on some serious weapons charges. Maybe Malcolm's murder, though I doubt anything can be proven.'

Maroc grinned at his friend.

'Bunch of amateurs. Can't see any more bother from them.'

Johansson nodded, then added.

'There's still the ordnance to take back.'

The Norwegian looked up, a wicked smile beginning to form.

'That leaves the lovely Emily to take care of. About time you two got things straightened out.'

Maroc shook his head, grinning at Johansson's persistence.

'OK, Cupid. First things first. Tomorrow, I'm taking you out on the town. Reintroduce you to a few drinking buddies. Then back here to complete the evening.'

'And Emily? You must show her the evidence. Give

383

her time to take it in. It won't be easy for her to accept that her brothers were scheming arseholes.'

Maroc nodded, then hesitated.

'Hope she doesn't shoot the messenger. After all, John and Malcolm are family. Family can get away with murder.'

He paused.

'Those two nearly did.'

'The two stopped being family when they tried to finish off their father. That's another thing. What about Max?'

Maroc nodded.

'I have unfinished business with Max. I doubt things will have changed between us.'

He thought for a moment.

'Just in case I need more evidence, I'm thinking of phoning the O'Connells in Manchester. They could back up everything I said about Malcolm.'

'Sure. But I doubt you need more than you already have.'

Johansson nodded to the open diary on the bench.

Not wanting to begin an evening's drinking on an empty stomach, Maroc suggested starting with a meal at a local restaurant.

Eating and talking, they found themselves on a well-trodden path down memory lane. Absent friends were duly toasted, adventures retold, each time with an increase in the body count.

They knew the stories by heart, but that mattered little. The ritual soothed. It deepened their bond.

The Heights was full and Johansson was greeted like an old friend. Maroc spotted the Beddgelert crowd and waved. Some of Maroc's closest friends had long guessed the Norwegian's connection with Maroc. It had made him more interesting.

They weaved their way up to the cabin a little worse for wear. The banter and leg-pulling continued. The evening concluded with a few more beers followed by JD chasers. They fell asleep just as the sun came up.

Around three in the afternoon, and still suffering, Maroc helped Johansson load his luggage into the four-by-four. He hoped his friend's blood alcohol level did not exceed the legal limit.

Embracing, they promised to keep in touch and to visit. Johansson would have plenty of time to catch his Manchester flight.

On his own for the first time in days, Maroc decided not to contact Emily till the following day. He needed to be fully rested, fully functioning. Besides, he was as nervous as a schoolboy.

He would walk the hills for a couple of hours; clear his head before driving over to Max's place. It had been so good seeing the old bugger after such a long absence.

Now there were things to discuss. Above all, he needed his father-in-law's advice on how best to approach Emily. He felt like a teenager embarking on his first date.

Maroc opened the black gate with its red dragon design. Stepping through, he entered the familiar world of the Southwell family. Memories flooded in, occupying their reserved spaces.

The front door of Plas Meurig greeted him, and he savoured its formal welcome. Still in possession of a front door key, he knocked out of courtesy.

Half a minute passed before Maroc heard footsteps.

The door opened, and Southwell appeared in his dressing gown. His mind returned to that first visit with Emily. Standing outside the same door, he remembered how intimidating this man had seemed then.

Southwell gestured Maroc inside. He entered, taking in the familiar smells and feel of the place. He felt at home in the old house.

'Am I still welcome?'

Maroc was smiling, but the older man could sense his uncertainty.

Southwell's answering smile put Maroc at his ease.

'Not sure if I should be left alone with you, Maroc. A trained killer and so on. How would you like your scotch? With or without green sludge?'

'The hell with it. I'll have it neat.'

The ritual over, he knew he was good with Max. Maroc dug into his jacket pocket.

'Bought you a book. It's a new one on neuroplasticity. How different mental states can change and form new neural pathways. Also, demonstrates how your thoughts can change you at a cellular level.

'New brain connections, eh?

Southwell accepted the book.

'Sounds like something you could use.'

Smiling, Maroc walked over to the big bay window and looked out onto the garden.

'You've certainly put some work in since I was last here.'

Southwell joined him.

'Katherine would be pleased, Peter. Labour of love, you know.'

His face brightened.

'It also gave me something to do since I wasn't having to look after you.'

'Cheeky bugger.'

They slipped comfortably into their old harnesses, each man enjoying the other's repartee.

Southwell was quiet for a while.

'Sorry about John. Should never have come out with that garbage.'

Maroc shrugged.

'Maybe he was being protective of you...'

Southwell stopped him mid-sentence.

'Now you're talking nonsense.'

His face softened.

'I know. You're trying to make things easier for me.'

Sadness vied with anger.

'I've long accepted it. My eldest son is a conniving bastard. If he wasn't of my flesh, I'd have nothing to do with him.'

Maroc smiled.

'Well, he's not a happy man. He's married to an iceberg. That should be punishment enough.'

Southwell was quiet for a moment.

'Ruth's all right.'

Maroc's eyebrows shot up.

'We are talking about the same person?'

'It's John. Nobody could live with him and not be affected. Over the years, the poor woman has learnt defensive strategies. Put up barriers.'

Maroc was slightly taken aback.

'But she's on his side, Max. She believes I did those things. Am that person.'

Southwell shook his head.

'Not a bit of it. We had a good chat, and… well, let's just say she saw through him years ago.'

Maroc shook his head.

'Bugger me! People always have the power to amaze.'

CHAPTER 57

Max accompanied Maroc to the front gate, waving him off after extracting a promise he would call his daughter. Driving back to Llanberis, he felt a slight sinking in the pit of his stomach. He could still see the expression of doubt on Emily's face, and he hated the memory.

Maroc realised how much he had relied on his wife's loyalty and trust. In his world of uncertainty and duplicity, he had seen her as a constant he could always depend on. A haven he could always return to.

Given he had embarked on such a life, was it fair to place on Emily such expectations? He knew he had no right to judge his wife. After all, he was the author of his questionable reputation. He was to blame for causing her present doubts.

Peter Maroc had believed he could have a marriage as well as the thrills of adventure and danger. He now realised he had built his life on a selfish premise.

Having showered and shaved at Max's place, Maroc decided he would phone Emily and request to see her that day. Using his mobile, he dialled the house number.

After it had rung for a while, with no answer, he decided he would try her mobile. He heard Emily's voice and began speaking. She continued speaking over him and he realised he had reached her voicemail.

Maroc decided not to leave a message. Rather than hanging around all day waiting until she was available, he decided to drive to the house. He had no idea what he would say to her. Sometimes, you just had to wing it.

Arriving outside the house, he saw her car parked in the drive. After ringing the front doorbell and getting no response, he knocked on the door. There was still no answer. Wondering where she could be, he used his key to let himself in.

The house was empty. Maroc thought for a moment and decided Emily had walked into town. He toyed with the idea of setting off to look for her. Would doing so place him in a desperate light? Did that matter?

His mobile rang just as he was about to close the front door. Maroc started to speak when a man's voice interrupted. 'Don't talk, Mr Maroc. Just listen.'

The voice was heavily accented and raspy, giving the impression the speaker was a heavy smoker. Unmistakably Eastern European, the man continued with brutal brevity.

'We have your wife. You have what we want.'

There was a pause, but Maroc failed to take advantage of it. The man continued.

'When we are ready, you will receive a text giving the address to where you will come.'

Maroc felt a sense of unreality. His mind struggled for an answer as to why this was happening. He started to speak when the man continued.

'There is no need for me to make unpleasant threats, Mr Maroc. You know what we can do if you try to...'

The voice paused meaningfully. In the meantime, you wait for our text which will come sometime tomorrow.'

Before Maroc could answer, the call was cut short. He stared at his mobile, wondering if he had returned to one of his nightmares. He prayed it was so and he would wake up to a kinder reality.

'Peter, everything, all right? Saw Emily go off with a couple of blokes first thing this morning. She looked upset.'

Alan Lewis, their nearest neighbour came towards him.

Maroc fought to sound normal.

'What time was that, Alan?'

Lewis made a face.

'Let's think. Got to be around eight, eight-thirty. They drove off in a black car. Merc, I think. Heard about her brother. No more bad news, I hope?'

Maroc thanked him, saying it was probably nothing. Emily, he said, was still deeply upset about Malcolm. He would keep him posted.

He knew it could not be Edon and his brother, given they were banged up in a British jail. Yet the accent was right. Definitely Albanian.

He knew the Fare in Manchester would have found out about Edon and Burim by now. But how the hell would they have found out about him? That he was alive? Surely not from the brothers. That piece of information would result in a death sentence for both.

So how had they found out where he and Emily lived? He would figure that one out later.

It was time to act. It was time to get Emily back home.

Conducting a firefight in a remote area like Llyn Llydaw was one thing. A city location would be another matter. The MOD would require a full breakdown of any operation carried out before they would sanction it.

The hell with that, he thought. Emily's life was at stake, and all discussions concerning this operation would have to be conducted after the event. He was getting her back with or without official approval.

Maroc dialled his old friend, John Tucker. He would present it to Tucker as unfinished business from the Llyn Llydaw encounter.

Tucker was eager to help and seemed more than willing to risk the consequences. Listening to Maroc's account, Tucker seemed sure the Fare was behind the abduction.

Maroc had his doubts. How had the Albanian Mafia managed to locate him and his family?

To the MI6 man, it seemed clear.

Edon and his brother had no other option than to call the Fare in Manchester and confess to everything. They had, in turn, informed the Krye in Lazarat.

Maroc had argued the brothers would be signing their death warrants. Tucker, with his extensive experience of Mafia mentality, held a different view.

The brothers would reason that by revealing Maroc's location, they might be spared or at least given a quick death. It was a plausible assumption.

Maroc's next task would be to recall Bill Gordon and Mark Fisher. Their wives would not be pleased. However, explanations and apologies would have to be postponed. At least until Emily was returned to him,

Except for Tucker, it was unanimous. The

authorities would be kept out of the loop. Maroc and Tucker would enter the house, relying on Fisher and Gordon to create a diversion. Hopefully, this would afford them enough time to get Emily safely out.

The strategy was makeshift and, perhaps, optimistic. It was the best they could come up with.

At least they had all of today, and perhaps more time tomorrow to refine the operation. In the meantime, it would be advantageous if they located the Fare's headquarters in Manchester. Ahead of the expected text message from Emily's abductors.

Maroc thought of the O'Connells at the Mogambo club. Given their background, they would have made it their business to discover the location of all potentially threatening elements in the city.

He thought he had gained enough trust with the brothers to approach them with such a request. If need be, he could always return the favour.

Bill Gordon was shocked to hear of Emily's abduction. He assured Maroc he would be over within the hour.

Fisher was just as obliging.

'Give me half an hour to get ready, and I'll be up there in about three hours, mate.'

And yes, he would have to make things up with his other half. Big time.

Five hours later, the four were in Tucker's large off-road vehicle, heading to central Manchester and the Mogambo Club. Arriving at the club, Maroc entered on his own.

Both brothers were in and were delighted to see him. Maroc explained the situation as briefly as possible. The London Irish club owners, realising the urgency, had the address and directions in Maroc's hands within minutes.

Michael O'Connell was apologetic, but he could not agree to give his men to this fight. Maroc nodded, saying he understood completely and it had never entered his head to ask. Once more, the men parted on good terms.

With both address and directions in their possession, the four would head over to Salford. There, they would begin putting into action their quickly fashioned extraction plan.

Tucker had stashed a couple of HK MP5 submachine guns in his vehicle. They were for Bill Gordon and Mark Fisher. He had correctly assumed the others would have their handguns.

Before setting off, Gordon had hinted he would bring a few useful 'toys' to the party. They had turned out to be a box of smoke grenades plus a half dozen flashbangs, thrown in for good luck.

Maroc had again reminded Tucker to delay calling the job in until Emily was safely out of the house. A hint of non-compliance with the Fare's terms and Emily would die.

Both men knew the Fare's culture. It was the same with all such organisations. Terms and Conditions were given, and if an agreement was broken, then blood would be shed.

They called it a matter of honour. Maroc recognised it as control.

'Has it occurred to you that Emily might not be at their headquarters?' Tucker asked.

'They might have her somewhere else?'

Maroc shook his head.

'We have to work on the assumption that she's there, John. If it turns out she's not, we rethink the plan.'

Tucker nodded.

'It's a big house. They could have a dozen, perhaps twenty men in there. We could wait until someone comes out of the house, then grab him. Give me five minutes, and I'll tell you whether Emily is there or not.'

Maroc grinned. He knew these were not empty words. Tucker was no sadist, but he could be very persuasive.

'We're working against time, mate. It's a good idea, but I need to present myself to the Kryetar within the next few hours.'

'OK, fine. We'll secure Emily and, with Mark and Bill's little distractions, get her out of the house. We're going to need serious backup.'

Tucker paused.

'A clean extraction, plus removing all these bastards off the streets, will take personnel. I mean, more than four.'

Again, Maroc shook his head.

'I know how you work, John. You'll have an armed response team called out before we make a move. Any sniff of that and Emily's gone.'

Tucker looked at his friend.

'Mate, I'm not talking about your street bobbies. Look, your SAS buddies are the best at covert surveillance. They'll relay full intel on what's happening. An armed response team will only come in when they see Emily outside the house. Christ, Peter, you've done more than your share of extractions. I'd never put her life in danger. You know that.'

Maroc was quiet. He looked at the MI6 man.

'Yes, OK, Tucker, you're right. Perhaps I'm too close to this.'

With an air of casual confidence, Tucker slapped him on the shoulder.

'We'll get Emily out, mate. No worries. It's all in hand.'

CHAPTER 58

It was dark. Bill Gordon's four-by-four was parked around a quarter of a mile from the Fare's Manchester headquarters.

Peter Maroc stepped out of the vehicle and started walking. He was unarmed. It had to be.

His three companions had left an hour before, giving themselves time to set up their sideshow for the Albanians. Tucker would find a way to enter the building before Maroc arrived.

He was glad to have Tucker on the team, especially tonight. He knew the man's skills.

Maroc always thought Tucker would have made an excellent cat burglar. There were few security systems his friend could not circumvent. However, Maroc guessed the Fare would challenge even his skills this evening.

As he neared the large house, Maroc became increasingly uneasy. He was entering enemy territory without a weapon. She was in there somewhere and in need of his help.

Mafia-style organisations had a certain code of conduct when it came to family. It indicated a strange morality. However, this sentiment did not stretch to others outside the family, where their brutality was legendary. He knew the Albanian mafia to be amongst the most vicious of these organisations.

The property had a long drive that curved to the left. Rounding the curve, Maroc had his first sight of the house. It was a large, tasteless building with little aesthetic appeal.

As Maroc approached the oversized front door, it opened. Two bulky men stepped out. They were followed by two more. Their build, together with their standard dark suits, shouted muscle.

Slight overkill, I wonder who they're expecting? Maroc thought with gallows humour.

No one laid a hand on him, instead, they formed an escort, leading the ex-trooper into the house. Once inside, he was led into a large living room. It was unoccupied.

He took in the ultra-modern furniture and fittings. The whole impression, at least in this room was, to Maroc, that of a show house. A place not lived in.

The men stood around the room, silent sentinels waiting for someone or something. The door opened, and two men walked in. One was tall and well built, his head shaved in a style that Maroc recognised as Eastern European macho.

The second was small, with short, badly cut grey hair. His face, heavily lined, spoke of a life badly lived. His pale blue predatory eyes hinted at a cruel nature.

The small man looked around the room. Maroc tried to read his expression. Contempt? At best, indifference. He guessed this was the Fare's main man in Manchester. The Kryetar.

Responding to an unspoken command, Maroc's escort quietly filed out of the room. This left only the Kryetar, and the man who, going by the expensive cut of his suit, was more than hired muscle.

Both men held handguns. Maroc saw they were Soviet-era semi-automatic Makarovs. Maybe not the fanciest, but, he thought, reliable as hell.

The Kryetar regarded him coldly. When he spoke, his accent was heavy Albanian.

'You have been big trouble for us, Mr Maroc. Cost our organisation a lot of money. A lot of…'

He searched for the right word.

'Bother, as you say here.'

'Where's my wife? We had a deal. Me in exchange for her.'

Maroc's voice was brusque, a man there to do business.

'Still think your big man in charge, I see.'

His grin was malicious, holding no trace of humour.

'She's a pretty lady. Very nice.'

Maroc, realising he was being baited, said nothing. Their plan had to work. There was little chance of this bastard honouring his promises.

He looked at the second man, wondering if he could rush the Kryetar and cannon him into his escort. It was not a serious consideration.

The door opened, and John Tucker walked in. His manner was casual, a man at ease and in the right place. Maroc, bewildered, wondered what part of the plan this was.

Turning back to the Kryetar, Maroc saw the small man holstering his weapon. The other man did likewise. Maroc moved towards the two, his intentions clear. Tucker spoke.

'Hold it, Peter. Don't do anything silly.'

Maroc spun around and saw Tucker had a pistol

levelled at his mid-drift. He looked up sharply at his friend.

'Sorry, Peter. Slight change of plan. Behave, and I'll try and persuade these nice people to let Emily go.'

Maroc felt momentarily disorientated. This was all wrong. He knew Tucker, they had a good history. Bloody good history. He spoke one word.

'Explain.'

His manner, still relaxed, Tucker shrugged.

'As you know, Peter, I operated a lot in Albania. I've come to know these people. They have their code of conduct. Well, let's just say, it works both ways.'

Maroc stood still, saying nothing. He would let this little drama play out on its own.

Tucker continued.

'I've never agreed with the restrictions on marijuana. It's a hell of a lot less harmful than alcohol, and you don't see our governments banning that cash cow. As for heroin and cocaine? Well, people should be allowed a lifestyle choice.'

Tucker turned towards the small man and smiled indulgently.

'The Krye in Lazarat came together with a few of us.

He gave Maroc a broad smile

Let's say, we came to a gentleman's agreement.'

At this, the Kryetar gave a dry laugh. To Peter Maroc, it sounded like rustling paper. Tucker continued.

'Chances are, once they get you to reveal a few things, they'll let you go.'

It was Maroc's turn to laugh.

'If they let me go, what happens to you?'

Tucker seemed to consider his question before

replying with a weary sigh.

'Good point, Peter. You may have just talked yourself out of a deal. Always been your problem. You find fault with everything.'

He grinned amiably at Maroc. Waving his gun in invitation, he continued.

'It's time you joined your wife. I know you've been dying to see her.'

He turned, the smile still in place.

'Try not to make that literal.'

Maroc felt a sense of unreality. Some men could not be bought. He had always placed Tucker firmly in that category. What the hell was going on?

The Kryetar was at his shoulder. He would love to throw caution to the wind. Finish the cocky little bastard with one blow. Did he have anything to lose? Taking a deep breath he stepped through the door. The three men followed him.

He could not just give up. Briefly, he toyed with the idea of ramming Tucker into the other two. He would leg it as fast as he could down the long corridor.

He sighed, realising he was not dealing with some ordinary heavy. John Tucker was a trained MI6 agent. With the reflexes of a cat, he was the best Maroc had come across.

He resigned himself to play the game further. Did he still have his friends on the outside? Maroc hoped so unless Tucker and his new business partners had managed to close down their main strategy. He was beginning to think there would be no SAS backup. No cavalry to save the day.

With Maroc its unwilling leader, the four continued down the corridor until Tucker called on him to stop.

His former friend kept the gun rock steady in his right hand. He nodded towards a smaller door to the left.

'Open it, Peter. And mind how you go. The steps are rather steep.'

His voice conversational, bordering on the light-hearted, he continued.

'There's a light switch up and to your left. That's it, now start down.'

Before switching on the stair light, Maroc thought he had seen a dim illumination below. Starting down, he finally reached the bottom step. Although not able to see much in the poor light, Maroc had the impression the room was spacious.

At the far end of the cellar, which he could now see was lit by one low wattage bulb hanging from the ceiling, he could make out a figure sitting on a chair. Emily?

He walked swiftly towards her. A shout from Tucker.

'Steady, Maroc. Mustn't rush things.'

The Kryetar spoke rapidly to his solidly built companion. The man nodded, giving Maroc a mocking smile before turning and climbing the steps back into the house.

Emily was bound to the chair by her wrists and ankles. Maroc noticed the cord was too tight and was cutting into her flesh. On seeing Maroc, she let out a cry of surprise.

'You OK, love?'

Stupid bloody question. How could she be OK?

Emily nodded and tried to smile. She started to speak, then stopped. Maroc read the fear in her eyes;

knew she would never admit to it. *My brave girl,* he thought. *I'll get us out of this bloody mess. Somehow.*

Thanks to Tucker, the extraction had gone tits up. He turned to face the man he had thought his friend. Tucker was still covering him, his gun hand as steady as ever. The duplicitous bastard.

The Kryetar had his back to them, speaking rapidly on his mobile phone. Tucker flipped the gun over, caught it neatly by the barrel and handed it to Maroc.

What the hell...?

Turning and walking stealthily, Tucker reached the small Albanian and stood still. The man finished his conversation just as Tucker delivered a swift hammer blow to the back of his neck. The Kryetar fell silently to the floor. He was out cold.

Without missing a beat, Tucker turned to face his baffled friend.

'Untie her, mate.'

He produced a fixed-bladed knife from its concealed sheath and handed it to Maroc.

'There's a door at the far end. The lock's a doddle.'

For a moment, Peter Maroc stood motionless, his head attempting to catch up with his rapid and baffling changes in fortune. Tucker turned to Emily and shrugged.

'The pension plan was pretty crap, anyway.'

She gave him a questioning look.

Working quickly, he cut through his wife's bonds. Before she stood up, he bent down and briskly massaged her wrists and ankles. On her feet, Emily began speaking. Maroc gently pushed her forward towards John Tucker, who was now at the far end of the cellar.

The MI6 man was bent over, working on the door lock with a small set of tools. Maroc, remembering his talent for lock picking, shook his head. This time, he was smiling.

'You bastard! You beautiful bloody bastard!'

The lock finally clicked. Tucker carefully opened the door, which led directly to the garden. It was dark outside.

Signalling to Maroc and Emily to stay put. He produced his mobile and punched in a number. Turning to Maroc, he hissed.

'Letting the lads know we're coming out. Give them a chance to stir things up a bit.'

Tucker pocketed the mobile, and, for a full minute, the three stood just inside the door. Maroc placed his arm around Emily, giving her a concerned look.

'Did the bastards hurt you?'

Still looking uncertain, the fear of the last few hours not having left her, she gave him a wan smile.

'Stop fussing. Just do what you're good at.'

He gave her an affectionate squeeze.

'Almost home and dry, Em. Just waiting for the pyrotechnics.'

As if on cue, there was a loud explosion from one of the wooden outbuildings. Smoke billowed from its roof. Emily jumped back to the safety of the cellar almost colliding with her husband.

A figure suddenly appeared at the doorway, and Maroc, realising he still had Tucker's gun, now raised it.

'Put that bloody weapon away, you Sassenach.'

Bill Gordon stepped into the cellar.

Maroc looked at him warily before turning to

Tucker.

'What bloody side is he going to be on?'

Tucker responded with a barking laugh. Maroc answered the MI6 man with an obscenity, then, looking at Gordon he added.

'He's the Sassenach in this setup, Jock. I'm a bloody celt!'

Bill Gordon was quickly joined by Fisher, who gave Maroc a relieved wave. With Gordon in the lead, they started through the cellar door.

They made their way across the grass, Gordon and Fisher throwing smoke grenades to left and right. They approached the main gate just as three figures lumbered towards them out of the smoke.

Tucker barked at the others.

'They're not armed. Try not to use your weapons.'

Big men, Maroc recognised them as part of his greeting party. The first made a grab for his gun. He was too slow, and Maroc viciously smashed his outstretched arm at the wrist with the heavy pistol.

The man yelped in pain as Maroc attacked his knee and head with two swift strikes. Using the pistol, he delivered a final blow to the side of his head.

The second man lunged toward Fisher, locking him in a bear hug. Maroc left Emily and stepped forward.

He delivered a short sharp punch to the man's kidney. He finished him off with a strike to the head with the pistol.

Gordon made short work of the third. He jabbed him in the throat and, while he gasped for breath, dropped the big man with a straight punch to the jaw.

John Tucker was occupied with his mobile while trying to keep up with the rest.

'You managing without me?'

He looked back at the fallen Albanians.

'You're making this look too easy, guys. I called in the cavalry. I suggest we lay low and wait.'

He turned to Emily.

'They shouldn't be too long.'

Maroc tapped Gordon on the shoulder, signalling him to stop. Gordon alerted Fisher.

The smoke grenades had done their job. With the poor visibility making things difficult and dangerous for both sides, they decided to stay put. The five crouched low on the neatly trimmed lawn. And waited.

A figure emerged from the smoke, and Emily, thinking it was help in the form of the armed response unit, stood up. Before Maroc could stop her, she had taken a step forward.

The Kryetar stepped into view, gun in hand. He appeared to sway, his weapon pointing dangerously at Emily. Maroc was on his feet and moving.

He reached his wife, pushing her to one side. Emily fell awkwardly onto the grass as Maroc continued towards the Kryeatar. There were three sharp cracks. Maroc gasped, taking a step back.

The Kryetar stood in a seeming daze and Tucker was quick to step in. He slapped the weapon from the small man's hand and then bent down to retrieve the fallen pistol.

Noticing the spread of blood on the man's shirt, Tucker could see there would be no further threat from the little Mafioso.

The Kryetar, his face distorted, uttered what could only have been a curse and spat at Tucker. As his body crumbled, the MI6 man stepped forward to support him to the ground.

John Tucker turned and saw Emily crouching over Maroc. Fisher stood as though protecting the scene. Gordon was desperately attempting to staunch the blood, rapidly turning his friend's white shirt a dark red.

They could see more figures approaching. Tucker quickly drew the semi-automatic Makarov he had recovered from the Kryetar. Mark Fisher had his 9 mm Zig.

Dressed in black, they emerged from the smoke. The breathing masks and goggles had turned them into entities from Dante's inferno.

But these devils were here to help. Gordon, Fisher and Tucker immediately dropped their weapons on the ground, lifting their arms in the air, ready to be identified.

Gently guiding Emily to one side, a member of the armed response unit signalled for help. Another appeared, carrying a compact first aid box.

He bent over the prone figure of Peter Maroc and got to work. A third man attended to the Kryetar.

As they made their way to the main gate, they could hear the sound of flashbangs coming from the large house. Tucker had stressed the body count be kept to an absolute minimum. The order had come from the top.

With one part of his mind, the MI6 man was trying to work out how the little Mafia boss had managed to appear so quickly in front of them. He guessed the cellar had a second entrance leading to the outside.

The Kryetar must have recovered and quickly

exited to another part of the garden. He should have hit the little bastard harder.

The medic had done his best for Maroc. Sedated and stretchered, he was flanked by his wife and friends.

Emily looked down at her husband. His pallor shocked her. Maroc's selfless act had undoubtedly saved her life. It afforded her little comfort.

Tucker looked over at the medic. The man shrugged his shoulders. It was not encouraging.

CHAPTER 59

For Emily and Max Southwell, it was Deja vu. They had played this scene before, and Malcolm's death had been devastating for both. Emily knew that losing Maroc would be a blow she might not survive.

Her husband was hovering between two worlds and Emily was afraid. Afraid of losing him all over again without having told him she was sorry. Sorry for her lack of faith. Of trust. She did not, could not imagine a life without him.

Maroc's ultimate act of selflessness had removed all of her lingering doubts. He had placed himself in the line of fire and had stopped a bullet. A bullet meant for her.

Maroc would give one of his derisive laughs on hearing such sentimental tripe. He would tell her to stop being a silly mare.

He had been rushed in a critical state to the same Manchester hospital where her brother had died. Had been seen by the same surgeon.

Two bullets had struck him. The first had lodged in his left shoulder, which the team had little difficulty removing. The second was proving to be a serious problem.

The 9 mm slug had passed through his lung and lodged near the thoracic vertebrae. There had been internal bleeding.

Mr Wood, the surgeon, remembering Emily was in the profession, had shown her Maroc's ex-rays. He explained how the second bullet had ended up close to his vertebra and was lodged behind a major artery.

Removing the bullet would prove difficult. If things did not work to plan, the procedure could kill or severely paralyse her husband. He had warned her the prognosis was not good.

The team worked on Maroc for six hours. Her father had been given a bed in a small sideward. Despite his protests, Emily had insisted he try to sleep. She had found a comfortable chair in a waiting room a corridor length from the operating theatre.

Emily woke with a start. Despite her determination to stay awake, she had dozed off. Mr Wood was standing over her. He looked exhausted, and Emily's first impulse was to tell him to sit down.

Wood gave her a small smile.

'Well, it's done. Now we have to wait. I must warn you, Doctor Maroc, the internal bleeding was worse than we thought. The bullet has been removed, but its travel was not without serious damage.'

'Will he pull through?' Emily was on her feet.

Wood looked at her for a long time.

'I don't know. His chances are not good.'

'But he has a chance? A fighting chance?'

The small surgeon shrugged.

'He's a strong, fit man. At least he has that in his favour. However, given everything I've told you.'

He looked at her directly.

'I have to suggest you prepare for the worse.'

Emily woke her father. Not to have done so would

have both upset and angered him. She explained everything as well as she could without alarming him. She told him that his son-in-law was now in a small recovery ward.

Max Southwell had firmly refused to return to his bed, and both he and Emily had been given comfortable chairs a few feet from Maroc's bed.

Emily was worried about her father. Worried this would set him back. Once again she marvelled at the change in the two men's relationship. The close bond that had grown between them.

The bleeping monitor picked up in tempo and Emily was up and at Maroc's side. His eyes were open. He was trying to speak.

Southwell arrived seconds later and Emily signalled him to give Maroc some space. Emily put her hand to her husband's cheek.

'Slowly, Peter. Take it slow.'

Southwell reached for Maroc's oxygen mask.

'Get that bloody thing off his face, Em. He's trying to say something. Give him some real air to breathe.'

Emily stayed his hand.

'Don't do anything till I get back, dad. I'll get someone.'

Emily left Maroc's bedside and went out into the corridor. A nurse was running towards her, perhaps alerted by the monitor. She deftly passed Emily and went to her husband's bed.

'Can you take the mask off? I think he's trying to say something.'

Southwell looked at the nurse who smiled her understanding.

'I'll take it off. Looks as though he's coming back to

us. Don't raise your hopes yet, Mr...?'

'Southwell. I'm his father-in-law.'

He looked at Maroc.

'You'd better make it, Maroc. You owe me a fishing trip.'

With his mask off, the nurse carefully lifted Maroc's head, allowing him a little water. Settling back onto the pillow, Maroc looked up into the anxious faces of his wife and father-in-law. He could hear the nurse's voice.

'I'll leave you with him. He's very weak. Don't overtax him.'

Emily felt slightly affronted by her comment, then realised how ridiculous she was being. The young staff nurse would have no idea she was a qualified doctor.

Maroc's smile was crooked; sardonic. He nodded at Max for more water. Emily stepped in, raising his head just as the nurse had done. He swallowed and coughed. Blood splattered onto the white bedsheet.

She fretted, using a napkin to absorb the spilt liquid. Emily tried to ignore the blood and what it might mean.

He was again trying to speak, his voice a whisper. Emily and Max bent over to listen. They could just about hear him.

'Tell Ellie May and little Joey I died thinking of them.'

Max, shaking his head in mock disgust, moved away from his grinning son-in-law.

'Do you ever get serious, Maroc? I mean. Even when you're supposed to be bloody dying?'

Emily was smiling through her tears. They fell on his face like warm rain. Using the napkin, she wiped away the salty liquid.

'Does this mean you're going to be OK, Peter? You'd better have.

She held his hand and squeezed hard.

'You'd better not die, you selfish sod.'

His eyes closed and Emily became momentarily alarmed. She bent her face close to his and felt his breath on her cheek. Maroc's breathing was even and regular.

Emily eagerly accepted this as a good sign. Her professional mind informed her of a bleaker reality.

There was the swish of a curtain, and Emily looked up as Wood entered the cubicle.

'I think he's sleeping, doctor. He talked to us, then he… dropped off.'

Wood was not the usual brisk physician. He had a softness about him that Emily appreciated.

Checking Maroc's monitor, the surgeon adjusted the rate of the IV drip. He lifted his patient's eyelids and carefully examined his chest with a stethoscope. Finally, he stood up.

'He's as strong as I've seen them.'

'Oh, I can vouch for that.'

He looked up at her, his expression was bleak.

'I don't wish to alarm you, Doctor Maroc, but don't hold out too much hope. He's in a bad way.'

Max Southwell looked like a man badly in need of sleep. He, together with his daughter had stood vigil on and off for the last twenty-four hours. Wood recommended they both get some rest.

Having already booked into the small hotel, a stone's throw from the hospital, Wood suggested they might at least take advantage of the comfortable beds.

Yes, they would be called if there was a change for the worse. The specialist, however, would not give either of them much hope or comfort.

Emily had never felt so defeated. The specialist's comments had left her bereft of hope. Her training informed her how serious Maroc's condition was. She feared his terrible injuries would take him from them.

Southwell refused to surrender hope. Maroc would fight for his life, just as he had.

Mark Fisher had telephoned home, explaining how he needed to stay at least another two or three days. Until his friend was out of danger. Yes, he would give him her love. No, dammit, he was not yet in the clear. Not by a long chalk.

Fisher had been invited to stay with Bill Gordon. They had kept in constant touch with the hospital, deciding not to visit. At least not until he was out of danger. The doctor's reluctance to give good news had disturbed them equally.

In another emergency unit within the same building, the Kryetar was also in a fight for his life. His chances of survival were about the same as Maroc's. Perhaps a little worse.

Maroc's bullet had lodged in the small man's chest cavity. It had missed the heart, puncturing his left lung. To Wood, who had operated on both men, the similarity in their cases was remarkable.

The small man had lost a lot of blood and needed an immediate transfusion. Both Fisher and Gordon had been informed of his condition.

Discussing it over a drink in Bill Gordon's kitchen, both wondered why the Health Service was bothering at all. Life for him would not be comfortable if he survived. His passing would suit everyone.

The Albanian brothers had been handed over to MI5 for interrogation. Talks with the Albanian authorities on their future had already taken place. Their counterpart in that country had been both embarrassed and grateful for their capture.

Edon and Burim Berisha were to be offered a reduction in their sentence in exchange for any helpful details concerning the Fare's operations in the UK and Albania.

The brothers would be deported back to their home country. There, they would serve out the remainder of their sentence. After all, as Tucker had said, why should the British taxpayer incur the cost of their incarceration?

The brothers' refusal to cooperate came as no surprise. Lacking in sophistication, they were not fools. If they did talk, either here in the UK or Albania, retribution would be swift and brutal.

Edon had decided his one phone call would be to the Manchester Fare. He had pondered long and hard on their position. After discussing it with his brother, they had arrived at a decision.

Edon would inform the organisation of Peter Maroc's continuing existence. He would throw in all the intelligence they had on the SAS man.

He hoped and prayed, that it might count in their favour. If nothing else, it was one way of getting revenge on the SAS pig, even if he and his brother did not live to see its implementation.

The voice at the other end had listened in silence. When he had finished speaking, it had told him he had done the right thing, the sensible thing. The knowledge would be put to good use.

CHAPTER 60

It had been three months since the Manchester episode. Max Southwell had moved in with his daughter and was preparing a meal in the kitchen. She had gone shopping in the village, promising to be back within the hour.

He looked at his watch. Maroc's watch. To him, it was an ugly thing with dials and functions he would never use. Still, he wore it like some would a friendship bracelet. It served the same purpose. The watch informed him she was running a little late.

Over the three months, father and daughter had grown even closer. Both had come to realise the transient and fragile nature of human existence.

They had been forced to accept one vital truth. Complete safety could never be a given, even in an orderly society such as Britain's.

It was a sobering thought how certain factions within the social order could have the power to significantly change the lives of others.

Southwell walked into the living room and made his way towards the large bay window to the front of the house. His eyes alighted on the new picture frame on the coffee table. Picking up the recent addition, he took it over to the window for a better look.

The photograph was of Emily and Maroc in front of the castle in Caernarfon. He remembered taking it with his old film camera. He still favoured the old camera above all the others he had since acquired.

A friend in Caernarfon still practised the archaic art of film development. He was always looking for new material for his hobby.

Moving to the large antique sideboard, he picked up his favourite. A large black and white photograph of Emily, Maroc and him. He remembered it being taken around four months previously. They had posed, slightly self consciously in the front garden. For the life of him, he could not remember who had taken the shot.

Maroc's face looked back at him. He noted how, even when smiling, his cynicism was never absent. Today, he realised how much more qualities he had missed in this man.

Southwell cast his mind back to when he and Maroc lived together. He was amazed at how quickly the two had adopted an undergraduate, almost existentialist lifestyle.

He viewed the period as being reminiscent of his college days, but with a slightly different curriculum. He shook his head and smiled. How he missed that time with his son-in-law.

He recalled the dark desolation that was his life after Katherine's death. Far from raging against the dying of the light, Southwell had welcomed it.

Maroc's sudden appearance had been an outrageous intrusion into his comfortable journey into oblivion. The young upstart had refused to let him be. Had dragged him back to face his physical and spiritual suffering.

Over the ensuing weeks and months, something

miraculous happened. Peter Maroc had initiated a process in which he, Southwell, had little faith. Systems he had always regarded as eastern mumbo jumbo were to become part of his life. Part of his daily reality.

Southwell smiled at the memory. Maroc had certainly sold him a bill of goods. From the beginning, when he was ready to give up, his son-in-law had somehow managed to paint a vision of a future worth fighting for.

To get there, Maroc first had to identify and work on an integral aspect of his, Max Southwell's nature. His perversity.

The man had thrown down a gauntlet. He had challenged Southwell to leave his death bed and fight.

What followed had opened a door to a better, brighter world, a hope for the future. The steady improvement in his physical well-being had been a bonus.

Replacing the picture frame, he again consulted his watch. Over half an hour late. Should he worry? Returning to the kitchen, he heard the key in the front door.

They came in laughing like teenagers. Having decided to pick a few bottles of wine in town, Peter Maroc bumped into his wife. Southwell heard his familiar Welsh lilt.

'Max? Look who I picked up in town? I believe the hussy was touting for trade.'

She kicked at him and was accused of assaulting an invalid.

There was a time when Max Southwell would have regarded such behaviour as facile, even embarrassing to those of a serious nature. But Maroc had robbed him of his seriousness.

He had no idea what he had replaced it with. But, by god, it suited him better.

Maroc turned and saw Southwell standing at the kitchen door. He was wearing Emily's apron and quite a lot of flour. His son-in-law gave a look Southwell had come to recognise.

He took off the apron, offering it to Maroc while jerking a thumb over his shoulder.

'To the kitchen, man. Much more your territory than mine.'

Although still not back to full health, Peter Maroc had made a good recovery. He had started his new job with Bill Gordon the week before.

Being back at work had boosted Maroc's confidence. It was noticeably contributing to his recovery.

Much of his job was physically demanding. It had aroused concerns in him whether he would be able to perform to his full powers. Bill Gordon had quickly recognised this and prudently lightened his daily schedule.

Most of the questions had been answered by the third day. With Gordon's encouragement, Maroc had become more certain there would be no real issues.

At home, the banter between the three was unforced. His brush with the reaper had brought them ever closer.

Looking at his smiling daughter, Max Southwell became more convinced Maroc was right. You only get one bloody life. Live it to the full. All else will follow.

ABOUT THE AUTHOR

Keith Williams

Keith Williams lives in a beautiful part of North Wales. Since retiring from a long and chequered career, his focus has been on writing.

He has published several self-help books and now devotes himself to writing action fiction based in Wales. When he is not writing, he is out exploring the hills and mountains of Snowdonia. This is his first novel.

Printed in Great Britain
by Amazon

14533436R10253